By J. A. Jance

J. P. Beaumont Mysteries

UNTIL PROVEN GUILTY • INJUSTICE FOR ALL
TRIAL BY FURY • TAKING THE FIFTH
IMPROBABLE CAUSE • A MORE PERFECT UNION
DISMISSED WITH PREJUDICE • MINOR IN POSSESSION
PAYMENT IN KIND • WITHOUT DUE PROCESS
FAILURE TO APPEAR • LYING IN WAIT
NAME WITHHELD • BREACH OF DUTY
BIRDS OF PREY • PARTNER IN CRIME
LONG TIME GONE • JUSTICE DENIED
FIRE AND ICE • BETRAYAL OF TRUST

Joanna Brady Mysteries

DESERT HEAT • TOMBSTONE COURAGE
SHOOT/DON'T SHOOT • DEAD TO RIGHTS
SKELETON CANYON • RATTLESNAKE CROSSING
OUTLAW MOUNTAIN • DEVIL'S CLAW
PARADISE LOST • PARTNER IN CRIME
EXIT WOUNDS • DEAD WRONG
DAMAGE CONTROL • FIRE AND ICE

Walker Family Thrillers

HOUR OF THE HUNTER • KISS OF THE BEES
DAY OF THE DEAD • QUEEN OF THE NIGHT

Ali Reynolds Mysteries

EDGE OF EVIL • WEB OF EVIL
HAND OF EVIL • CRUEL INTENT
TRIAL BY FIRE • FATAL ERROR

J.A. JANCE

PAYMENT IN KIND

A J.P. BEAUMONT NOVEL

HARPER

An Imprint of HarperCollins*Publishers*

This is a work of fiction. Names, characters, places, and incidents are products of the author's imagination or are used fictitiously and are not to be construed as real. Any resemblance to actual events, locales, organizations, or persons, living or dead, is entirely coincidental.

HARPER

An Imprint of HarperCollins*Publishers*
10 East 53rd Street
New York, New York 10022-5299

Copyright © 1991 by J. A. Jance
ISBN 978-0-06-208636-5

First Harper premium printing: January 2012
First Avon Books mass market printing: March 1991

HarperCollins ® and Harper ® are registered trademarks of Harper-Collins Publishers.

Printed in the United States of America

Visit Harper paperbacks on the World Wide Web at
www.harpercollins.com

HB 05.11.2023

For Penny,
and in memory of
Paul

CHAPTER 1

THE FIRST THING I NOTICED THAT MORNING WAS THE quiet, the deathly quiet. And then I noticed I was cold. For the first time since Karen divorced me, leaving me in sole possession of the covers and taking her perpetually frigid feet elsewhere, I woke up with cold feet, and not just feet, either.

It took a while to figure out that what was missing was the comforting rumble of the building's heat pumps on the roof outside my penthouse apartment. It was not quite sunrise on a wintry early January morning, and those warmth-giving pumps were definitely off. Had been for some time. My bedroom was freezing.

I put in an irate call to the manager, who confirmed what I already knew. The heat pumps had "gone on the blink." For some unaccountable reason, the heat pumps in Belltown Terrace, a luxury high-rise condominium in downtown Seattle, are built to function fine in temperatures all the way down to fourteen degrees Fahrenheit. Down to, but not below.

So when the thermometer hit a record-breaking six degrees above zero sometime during the late night hours of January second, Belltown Terrace's over-worked heat pumps kicked off entirely. By the time I woke up several hours later, the thermometer in my apartment read a chilly forty-five.

Leaving the manager to summon the proper repairmen, I headed for the warmest spot in my house—the two-person hot tub in the master bathroom. I turned on the air jets and climbed into the steaming water, fully prepared to stay there for as long as necessary.

I lay in the tub with my eyes closed and my head resting comfortably against one of the upholstered cushions. Reveling in luxurious warmth, I was jarred from my torpor by a jangling telephone in the chilled bedroom behind me. Weeks earlier, Ralph Ames, my gadget-minded attorney in Arizona, had hinted broadly that I might want to consider buying myself a cordless phone, but I hadn't taken his advice. Now I wished I had.

"Smart ass," I grumbled for Ralph's benefit as I threw myself out of the steamy tub, grabbed a towel, and dashed for my old-fashioned and very much stationary phone.

If my caller had been Ralph Ames, I would've had to tell him his suggestion had a lot of merit, but it wasn't Ames at all. Instead, the person on the phone was Sergeant Watkins, my immediate supervisor from Homicide at the Seattle Police Department. When Watty calls me at home, it usually means trouble, but surprisingly, he didn't launch into it right away.

"How's it going?" he asked with uncharacteristic indirectness.

"Colder 'an a witch's tit," I answered tersely. "Our heat pumps went off overnight. I'm standing here dripping wet."

"Your heat pumps went off?" he echoed with a laugh. "What's the matter? Did one of you fat cats forget to pay the bill down at City Light?"

Sergeant Watkins doesn't usually beat around the bush discussing the weather. "Cut the comedy, Watty," I snapped. "I'm freezing my ass off while you're cracking jokes. Get to the point."

"I've got a case for you, Beau. Initial reports say we've got two stiffs on Lower Queen Anne Hill. We've got some people on the scene, but no detectives so far. You're it."

"Where?"

"In the Seattle school district office. Know where that is?"

I was already groping in my dresser drawer for socks and underwear. "Not exactly, but I can find it," I returned.

"The streets outside are a damned skating rink," Watty continued. "It might be faster if you go there directly from home instead of coming into the office first."

During the call I had managed to blot myself dry with the towel. Now I held the phone away from my ear long enough to pull a T-shirt on over my head. I returned the phone to my ear just in time to hear Watty continue.

"Do that. Detective Kramer'll meet you there as soon as he can. The guys in the garage are trying to find another set of chains. One broke just as he was starting up the ramp."

"Kramer?" I asked, hoping I had heard him wrong. "Did you say Detective Kramer? What about Big Al?"

I can get along all right with most of the people in Seattle P.D., but Detective Paul Kramer is the one notable exception. When it comes to my list of least favorite people, Kramer is right up there at the top— just under Maxwell Cole, the lead crime columnist for our local news-rag, the *Seattle Post-Intelligencer.*

"I thought someone would have let you know," Watty returned. "He and Molly both came down with a bad case of food poisoning after a Daughters of Norway dinner Saturday night. They ended up in the Ballard Hospital emergency room along with fifteen or twenty other people. He's still in no shape to come back to work. And Kramer's partner called in sick as well."

"So we're stuck with each other?"

"For the time being."

Having to work a case with Detective Kramer was a bad way to start a new week and an even worse way to start a new year. If I were superstitious, I might have seen it as an omen.

"Swell," I grumbled. With that, I hung up on Watty and dialed the concierge, making sure someone was working on the heat pump problem and asking her to call for a cab while I finished dressing.

People in the Pacific Northwest are used to clouds and rain in winter. That kind of weather is expected and comes with the territory. Arctic cold isn't, and nobody here knows what to do when it comes. I put on an extra sweater over my shirt before adding the shoulder holster for my new 9-mm Beretta automatic. My old faithful .38 Smith & Wesson was still gathering dust in some evidence room in Prescott, Arizona.

With a wool tweed sport coat over both sweater and automatic, I rummaged around my apartment until I located the fur-lined leather gloves and gaudy muffler my kids had sent me for Christmas several years earlier. Fortunately I wasn't working undercover, because that muffler is anything but unobtrusive.

By the time I raced downstairs and into the clear bitter cold, a green Farwest cab with white smoke billowing from its exhaust system and chains on its worn rear tires was stopped in the passenger loadzone in front of the building. I was glad I wasn't driving. In my experience, cab companies don't mess around with chains until well after it's absolutely necessary.

"The school district office," I said as I climbed inside. "South slope of Lower Queen Anne. Just off Mercer Street."

The cab driver obviously didn't need an exact address. With a nod, he slipped the car into gear and we crunched away from the sidewalk.

City crews had been working through the night to clear main arterials of the seven or eight inches of snow that had fallen Sunday afternoon and evening. The snowstorm had been followed by a frigid cold front that had swept down out of Alaska, bringing with it record-breaking lows. The main thoroughfares, some of which had been cleared of snow earlier, were now glazed over by a thick layer of ice. The taxi rumbled along like a slow-moving tank.

If you live in Chicago or upstate New York, seven or eight inches of snow followed by treacherous ice is no big deal because those cities are flat. Seattle isn't. Steep glacial ridges create streets that resemble roller coasters under the best of circumstances. Combined with ice and snow, the city's rough terrain becomes a bumper-car disaster.

At the first hint of snow, many Seattlites head home at once and stay there for the duration. It beats crashing and burning your car on some ice-bound street. Stores quickly sell out of the essentials—milk, bread, and videos. With four inches on the ground, the city comes to a standstill. That morning's eight inches was double that. Except for my solitary cab, Second Avenue all the way down to the central core was entirely deserted.

"Understand they let all the kids out of school today," the driver said conversationally as he turned off Second onto Cedar and made his way across an equally deserted Denny Way. "But I guess the grownups ain't that lucky. Right?"

"Right," I said briskly, leaving intact his erroneous conclusion that I was some kind of school district bureaucrat. The driver, in his late thirties, was prematurely potbellied and friendly. He negotiated the steep, icy streets with the kind of casual aplomb born only of years of experience.

"What the hell's going on?" he asked when we were stopped cold on Mercer by a scatter of emergency vehicles parked helter-skelter on the icy street. A parking enforcement officer, huddled in her curtained cart, motioned firmly for him to move on.

"Just let me out," I told him, passing my fare across the seat. "I can make it from here on foot."

Before the cabbie could give me my change, an impatient horn blared loudly behind us. "Hold your horses, fella," the driver muttered under his breath while he deliberately counted out my change.

When the horn sounded again, I looked around. The driver of a medical examiner's van was waving for us to move aside. Shaking her head with annoyance, the parking enforcement officer stepped out of her cart and was headed in my direction by the time I climbed out of the cab. Once on the slick pavement, I lost my footing and almost slid under the cab before catching myself on the door handle.

The driver of the van honked furiously a third time, but the cabbie studiously ignored him. It was a practiced pretense.

"Take care, fella," he said to me, acknowledging my generous tip with a partial salute. "And if you need a ride home after work, be sure to give a call. I'm pulling a double shift today."

He paused long enough to carefully place the money in his wallet before finally, deliberately, moving out of the van's way. He slid away from the curb just as the parking enforcement officer pounced on me.

"I'm sorry, sir, but this is a crime scene. You'll have to move along. We're not allowing anyone beyond this point."

I flashed my badge in her direction. She mumbled

something and retreated, scuttling hurriedly back toward the welcome warmth of her plastic-enclosed cart. My slick-soled leather dress shoes filled with snow as I slipped and slid over to the sidewalk and up the hill, where, despite the steep grade, ice-crusted snow made for somewhat less hazardous footing.

Out in the street, I could see the tracks where some crazy urban winter athlete had taken advantage of the incline for a little early morning skiing. Shaking my head in wonder, I kept on walking.

The unimposing two-story building that houses the administrative offices of the Seattle Public School District on Fourth Avenue North sits on the flank of Lower Queen Anne Hill, near an invisible boundary where the city's commercial zoning gives way to residential. Its construction of Roman brick and great expanses of glass may have been wonderfully modern years ago when the complex was built, but now, with a skeleton of dead pyracantha clinging stubbornly to its walls, it looked like a frumpy, aging dowager.

I had reached the front door and was in the process of shoving it open when Dr. Howard Baker strode past me. The white-haired head of King County's medical examiner's office shouldered me out of the way and lumbered into the building without any kind of acknowledgment. Doc Baker's personal presence at the crime scene suggested that whatever had happened was probably something out of the ordinary.

Inside, although a number of uniformed police officers were scattered throughout the granite-floored reception area, the room was deathly quiet except for the occasional uncontrolled sobbing of a young woman who huddled in the far corner of the room with a Medic One attendant kneeling solicitously beside her. Doc Baker's wide-backed frame filled the doorway of what appeared to be a janitorial closet just to the left of the front door.

As I stepped closer, I could smell the unmistakable odors of industrial-strength cleaners, polishes, and disinfectants. But underneath those innocuous smells was a hint of something else—the sharply acrid aroma of burnt gunpowder and the far uglier coppery stench of blood. Death was present in that closet as surely as mops and brooms.

I moved close enough to Baker's broad backside so I could peer over his shoulder. At first all I could see was a woman's bare leg extending into the room from the closet. From the position, it looked as though the closet door had been closed with her leg pressing against it. When the door had been opened by some unsuspecting person, the leg had sprung out into the room and slammed down to the floor like a grisly horror-movie jack-in-the-box.

She wore a maroon full skirt of some heavy, wool-like material and a matching long-sleeved turtle-neck. The skirt was hiked up around her waist. She wasn't wearing any panties. Graceful but lifeless fingers almost touched a .38 Special that lay on the white tiled floor a few inches inside the doorway.

Baker knelt down to examine the gun. That's when I saw the other leg, a man's leg, underneath the woman's. I moved to a slightly different angle to get a better look. Other than a pair of socks whose elastic had gone to seed, the man too was naked from the waist down. He was wearing a shirt, however, one that made me think of our own at S.P.D. Then I saw the blue striping and breathed a sigh of relief. A blue shoulder patch identified it as belonging to Seattle Security Service, one of the largest security guard companies in the city.

Baker got up quickly, nearly knocking me over in the process, and glared around the room, searching for someone. He seemed surprised to find me standing directly behind him.

"Hello there, Detective Beaumont. Have you seen that damn photographer? She was supposed to be here a long time ago."

"Haven't seen her," I answered. "I've only been here a few minutes myself."

Shaking his head, Baker headed for the outside door, while I took his place in the doorway of the murky, dimly lighted closet.

I stepped closer and warily examined the dead man's face. Years before, I too had spent some time working for Seattle Security, moonlighting to earn a little extra money when the kids were young and my meager paycheck never stretched quite far enough. Further investigation might still identify the dead man as another financially strapped police officer, but for now I was relieved that his face wasn't one I immediately recognized. The name tag pinned to his breast pocket said, "A. Chambers." That didn't ring any bells either.

In death, A. Chambers sat with his back propped against a deep janitor's sink. His slack-jawed chin hung down, resting on an ample chest. A huge brown stain had spread across his lower chest and belly. Blood had pooled on the floor around and beneath him. I've seen enough murder scenes to know that A. Chambers had bled to death.

I turned my attention back to the woman who lay in a tangle of fallen brooms and mops, staring sightlessly at Chambers from across the small, evil-smelling closet. The almost delicate hole in her chin was in direct contrast to the spattered gore on the wall and mop handles behind her. The condition of her body had all the earmarks of a self-inflicted wound.

If the woman was a suicide, she was one of the selfish kind—unhappy people who aren't content to go out alone. They always insist on taking one or two others along with them, the more the merrier.

That being the case, she had taken far more care with the placement of her own bullet than she had with his. The woman had died quickly, probably painlessly, while A. Chambers' lifeblood had slowly ebbed away.

Repulsed by the woman's strikingly calm face, which belied the shattered mess behind it, I looked down at the floor where the two sets of naked legs, one wearing pitifully sagging socks, lay both open and entwined together like those of a pair of abandoned rag dolls left behind by some forgetful child.

Baker came hurrying back with the photographer firmly in tow. Unceremoniously he shoved me aside. I let him do it without protest. I went over to a window and stood looking out at the snow-shrouded city below me. It was a glistening, blinding white—beautiful, peaceful, and serene. That pristine beauty seemed totally at odds with the terrible darkness that had exploded during the night and left two people dead in that gory closet behind me.

Who is dead, and why, are the fundamental questions at the bottom of every homicide investigation. What terrible passions and connections drive human beings to kill others and then turn the murder weapons on themselves? I know from firsthand experience that the answers to those questions, once we unravel them, wreak havoc among the living long after the dead are buried and decaying in the ground.

For some unaccountable reason, as I stood looking out at the glistening city, the lyrics from that old Ethel Merman song came bubbling into my head. It's from *Annie Get Your Gun*, I think, and the words say something to the effect that you can't get a man with a gun.

You can, actually, but if you do it with a .38 Special, what's left over won't be good for much of anything.

CHAPTER 2

SEASONED OLD-TIMERS ON THE HOMICIDE SQUAD KNOW all too well that there is a time to approach Doc Baker and there is a time to leave him alone. As he talked to his assistants, I heard him mention that he believed the man had been shot in the reception area and then dragged into the closet, where he subsequently died. I looked at the shiny granite floor. Someone had taken the time to clean it very, very thoroughly.

As the irascible medical examiner bustled around the crime scene that bitterly cold morning, rumbling orders at the hapless woman photographer whose misfortune it was to draw this particular assignment, I knew enough to keep a very low profile. Detective Paul Kramer didn't. Relatively new to Homicide and already saddled with a reputation as a headstrong go-getter, he showed up late and immediately started rocking the boat.

Pausing barely long enough to stomp the layer of crusted snow off his shoes, Kramer, bullnecked and bullheaded as ever, charged up behind Doc Baker with his feet still wet. The medical examiner was still totally involved in working one-on-one with the police photographer.

Seeing the bodies, Kramer whistled. "What were they doing, getting it on in the janitor's closet?"

Doc Baker reacted like an awakened bear summoned too early from his darkened winter cave. He's a big man, one who requires far more than the average amount of personal space not only because of his girth but also by virtue of personal preference. He doesn't like to be crowded, physically or mentally.

Angered now by what he must have regarded as gross impertinence on the young detective's part, Baker turned and erupted out of the closet in one surprisingly fluid motion. The crook of his elbow caught Kramer full in the midsection, and the younger man doubled over in pain. It could have been an accident, I suppose, but then again . . .

"Your shoes are still wet, Kramer. Anybody ever teach you to watch out for trace evidence, for Chrissakes? Now, go dry those damn shoes and stay out of my way until I'm ready for you. Understand?"

Diplomacy has never been one of Baker's long suits, nor is he known in local police circles for professional courtesy. Chagrined, Kramer turned away, glancing around the room to see exactly how many other people had witnessed Baker's sharp-tongued put-down. There were several.

When Kramer caught sight of two uniformed officers exchanging knowing grins, the detective's face turned several shades of red. Without a word he retreated to the rubberized mat near the door and, as ordered, thoroughly dried his shoes. Finishing that, he spied me standing near the window. He was seething with suppressed anger as he strode over to me.

"So what the hell are we supposed to do, stand around here all day? Wait with our thumbs up our asses?"

"You're damned right we're going to wait," I counseled reasonably. "Until hell freezes over or until Doc Baker gives us the go-ahead, whichever comes first. The last thing we need to do in this investigation is to get crosswise with Baker at the outset."

The already florid color of Kramer's face darkened appreciably. Frowning, he scanned the room until his eyes stopped abruptly at the quietly weeping woman sitting in the corner. Her hyperventilating sobs were slowly subsiding. An emergency medical technician had just walked away, leaving her alone.

"Who's she?" Kramer asked, directing his curt question at me, but nodding in the woman's direction.

I shrugged. "A secretary or receptionist, I presume. From her reaction, my guess is that she's the one who discovered the bodies."

"Your guess?" Kramer demanded irritably, his tone laced with sarcasm. "Don't you think we ought to start by finding out for sure?"

She wasn't going anywhere. "Suits me," I told him. "Until Baker gets freed up, I don't have anything better to do."

Kramer glowered at me and then started off toward the corner where the woman was sitting.

Little more than a girl, twenty, or twenty-one at the most, she was a study in contradictions, a walking-talking-breathing oxymoron. She was small and pert, cute almost, despite the muddy tracks left on her face by smeared and smudged makeup. Her shoulder-length straw-blond hair was frizzed around her face in that uncontrolled, finger-in-the-electrical-outlet look affected by so many younger women these days. She wore a high-necked lacy white blouse that would have done a straitlaced Victorian lady proud, but two shapely knees showed several fetching inches of nylon-swathed flesh beneath the hem of a black imitation-leather miniskirt and above the tops of matching winter boots. The tiny skirt left little to the imagination, but the exposed knees and thighs were primly glued together.

Like the paradoxical lace and leather, the tearful shudder that passed through her body as Kramer approached was at the same time both genuinely grief-stricken and poutily sexy. She examined Kramer with a none-too-bashful appraisal that he clearly read as an invitation.

"I'm Detective Paul Kramer," he said, holding out his identification long enough for her to glance at it. "And this is my . . ."

Motioning vaguely toward me, he started to say partner and then backed off. At least we were agreed on that score. We may have been stuck working together temporarily, but partners we weren't.

"This is my associate, Detective Beaumont," he continued after a somewhat awkward pause. "We'll be handling this case together. Mind if we ask you a few questions?"

She shook her head. "Okay," she said huskily. "Go ahead."

"Detective Beaumont here is under the impression

you're the one who discovered the bodies. Is that true?"

She nodded, vigorously.

With a reluctantly acknowledging glance at me, Kramer took out notebook and pencil. "What's your name, please?"

"Jennifer," she replied. "Jennifer Lafflyn."

"And you work here?"

"I'm the morning receptionist. In the afternoons, I'm a traveling secretary. I go to whichever department needs help at the moment."

"This is your desk?" I asked.

She nodded and glanced uneasily toward a desk that faced the front door. The side of the desk was almost parallel with the open closet door, and it stood less than five feet from it.

"That's where I usually sit, but today . . ." She broke off, and I nodded understandingly. I wouldn't have wanted to sit there right then, either.

"Where do you live, Miss Lafflyn?" I asked.

She didn't answer at once. Her eyes became instantly brittle and surprisingly hostile. Despite the virginal blouse, I had the unmistakable impression that this was a young woman with some heavy-duty mileage on her.

"It's a routine question, Miss Lafflyn," I added quickly. "We need your address for our incident reports."

"Ms.," she corrected sternly. "It's Ms. Lafflyn, not Miss."

So that was it. I had unwittingly stumbled into the mystifying Miss/Ms. quagmire.

Old habits die hard, especially those rock-solid

edicts of polite behavior that mothers pour into their sons' innocent minds along with the daily doses of equally solid bowls of oatmeal they pour into growing bodies. Unfortunately, the things mothers brainwash sons into believing don't necessarily change with the times.

My mother had ordered me to always address a young woman as Miss until absolutely certain she was a Mrs. That may have been true once, but it certainly wasn't true as far as Ms. Jennifer Lafflyn was concerned, a pissed Ms. Jennifer Lafflyn. There didn't seem to be much I could do to redeem myself in her eyes.

In the meantime, Detective Kramer was getting a huge bang out of every moment of my discomfort. With an ill-concealed smirk tugging at the corners of his mouth, he wrote down the address of a studio apartment which Ms. Lafflyn told us was located off Broadway near Seattle Community College.

"Tell us about this morning," Kramer urged.

"Alvin wasn't here at the door when I got to work this morning."

"Alvin?" Kramer asked.

"Alvin Chambers. The security guard."

Kramer nodded. "I see. And what time was that?"

"Seven," she added. "I was right on time, even with the weather. I come in at seven. That way I can leave at three. Anyway, when I arrived, Alvin wasn't here, and his table was still out, too. That seemed odd to me at the time. I mean, by the time people started coming in each morning, he usually had his table and chair put away and was there at the door, cheerful as could be, greeting people as they came in, opening the door for anyone who needed it. He was such a nice man."

Her eyes brimmed with sudden tears and she had to break off for a moment before she took a deep breath and was able to continue.

"Anyway, when I got here this morning and saw the table and chair were still out, I thought maybe he'd just gone to the bathroom or something."

"Are those them?" I asked, nodding toward a forlorn card table and an equally shabby folding chair that were stacked against the wall behind the receptionist's desk.

Jennifer nodded. "When he still wasn't here by seven-fifteen, I put the logbook away in the desk. I started to put the table and chair away too, where they're stored, in the closet."

Jennifer's story faltered to a fitful stop while she sent an uneasy sidelong glance at the still-open closet door. Again an involuntary shudder passed through her body.

"Is that when you found them?"

Unable to speak for a moment, Jennifer could only nod while she struggled to regain control. At last she did so and continued in a voice that was little more than a tremulous whisper.

"I'll probably have nightmares about it for the rest of my life. I mean her leg just fell out at me. Popped out into the room like toast from a toaster. It scared me to death." She put her hand to her mouth, and for a moment I was afraid she was going to be sick.

"And then what happened?"

"I screamed. At least somebody told me later that I screamed. I don't remember it at all. And then I guess I fainted. Mr. Jacobs from Curriculum was just coming through the door as it happened. He caught me and kept me from falling. He's the one who placed the call to 911."

"What's this about a logbook?" I asked.

"There's not much to tell. Security keeps a log of whoever comes and goes after hours and on weekends. People have to sign in and out."

"You said you put the logbook away. Where is it now?"

She pointed back toward the still-unoccupied receptionist's desk in the middle of the room. "Right there," she said. "In the bottom drawer. Would you like me to get it for you?"

"No," I replied. "Leave it there for right now. Did anyone else besides you touch the book or the table or chair?"

"Not that I know of."

"We may need to have a sample of your fingerprints," I said.

Up till then, the interview had been rolling along fairly smoothly, but at the mention of fingerprints, Jennifer Lafflyn balked. "Why? What would you need my fingerprints for? I haven't done anything wrong. I was just doing my job."

Kramer moved in soothingly to calm troubled waters. "It's standard procedure, Ms. Lafflyn. We take prints and have them available. For comparison purposes."

"Oh," she said, sounding somewhat mollified, but she was still glaring at me when she said it. I hadn't gotten off on the right foot with the young lady, and it wasn't getting any better.

"Let's talk about the victims for a moment," I said. "Do you know anything about them?"

Jennifer Lafflyn nodded authoritatively, jutting her chin. It was almost as though the stupidity of my question had somehow stiffened her spine. "Of course I do. Everybody here knows them. Alvin's the security guard I was telling you about."

"And the woman?"

"Mrs. Kelsey," she answered confidently.

"Who?"

"Marcia Louise Kelsey, from Labor Relations."

Doc Baker, finally satisfied with the photographer's work, emerged from the closet for the last time and directed two of his technicians to cover the bodies. Seeing that, Kramer abruptly snapped shut his notebook and strode off across the room, catching up with the medical examiner as he neared the door.

Kramer may have been ready to cut short the interview with Jennifer Lafflyn, but I wasn't. She watched with undisguised interest as Kramer walked across the room, and she seemed surprised when she looked back and found me still standing there.

"What time did Alvin Chambers usually get off work?" I asked.

Jennifer frowned. "What do you need to know that for?"

"We have to know what was usual in order to figure out what was different in the pattern, where there are any discrepancies."

"Seven-thirty," she answered. "And he always left right on the dot, never early and never late."

"So you were here together for half an hour or so nearly every morning?"

She nodded.

"How long had you known one another?"

Jennifer shrugged. "I don't remember exactly. Two or three months maybe. A long time for that job. It seems like all the other guards change every week or so. Everybody but Alvin. He seemed to really like it, to enjoy what he was doing."

"So is it busy around here in the mornings, or did you two have a chance to talk?"

"Some," she said. "Alvin was friendly. He liked people."

Jennifer Lafflyn was as changeable as Seattle's weather. Once more her eyes filled with tears that spilled over and ran down her cheeks. "I liked him a lot. As a friend, even though he was old enough to be my father. I really respected him, know what I mean?"

"And what did the two of you talk about?"

"Work, the weather, dumb stuff like that. Sometimes we talked about God."

"God?" I asked.

"Alvin was very religious. He used to be a minister, you know."

"No, I didn't know that. Did he retire?"

Jennifer shook her head. "I don't think so. He told me he quit. Just like that, but he was real religious all the same. Sometimes I thought maybe he was trying to convert me, but mostly we just talked."

"Did you ever see him with Mrs. Kelsey?"

"What do you mean?"

"I mean did you ever see them together, talking together, coming and going at the same time?"

"No," she said firmly. "Never. Why?"

It was my turn to shrug, surprised that she hadn't put two and two together on her own.

"If you find two people dead in the same closet, it's not too far-fetched to think that there might be some kind of connection between them."

During interviews, detectives are trained to watch for every nuance of expression. The twitch of an eyelid can be vital. A sudden anxiety exhibited by fluttering hands may indicate that questions are probing too near some painful truth. In answer to my comment, I saw a flicker of something blaze briefly in Jennifer's eyes before she blinked and sent a curtain of disdain over her face.

She struggled to her feet. "No," she said. "Absolutely not! There was never anything like that between them. You have a really nasty mind, Detective Beaumont. Now, if you'll excuse me, I'm going to go to the rest room and wash my face."

I watched her flounce off across the reception area, tottering a little in her high-heeled boots. She disappeared into a ladies' washroom. From her reaction, there could be no doubt that my suggestion of a relationship between the two dead people had sent Jennifer Lafflyn running for cover.

I wondered why that was, because if Alvin Chambers and Marcia Louise Kelsey hadn't had a relationship before they died, they sure as hell had one now.

CHAPTER 3

I WAS ON MY WAY TO THE DOOR TO JOIN DOC BAKER AND Detective Kramer when I almost collided with a lady who came rushing down the stairway into the reception area. She was a horsefaced woman wearing a severe suit that matched her iron gray hair. She stopped directly in front of me, pausing uncertainly and looking anxiously around the room.

"May I help you?" I asked.

"Oh, my, yes. Are you with the police?"

"Yes. My name's Detective Beaumont. What can I do for you?"

"I'm Doris, Doris Walker, Dr. Savage's secretary."

Dr. Kenneth Savage, the superintendent of schools, was the one employee of the school district whose name I recognized without any prompting. He had come to Seattle from Boston several years earlier and was trying to help the district cope with its twin perennial problems of decreasing enrollment and decreasing revenues. The fact that Savage had lasted for five whole years in a mostly thankless position not known for job security probably meant he was doing a reasonably good job.

"I just don't know what to do," Doris continued distractedly. "With all that's happened here this morning, Dr. Savage is having all the calls routed through us upstairs, and . . ." She stopped in midsentence, seemingly overcome by indecision.

"And what, Doris?" I prodded. "We can't help you if you don't tell us exactly what the problem is."

"Mrs. Chambers is on the phone," she blurted suddenly, nodding toward the janitor's closet without actually looking at it. "You know. His wife."

Although she seemed close to tears, she kept her voice discreetly low. I glanced cautiously around the room to make sure I was the only one listening to what she said.

"She told me that she has his breakfast on the table ready for him to eat it but that her husband still isn't home. He's more than an hour late, and she wanted to know if he had left here. That means she doesn't know anything at all yet, and I don't want to be the one to tell her. I mean what can you say when something this terrible has happened?"

I could have told Doris Walker that years of doing it, years of bringing people that kind of devastating news, doesn't make it any easier.

Instead I said, "Get the phone number and address of wherever she is right now. Tell her there's been a problem here at the office, and that you'll have someone check and get back to her as soon as possible. All right?"

Doris Walker nodded gratefully, heaving an immense sigh of relief. "So you don't want me to tell her. I don't have to?"

"Absolutely not!"

"Oh, good. I was afraid it was going to be up to me."

"Go back and talk to her now," I urged. "And when you get the information I asked for, come straight back here and give it to me. We'll handle it from there."

"Of course. Right away." Doris Walker hurried toward the stairs with the step of someone whose shoulders had just been relieved of the weight of the world. I in turn joined Kramer and Doc Baker near the door.

"Where've you been?" Kramer asked. "We don't have all day, you know."

Behind Kramer's back, Doc Baker gave an almost imperceptible shake to his head. The blatantly sympathetic look told me he found Detective Paul Kramer almost as tiresome as I did.

"What have we got, Doc?" I asked.

"Looks like homicide/suicide so far, although we haven't found a suicide note yet," Baker replied. "My guess is she got him first and then turned the gun on herself. She died right away. He took his time."

"IDs?"

Baker nodded. "Tentative. We'll have to have them confirmed by relatives as soon as possible. The male was wearing a name badge."

"I saw that," I said.

"People here say his whole name was Alvin Chambers. He worked for Seattle Security. They're the company with the security contract for the school district. The woman's name is Marcia Louise Kelsey. She was head of Labor Relations for the district here. We noticed her purse wasn't here. You may want to see if it's upstairs in her office when you go up to secure it."

I nodded. "Thanks for letting us know."

Baker waved and started away. "No problem."

"By the way," I added. "Those are the same names we were given by the receptionist."

Baker stopped and turned, raising one bushy eyebrow. "Who's that? Jennifer Lafflyn, the young woman who found the bodies?"

"That's right."

The medical examiner nodded his massive head. "I see, but we still have to regard the identification as tentative for right now. Did she have any idea about what kind of links might exist between these two people?"

"As a matter of fact, I asked her that very question just a few minutes ago," I replied. "According to her, there was no connection whatsoever."

I could have added that Jennifer's exaggerated nonresponse to my question had made me wonder, but it was such a tenuous hunch on my part that I didn't bother. I wouldn't have minded passing the idea along to Doc Baker, but I wasn't in favor of giving Kramer the benefit of my theory. Sharing hunches with people you neither like nor respect can be lots tougher in the long run than simply keeping your mouth shut.

"Well," said Baker, "I was just giving your partner here what we assume to be the victims' names and addresses. After you finish up, you may want to track down next-of-kin, notify them officially, and bring them by my office for the positive ID. Just give us an hour or so to get the bodies back downtown."

At that point, one of the medical examiner's technicians came over and waited patiently to be acknowledged. "What is it, Stevens?" Baker asked.

"There was something under one of the stiffs. Thought you and the dicks ought to take a look."

We walked back over to the closet. Marcia Kelsey's body had been removed altogether. Alvin Chambers' body-bagged corpse had been hefted onto a gurney nearby.

"It was under his ankle," Stevens said. "Anywhere else and it would have been covered with blood."

On the floor of the closet, in a small area where the tile hadn't been stained brown, lay a little yellow Post-it sheet. Grunting, Baker knelt down, studied the paper for a moment, then got up and moved out of the way, letting Kramer and me go by turns.

It was one of those cute little notepad things that says "From the desk of Marcia Kelsey." The handwriting was firm and perfectly legible: "A, See you tonight at the usual time. M."

"So they were getting it on in the closet," Paul Kramer crowed once he had read the note. "I told you."

Baker shot him a withering glance.

Something was bothering me, nudging my thinking. "Why did she do it in the closet with the door closed?" I asked, looking back inside at the grungy room with its dirty, deep sink. The only light was from a dim, unshaded forty-watt bulb hanging on the end of a rubberized cord with a chain pull for turning it off and on.

"You're right," Baker agreed. "That closet's not a very nice place, but maybe she wanted to muffle the noise."

But I was still studying the hanging lightbulb. Suddenly another bulb switched on in my head. "Wait a minute, Doc, was this light off or on when you got here?"

Frowning, Baker peered at me over the tops of his thick bifocals. "Off," he said. "Why?"

"Had anybody messed with it?"

"They all said they hadn't," he answered, giving me his undivided attention and nodding as the light dawned for him as well. "Now that you mention it, Beau, you're right. The light was definitely off. I'm the one who turned it on so we could see what we were doing in there."

"What's the light being off or on got to do with anything?" Kramer asked impatiently.

"People hardly ever kill themselves in the dark," I replied.

"Wait a minute. Are you trying to tell me that some poor son of a bitch who isn't worried about blowing his brains out would be scared of doing it in the dark? Get off it. Once they're dead, what does it matter?"

Paul Kramer had walked me right up to the very edge of my patience. "Let's leave interpretation up to the shrinks, shall we, Detective Kramer?"

Before Kramer could reply, Baker broke in. "Thanks for pointing out the light thing, Beau. It'll keep us on our toes when we do the autopsies."

"And when will that be?"

"This afternoon, probably. With the lousy weather, business is a little slow for us right now. Except for this, it's been too damned cold for people to be running around killing each other. For a change we don't have cases lined up and waiting. Even if we did, though, this would be a priority. After all, these people are supposedly fine, upstanding members of the community. There's going to be a whole lot of heat from the public and the media wanting to see results fast. This one isn't going to be any picnic for us, or for you either."

Baker wasn't saying something I hadn't already figured out for myself. Bums can get murdered every day of the week and nobody gives a damn, but let the victim be an ordinary bill-paying, tax-paying citizen, and people get a whole lot more interested. Throw in a dash of infidelity and you have a case that's going to be conducted in a white-hot spotlight of public scrutiny. Believe me, those kinds of cases are difficult for everybody concerned. They have minimal opportunity for glory and unlimited potential for disaster.

"Any idea when this happened?" Kramer asked.

"I can't say right now. We'll know better after the autopsies."

"And the gun?" I asked.

"A .38 Special. Probably belonged to Chambers or maybe the security guard company. He's wearing a holster, but it's empty."

"Why would a security guard in a school district need to be packing a piece?" Kramer asked.

Baker shook his head. "Beats me."

"We'd better stop by and ask the Superintendent

of Schools about that," I said. "We'll ask him about the logbook as well."

"Logbook?" Baker asked quickly.

"According to Jennifer Lafflyn, the security guards were required to log everyone who came through the building after hours. She said the book itself is safely put away in the bottom drawer of the receptionist's desk. She took care of that before she had any idea something was wrong."

"No doubt we'll need to take a look at it," Baker said.

The crime-scene investigators showed up right about then with their little bags of tricks. Crime-scene specialists sift through everything, dust for prints, preserve evidence, and do all the fine detail work made possible and necessary by advanced technology. Their work, combined with what happens later at the crime lab, is absolutely essential in successfully bringing cases both to court and conviction.

That's fine for them, but not for me. I'm glad those guys can analyze the hell out of threads found in carpets and traces of blood found on shoes, but I'd much rather be out on the streets talking to people—asking questions and getting answers—than being locked up in a lab someplace examining DNA fingerprints under a microscope.

We were almost finished when Doris Walker reappeared at my elbow.

"Here's the number you asked for," Doris said, handing me another slip of yellow paper. Post-its are evidently very popular at the school district office, and this one was larger than any I'd seen before.

"Mrs. Chambers said she's at home and will wait for a call back."

"Good," I said. "Thank you."

"When I told him I was bringing this down to you, Dr. Savage asked if you could stop by his office and talk to him for a few minutes before you leave. If it's not too much trouble, that is."

"Certainly," I said. "No trouble at all. We'll be glad to. We need to see him anyway."

Doris nodded and returned the way she had come.

"Who was that?" Kramer asked, watching her walk away.

"Doris Walker, the superintendent's secretary. She came down a few minutes ago and told me that Alvin Chambers' wife was on the phone wondering why he was so late coming home for breakfast. I told her to take a message about where we could reach the wife later and that we'd be in touch."

"Who's this doctor who wants to talk to us?"

"Dr. Savage. The superintendent of schools."

"Oh," Kramer said.

While the crime-scene team began work on the closet, we were taken upstairs and shown Marcia Louise Kelsey's office. It wasn't a plush executive-suite kind of place. The place was messy and cluttered, but there was no sign that it had been ransacked, and there was no indication that a struggle had taken place there. A pencil lay at an angle on a blue-lined tablet, looking as though the writer had stopped working for only a moment to do something else.

Offices usually have a certain amount of personal junk in them—family photographs, children's scrawled crayon Mother's Day greetings, personalized cups.

Marcia Kelsey's office had a curiously impersonal air about it. Neither the cluttered desk nor the faded yellow walls held any artwork or family photographs, only a collection of framed diplomas. Several unfaded oblong spots showed where pictures might have been once, but they weren't there any longer.

A sagging brown couch stood against the far wall under a window, its cushions piled high with computer printouts and other work-in-progress-type debris. For the first time I felt like I was being given some valuable insight into the dead woman's personality. I have a hard time relating to people who have to work in perfectly orderly offices.

There was plenty of physical evidence that Marcia Kelsey had left the room with every intention of returning. An open briefcase lay on the floor behind the desk, along with a shoulder-strap purse, a pair of panty hose, two heavy orange and gray woolen socks, and a pair of much-used snow boots.

Kramer pointed meaningfully at the panty hose. "If she started undressing here, how come they ended up in the closet downstairs? Why not clean all that crap off the couch and use that?"

Why not indeed?

When we finished with Marcia Kelsey's office and sealed it with crime-scene tape, Kramer was anxious to hit the road. "We ought to do like Baker said and get cracking on the notifications right away."

"First we go see Dr. Savage. I told Doris Walker we would, and that's what we're going to do." I started off down the hall, and Kramer followed reluctantly, complaining all the way.

"I don't know why we have to do this. Wait a minute, Beaumont. This Dr. Savage doesn't happen to be one of your high-toned cronies from outside the department, does he?"

Ever since I came into a fair amount of money and moved into Belltown Terrace, a high-rise downtown condo, there's been a certain sour-grapes element at work among some of my cohorts at Seattle P.D. A few of those folks can't seem to let go of what they presume to be my rarified social status. Mostly that so-called status is nothing more than a figment of overly active imaginations, but it doesn't make the ongoing antagonism any less real or any less annoying.

"I've never met the man before," I answered stiffly. "I assume he's interested in being apprised of what's going on here. After all, he is the school district's head honcho. We're here working on his turf, remember. It can't hurt for us to show him a little common courtesy."

"It'll be a waste of time," Kramer grumbled.

"Courtesy is never a waste of time," I assured him.

If she had only lived long enough, hearing that comment coming from her diamond-in-the-rough son would have made my mother proud. Astonished and proud.

When we appeared in front of Doris Walker's desk, her phone was ringing, ablaze with several blinking lights that indicated calls waiting on hold. As soon as she saw us, however, she dropped the handset back into its cradle, jumped to her feet, and left the telephone ringing unanswered while she escorted us to the door of the superintendent's private office.

"He told me you were to be shown in as soon as you got here," she explained.

I had seen Dr. Savage once or twice on television, usually standing in front of a podium addressing either the press or a group of citizens. In person he turned out to be surprisingly short. Well dressed and rotund, he spoke in flat, nasal tones that betrayed his proper Bostonian origins. He stood to shake hands across his desk and then waved us into chairs as Doris made the introductions.

"This is awful," he murmured, resuming his seat. "I can't imagine anything worse. How could such a terrible thing happen? The phone lines have been going like crazy all morning. Of course, we haven't given out any information, none at all. I hope that's correct. It's what we were told by the first officer who came here this morning. He said not to release anything, not a single word, until someone has a chance to notify next-of-kin."

"That's exactly right," I said reassuringly. "And we'll be doing that as soon as we possibly can, but in the meantime, there are a few things we need to clear up. Miss Lafflyn told us that your security guards keep a logbook and that it's currently located in the receptionist's desk downstairs. The crime-scene investigators will be picking that up and taking it along downtown with them."

"Certainly. That's fine. I'm sure we can scare up another one for whoever Seattle Security sends over to take Mr. Chambers' place. It's terrible for the families, of course, and I don't want to seem incredibly hard-hearted, but my main concern has to be to get this dreadful matter straightened out as soon as possible. We're an inner-city school system, you know. This kind of tragedy will make headlines all over the country. We can't afford that kind of PR. We simply cannot afford it."

Savage paused, seemingly winded by the vehemence of his speech. "Is there anything else you need?"

"Yes," I told him. "We'll need to have an opportunity to interview any number of your personnel, although we can't tell at this time the exact identity of the people involved, how many there are, or how much time we'll need to spend with each one of them," I added. "First on the list would be Mr. Jacobs, the fellow who called 911. There are probably numerous others as well."

Savage nodded thoughtfully. "I sent Martin, Mr. Jacobs, that is, home this morning right after it happened. He had quadruple bypass surgery six months ago. I didn't want to take any unnecessary chances. We'll give you his home number, though. He said he'd be happy to talk to the authorities whenever they needed him. And if there are any other phone numbers you need, phone numbers or addresses, we'll be happy to provide them—unless they're unlisted, of course. Those would be off limits. We'd have to get permission from each individual employee before we give those out."

He punched a button on his phone, and Doris Walker's disembodied voice came floating through the intercom. "Yes, Dr. Savage?"

"Write a memo to Personnel," he ordered. "Tell them that they are to cooperate fully with these detectives." Savage turned to us with a frown. "What were your names again?"

"Detectives Beaumont and Kramer," I told him.

He repeated the names into the intercom. "Whatever information they require is to be given the highest possible priority. Be sure to make that clear. As soon as you have the memo typed up, bring it in for my signature, and then I want you to deliver it personally. No. Absolutely not. Don't send it through interoffice mail. You make sure it gets to Kendra Meadows herself. Today. This morning if at all possible."

He switched off the intercom and turned back to us, obviously pleased with himself and the way he personally was handling this crisis. "Is there anything else I can do to be of service, gentlemen?"

I glanced at Kramer, who shook his head and glanced pointedly at his watch. "We really ought to be going," he said, rising to his feet.

"There is one more thing you could clear up for us, Dr. Savage. To my knowledge, most security guards in this area don't usually wear weapons, but Mr. Chambers was wearing a holster, and a gun was found at the scene. That troubles me. Why would a weapon be necessary in a situation like this, where he was functioning primarily as a night watchman?"

Savage's easy affability retreated somewhat. He looked at me warily for several long moments before he answered.

"This district is currently faced with any number of difficult crises, Detective Beaumont, one of which involves closing several schools. That's always a very emotional issue. We've also had our share of union difficulties."

From his obvious discomfort, I sensed that his

initial answer wasn't the whole answer. "I know about the strike last fall," I said. "But having a security guard on overnight and on weekends would indicate some kind of ongoing problem."

He shrugged as if to downplay the importance of what was being said, but the seriousness of his concern was plainly written across his face. Kenneth Savage wouldn't have been any better at playing poker than I am.

"We've had some threats now and again," he said quietly. "Nothing serious of late," he added lightly with a quick smile.

"Threats? What kind of threats?" I pressed.

He shrugged. "Oh, you know. The usual kind of crazies."

"There's no such thing as a 'usual' crazy," I returned. "They're all one of a kind. Exactly what sort of threats?"

"Bomb threats," he answered with pained reluctance.

"And they haven't been reported?"

For an answer he made a waffling motion with his hand.

"Have they or haven't they?"

"To the authorities, yes, but we've tried to keep it out of the media, and so far we've been successful."

"Why keep it quiet?"

"As I said before, gentlemen, we're a troubled district." He sat up straighter in his chair, delivering his words with guarded intensity. "As such, we can't afford any adverse publicity. We've been handling this situation the best we know how, monitoring the situation, keeping things under control."

"I hate to be the bearer of more bad news," I told him. "With those two murders downstairs, 'adverse publicity,' as you call it, is here to stay. You'd better brace yourself for it."

Dr. Savage seemed to have shrunk into himself. "What do you want me to do?" he asked.

"When Doris finishes that memo," I said, "you have her gather up every bit of information you have on those bomb threats and have it ready for us to pick up when we come back later on this afternoon."

"But why? I thought you were investigating the murders. What does that have to do with the bomb threats?"

"Maybe nothing, but then again, maybe they are connected. I want everything you have, regardless of its seeming importance, understand?"

Savage nodded. "Right," he said. "Everything. You'll have it."

Detective Kramer was already standing poised by the door when I got up to follow him.

"Way to go," he said under his breath as I followed him out the door and down the hall. "Glad to see you can put the screws to somebody when you feel like it."

I'm sure Paul Kramer intended that remark as a compliment, but to me it didn't feel like something to be proud of. My mother wouldn't have liked it either.

CHAPTER 4

THE ADDRESS DORIS WALKER HAD GIVEN US FOR ALVIN Chambers was in the North End. With the streets blanketed by snow and ice, getting there proved both difficult and hazardous.

It was midmorning now. The City of Seattle no longer appeared to be a ghost town. Despite the frigid cold, the pale crystal blue sky lit by brilliant sunshine had tempted at least a few intrepid souls into venturing outside. Some were making justifiably belated attempts to get to work, while others, especially children in a holiday mood, took advantage of their unexpectedly lengthened Christmas vacation to play in the morning's winter wonderland.

Seattle drivers don't get nearly enough experience at driving on snow and ice to be any good at it. What little they learn during one year's major storm never carries over to the next. We didn't even make it off Queen Anne Hill without passing several minor spin-outs and accompanying fender benders. A departmental traffic advisory warned us that both Aurora Avenue and northbound I-5 were tied up with accidents, so we cut across town on Mercer Street, aiming for Fifteenth Avenue.

With Kramer driving, we had just passed the intersection where Queen Anne Avenue North meets Mercer when a sled loaded with two laughing kids came flying down Roy Street and zipped across the street directly in front of us. It was sheer luck that we didn't crush them under our tires. Had the timing been even so much as one microsecond different, there would have been nothing Kramer or anyone else could have done to avoid hitting them.

"Jesus Christ!" Kramer grumbled. "What the hell do those crazy kids think they're doing?"

"Stop the car," I told him. "I'll go set them straight."

"Bullshit," Kramer responded. Instead of slowing down to let me out, he accelerated and reached for the radio. "Kids on sleds are Traffic's problem, not ours. We're Homicide, remember?"

"If someone doesn't stop them, it could very well become Homicide's problem," I returned grimly.

In fact, during the past few years, the number of snow-related deaths in the city had taken an alarming swing upward, particularly due to sled/motor vehicle accidents.

It would have taken only a moment to give those kids the dressing down they so richly deserved, with the added side benefit of maybe saving their young lives, but Detective Kramer was driving. Intent solely on the case at hand, his type A personality allowed for no diversions or distractions, not even potentially lifesaving ones. Disgusted, I listened while he reported the near-miss incident to an already vastly overworked traffic dispatcher.

"They're not going to have time to do anything about it," I muttered when he finished.

"We're not either," he replied.

I could see that working together wasn't going to be a picnic for either one of us.

It took us more than an hour to make what normally would have been a simple twenty-five-minute ride to the North End. The object of our drive turned out to be a modest two-storied complex called Forest Grove located a block off Aurora on Linden Avenue. The weathered shingle structures looked like an early failed attempt at condominiums, one that had deteriorated into lower-middle-class apartments with the passage of time and the dwindling of enthusiasm. Even the pristine mantle of snow couldn't disguise an overall air of near hopelessness, of abject poverty held only partially at bay.

The complex's driveway dipped steeply down from the street, with plenty of spinning tire tracks in evidence to show that those few drivers who had managed to escape the parking lot that morning had struggled mightily to make their way up to Linden. We parked on the street and walked and slid down into the complex past a grove of evergreens, their branches drooping under the weight of fat clods of snow.

Number 709 was in the third building and on the second floor. Unable to use the snow-laden railings, we gingerly climbed a rickety set of stairs that groaned and creaked ominously beneath us and the added weight of heavy snow.

Once on the small landing outside the apartment, we saw that the curtains were solidly closed against the brilliant daylight. The varnish on the flimsy front door was faded and peeling. From inside we could hear the droning hum of a television set. Kramer tried ringing the bell. Predictably, it didn't work, but Kramer's determined knock, curiously muffled by the snow around us, eventually produced a reaction—the audible lowering of the volume on the TV.

"What's the matter? Forget your key?" a woman's voice demanded as the door was flung open. "Where've you been?"

The sour-faced woman standing before us was improbably fat and wearing a terry cloth robe that gapped open over her more than ample boobs. Hastily she pulled the robe shut and stood on her toes to peer anxiously over our shoulders toward the parking lot. I knew who she was looking for. She didn't know yet that he wasn't coming. Not then, and not ever.

"Sorry," she mumbled. "Thought you might be my husband, Alvin. He's late getting home from work, and he never called, either. Who are you?"

"Police officers, ma'am," I began, reaching for my ID. "Are you Mrs. Chambers?"

"Yes."

"Would you mind if we came in?"

"Yes, I mind. Couldn't you come back later? I'm right in the middle of *The Young and the Restless*."

"It's very important, Mrs. Chambers," I insisted.

"Oh, all right," she said grudgingly. "Come on in

then, but I don't want you to stay very long, not when Alvin's not here. People might talk, you know."

She turned and waddled away from the door, clutching the robe around her. Kramer and I followed, making our way through a heavily curtained room whose only light came from the flickering images on a color television set in the far corner. Before my eyes adjusted to the lack of light, I stumbled into a chair and sent a pile of something crashing to the floor.

"Don't worry about that," Charlotte Chambers said. "It's only Alvin's books. I keep waiting for him to put them away. Stay there a minute and I'll turn on a light."

She switched on a table lamp on an end table by the couch and punched the mute button on the television set's remote control. The room looked like it had been in an earthquake. Boxes with stacks of contents spilling out of them were scattered everywhere. Every available flat surface was covered with junk—clothing, soda cans, dead newspapers, books. A narrow path threaded its way through the debris to where two decrepit recliners sat in front of the television set. Before one of them sat a TV-tray, and on it was a plate with someone's breakfast—two congealed eggs and two pieces of dry toast.

"Alvin's breakfast," Charlotte Chambers told us when she noticed I was looking at the plate. "He usually likes to eat just as soon as he gets home, but like I said, he's late today, and he didn't even call. That's gratitude for you, when I got up special to cook for him. You'd think he'd show a little consideration."

She flopped into the other recliner, picking up a

huge bowl of popcorn as she did so and thumping the protesting chair back into a full reclining position. "Want any popcorn?" she asked. "I popped it just a little while ago. It's fresh."

She held out the bowl of popcorn, but both Kramer and I declined. The idea of eating popcorn for breakfast is totally foreign to me. I watched in horrified fascination as she shoved a huge fistful of popcorn into her own mouth, totally heedless of the stray kernels that leaked out of her hand and dribbled down her multitudinous chins only to fall unnoticed to the floor and disappear into the matted orange and green shag carpeting.

"What is it you wanted again?" Charlotte asked, with her mouth still full.

"We're here concerning your husband," I told her.

"You're out of luck then. I already told you he isn't here. Have a chair if you want to."

Kramer made a quick dive for a kitchen chair that was sitting against a wall. He removed a tangle of unfolded clothes and took that chair for himself, leaving me no option but the other recliner—the one with the plateful of greasy, petrifying eggs sitting in front of it.

"Who did you say you are again?" she asked, munching on a mouthful of popcorn. "And what's this all about?"

"We're police officers, ma'am, and we're here about your husband."

"What about him?"

"Mrs. Chambers," I said quietly. "There's been a serious incident down at the school district office. I'm afraid we have some bad news for you."

She had just stuffed another handful of popcorn into her mouth. At least she stopped chewing. "What kind of bad news?" she asked.

"A man has been murdered," I said, unable to find any less damaging way to give her the news. "We have reason to believe that man is your husband."

Charlotte Chambers looked from me to Kramer and back again. "This is some kind of joke, isn't it?" she said.

I pulled my ID from my pocket and waved it in front of her, but she didn't bother to look at it.

"It's like some sort of newfangled *Candid Camera*, isn't it? I've heard about this program. You're waiting to see what I'm going to do."

I wasn't making much progress. I took another shot at it.

"Mrs. Chambers, I can assure you, this is no joke, and it's not a television program either. A man has been killed. He's been tentatively identified as your husband. We've been sent to notify you and to bring someone along down to Harborview who can positively identify the body."

Charlotte Chambers shoved another deliberate handful of popcorn into her mouth. She chewed thoughtfully, shaking her head all the while. "You're mistaken," she said at last. "Alvin is at work. I'm sure he's on his way home by now."

I looked at Kramer, appealing for help, but he shrugged his shoulders and left it for me to handle. Clearly Charlotte Chambers' ironclad denial wasn't any of his concern. I probably could have pounded my way through her defenses, but that didn't seem like a reasonable thing to do. Instead, I tried yet another tack.

"Perhaps you're right," I conceded. "Maybe he isn't your husband. He was found in a janitor's closet down at the school district office along with a woman."

"You say this man was with another woman? That settles it then," Charlotte Chambers responded triumphantly. "My husband's a happily married man, a man of the cloth, at least he was until he quit. He's not like those despicable men on television and in the movies. Alvin wouldn't be caught dead with another woman."

It was an unfortunate choice of words. The ghost of a smile appeared in the corners of Detective Kramer's lips, but I managed to keep a straight face. After all, this was no laughing matter. One way or the other, I had to get Charlotte Chambers to agree to accompany us to the medical examiner's office. We needed her verification.

"Then you'll come along with us downtown?" I asked. "That's the only way we can be sure it's not your husband."

She nodded and heaved herself off the couch. "Sure. I'll have to get dressed first," she said. "We'll leave a note for Alvin so if he comes home while we're gone, he'll know where I am."

"Right," I said.

She grabbed up the pile of unfolded clothes Kramer had removed from the chair and carried it into a bedroom, closing the door behind her.

Kramer clicked his tongue. "This dame's a real

Loony Tunes," he said. "Even if he is her old man, who's to say she'll recognize him?"

"She'll recognize him, all right," I replied grimly, "but only if we get her down there in the first place."

We fell silent and waited until the bedroom door opened again and Charlotte Chambers emerged. She was wearing the standard fat lady uniform of black polyester stretch pants expanded to their absolute maximum under a tent-like red blouse that came almost to her knees. She moved away from us, hiking the pants up and smoothing the top down as she went.

Stopping by her chair, she pulled a pair of snow boots out from under a stack of yellowing discarded newspapers and sat down to pull them on, wheezing with effort at the physical exertion. Once she had the boots on her feet, she made no attempt to fasten them. I could see the fasteners would never close around her wide calves.

"There," she announced. "I'm ready."

She waddled to an entryway closet and dragged out a knit cap. Putting it on, she stuffed her stringy hair inside it, wrapped a matching scarf around her neck, and then pulled on an enormous coat that reached all the way down to her ankles.

I held out my arm. "This way, Mrs. Chambers. Let me help you. It's slippery out there."

She clung to my arm with a deathlike grip all the way down the stairs. I took it slow and easy. I sure as hell didn't want her to fall. If she had landed on top of me, Charlotte Chambers would have mashed me flat.

It took both Kramer and me to help her up the

steeply graded drive that led out of the parking lot. By the time we reached the car, she was panting and out of breath. So were we. Rolling his eyes in relief as I handed her into the backseat of the car, Kramer hurried around to the driver's door, climbed in, and started the engine.

The trip downtown was made in almost complete silence. Since Charlotte Chambers had not yet conceded that the dead man was her husband, there wasn't much sense in launching into any kind of questioning process. That would have to come later.

Halfway downtown, I heard the rustle of paper and looked back to see that Charlotte Chambers had pulled a Snickers bar from her cavernous purse and was starting to unwrap it. She caught me watching.

"Would you like one?" she asked guiltily. "I've got two more just like it in my purse."

"No, thanks," I said. "I'm not very hungry right now."

"Me either," Kramer added.

When we finally managed to creep up the snow-bound hillside to Harborview Hospital and the medical examiner's office, the two parking spots reserved for police vehicles were both occupied by nonpolice cars.

"Take her on inside," Kramer said, pausing near the door. "I'll drop you two off here and then go find a parking place."

"Thanks," I muttered to him once Charlotte Chambers was safely on her feet and standing outside the car. "You're all heart," I added.

Naturally the receptionist was Johnny-on-the-spot. Naturally there was no wait for an available technician. We were ushered directly into the morgue. Kramer managed to stall his entrance long enough so that by the time he came into the room, a slack Charlotte Chambers had collapsed weeping into my arms. It was all I could do to hold her up.

Despite his widow's lofty claims to the contrary, Alvin Chambers had indeed been caught dead with another woman.

My job now was to find out why.

CHAPTER 5

KRAMER ENTERED THE ROOM AND IMPATIENTLY MO-
tioned me aside with a jerk of his head.

"What's up?" I asked.

"Doc Baker wants to talk to both of us. Outside.
On the double."

Put that way, it sounded like an invitation to a be-
heading, but then, Doc Baker's corpse-side manner
has never won any prizes for tact.

Nodding, I led the still-sobbing Charlotte to a
nearby chair and eased her into it.

"You wait right here, Mrs. Chambers," I said gently when she looked up at me in tearful dismay, "We'll
be back just as soon as we can."

Howard Baker was waiting for us outside. We
found him pacing back and forth in the highly polished corridor, pacing and fuming, with his mane of
unruly white hair almost standing on end and his
hands shoved deep in his pockets. He barely waited
long enough for the heavy swinging door to whisper
shut behind us before he lit into us full bore.

"Why for God's sake did you go after the damn security guard's family first? I thought you'd have better sense. I told you earlier. Marcia Louise Kelsey was highly thought of down at the school district. If you don't get to her family pretty damn soon, word's bound to leak out. What the hell are you two guys using for brains these days?"

Despite what the Constitution says, all men are not created equal—not in life and not in death either. Rank hath its privilege, even in the medical examiner's wagon. In the world of social standing, labor relations specialists may not count for much up against the likes of, say, Lee Iacocca, but they do if it's a contest between them and a lowly security guard. According to Doc Baker's rules of order and propriety, Marcia Louise Kelsey's death demanded a prior claim on the homicide squad's time and attention. The death of a mere peon like poor old Alvin Chambers didn't count for much.

Usually I don't let Doc Baker's penchant for public relations bother me, but for some reason this time it got me good. After all, Alvin Chambers' job title may not have sounded as important as Marcia Louise Kelsey's, but he was sure as hell equally dead. I was working up a sarcastic rejoinder, but Kramer spoke up before I had a chance to spit it out.

"We had to go there first, Doc. The Chambers woman was on the phone raising hell in the superintendent's office because her husband was late getting home for his toast and eggs."

"Oh," a somewhat mollified Baker replied. "I see. Well, get the hell out of here now and find Mr. Kelsey. Do it quick before somebody else does."

"Wait a minute. What about Charlotte Chambers?" I demanded. "After bringing her all the way down here, we can't very well just go off and leave her like this."

"Don't worry about Mrs. Chambers," Baker replied. "I'll get someone from my office to drive her home."

"But we haven't interviewed her yet," I objected.

"There'll be time enough for that later," Baker said, herding us unceremoniously toward the door. "After you talk with Mr. Kelsey."

Some things aren't worth going to the mat for, and this was one of them. I sidestepped Baker and poked my head back into the room where we had left Charlotte Chambers long enough to explain that one of Dr. Baker's staff members would take her home. Still sitting exactly as I'd left her, she nodded gratefully. I hoped whoever Baker sent would be big enough and strong enough to handle her.

When we got out to the car, I found that Kramer had parked with the rider's door opening directly onto a pile of dirty sanded snow left behind by a snowplow. By the time I managed to climb inside, my shoes and socks were covered with the stuff. Disgusted, I brushed it off as best I could.

"It's only snow," Kramer observed with a laugh. "It won't kill you."

I had seen Kramer coming to work both winter and summer in a little blue RX 7 equipped with a permanent set of ski racks. I knew from coffee break chatter around the office that he fancied himself as something of a ski-slope expert. That in itself would have been enough to keep me away from visiting Seattle's nearby slopes even if I could have overcome that most basic of all objections—the one against breaking your neck.

"Just drive, would you?" I asked. "What's the address?"

"Thirteen fifty-two East Crockett," Kramer replied, heading off in that direction. Considering road conditions, we were lucky that the Kelsey home was in generally the same part of town as Harborview Hospital.

East Crockett Street, at the far north end of Capitol Hill, is one of those city planner's nightmares that hops and skips its way east and west across town from Puget Sound to Lake Washington without ever being a through street. There are little chunks of Crockett on Magnolia Bluff, on Queen Anne Hill, and on Capitol Hill as well, but none of them connect.

We headed east on Boston, aiming for Thirteenth, one of two tiny streets that would take us up the hill to the single, block-long section of Crockett. As we neared the intersection, however, I noticed an aging, burnt-orange Volvo parked haphazardly on the side of the snowy street. The beat-out junker looked more than vaguely familiar.

Not Maxwell Cole, I thought with a sinking feeling in my gut. Please not Maxwell Cole, but as we came even with the car, I caught sight of a series of *Seattle Post-Intelligencer* parking stickers glued in the back window.

"Damn!" I muttered.

"What's the matter?" Kramer asked, glancing at me as he swung the car out of the fairly well-traveled snowy tracks on Boston and shifted down for the steeply inclined and much-less-traveled Thirteenth.

"That old Volvo parked back down there. It's Maxwell Cole's car," I answered.

"Maxwell Cole? The crime columnist for the *P.-I.*?"

"One and the same."

"But how do you know for sure it's his car?"

"Believe me, I know," I told him.

Kramer would have recognized the Volvo too, if he'd spent as many years as I have with Max, a perpetual fraternity brother who has never grown up, dogging my every step.

Kramer groaned. "That's great! Just what we need, a damn reporter on the scene before we are."

My sentiments exactly.

The 1300 block of Crockett consisted of a row of three originally identical and ersatz Victorians perched like so many birds looking down on the Montlake Cut, a man-made waterway connecting Lakes Union and Washington. Angular rooflines on the narrow houses seemed to grow up out of the hillside like so many gaunt plants potted in fair-sized two-car garages far below.

Two of the houses were a faded gray, but 1352 showed every evidence of having been recently and lovingly repainted, although it must have been a killer of a job. The wooden shingles gleamed like the surrounding snow. The trim was a deep green. Two stately but snow-shrouded holly trees stood guard on either side of the old-fashioned front porch, while the wide front door itself was decorated by a huge red-bowed Christmas wreath. The place looked as though it might have been lifted from some old-time, gilt-lined greeting card.

The whole effect would have been picture-perfect if it hadn't been for the overweight man with an open, flapping coat who was clutching the handrail and gingerly working his way back down the steep steps toward the sidewalk. Seeing him confirmed my worst suspicions—mine and Doc Baker's as well. The media had indeed beaten us to the punch. The man picking his way down the stairs was none other than my old nemesis, crime columnist Maxwell Cole himself.

I scrambled out of the car, intent on stopping Cole before he managed to slip away. We needed to find out exactly how much damage he'd done. He blundered off the steps and was heading back down Crockett toward his car when I stopped him.

"Hold it right there, Max. We want to talk to you."

At the sound of my voice, Max froze, standing knee-deep in the snow. Slowly he turned back toward me while an expression of profound dismay washed over the reporter's face. He looked like the kid caught with his hand in the proverbial cookie jar.

I didn't waste time on polite formalities. "What are you doing here, Max?"

He glanced anxiously from me to Kramer and back again. Max was out of shape and puffing from exertion just from walking back down to the street. "I stopped by to see Pete," he managed.

"Pete who?" I demanded.

"Pete Kelsey," he replied.

"Why?" I asked.

Max took a deep breath and tried to regain a little

of his dignity. "He's a friend of mine," he replied, squaring his shoulders. "A very good friend."

That didn't sound likely, not coming from the Maxwell Cole I knew.

"Is he now," I responded. "And how is it that you just happened to stop by to see him today of all days?"

"I did, that's all," Max insisted petulantly, his voice lapsing into its characteristic whine. "You can believe that or not."

"I choose not, Max. I know you too damn well. Your stopping by here wouldn't have anything to do with Pete Kelsey's wife, now would it?"

He eyed me warily. "What if it did?"

"This is a police matter, Max. Don't screw around with us."

Shrugging, Maxwell Cole caved in. "I heard about Marcia as soon as I got to work," he said. "You know how these things get around. I stopped by to see if Pete needed anything. That's all"

"Am I to understand that you know these people? As in friend of the family?"

He nodded.

"So tell me the truth, Max. Was this really a Good Samaritan call, or are you really out here chasing after a scoop, an exclusive interview maybe?"

Maxwell Cole's eyes narrowed in anger. Although there was no hint of a breeze, the drooping tips of his handlebar mustache trembled with suppressed rage. "I'm telling you, J. P., these people are friends of mine. I thought I might be able to help. Besides, Pete wasn't home. Nobody's there."

"Any idea where we'd find him?"

Cole glanced surreptitiously at his watch and then

shook his head. "I can't think of any place at all," he said. "Now, let me go before I freeze to death."

I nodded. "Go on."

Without hesitation, Cole clambered on down the street toward Thirteenth, leaving a dented trail of steps in the snow.

As soon as Max was out of earshot, Paul Kramer wheeled on me. "Wait just a goddamned minute here, Beaumont. How come you're letting him go? You saw the way he looked at his watch. That guy knows something, and he's not telling."

"Right," I said. "And all we have to do is follow him to find out what it is."

Kramer looked at me speculatively for only a moment, then he nodded and got back into the car. "We'll just see about that," he said curtly.

It turned out I was right.

Although Crockett wasn't posted as a oneway street, most of the residents seemed to treat it that way, entering on Thirteenth and exiting by way of Everett Avenue. When we got back to Boston, Maxwell Cole's laboring Volvo was disappearing over the crest of the hill. Both Max and Kramer had their hands full negotiating their vehicles through the hazardous streets. I rode shotgun and had no trouble keeping the Volvo well in sight.

Cole led us back down off Capitol Hill, through the bungled I-5 interchange known locally as the Mercer Mess, then north to the Fremont Bridge. Max turned off onto Phinney North and stopped on the street next to the Trolleyman Pub, a factory outlet store for one of the city's better-known microbreweries where they make Red Hook Ale. By then we were little more than a block behind him, but Max was oblivious to our presence. Without bothering to pause and look around, Max hurried inside.

The Trolleyman is a little too trendy for my taste. From the unexpected *NO SMOKING* sign on the front door to the brightly lit interior decorated with all-too-modern art, it's hardly the kind of tavern where any self-respecting serious drinker would choose to hang out. Due to the weather, the white-formica-topped tables with their oak chairs were mostly deserted. A single couple was cuddled cozily on an old-fashioned sofa in front of the roaring corner fireplace.

Kramer and I entered the room just as Maxwell Cole was sidling confidentially up to the bartender, a craggy-faced man in his midforties, a junior Willie Nelson type whose shoulder-length, graying hair was drawn back in a scrawny, rubber-band-held ponytail.

As he caught sight of us, Maxwell Cole's mouth dropped open in dumb amazement. Whatever words he had planned to say died on his lips.

I took the bull by the horns. "Pete Kelsey?" I asked.

The bartender looked at me appraisingly, his head cocked to one side while he absently polished the already gleaming surface of the bar.

"That's right," he said. "What can I do for you?"

Pulling out my ID, I tossed it to him. He caught it in midair, looked at it, and tossed it back without comment.

"We're police officers," I explained. "I'm Detective Beaumont and this is Detective Kramer. We'd like to have a word with you. In private, if you don't mind."

Kelsey glanced around the almost-deserted room

and grinned engagingly. "It's already pretty private in here today. I have a feeling most of the regular lunch crowd didn't bother to come to work, and neither did my helper, so this will have to do. Besides, Max here is an old friend of mine. What do you want to talk about?"

"This is confidential, Mr. Kelsey," I insisted. "Really, I . . ."

Kelsey shrugged impatiently. "I already told you. Max is a friend of mine. Whatever you have to say, you can say in front of him."

"It's about your wife."

The friendly, easygoing look on his face disappeared. In its place a hardened mask slipped over his otherwise handsome features. "What about her?"

"Two people were found dead at the school district office early this morning, Mr. Kelsey. I'm sorry to say that one of them may very well be your wife."

Pete seemed to stagger under the weight of the news, leaning against the bar for support. For confirmation, he glanced briefly at Maxwell Cole, who nodded wordlessly and ducked his head.

My heart went out to Pete Kelsey. My guess was that this would prove to be one of those cases where the death itself would be only the tip of the iceberg. If he wasn't already aware of it, by the time we finished uncovering all the sordid details surrounding the deaths of the two nearly naked people in the closet, I imagined Pete Kelsey would have a whole lot more to grieve about than a simple, unexpected death. He'd have to learn to live with betrayal as well.

He lurched backward and settled on a stool behind the bar. "How?" he whispered hoarsely. "How did it happen?"

"We don't know that yet and won't until after the autopsy."

At that, Pete Kelsey bent over, burying his face in his hands while his wide shoulders shook with uncontrollable sobs. The gray-flecked ponytail flopped up and down like a landed fish. He was mumbling to himself through the sobs, and I strained to hear the words.

"I never should have . . ." was all I could make out.

Kramer and I waited patiently for a break in the emotional storm. At last there was a letup.

"What do you want me to do?" he asked hopelessly, looking up at us only after wiping his tear-stained face on the shoulders of his faded blue work shirt.

"If you could accompany us downtown, we need to have someone make a positive identification."

He nodded. "It'll take me a few minutes to close up. And I should call my manager . . ."

"I'll do that," Maxwell Cole offered. "I can call Nancy and let her know. You do whatever else needs to be done."

By this time the couple in the corner had become aware of the situation. With hurried words of clumsy condolence, they paid their tab and left. Pete Kelsey seemed to have regained control of himself as he turned off coffeepots, emptied the cash register, and turned out lights.

"Nancy said to leave the change in the bottom drawer of her desk," Max reported when he got off the phone. "She'll be in to reopen about four. She's waiting for someone to come put chains on her car." Max paused for a moment before adding, "She says to tell you she's sorry."

Pete Kelsey nodded, but he went on with what he was doing, stopping by the window long enough to turn the orange and black *CLOSED* sign so it faced out. Then he opened the door to let us back out onto the street.

"Me too," he murmured fiercely under his breath. "Me too."

CHAPTER 6

OUTSIDE, STANDING IN THE SNOWBOUND AND ALL-BUT-deserted street, we suggested that Pete ride with us as far as Harborview Hospital, but he declined, saying that he didn't want to have to come all the way back across town to pick up his car from the tavern. Considering the hazardous driving conditions, I didn't blame him. It was time for compromise.

"I'll ride with you then," I suggested. Pete nodded in agreement, pulling car keys from the pocket of a faded sheepskin-lined denim jacket as he started toward the cars.

Meanwhile, Maxwell Cole, who was still hovering solicitously in the background, tagged along after us. "Want me to come too?" he asked hopefully.

"No, Max," Pete answered. "I'll be all right."

Max's heavy features sagged with disappointment at the idea of being left behind. "I'll give you a call later then," Max added. "Just to see if there's anything you need me to do."

"Sure," Pete said.

His car, parked in Seattle's peculiar *BACK-IN-ANGLE-ONLY* fashion near the buried curb, was a bowlegged old Eagle station wagon. Nut brown in color, it was the kind of nondescript vehicle used-car dealers call "transportation specials," a means of getting around rather than an extension of the owner's ego. It also had the lived-in look of a one-person car.

I waited while Pete Kelsey sorted through the accumulated debris on the rider's seat, which included several sets of blueprints, a series of empty coffee cups, and a massive old-fashioned satchel that evidently functioned as a briefcase. All this he tossed carelessly onto the floor behind the front seat. The backseat had been folded flat, and the entire rear of the car was occupied, from side to side and back to front, by an enormous old-fashioned, claw-footed tub.

"Sorry about the mess," Pete apologized. "I picked the tub up from the refinishing company Saturday afternoon and was supposed to drop it off at a remodeling job today, but with the weather and now this . . ." His voice trailed off.

"Don't worry about it," I said. "Let's go."

The four-wheel-drive Eagle may have looked ungainly, but properly equipped with snow tires, the station wagon was as agile and surefooted as a mountain goat, and Pete Kelsey was a capable driver. He knew the streets of the city well enough that we got to Harborview Hospital a good two minutes before Detective Kramer did.

While we waited for Kramer to arrive, I sat there knowing what was to come and dreading it. You can't be human and not feel some empathy for the people whose broken loved ones lie on cold, hard slabs in

morgues waiting for someone to come identify them.
Often the survivors' shattered hopes and dreams lie
there dead as well.

Leading Charlotte Chambers through the process
had been bad enough. Fortunately for her, the bloody
wound on her husband's chest had been mercifully
concealed, hidden from view beneath the antiseptic
covering of the body sheet. With Pete Kelsey it would
be different. There was no way to conceal Marcia's
ugly head wound. It would be fully visible. My heart
went out to her husband. So far, he was bearing up
pretty well, but I couldn't, in good conscience, allow
him to walk unprepared into the medical examiner's
office. I felt a moral obligation to give him some advance warning about what was coming.

"Have you ever seen a gunshot victim?" I asked.

It was a moment before he replied. "Yes," he answered dully without elaborating as to where or when.
"I have."

"So you know what to expect?"

He nodded grimly.

"It'll probably be pretty rough, Mr. Kelsey. The
bullet went in through her chin and came out the
back of her head."

"Oh."

The single word wrenched out of him as an involuntary groan. Pete's fingers closed around the steering
wheel in a white-knuckled grip, but he kept himself
under control.

"I'll be all right," he said at last, loosening his fingers from the steering wheel and unclenching his
stiffened jaw. "Thanks for letting me know."

Frigid air had crept into the car. We were both

getting cold. I led him inside, and Kramer caught up with us in the reception area. The three of us walked into the morgue together. When the attendant pulled out the body and removed the sheet, Pete Kelsey took one quick look, then turned away and dashed for the door, his face ashen, his throat working convulsively.

I found him standing outside the building, gulping in deep, shuddering breaths of the icy air.

"Couldn't they have done something to clean her up?" he whispered hoarsely.

"Not until after the autopsy," I explained. "It's a matter of preserving evidence."

He shook his head miserably. "Her hair," he murmured in a voice choking with raw emotion. "I can't believe her hair. Marcia was always so vain about it. She loved being a blonde, a real, natural blonde. When the gray crept up on her a few years ago, she hated it and started dipping in the dye."

Suddenly, thinking about his wife's once beautiful hair proved to be too much. There was no way for him to reconcile the memories of what Marcia Kelsey had once been with the terrible ruin in the morgue behind us. Kelsey plummeted over the edge of control. Leaning against the building, he stood with his face averted from me, sobbing uncontrollably.

I couldn't help him. No one could have. That kind of wild grief is beyond the reach of comfort. I waited until the worst of the tears had spent themselves.

Finally he straightened up and squared his shoulders. "I'm all right now," he said shakily. "What happens next?"

"We'll need to ask you some questions. It's cold

out here, Mr. Kelsey. Let's go back inside." The frigid air sliced through my clothing, chilling me to the bone, but I don't believe Kelsey even noticed. I pulled open the door and made as if to lead him back inside.

"No," he said, jerking his arm out of my grasp. "I don't want to go back in there. I can't."

"But we must ask you some questions," I insisted. "We need to get as much information from you as we possibly can. We'll need you to tell us everything you remember about your wife's activities during the last few days."

"Yes, of course," he answered reasonably. "I understand all that, but just not in there, okay? Can't we go to my house? It's not far from here."

I didn't tell him that Detective Kramer and I had been to his house once already that morning. "Just let me tell my partner," I said. "He can meet us there. Would you like me to drive?"

"No," he said. "I'm okay now. Really."

Once back in the cars, Kelsey and I led the way in the Eagle, with Kramer following behind. When we turned onto Boston, we found the lower street almost totally blocked with haphazardly parked vehicles. The collection included minivans and cars bearing radio station and newspaper logos. There was also a small knot of people milling disjointedly around on the snowy street carrying video cameras and handheld recording equipment.

Pete Kelsey's eyes narrowed when he saw them, but he said nothing. Without being told, he knew at once who they were and what they wanted. Moving steadily through the vehicles and people, he turned up Everett, going the wrong way up what was ostensibly a one-way street. A smaller group of people stood in the street at the corner of Crockett and Everett. Grudgingly they moved aside as we came up behind them.

While we were still a good half block away, he dropped the sun visor and punched the button on a garage door opener. By the time we reached the two-car garage, the door was already open. We pulled into it before the media ambushers realized who he was or what he was doing. Kramer parked in the street and dashed into the garage just as the door started back down. The startled welcoming committee was left stranded on the other side.

It was a neat maneuver on Pete Kelsey's part. Despite the tragic circumstances, it almost made me smile. In the long-term continuing warfare between J. P. Beaumont and the media, Pete Kelsey's garage-door-opening Genie had just won a round.

As I climbed out of the car, I glanced around the garage, expecting to see the usual suburban garage clutter, but I was disappointed. In my experience, most people's garages are similar to those old-fashioned rolltop desks whose lids can easily conceal months and years of accumulated junk and disorder. Pete Kelsey's garage was not like most people's. It was, in fact, disgustingly neat and well organized.

Not only was it totally free of garage-type clutter, it was also a whole lot bigger than I expected. Two thirds of the way down the wall, there was a dividing line between new and old concrete that showed where the side of the hill had been carved away, making the garage deeper by half a car length. A set of ancient yellow kitchen cabinets with all doors removed had been installed in the newly created area. Arranged neatly on the open shelves was an enviable collection of tools and tool chests.

As Pete Kelsey got out of the car, he paused long enough to extricate a red toolbox and the several sets of blueprints from the back of the Eagle. On his way toward the door that led into the house, he slipped the chest onto one of the shelves, where it fit perfectly into a gap between two others. He shoved the rolls of blueprints into a series of open blueprint-sized openings—slots that had been built into the cabinets where drawers had once been.

I couldn't help but feel a growing curiosity about the man. News of his wife's death had rocked him, but it hadn't kept him from conscientiously closing up the Trolleyman before he left, and it didn't keep him from properly putting away his tools and equipment, either.

"Come on in," he said, leading the way.

As I followed him, I was struck by the contrast between Marcia Kelsey's messy office and the pristine condition of Pete Kelsey's garage. Cupid must get a helluva kick from linking up poor unfortunate odd couples and watching while they try to work out a lifetime's worth of differences.

The door from the garage led to a stairway and up into a back-door entryway that also served as a pantry. From there we followed Pete Kelsey into what the real estate ads always refer to as a country kitchen. This one had been spectacularly remodeled, from the recessed lighting in the ten-foot ceiling to the glossy finish on the hardwood floor. Both the cabinets and the countertops were made from the same light-colored Swedish-finish wood, and both were varnished to a lustrous shine.

I'm not a cook, nor do I consider myself a connoisseur of kitchens, but in my uneducated opinion, this one clearly possessed all the modern conveniences. The whole effect was one of quality design executed by highly skillful workmanship. Maybe Pete Kelsey looked like an old-fashioned hippie, but the house screamed of advanced yuppiedom, and I sensed from his casual pride in ownership that we were looking at a Ph.D.-level do-it-yourself project.

"Coffee?" Pete Kelsey asked, motioning us onto chrome-legged stools grouped around an island counter.

I nodded. It had been a long morning, with no time out for a single cup of coffee, to say nothing of breakfast.

While we watched in silence, Pete ground fresh, gourmet-type beans, started a pot of coffee, and put a hunk of crusty homemade bread on the countertop in front of us along with a container of butter and a pot of homemade apricot jam. He moved with the easy assurance of someone accustomed to working in a kitchen.

"Help yourselves," he said, handing us knives and napkins. "I've got to make some calls first. Our daughter is in school at the U of O down in Eugene. I need to get hold of her. And then there's Marcia's parents," he added bleakly.

Rather than retreating to the relative privacy of another room, Pete made the two calls from a wall phone in the kitchen. He reached Erin, the daughter, first.

Munching on the delicious brown bread and helping myself to the robust, black coffee, I heard only one side of the difficult conversation. Pete Kelsey delivered his shocking news as humanely as possible. After a short pause punctuated by murmured words of comfort, he went on to arrange the businesslike details of how and when Erin should get back home.

His judgment, one with which I heartily concurred, was that the roads were far too hazardous for her to risk driving. He advised her to catch the first available plane and that he'd be sure someone was at the airport to meet her when she got in.

The next call was to Marcia's parents, who, he explained, were retired and wintering on the Arizona snowbird circuit. Kelsey handled himself well through both difficult calls, but once he got off the phone with his mother-in-law, his face was chalky gray and his eyes red-rimmed. He looked totally drained. For a moment, he stood leaning against the doorjamb, covering his eyes with his hands. When the front doorbell buzzed from two rooms away, he jumped as though he'd been shot.

"Would you mind getting that?" he asked. "I don't want to see anybody just now, I don't care who it is."

I was only too happy to oblige. I had a pretty good idea of who would be ringing his bell right about then. It had taken some time for the locked-out reporters to get organized and work up their considerable nerve.

I've always thought it takes a hell of a lot of gall to

try for a firsthand interview with someone whose life has just been jolted by some terrible tragedy. In this instance the circling pack of newshounds had evidently decided that sending one emissary was a better tactic than having everybody show up at once.

The person standing with her finger poised on the bell preparing to ring it yet a third time turned out to be one of the more attractive distaff members of Seattle's electronic media. I recognized her from other crime-scene gatherings, but when I opened the door, she didn't know me from Adam. That was probably just as well.

"Mr. Kelsey?" she asked sweetly.

"No," I answered.

She gave me a charming, white-toothed smile, a win-friends-and-influence-people-type smile. "I was wondering if I might speak to him," she said carefully. She was pushy, but doing her best to temper it.

"Mr. Kelsey isn't seeing anybody right now," I replied. I started to close the door, but she wasn't about to be dismissed quite that easily.

"Are you a member of the family?" she asked quickly, somehow insinuating herself between the closing door and the frame. She could have taken her training from Fuller Brush.

Some of the other newsies had worked their way onto the sidewalk, warily edging onto the porch and within earshot.

"I'm a police officer," I answered shortly. "Mr. Kelsey would like all of you to leave. Now. He won't be making any statements at this time."

With that, I bodily elbowed her out of the way and shut the door in her face.

My former partner, Ron Peters, the one who's working in Media Relations, keeps telling me that I need to learn to cultivate a better interaction with reporters. Not bloody likely, I tell him. I'm too old and too set in my ways.

By the time I got back to the kitchen, Pete Kelsey had refilled our cups with the last of the first pot of coffee and had started another one brewing. Performing those mundane tasks seemed to calm him, to provide some relief in the face of the roiling emotions that swirled around him.

"All right," he said at last, easing himself onto a stool across the counter from us. "You guys said you had questions. What are they?"

I had been dimly aware that while we waited for Pete Kelsey to finish his phoning and get squared away, Paul Kramer was becoming more and more agitated, although I hadn't been able to see any reason for it. Now, drumming his fingers steadily on the table, my reluctant partner leaned far back on his stool and eyed Pete Kelsey speculatively.

"You might start by telling us what you know about Alvin Chambers," Kramer said.

Pete Kelsey had been nothing if not cordial and hospitable to us, and that under the most difficult of circumstances. Yet the first question Detective Kramer lobbed across the net to him was a powerful, game-stopping spike about a man assumed to be the dead woman's lover. Talk about sensitivity! In that department, Detective Kramer took the booby prize.

But Kelsey didn't take the bait. "Who's Alvin Chambers?" he asked blandly, returning Kramer's hard-edged stare with an unwavering blue-eyed gaze of his own. Pete Kelsey seemed genuinely puzzled.

"Wait a minute," I said, holding up my hand. "We can get to that later."

Shaking off my interruption, Kramer continued undeterred. "Who *was* Alvin Chambers is more like it. He's the dead man we found in the closet along with your wife."

Kelsey frowned thoughtfully and shook his head. "The name doesn't ring a bell. I don't recognize it at all."

I could see that it annoyed the hell out of Detective Kramer that Kelsey remained unperturbed. "It's possible," Kramer added slyly, "that Chambers and your wife were lovers."

Kramer dropped his bomb and waited for a reaction. The kitchen around us was suddenly deathly quiet except for the cheerful gurgling of a new pot of coffee as it finished brewing. I more than half expected Pete Kelsey to reach across the counter and punch Kramer's lights out.

Instead Pete set his cup down carefully on the counter and nodded while the ghost of a bittersweet smile played around the corners of his lips.

"Is that right? It's entirely possible, I suppose," he added ruefully. "That woman was always full of surprises. Anybody ready for more coffee?"

CHAPTER 7

I WATCHED PETE KELSEY'S FACE AS HE MOVED ACROSS the kitchen, walking that precariously thin line of control between grief and anger. If he fell off the tightrope, there was no telling which side he'd come down on or which side would be more helpful to our questioning process.

"What do you mean, full of surprises?" I asked, holding out my cup for him to refill it.

He poured the coffee carefully, deliberately returning the pot to its stand on the counter before he answered.

"We've been married for twenty years," he replied evenly. "Marcia's always had a mind of her own as well as her own . . . shall we say, outside interests?"

Kelsey returned to his chair and flopped into it as though the bones in his body had suddenly turned to rubber.

Talking about a flawed relationship after the death of one of the partners is never easy. No matter how awful the reality may have been, after the fact,

survivors tend to idealize their marriages, pretending everything was smooth and tranquil even if it
wasn't. Especially when it wasn't. There seems to be
a generally held belief that a blissfully happy past
is somehow a prerequisite for grieving. I gave Pete
Kelsey full credit for going against the trend and not
trying to duck a painful issue.

"I take it you don't mean your wife's job," I commented.

"No," Pete replied, staring morosely into the
bottom of his coffee cup. "I don't. It has . . . had
nothing to do with her job, and yet everything, too,
I suppose."

"Look," Detective Kramer put in sharply. "Two
people were found half-naked and dead in a closet.
One of them was your wife. Would it be safe to assume
that you and your wife were having marital difficulties, Mr. Kelsey?"

Pete Kelsey's eyes narrowed. "No," he answered.
"I've been trying to tell you. That's just the way
things were for us, right from the beginning. Didn't
you ever hear the term 'open marriage'?"

Detective Kramer snorted derisively. "I've heard
of it, all right, but I thought it was extinct, gone the
way of Hula Hoops and dodo birds."

Kelsey shrugged. "It probably should have, the way
things are going, but ours never did, at least not altogether. Back when we started out, we were the
leading edge and well ahead of the times, and that
was fine with both of us to begin with." He paused,
then added, "Things change, people change.
Maybe . . . probably I changed more than she did.
Eventually I wanted something else, something more

than Marcia was capable of giving. And after the AIDS scare . . ."

He lapsed into a momentary brooding silence. "I haven't slept with my wife for the past four years," he added softly. "It wasn't worth the risk."

An undisguised look of pained disbelief passed over Detective Kramer's broad face. "Maybe you should have thrown her out," he suggested.

For the first time, Pete Kelsey bristled. "What I did or didn't do is my business and nobody else's."

"Let's just say your reaction's a little unorthodox," Kramer allowed, backing off slightly. "All we're trying to do, Mr. Kelsey, is to get a handle on this situation and on the people involved. It's important that we establish motivations, that we understand personalities, and so forth. This sounds like a situation that would have driven most men to a divorce court."

Kramer's underhanded cut, a psychological jab that said real men don't put up with this crap, wasn't lost on Pete Kelsey.

"I'm not most men," he answered stiffly. "I loved my wife, no matter what. Erin had already lost one mother. I didn't want her to lose another. Whatever else you can say about her, Marcia is . . . was a hell of a mother."

I had been stunned into shocked silence by Detective Kramer's ugly insinuations. Now Kelsey's comment caught my attention and I leaped back into the fray. "You're saying Erin isn't Marcia's natural child?"

Kelsey shook his head. "No, she's mine. My first wife died in a car wreck in Mexico when Erin was only two. I came to Seattle shortly after that and was trying to put my life back together. That's when I met Marcia. In fact, Max, the guy you met at the Trolleyman this morning, is the one who introduced us."

I almost choked on a misdirected sip of coffee. "Maxwell Cole?" I spluttered, trying to keep the drips from falling on my sweater.

"You know him?" Kelsey asked.

I nodded. "Yes, I do. We went to the U-Dub together."

"It's a small world, isn't it? At the time I was just starting out doing remodeling jobs. I had stopped by to give Max's mother a quote on some work she wanted done. I had Erin along with me because I couldn't afford to leave her with a sitter. Marcia happened to drop by the house that afternoon. She and Max were old friends, you see, from high school. She was back in town after a brief failed marriage and looked him up for old times' sake. By the time I finished talking to Mrs. Cole, Erin and Marcia had become great pals. That was the beginning of it. Of us as a family, I mean. Max ended up being best man in our wedding. He's also Erin's godfather."

So Maxwell Cole had been giving it to us straight when he claimed to be a good friend of the family. That was important to know, although I didn't much like the idea of that scuzzbag being a potential source of valuable information.

I looked across the table, trying to assess what was going on with Detective Kramer, who sat there tapping his fingers impatiently. "Tell us more about your wife," he said. "Aside from what you've already told us, what was she like?"

"What do you want to know?" Kelsey asked hopelessly, rubbing his eyes with both hands. The process was wearing him down. The strain was beginning to show in his handsome but haggard face.

"Do you want me to tell you that she was bright and ambitious? Funny and single-minded? Stubborn and selfish? Messy as hell and wonderful at the same time? Is that what you want to know?"

He broke off and didn't continue while his eyes clouded over with unshed tears. Letting his shoulders sag, he seemed to shrink back into himself.

"But your wife never mentioned this Alvin Chambers to you by name?" I asked, feeling like a surgeon unnecessarily probing a tender abdomen to verify the presence of a swollen appendix.

"No. She didn't." Pete Kelsey choked back a hoot of involuntary laughter that was anything but funny. "I'm sure this will sound strange to you, considering the circumstances, but Marcia was more honorable than that. A perverted sense of honor if you will, but she never rubbed my nose in whatever it was she was doing, not once."

While Kramer remained focused on the sexual implications, I realized that we still hadn't touched on the suicide angle, and despite the doused lights in the closet, it was time that we did that, just for drill.

"How did your wife seem to you these past few weeks?" I asked casually.

"She had been preoccupied for several months," Kelsey admitted.

"Was it her job?" I asked.

"No. I don't think so. She loved her work, the more the better."

"What about her health?"

"Good. Excellent, in fact. She had some problems off and on over the years, mostly female-type stuff. She had a hysterectomy when she was barely twenty-one, but generally speaking, she was fine both mentally and physically."

"Had your wife ever been despondent?" I asked.

"Despondent?" He frowned. "Like depressed? You mean as in suicide? Wait a minute, is that where this is all leading?"

I nodded.

"Let me get this straight. You're implying that Marcia did this, that she killed herself and this other guy as well?"

"That's how it looks right now."

Kelsey shook his head emphatically. "No. Impossible. Absolutely not!"

His instantaneous response reminded me of Charlotte Chambers' reaction when we had mentioned the possibility of her husband carrying on with another woman. She hadn't thought Alvin capable of such a thing. Why are husbands and wives always the last to know? I wondered while in the background, Pete Kelsey continued his angry, categorical denial.

"You don't understand. Marcia was opposed to violence of any kind for any reason. She was a *vegetarian*, for Christ's sake. She didn't believe in killing animals, not even to eat. How could someone like that take someone else's life, or her own either for that matter?"

Pete Kelsey wouldn't have liked my stock response to that question. I know from experience that homicide is no respecter of philosophy or religion. At the moment of crisis, those who pull the triggers of murder weapons are far beyond the pale of their own moral imperatives, to say nothing of society's as a whole.

"Let's set that aside for right now," I said gently. "Let's go back to last night. Now, exactly what time did your wife leave the house?"

"Seven-thirty or eight. I'm not sure which. It was right after dinner."

"Did she tell you where she was going?"

"To the office. That's what she said, to work on her report for the retreat."

"Retreat? What retreat?"

"The school district's annual administrative retreat. Once a year about this time they all go out of town and huddle at a resort somewhere to try and figure out what they're going to do next. This year's retreat is scheduled for Semi-ah-moo, a place up near Blaine. It's supposed to be Wednesday, Thursday, and Friday of this week."

"You said annual retreat. So this isn't something out of the ordinary?"

"Hardly. It's the same old thing every year— declining enrollment, budget cuts. As head of Labor Relations, Marcia was supposed to make one of the major presentations. She liked doing it, thrived on it, in fact. Saw creating order in that kind of mess as a challenge. She had been working on her presentation all during Christmas even though Erin was home."

"Didn't it bother you?" Kramer asked.

"Didn't what bother me?"

"Your wife working so late on a Sunday night, especially in such terrible weather?"

Every time Kramer opened his mouth to ask a question, there was a not-so-subtle undercurrent of sarcasm. I'm not sure if Pete Kelsey noticed it, but I sure as hell did.

"It *did* bother me, as a matter of fact," Kelsey answered testily, "but that didn't make any difference. I already told you, Marcia was her own woman. She did what she wanted when she wanted. She liked to ski. She was used to driving in snow. I helped her put chains on the Volvo before she left."

Right up until then, I had felt that Kelsey's answers had been straightforward, but this one set off a chain of alarm bells in my head. Why was he suddenly being evasive and focusing on the side issue of the weather without addressing the important part of the question? Detective Kramer noticed it too and wasn't about to be misled.

"Why was she working?" he asked again.

A slight tremor came into Pete Kelsey's voice. "Actually, we had a quarrel about it before she left."

"What kind of quarrel?"

"About her going. I really didn't want her to."

"But you just said . . ."

"It wasn't because of the weather. There was something else."

"What?"

"It's probably not important."

Kramer was becoming more and more impatient. "Let us judge what's important, Mr. Kelsey."

As Kelsey struggled with how to respond, the atmosphere in the room became so charged with tension, it felt as though someone had flipped a switch.

Whatever it was Pete Kelsey didn't want to tell us about was something Kramer and I were both equally convinced we wanted to hear. Had to hear.

"I was just feeling . . . well, you know, uneasy. I wanted her to stay home. That's all."

"You were feeling uneasy? Why?"

"We've been having some strange phone calls lately," he answered reluctantly. "Nothing all that bad, I guess, just worrisome—the kind of thing where the phone rings in the middle of the night and you pick it up and you can hear someone breathing but they won't talk to you. And then . . ."

"And then what?"

"Nothing, just that whole series of harassing calls."

"Did you report them?"

"No. Marcia didn't want to, and they didn't seem all that important at the time, at least not until yesterday afternoon. When Erin left to go back to Eugene. I wanted her to be ahead of the storm."

"What happened then?"

"I was helping her load her things into the car and she happened to mention that she'd been getting calls like that too. At her apartment in Eugene. I told her flat out to change her number. To get one that's unlisted. She was planning to do it today. Before all this . . ." For some time he sat silently with his chin resting cupped in his hand, staring down at the countertop.

"Go on," I urged.

"So I tried to talk to Marcia about it, tried to talk her out of leaving the house and going anywhere, but she said it was just a weird coincidence and that

I worried too much. We had words about it." He paused for a moment before adding, "I never even kissed her good-bye."

Detective Kramer's pager went off right then. There are times when I hate those goddamn things. Kramer asked Kelsey if there was another phone he could use besides the one in the kitchen so he could return the call without disturbing the interview further.

Interviews are delicate things. Fragile almost, with a rhythm and life all their own. Before the pager sounded, I had sensed that we were verging on something important, but now, with the interruption, I doubted we'd ever get back to it.

Pete obligingly led Kramer away through a swinging door that opened into a large dining room. They continued on through another doorway, disappearing into the living room beyond that.

Left alone in the kitchen, I realized that now my coffee cup really was empty. I got up to fill it. The coffeepot sat on the counter next to a state-of-the-art down-draft gas stove top that was very like my own except for the fact that this one was absolutely spotless.

Pete came back. He seemed to have lost some control while he was out of the room. He walked over to the sink and stood with his face averted and his shoulders hunched, staring out the window.

"I'm glad you helped yourself to the coffee," he said at last. "Your partner said to go on without him. He could be a while."

With backhanded swipes at his reddened eyes, Kelsey settled back on his stool while I attempted to pick up the scattered threads of the interview. "So that's the last you talked to your wife? When she left the house right after dinner?"

"Yes. I never saw her or talked to her after that."

"Were you here all the rest of the night?"

The minute pause before he answered made me wonder if he was telling the truth.

"Until around ten-thirty or so," he said. "It was getting late and she wasn't home. I tried calling her direct line, but there was no answer, so I drove over to her office. Her car was there, but I couldn't raise anybody, not even the security guard. I checked a couple of other places and went back by her office again around midnight. By then her car was gone from the lot and I thought maybe we had just missed each other in transit, but when I got back here, she still wasn't home. I realized then that wherever she was, she didn't want to be found. I went to bed. There was no point in staying up any later. I had some contracting work to do early this morning."

"You said you noticed her car was missing from the parking lot?"

"That's right. Marcia has . . . had an assigned spot, and she always parked there, even at night. It's a good one, close to the door, and the snow wouldn't have kept her from using it."

A possibly devious husband and a missing car were two more things that didn't fit with Doc Baker's suicide theory. I asked for the make and model of Marcia Kelsey's turbocharged Volvo. With vehicles abandoned in the snow all over the city, someone's misplaced car could be illegally parked directly in front of Seattle P.D.'s headquarters in the Public Safety Building and it wouldn't be discovered for days.

Kramer returned to the kitchen, announcing that a call had come in for Pete Kelsey, that Erin wanted to give him her arrival times and flight numbers. While Pete went to pick up the phone in the other room, Detective Kramer edged his way over to me.

"I've got some news for you," he said under his breath. "From Doc Baker. They haven't completed the autopsies yet, but he did have one gem for us, a preliminary finding that he thought we ought to know about."

"What's that?"

"The doc says we've got a double on our hands."

"You mean Pete Kelsey's right? Marcia didn't commit suicide after all?"

Detective Kramer nodded. "That's right. And how do you suppose he figured that out before anybody else did? You can bet it's got nothing whatsoever to do with her being a goddamn vegetarian! It's because he did it. He caught 'em in the act and decided to put an end to it."

Even though I suspected Pete Kelsey had lied to me about something, that didn't necessarily make him a killer. "Wait just a minute here, Kramer. Did Doc Baker tell you something more about Pete Kelsey, something I ought to know?"

"Doc Baker treats me like shit. He didn't tell me a goddamned thing, but I'm smart enough to put two and two together. That longhaired freak invites us in here and serves us homemade bread and coffee like we're some kind of visiting royalty instead of cops investigating his wife's murder. He admits he knows she's been whoring around on him, but he still acts grief-stricken. What a load of crap! I'm not falling for it. Kelsey's cool. Too damn cool, if you ask me. All we have to do is wait. He's bound to trip himself up."

Kramer's absolute conviction that Kelsey was our man caught me off guard. Jumping to those kinds of conclusions so early in an investigation is bad for everyone concerned. It's too easy to go looking for answers that will match some preset scenario, to create a set of erroneous self-fulfilling prophecies, rather than focusing on what really happened.

"Hold up a minute, Kramer," I cautioned. "Let's back off a little."

He shook his head stubbornly. "I'm not backing off an inch," he declared. "Not one goddamn inch!"

As he said the words, Kramer reached across the counter to the place where Pete Kelsey had been sitting. Without touching the handle, he picked up a teaspoon that had been lying in Kelsey's saucer. With a single smug look at me, he placed the spoon in a glassine bag and dropped it into his pocket.

"What the hell are you doing?"

"Fingerprints," Kramer responded with a smile. "Maybe our friend Kelsey has a police record someplace and his prints are on file with AFIS. If not, we'll happen to have a couple handy. Just in case."

AFIS is the state of Washington's new Automated Fingerprint Identification System, a computerized program that's turning previously unusable fingerprints into valuable crime-solving evidence.

"That's not entirely legal," I pointed out.

"Neither is homicide," Kramer returned. "If you

want to squeal about it, Detective Beaumont, go right ahead. Be my guest. Meanwhile, I'm going out to start the car."

Kramer left, taking the pilfered spoon with him, and I didn't try to stop him.

Kramer didn't have to convince me. Between lifting a spoon and nailing some creep who was responsible for the cold-blooded execution of two people, there was absolutely no contest.

Sometimes you have to fight fire with fire.

CHAPTER 8

I WAITED UNTIL PETE KELSEY RETURNED TO THE kitchen. He paused in the doorway and gave me a long, searching look. It seemed to me that he somehow sensed that things had changed between us. He was right. They had, and not for the better.

"We're going now," I said, handing him one of my business cards. "Call me if anything comes up that you think I should know about."

He nodded, but he tossed the card on the countertop in an offhand, don't-call-us-we'll-call-you fashion. "Do you need me to show you the way out?" he asked.

"No. I'm sure I can find it." I made my way down the stairway and through the immaculate garage. I let myself out onto the street, where Kramer was sitting in the already idling Reliant.

I looked around. The crowd of eager newsies no longer jammed the neighborhood. It was too damn cold. Either they had retreated to the warmth of their vehicles parked a block below on Boston or they had abandoned the field entirely and returned to their individual newsrooms.

"Well?" Kramer asked as soon as I climbed into the car and fastened my seat belt.

"Well what?" I returned.

"What do you think? Do you agree or not?"

"You mean have you convinced me that Pete Kelsey's our man? No, you haven't. It's all conjecture, Kramer, without any supportive facts. He may have lied to us about some things, but so far I can't see that we have a smidgen of solid evidence."

Kramer shook his massive head. "Come off it, Beaumont. Show me your stuff. Ever since I got to Homicide, everyone's told me about you and your terrific hunches."

"My 'terrific hunches,' as you call them, sure as hell aren't telling me that Pete Kelsey is a killer."

Kramer didn't bother to mask his disgust. "You know what's the matter with you? You fell for all that open marriage bullshit. That doesn't mean the poor bastard wasn't being led around by the balls. He was. That wife of his must have been a real piece of work, but then, so's Kelsey.

"I think he fed us that whole line of crap just to throw us off track, to make us think he knew what she was up to the whole time. My guess is, he didn't. I'll lay you odds he just found out his wife was two-timing him and decided to put a stop to it once and for all. Where I come from, jealousy's still a pretty damn good motive for murder."

We were headed back to the department. I suppose I could have argued with Detective Kramer on the way, told him that he was being premature and lectured him about jumping to conclusions, but I didn't. Reluctantly, and based on my own observations, I was forced to admit that there was some plausibility in what Kramer was saying.

By then, Kramer was wearing on me, getting on my nerves. I'm basically an impatient person. I always have been, and sobering up hasn't made any difference. Through my work in the AA program, I've been trying to learn to accept the things I can't change and to change the things I can.

I couldn't change Detective Kramer, couldn't keep him from running off at the mouth, but I could and did get out of the car. I had him drop me at the garage entrance. Bypassing the elevators, I took to the stairwells and pounded my way up to the fifth floor while Kramer parked the car.

Margie, my clerk, had two messages for me. One was from Big Al telling me not to worry, that he was much better, but that he was taking a few days of personal leave to help Molly while she finished recuperating. The other was from a lady named Kendra Meadows, who identified herself as the director of Personnel for the Seattle school district.

It was after three. With the midwinter afternoon waning fast, I figured I'd better hurry and get back to Kendra Meadows before she left her office and headed home.

As soon as she answered the phone, I could tell from the low, husky timbre of her voice that Kendra Meadows was a middle-aged black woman. She was all business.

"I have a memo here from Dr. Savage telling me that I'm supposed to render whatever assistance you may find necessary, Detective Beaumont. Phone numbers, addresses, that sort of thing. I'll be here the rest of the afternoon if you want to stop by. My directions are to stay as late as you need me to."

Dr. Savage had pulled out all the stops on this one. Kendra Meadows was ready and willing to help, but I didn't yet know exactly what help we would need. Not only that, we had a mound of paperwork to tend to before we called it a day. I hedged for time.

"Things have gotten pretty hectic around here today," I said lamely. "Will you be in your office tomorrow?"

"I don't see any reason why I wouldn't," she countered.

If Kendra Meadows had a sense of humor, none of it leaked into her telephone presence. "I come to work every day, Detective Beaumont, rain or shine."

"Good," I said. "Either Detective Kramer or myself will be in to see you tomorrow then."

Over my desk I keep a ribald poster featuring a bare-assed kid sitting forlornly on a pot. The caption says, "The job's not finished until the paperwork's done." The same can be said of police work. I was reaching in one of my drawers for a blank report form when Detective Kramer's bulky frame appeared in the door of my cubicle.

"Boy, do I have a deal for you," he said.

"What's that?" I turned to look at him. He was holding up his own fanfold of messages.

"How about if I push the papers around here and you go back up to the district office and pick up their bomb threat file? Doris Walker called three different times to say it was ready and were we going to pick it up today."

I found it interesting that although I had been the one who had actually talked to Doris Walker, somehow all three of her messages had been shuffled to Kramer. None had come to me. I had heard rumors from one or two of the other detectives who had been stuck working with Paul Kramer that he had developed a system for hogging important messages and that he loved doing reports. All of them. Believe me, for homicide cops, this is *not* normal behavior.

Both items had raised eyebrows, although to my knowledge, no one had filed an official grievance on the issue. The report-writing incidents in particular had provoked numerous derogatory comments, the general consensus being that Kramer volunteered to do the paperwork so he could write things his way and make Detective Paul Kramer look good. Officially. That didn't scare me in the least. No matter what he wrote, it wouldn't be any skin off my nose. I sure as hell wasn't lobbying for a promotion, and I hate paperwork.

"You bet," I told him. "Sold."

I took long enough to put in a "Locate Car" call to 911 on Marcia Kelsey's vehicle in the hopes that somebody might stumble across it. The dispatcher took my "Homicide Hold" request seriously, but he didn't offer much hope of success.

"You want us to locate a misplaced car in this weather? Go ahead and give me the info, Beaumont, but don't hold your breath. With the streets the way they are, I'd say the chances of our finding it are slim to nonexistent."

Two minutes later, I was on my way. The streets were still relatively deserted, and the people who were out seemed to be in a jovial holiday mood. I grabbed one of the Queen Anne-bound buses on Third Avenue rather than go through the hassle of checking out a departmental car. That way, once I had Doris Walker's file in hand, I could go directly home, settle into my user-friendly recliner for a while, and maybe get a little perspective on the day.

It was something to look forward to, a bright spot on the horizon.

Doris Walker was waiting for me at her upstairs desk. The file folder in question had been placed in a large, unmarked manila envelope, which she handed over to me with a relieved sigh.

"Did you ever talk to that poor woman?" she asked.

"You mean Mrs. Chambers?" Doris nodded.

"Yes," I said. "We told her. Right after we left here this morning."

Doris seemed immensely relieved. "Good. And is she all right?"

It was a somewhat naive question. I'm afraid my response was more curt than Doris Walker deserved. "As right as she's going to be, for someone whose husband just died."

"I'm sure," Mrs. Walker said with an embarrassed duck of her chin. "It must be terrible for her. I can't imagine how I'd deal with it if something like that ever happened to my Donald."

"With a little luck," I told her, "you'll never have to."

Taking the envelope she gave me, I left the office and headed for home. I could have gone to see Kendra Meadows, but I still didn't know what to ask her. Rather than wait for yet another bus, I wrapped the ugly glow-in-the-dark scarf around my neck, shoved gloved hands deep in my pockets, and set off down the hill, cutting through a winter-wonderland Seattle Center. Except for the muffled shouts of a few children having a snowball fight near the frozen International Fountain, the place was almost totally deserted.

As I walked, my fondest hope was that Belltown Terrace's recalcitrant heat pumps were once more working properly. I came to the corner of Second and Broad and paused, waiting for the light to change. Suddenly, behind me, somebody yelled, "Look out!"

Luckily for me, my reflexes still work fine. I dodged out of the way just in time to avoid being creamed by a tightly packed snowball that had been lobbed off the sixth-floor running track of Belltown Terrace. I looked up and saw Heather Peters grinning down at me and getting ready to take another potshot.

"Heather," I yelled, "knock that off before someone gets hurt."

The happy grin disappeared from Heather's face. "See there?" I heard Trade's high-pitched reproving voice. "I told you we shouldn't. Now we're in for it!"

"Meet me at the elevator, you two," I ordered, fully prepared to march upstairs and chew ass.

"Don't be too hard on them," a woman's voice said. The voice that had called out the timely warning belonged to an elderly lady who, leaning heavily on a cane, was making her way slowly along the snowy sidewalk.

"They're only young once, you know," she added with an understanding smile. "Remember, it doesn't snow here all that often."

Mollified a little by her wise counsel, I toned down the rhetoric enough so that once I found them, all the girls got was a good talking to about the dangers of throwing anything at all off high-rise buildings. The bawling out was followed, in short order, by steaming mugs of hot chocolate all around.

Disciplinary lines tend to get a little fuzzy when the miscreants don't happen to be your own flesh and blood, or maybe I'm just turning into a middle-aged softy.

After drinking their cocoa, the girls left my apartment to return to their own, and I retreated to the comforting confines of my ancient recliner, reveling in my living room's toasty seventy-degree temperature. I was sitting there lapping up creature comforts when the phone rang.

"Hey, Beau. You going tonight?"

At once I recognized the thin voice as that of Lars Jenssen, a retired halibut fisherman who serves as my sponsor in the Regrade Regulars, an AA group that meets each Monday night in a restaurant just up Second Avenue from where I live.

My doctor-ordered stay at the Ironwood Ranch dryout farm in Arizona may have been cut short through circumstances beyond my control, but I had decided that I owed it to myself and to my ailing liver to straighten up and fly right. For the time being, anyhow. Working on my own and with Lars Jenssen's continuing help, I was halfway through the prescribed ninety meetings in ninety days that are supposed to get boozy lives back on track again.

Lars lived another block up Second in a fourth-floor brick walk-up apartment that was a long way from my penthouse luxury, but he never complained.

"I'll stop by for you around six-thirty," he said, not waiting for me to say yes or no.

I thought of my shiny little 928 securely parked in the garage downstairs. It was safe and sound, and considering road conditions, I wanted to keep it that way. Nevertheless, I felt a moral obligation to offer Lars a ride in the frigid weather.

"Look, Lars, I don't much want to drive. Someone will end up creaming my car if I do, but we could always take a taxi. How about if I grab a cab and stop by to pick you up?"

"Take a cab?" he echoed. "Hell, man, it ain't but six blocks or so. Walkin'll do us both a world of good."

He hung up on me then, without giving me a chance to argue. But then again, I wouldn't have had the nerve. Lars Jenssen was seventy-nine and ten months. I was forty-four. If he could walk six blocks in that kind of weather, then by God, so could I.

Rather than rush into the contents of Doris Walker's envelope, I sat there with one last cup of cocoa, enjoying the warm quiet of my snug apartment, trying to sort back through the long interview with Pete Kelsey.

Part of the problem was that, liar or not, he was such a likable guy. At least he struck me that way, although the same thing obviously didn't hold true for Detective Kramer. He found something ominous, something underhanded, in Kelsey's forbearance with regard to his messy, and by Kelsey's own admission, sexually promiscuous wife. But atypical reactions do not necessarily a killer make. I tried to put all personal feelings aside and examine only those things we had learned in the interview.

I had to agree with Kramer that there were things about Pete Kelsey that were puzzling and contradictory. He seemed to be a fairly intelligent sort, well spoken, and reasonably well educated, yet he worked at a series of lightweight, pickup jobs, and he had evidently done so for many years, had made a career out of it. Why? Had he gone to college? If so, where, and what had he majored in? I made a note to call Nancy, the lady at the Trolleyman, to find out whatever I could from her.

And then, much as I hated to, I made another note, this one reminding me to call Maxwell Cole. I didn't relish the idea of having to ask him for help, but that appeared to be unavoidable. After all, he had been best man at Marcia and Pete's wedding. And he had been appointed Erin's godfather even though he hadn't laid eyes on the child until she was at least two.

Historically, Max may have started out as Marcia Kelsey's friend, but he obviously felt close to Pete as well, close enough to guess that if Pete wasn't at home that morning, he'd most likely be at the Trolleyman, and he had cared enough to try to break the bad news himself.

I needed Max to tell me what he knew about Pete Kelsey, and also to shed what light he could on Marcia.

Other than being less than fanatically neat, what I had learned so far hadn't given me any kind of clear fix on the kind of person she had been.

That's one of the strange things about this job. Homicide detectives always learn about victims after the fact, after they're already dead, through the eyes and words of those they leave behind. Sometimes we learn to love them; sometimes we hate them. Strong feelings in either direction can be valuable motivating tools for keeping investigations focused and energized and moving forward.

With Marcia Louise Kelsey, I was up against an enigma. Who was she, this avant-garde proponent of open marriage? What had she been like? What kind of mother had she been? What had she seen in Alvin Chambers? Compared to Pete Kelsey's rugged good looks, a fifty-year-old failed minister turned security guard couldn't have been such great shakes.

What little we had learned about Marcia had come through Pete Kelsey's eyes, and the resulting portrait was a confusing mishmash of love and hate that gave us few clues about the woman herself. Was she some kind of oversexed monster who had somehow kept Kelsey tied to her even though he had more than ample reason to walk away? Or was she something else entirely?

I sensed that there was something important lurking in the tangled relationship between Marcia Kelsey and her long-suffering husband, perhaps even something sinister. Right then and there, I made up my mind to find out what that something was.

The idea that involvement with Marcia Kelsey

might have lethal side effects inevitably led me to consider Alvin Chambers. He reminded me of some poor, hapless boy black widow spider who knocks off a casual piece of tail only to wind up topping his lady friend's dessert menu shortly thereafter. Male black widows never get a chance to sit around swapping locker-room conquest stories, and neither would Alvin Chambers. That poor bastard couldn't tell us a thing.

What had gone on between them? What was the appeal? I remembered the Kelseys' spotless kitchen and mentally compared it with Alvin Chambers' slovenly apartment and his equally slovenly wife. It was easy to imagine what the somewhat over-the-hill Alvin might have seen in Marcia Louise Kelsey. It was far more difficult to understand the reverse—what a bright intellectual, a highly thought of professional school administrator, would have gotten out of a clandestine relationship with the security guard. I wondered if Charlotte Chambers would be able to step out of her denial of Alvin's infidelity long enough to help us find any clear-cut answers.

I fully intended to spend some time looking over the contents of the envelope Doris Walker had given me, but by then the warmth of my apartment and the comfort of my familiar chair proved to be too much for me. I fell into a sound sleep with the enve-lope resting unopened in my lap. I didn't waken until much later when the phone rang. Lars Jenssen was calling from the security door downstairs.

"Hurry up, will you?" he bellowed impatiently into

the phone. "It's cold enough to freeze the ears off a brass monkey down here."

If Lars Jenssen thought it was cold, that meant it was damn cold indeed.

I did as he asked and hurried.

CHAPTER 9

DESPITE THE WEATHER, THERE WERE STILL TWENTY OR so people at the weekly meeting of the Regrade Regulars. Attendance didn't vary much from what it usually was since most of the regular Regulars live somewhere close by in the downtown Seattle neighborhood known as the Denny Regrade.

Like downtown dwellers everywhere, many refuse to own cars. Some of them attribute their aversion to driving to high-blown philosophical reasons replete with ecological one-upmanship. Others don't own cars because they simply can't afford them. Still others, I suspect, lost their driver's licenses in legal proceedings of one kind or another long before they hied themselves off to their first AA meeting. In the ensuing years some have never gotten around to getting another.

Oddball that I am, I don't exactly fit into any of those specialized categories. My main problem with driving downtown is parking downtown.

Lars and I showed up on foot a few minutes prior

to the beginning of the meeting. Ironically, the Re-grade Regulars meet in a seedy upstairs room over a restaurant and bar which continue to do steady business with a habitual and often raucous crowd of serious and not-yet-repentant drinkers.

I've been told that there's nothing worse than a reformed drunk. That may well be true, but three months into the program, I'm a hell of a long way from reformed. The whole idea of having to quit drinking pisses me off. When the world is full of spry old codgers, seemingly healthy people like Lars Jenssen and some of his aging cronies, who've been drinking steadily way longer than I've been alive, it irks the hell out of me that here in my midforties I'm stuck with some kind of lame-duck liver.

I don't like going to meetings, and I sure as hell don't look forward to them, but they beat the alternative as outlined in grim physical detail by the inscrutable Dr. Wang. And so I go.

The meeting itself was over by eight-thirty, and Lars and I made our way downstairs to the smoky restaurant for our ritual postmeeting rump session and greasy spoon dinner.

Lars Jenssen was already in the Navy prior to World War II. He missed being on the USS *Arizona* because a ruptured appendix had him confined to a room in a naval hospital in Pearl Harbor on December 7, 1941. Once he got out of the hospital, his luck continued to hold.

During the war in the Pacific, Lars survived having two other ships shot out from under him. A confirmed nonswimmer, he still carried in his wallet the frayed and brittle one-dollar bill that had floated by him in debris-littered water off the Philippines while he clung to a life preserver waiting to be picked up after the sinking of the second one, the destroyer *Abner Read*.

Lars stayed on in the Navy after the war, retiring with twenty years of service, and had gone on to a second career as an Alaska halibut fisherman. A lifetime drinker, he had managed to make it through the death of his only child, a son, who was shot down during the Vietnam War, only to fall apart completely during the five years it had taken for his wife, Aggie, to succumb to Alzheimer's disease.

Sober now for six years, he lived just up the street from me, subsisting on a small naval pension and Social Security in a subsidized apartment building called Stillwater Arms. He prided himself in both his unwavering independence and his good health.

His most prized possession was a videotape copy of a television news broadcast that featured an interview with him done by the local CBS affiliate during Seattle's famed five-day Labor Day Blackout of 1988. A misguided construction project had shut off the electricity to much of the downtown core, paralyzing businesses and stranding high-rise dwellers, many of whom were far too old and frail to negotiate the long, darkened stairways in their buildings.

The camera had caught Lars Jenssen at the bottom of a nine-story stairwell. He had affixed a flashlight to his cane and was loaded with a backpack full of sack lunches, which he was about to deliver to unfortunate and less able high-rise strandees.

"Somebody's got to take care of all those old people," he had grunted pointedly into the camera, and then set out determinedly to clump up the nine stories to deliver his goodies.

I hadn't seen the interview at the time—hadn't even known Lars Jenssen then—but he had shown it to me once after we met, venturing shyly into my condo to play it for me on the VCR.

"Offered to let that young guy come with me, but he said he didn't want to climb all them stairs. Ha!" Lars had snorted derisively when he showed me the tape. "That's what's the matter with kids these days. No gumption."

We ordered our usual postmeeting dinners—a chili-burger for me and a plate of sliced tomatoes and cottage cheese for Lars. It was to this unvarying evening repast, cholesterol doomsayers to the contrary, that Lars Jenssen attributed both his good health and his longevity.

Spooning half a pitcher of cream and several heaping spoonfuls of sugar into his coffee, he eyed me thoughtfully.

"How come you never talk about your family none, Beau?" he asked. "You had a chance tonight, and you blew it. Oh sure, you talked about your kids and all, but when it comes to the rest of your family, it's like you fell off a turnip truck somewhere all growed up."

"That's not too far from the truth," I told him with an uneasy laugh.

My family history, or lack thereof, isn't something I'm particularly eager to talk about. It's nothing to be ashamed of, I suppose, but it's not something to brag about, either.

"My mother's dead," I said flatly after taking a

forkful of my chili-burger. "I never knew my father. He died during the war. They weren't married."

With an oath, Lars flung his fork back onto his nearly empty plate, where it bounced on a wilted lettuce leaf.

"See there?" he demanded loudly. Encroaching deafness had disabled Lars Jenssen's volume control years before. "No wonder you're all screwed up, Beau. You never had no men around, did you? You know, what they call one of them role models."

Rather than being provoked by Lars Jenssen's probing interference, I was instead slightly amused. For a whole lot of money, the department gladly would have paid to send me to a genuine shrink. So here I sat in a dingy restaurant being psychoanalyzed by a meddlesome near-octogenarian who had probably never even heard of Sigmund Freud.

Lars leaned back in his chair and squinted nearsightedly across the table at me. "What about your grandparents?" he persisted stubbornly. "You musta spent at least some time with them."

My amusement disappeared as I felt my hackles rising. I could talk about my father. The motorcycle accident that had killed him was just that—an accident. And so was I, for that matter. It was a cruel twist of fate that those two young lovers, my parents, had never had the chance to marry. The fact that my mother never married anyone else during the lonely years afterward testified to the enduring love she must have felt for her dead sailor/lover.

And I could talk about my mother, too. She had done it all and done it by herself, with no help from anyone. She had kept me and raised me at a time when that simply wasn't done in polite society. She had brought me up with unstinting devotion and a self-less, gritty determination. I've seen a lot of action in my years on the force, but those two qualities still form the basis for my definition of heroism.

Talking about my mother and father was fine, but I could not, would not, talk about my grandfather—a man whose name I bore—about Jonas Piedmont, that stiff-necked, stubborn Presbyterian son of a bitch who had turned his pregnant sixteen-year-old daughter out of the house and who had never once, in all the difficult years that followed, lifted a single solitary finger to help her.

The sudden unexpected flood of resentment that washed through me made it difficult to remember exactly what Lars Jenssen's question had been, to say nothing of answering it.

"No," I said finally. "I never did."

"How come?" Lars wasn't one to let sleeping dogs lie.

"We just didn't, that's all."

"They dead?"

"Goddamn it, Lars. What's the point of all this third degree? No, they're not dead, not as far as I know, but they could just as well be. For all I know, they probably still live somewhere right here in Seattle, but you couldn't prove it by me. I've never met them, never laid eyes on them, never wanted to. Once they found out my mother was pregnant with me, they crossed us off their list. Permanently."

"I see," Lars Jenssen said, nodding sagely. "Maybe you ought to pay them a visit."

"Like hell I will!" I snorted.

AA has strict live-and-let-live rules that decree members should not interfere in other people's lives, rules that create psychic nonaggression pacts which allow each member, supported by the invisible group behind him, to work his way through his own nightmare of self-imposed darkness.

If anyone had ever told Lars Jenssen about those rules, he had long since forgotten them, or maybe he did remember but was simply ignoring them.

"The thing is, Beau, you gotta give 'em credit for doing the best they could."

"I don't have to give them anything," I insisted.

Lars shook his head. "Just a minute here," he said. "Take my boy Daniel now. He didn't get drafted, you know. He up and volunteered, for Chrissakes. He went over, to Vietnam and got hisself blasted to pieces all for nothing. I cussed him for that, cussed him good, too. Not just after he was dead neither, but right then, at the time, when he was leaving.

"I cussed Danny and told him he was too god-damned stupid to be any son of mine. Course, it wasn't true, and it like to broke poor Aggie's heart, me carrying on that way all the while her only son was packing up his stuff to leave home and go off to war. And I cussed him later on, too, when I'd be out in the boat, just me and God and the ocean . . ."

Lars broke off suddenly, stopped cold, and didn't continue.

Any mention of the Vietnam War always gets to me, because when the war came, I didn't go. It wasn't that I was a draft-dodger or a protester. I simply didn't get drafted, although God knows I was prime cannon fodder material, and you can be damn sure I didn't volunteer, either. By the time I was in college and eligible for the draft, my mother was already sick and dying. I've wondered sometimes if maybe one of her friends wasn't on the local draft board. Maybe that would help explain why I'm still walking around in one piece when lots of other people aren't, including Lars Jenssen's son, Daniel. Lately I've wondered if going into law enforcement wasn't a way to make up for what I have somehow come to regard as dereliction of duty.

We had been sitting there quietly for a very long time when I realized at last that Lars Jenssen was waiting for me to spur him forward. "So what happened then?" I asked.

He shrugged. "I got over it, I guess. Finally figured out that it wasn't doing me no good. All that resentment was just eating up my insides. Except . . ."

"Except what?" I prompted again.

"By then Daniel was already long dead and buried. Getting rid of all that poison helped me some, but it didn't do poor little Danny no good, or Aggie neither. By then she was so far gone that she didn't understand. I'll tell you this, Beau, if I got me one regret in life, that's it. Once they're dead, you can't do nothing about it, nothing at all."

For a moment Lars Jenssen seemed adrift again, lost in a sea of thoughts about the past and what couldn't be changed in it. Then he sat up and put both hands on the table.

"How're you doing on your list?" he asked brightly, seeming to change the subject. I realized belatedly that he hadn't changed the subject at all. That cagey old goat was simply taking a run at me from another direction.

Anyone who thinks the Alcoholics Anonymous program is a walk in the park hasn't sat down to do Step 4, which entails making a searching moral inventory of yourself, or Step 8, which involves making a list of all the people you have wronged in your lifetime, people to whom you ought to make amends while you still have a chance.

I was on Step 8, and Lars Jenssen's message was clear.

"Look, Lars," I said patiently. "You've got it all ass-backwards. I didn't wrong my grandparents, they wronged me, us—my mother and me both. If that happened to Kelly, if my own daughter got pregnant, you can bet I wouldn't throw her to the wolves like that."

"Oh?" Lars Jenssen asked.

And suddenly I had a vision, a flashback of me standing nose to nose with Kelly in Arizona a few months earlier, of my telling her that the young man she had been interested in was nothing but a creep and a bum. In the dim restaurant light my ears reddened at the thought. I wondered if Lars saw them change color, if he had spoken about this because somehow he had direct knowledge about my confrontation with Kelly or if his comments came from the general pool of human experience that goes with being a parent.

To shut down the discussion, I reached for the check, which Lars Jenssen always insisted on splitting right down to the last penny. "Let's head home, Lars. I've got a case I'm working on."

As soon as the words were out of my mouth, I knew I had stumbled into yet another one of Lars Jenssen's pet peeves where J. P. Beaumont was concerned.

"What time did you go in to work this morning?" he asked, pushing back his chair and taking up the cudgels.

"A little after seven," I answered. "Why?"

"And what time did you quit tonight?"

"Five. Right around there."

"And you're going to work some more tonight? One of the biggest mistakes a man can make is to work too goddamned much. First you drank so much it got you in trouble, and now you're gonna work so much it'll be the same damn thing. Society ain't as hard on workaholics as it is on the other kind, but it's still just as bad for you in the long run, just as hard on your system, you mark my words."

The conversation had done a complete circuit. We had gotten beyond the sticky family part of my life. Once more I was able to regard Lars Jenssen's well-intentioned concern as nothing more or less than an amusing, harmless foible.

"I'll bear that in mind, Lars. Come on."

We got up and left. Once outside, we found the air was brittle and cold. Lars paused on the sidewalk outside the restaurant and sniffed the air.

"It's gonna rain," he pronounced. "Take maybe a couple of days, but it'll rain like hell."

I glanced up. The air was so still and clear that

even with the downtown glow washing against the sky, a few faint stars were visible.

Shaking my head in disbelief, I took him by the arm. "Snow maybe, Lars, but it's too damn cold to rain."

He looked at me with a kindly but disparaging glance. "These young kids," he mumbled. "They don't know nothing about nothing."

Me? A young kid? I'd already spent almost twenty years on Seattle's homicide squad, but in Lars Jenssen's vernacular, I was nothing but a misguided young upstart. Chuckling inwardly, I didn't bother to reply.

We walked home through the biting cold. Even with his cane, Lars Jenssen had little trouble keeping up. He had told me that he used the cane more for balance than anything else, and striding along beside him, I could see that was true. I walked on with him as far as his apartment and then backtracked the single block to my own building.

There was one lone light blinking on my answering machine. One call had come in. And when I listened to the recording, the voice on it belonged to Detective Paul Kramer.

"Give me a call," it said. "It's nine-thirty, but I'm still at the office."

At least I wasn't the only workaholic in the crew. As far as I knew, Kramer was married, but he was nonetheless working bachelor's hours. Picking up the phone, I dialed his number. He answered before the second ring.

"Beaumont here," I said. "Why the hell are you still working, or did you switch to graveyard without telling me?"

"I was working on the reports until just a little while ago," he answered lightly. "But I thought you'd want to know that Baker's finished the autopsies and I can pick them up early tomorrow morning. They actually said I could get them tonight, but it's late, so I said what the hell."

"Right. Anything else?"

"We may have some preliminary stuff from the crime lab by then as well. Other than that, there's not much to tell. You'll be happy to know that our reports are completed and on Sergeant Watkins' desk."

I resisted the temptation to say, "Pin a rose on you."

"Good," I said. "That should make his day."

There was a pause, a pregnant pause, as though Kramer had something else to say and couldn't make up his mind to spit it out.

"What's going on, Kramer? Is there something more?"

"No, not really. Did you pick up the bomb-threat info from Doris Walker?" Kramer asked.

"Yes, I got it."

"Well? Have you looked at it yet?" Kramer demanded impatiently. "What does it say?"

Lars Jenssen's warning about becoming a workaholic came back to me. The devil made me decide that in a world of workaholics it was time for an ounce of prevention.

"No, I haven't looked at it yet, and I'm not going to, either, not until morning. The city doesn't pay enough for me to work twenty-four hours a day, and they don't pay you that much either. We'll go over it in the morning."

"Good enough. I'm heading out of here too. See you then."

Kramer sounded casual and almost friendly, and phony as hell. "Right," I said, and put down the phone.

Nothing of what he'd told me had been important or urgent enough to merit an after-hours phone call, and Detective Kramer and I certainly weren't on the kind of chummy basis that makes for pass-the-time phone calls going back and forth. I couldn't help wondering what the hidden agenda had been in his calling me, but when no obvious answers immediately presented themselves, I let it go and headed for bed.

What I needed right then more than anything else was a good night's sleep, but that was something easier said than done. Once in bed, I fell asleep within minutes, but shortly after that, some outside noise disturbed me enough to bring me fully awake. After that, I couldn't go back to sleep for any amount of money.

I tossed and turned, waiting for sleep to return while my guts roiled inside me. That late night chili-burger was at war with my innards, and the roaring battle kept me wide-awake no matter how tired I was.

I lay there for what seemed like hours, listening to the rumbling of the building's heat pumps on the roof outside my penthouse. No longer were they an anonymous part of the building's white noise. I was consciously aware of them now, aware of the implications behind their presence and absence—heat or cold, comfort or not. The ongoing roar was down-right soothing, but I still couldn't sleep.

For a while I kept my restless brain at bay by focusing on the case, by doing a series of mental lists about what would need to be accomplished the next day—locating the missing Volvo, interviewing the Chambers woman and Maxwell Cole, getting a look at the autopsy results, and talking to the lady at the school district.

But thinking about the case was really only a futile effort to jam my mental frequencies and hold other more disturbing thoughts at bay. Because Lars Jenssen had, knowingly or not, let one of my very own personal demons out of the jug.

"Damn you," I mumbled aloud as I finally drifted off to sleep in the wee hours. Only, it wasn't Lars Jenssen I was thinking about and cursing. It wasn't him I was damning.

It was that selfish son of a bitch himself—my grandfather, Jonas Piedmont.

CHAPTER 10

THAT NIGHT, FOR THE FIRST TIME IN MY LIFE, I DREAMED about my grandfather.

I was in a cemetery, a cold, wind- and rain-swept cemetery, not a real one, and not one I'd ever seen before. Across a wide expanse of grass, I could see a wooden casket poised over a newly dug grave, waiting to be lowered into it. Around the grave a group of men, some leaning on picks and shovels, stood waiting and talking.

Somehow I knew at once that Jonas Piedmont was lying dead in that coffin. Filled with a terrible and inexplicable urgency, I hurried toward the group of men, rushing because I knew I was late. Long before I could cover the distance between me and the grave, however, the casket began sinking slowly and inevitably into the ground. I shouted for them to wait for me, but instead, they all turned and started throwing dirt onto the vanished coffin.

I shouted again, pleading in vain for them to stop, but they wouldn't. They kept right on flinging the heavy, wet dirt into the hole in the ground. By the time I reached the group and recognized the men as members of the Regrade Regulars, the grave was completely filled in and slivers of grass were already sprouting up through the muddy ground even as Lars Jenssen himself heaved the last shovelful of dirt onto the grave. When he saw me standing there panting, he leaned on his shovel again, pointing and laughing.

I fought my way out of the dream and found that the sheet had somehow come loose during the course of that restless night. It was bunched up and wrapped around my neck. I fought my way out of that too, throwing it on the floor beside the bed, and made my way into the bathroom. I didn't need an interpreter to explain that particular dream. What I really needed was a steaming hot shower to wash it away.

As I shaved, the radio in the bathroom reported that another day had dawned clear and cold. There was a slight warming trend, all the way up into the low twenties—a big help for Belltown Terrace's heat pumps, which still rumbled away outside—but the slightly higher temperatures wouldn't make things that much better for anything else.

I was glad not to have to pay attention while the announcer went through the long list of school closures that would extend holiday vacations for most Puget Sound youngsters for yet another day. And I was relieved to hear that no new incidents of sled/vehicular fatalities had occurred the day before.

Armed with a cup of coffee, I stood at my living room window gazing across the snow-wrapped city. From the penthouse level of Belltown Terrace, the snow-covered hillsides still looked picture-pretty, but that sense of beauty changed drastically once it was closer at hand.

Down on street level, standing outside in it, shivering in snow up to my calves, that seemingly pristine white stuff took on a hard and brittle texture. It was dirty and crusted over by the mottled leavings of sanding crews. I waited for the bus in front of Belltown Terrace.

With a badge and ID, police ride free on city buses. "Pray for rain," the driver of the overloaded Metro bus told me with a cheerful grin as he glanced at my badge. "Rain's the only thing that's going to help."

I was sure that was true, but despite Lars Jenssen's prediction to the contrary, that morning's biting cold didn't make rain a likely possibility.

The slow-moving bus was jammed to the gills. The almost carefree holiday attitude from the day before was completely gone, wiped out by that second frigid morning. There was no lighthearted camaraderie and banter among the people pressed together in the hot, steamy bus. Those few who did talk were mostly weary mothers, comparing the logistics of hastily arranged child care. Along with unaccustomed heavy-duty coats, gloves, and scarves, people wore frowns of grim determination. This was winter, real winter for a change, and the grownups of Seattle weren't having any fun.

Once on the fifth floor of the Public Safety Building, I went directly to my cubicle, opened Doris Walker's envelope, and dragged out the bomb-threat folder, which, out of deference to Lars Jenssen, I hadn't even cracked open before coming to work.

There in my office, I read through it quickly. According to the file, there had been a total of seven threats in all, starting and ending back during the teachers' strike at the beginning of the school year earlier that fall. Most had come in at night or on weekends, two by phone on the district's answering machine and the others wrapped around rocks and tossed through plate-glass windows. All of them had targeted the school district administration office itself.

Despite seven thorough searches, no bombs had ever been found. After the first one, round-the-clock security guards had been instituted at the office complex on Queen Anne Hill. That surveillance continued for some time, even though the threats themselves had ceased about the same time striking teachers had returned to work. Now, several months later, round-the-clock coverage had been replaced by two consecutive after-hours shifts.

I was surprised to learn that each of the several incidents had indeed been reported to the school authorities and then passed on to the proper personnel at the Seattle Police Department. The report specifically mentioned the names of several members of the Fraud and Explosive squad. Try as I might, I couldn't remember anything at all about the case coming through official departmental pipelines. Nor, to the best of my knowledge, had there been any mention about it in the media. That seemed odd to me. Local school district bomb threats are always big news, but these seemed to have fallen into a black hole without a single reporter noticing. I wondered why.

I don't pretend to understand media people, and when I need help in that department, I always turn to Ron Peters, the man who was my partner until a permanent back injury made his return to regular duty as a homicide detective a physical impossibility. Back on the job after months of hospital treatment and rehabilitation, Peters was now ensconced, not entirely happily, in his new job with the Media Relations Department.

Unfortunately, when I called down to talk to him, Peters was closeted in that champion bureaucratic waster of time—a morning-long meeting. He was there, and so was everyone else from his unit. Did I want to leave a message?

I've long held the revolutionary belief that if all staff meetings in the world were totally abolished overnight, not only would civilization as we know it survive, it would actually thrive.

"No," I said. "I'll call back."

My next call was to the F & E squad itself, where I reached Detective Lyle Cummings, affectionately known around the department as Officer Sparky.

Lyle Cummings had been plain old Lyle Cummings for his first eight years at Seattle P.D. The Sparky handle had come to him in midcareer as the result of an unfortunate incident in which Lyle and his partner, Dave Cooper, had been out test-driving the department's brand-new $150,000 bomb-disposal truck. Crossing the Spokane Street Bridge, a missing three-cent grommet caused an electrical short circuit in the radio wiring. Unable to summon help, the truck wound up as a smoldering ruin parked in the far right-hand lane of the West Seattle Freeway.

When the smoke cleared from around the charred remains and when the dust settled on all the paperwork, it turned out that the damage to the vehicle was completely covered under the truck's original warranty, but the damage to Cummings' name and reputation proved to be permanent. The "Sparky" handle was liberally applied, and it stuck. Cummings managed the teasing with a combination of humor and good grace.

"Hello, Sparky. This is Beaumont from Homicide," I said.

"Top of the morning, Beau," he said. "What can we do for you?"

"I'm calling about the school district bomb threats."

Instantly his tone became markedly guarded. "School district bomb threats? What do you know about that?" he demanded.

"Not much, but I've got the file right here and . . ."

"What the hell are you doing with it? That file's not supposed to be out of this office."

"Hold on," I countered. "I don't have your file, Spark. I have the school district's file."

There was a long pause before he said, "Ouch. Me and my big mouth. I guess I blew it, didn't I?"

"You could say that," I returned lightly, knowing I had him dead to rights, but I didn't rub it in. "Look, I'm working yesterday's school district case. That file of yours may have something to do with it."

"You mean the suicide/homicide? How could it? I got the distinct impression from what I read in the paper this morning that it was some kind of love-triangle thing. What does that have to do with bomb threats?"

"Beats me," I answered, "but it's our job to check all the angles. I want to see that file. ASAP."

There was another long, thoughtful pause. "Hang tight, Beau. I'll see what I can do and get back to you."

Ten minutes later Detective Cummings appeared in my cubicle, file in hand.

"I got the word from upstairs," he said, handing it over to me. "You can look at it all you want, but only while I'm here. You can take notes if you like, but nothing gets copied, and nothing gets taken out."

"Wait just a goddamned minute here," I objected. "What is this? I'm a homicide detective working a case and I can't have unlimited access to one of Seattle P.D.'s own files?"

Sparky shrugged. "It's the best we can do under the circumstances. If you'd like a word of friendly advice, I wouldn't make too many waves about it either. Rumor has it that some of the brass are getting their chains yanked real good on this one by person or persons unknown. My guess is it's somebody important from across the street."

"Across the street" was the department's sarcastically euphemistic reference to the city's administrative offices located on the other side of Fourth Avenue.

"You mean as in the mayor's office or somebody on the city council? We're supposed to be talking squeaky clean Seattle here."

"We're also talking partisan politics," Cummings replied meaningfully. "Now, are you interested in looking at the file or not?"

Silenced, I scanned through the incident reports. The information contained in them wasn't very different from what I already had received from Doris Walker, with one notable exception—the actual texts of the threats themselves. There were typed transcripts of the two that had come in over the phone.

One said: "Start school now or else this place is history." The other: "Education delayed is education denied. Dynamite is the cure."

"Cute," I said, tossing the transcripts back in the file. "The guy must think he's a comedian. It is a guy, isn't it?"

Cummings nodded. "Young male Caucasian, that's about all the experts have been able to tell us so far from listening to the tapes."

Also included were Xeroxed copies of the other threats, the ones that had been tossed through the windows. The poorly spelled notes had been stitched together, some with whole words and others with individual letters clipped from newspapers and magazines, a real cut-and-paste job. One said, "Teachers should teach. Strikes waist lives. Get school open before I blow this place to peaces." Another said, "All I need too know is availible in *The Anarchist's Handbook*. Pipe bombs rule." Still another said, "You guys are fuking with my life. I want my education now!"

I looked up at Cummings. "This dude can't spell for shit, and he reads too many kidnap novels."

Sparky Cummings nodded. "If he reads at all. The more we pay for education, the less we get. Go on."

"Whose the boss, you or the teachers?" and "I am loosing patients. Stop the strike now."

"If he's so opposed to the teachers' union, how come he's threatening to blow up the school district office? Why not the union's office instead?"

"Beats me," Cummings replied. "Where is it written that kooks have to be smart or logical?"

"Who sat on this report, Sparky? I need to know."

"All of the above," Cummings answered. "At the time it was happening, both the teachers' union and the district asked that we not release the information because they were deeply involved in negotiations. I don't know who had the horses to keep a lid on it after the strike was over, but of course, by then the threats had stopped as well. There probably wasn't much reason to raise a hullabaloo after the fact."

"Particularly not when Her Honor's primary interest is maintaining the status quo," I added.

Cummings shot me a warning frown. "You said that, Beau. I didn't."

Although the two shouldn't have been linked, the previous year's mayoral election had been won and lost with the school district's future as the central focus of the bitter campaigns. A group of angry and very vocal parents, tired of years of mandatory busing, had brought in some new political blood. Much to the consternation of long-term political lights, the new kids on the block and their off-the-wall candidate had played havoc with what should have been a shoo-in election for the retiring mayor's handpicked successor.

Elected by such a minute margin that a legally mandated recount had been necessary, the new mayor was now trying her best to keep city government running smoothly while she fought to regain lost ground among the grass-roots electorate. Meanwhile the school district was doing away with busing an inch at a time while student population dwindled, as did money, and those same disillusioned parents, beaten but still pissed, continued to take their children elsewhere.

Her Honor's press aide had recently announced that Seattle was once more among the top three contenders for "The Most Livable City Award." Participants in that kind of national competition can't afford to wash their dirty underwear in public, and trouble in a school district is civic soil of the worst kind. If you don't believe it, try asking the City of Boston.

Scanning through the file wasn't telling me much of anything new. "So what did you guys finally find out about this?" I asked at last.

Cummings shrugged. "For a while the pet theory going around was that someone opposed to the teachers' union was posing as a student and making the threats, but we couldn't find any likely possibles. A disgruntled student was the most we ever came up with, although why a "disgruntled student" would be so damn eager to have school get started, nobody was ever able to figure out. After the strike was over, though, since no bombs were ever found and since no one was hurt, the case got shifted to low priority."

"Fast?" I asked.

"You mean did it get shifted fast?" he asked. I nodded. "You bet. It was fast, all right."

"And nothing's happened since?"

"That's right," Sparky replied. "Zippo."

"Well, something's happened now. That security guard is dead. So's the woman. Maybe it wasn't a love triangle at all. Maybe it was made to look that way, just to throw us off," I suggested.

"I suppose that's possible," Detective Cummings agreed, "but not very likely. I still can't let you have the file."

While Sparky Cummings sat there waiting, I went back through the file once more and took some notes, paying particular attention to the threats themselves, which I took down verbatim, sloppy spelling and all. As I went through the exercise, something struck me as strange.

"How many kids do you know who can't spell the word 'fuck'?" I asked.

"Not many," Cummings admitted with a grin. "It goes with the territory. They usually spell it right when they spray-paint it on bridges and overpasses."

"So how come this joker doesn't know it's got a *c* in it?"

"My specialty is bombs," Sparky Cummings said seriously. "I don't know beans about teenagers, my own included."

I finished copying what I wanted from the file and tossed it back across the desk to Detective Cummings.

"Thanks for bringing it down, Spark. I'll try not to make any waves for you guys, unless I have to."

He waved. "Sure thing, Beau. Glad to help."

I sat there for several minutes after Cummings left, thinking that it was odd for someone so eager to be in school to be such a rotten speller. The two didn't seem to mix. People who actually liked school and wanted to be there were usually insufferable teachers' pets, brownnoses who spelled everything perfectly.

I remembered that back when I was in school, perfect spelling was never one of my problems.

CHAPTER 11

I SAT THERE FOR SOME TIME THINKING ABOUT THAT MYS-terious *C*-less fuck, and wondered idly if it was related to Erica Jong's zipless one. I had meandered on into some self-pitying woolgathering and was mulling about how long I had done without same, with or without the zip or the *C*, when my phone rang.

"Beaumont? This is Kramer. I'm down in the garage. I finally got us a car. Come on down so I don't have to turn loose of it. Hurry up, will you?"

Nobody had told me we were scheduled to go touring that morning, but I decided to be agreeable. "I'll be right there. By the way, where are we going?"

"Back up to the school district office. To see Andrea Stovall."

Another new person at the Seattle school district. "Who's she?" I asked.

"Just get down here, would you? I told them we'd be there by nine and we're going to be late. I'll tell you about her on the way."

I threw my notebook into the first available pocket,

locked the school district's bomb-threat file folder in my desk, and made my way down the stairs, bypassing the building's more and more glitchy elevators. Detective Kramer was pacing the floor of the garage near an idling Reliant, hands planted belligerently on his hips, an impatient frown imprinted across his broad forehead.

"So who's Andrea Stovall?" I asked again as I got in the car.

"I got her name off the logbook sheets," he answered.

"Logbook sheets?" I asked. "We've got those back already?"

"I thought I told you about them last night."

"You told me Doc Baker had preliminary autopsy reports ready for us to pick up this morning. I don't remember anything at all about the logbook."

Kramer fastened his belt with a shrug. "No kidding. You mean I didn't tell you about that? I meant to. It must have slipped my mind or maybe it happened after you called. Mark Fields brought them up from the crime lab last night." He tossed a manila envelope across the seat at me.

"They're in there, copies of the logbook sheets, an unofficial copy of Doc Baker's findings, and whatever the crime lab has done so far."

"Slipped my mind" my ass! Fighting to control my anger, I opened the envelope and thumbed through the three separate sets of papers I found there. I focused first on the cleanly typed forms from Doc Baker's office. There's nothing like reading autopsy and crime lab reports to help whittle your own troubles down to size and make you count your blessings. The impassive technical terminology condensed Alvin Chambers' and Marcia Kelsey's brutal deaths down into dry, bare-bones anatomy class specifics.

Doc Baker estimated Chambers' time of death as somewhere around midnight, although he had probably been shot well before that. He had been shot in the back and then dragged, still alive but possibly unconscious, into the closet, where he had bled to death. A .25-caliber CCI-Blazer slug, shot at point-blank range, had severed his spine and then inflicted surprisingly terrible damage as it ripped through vital internal organs and exited near his belly button. People who don't want to think about outlawing handguns haven't seen firsthand the kind of damage they do.

It took a second for the information to sink in. I looked over at Kramer. "The gun we found was a .38, but this says a .25."

"That's right."

"So we're dealing with two weapons, not one."

"Right again."

I continued reading. There were signs of a blow to the head on Chambers, but it was Doc Baker's assessment that although the blow may have rendered him unconscious, it had in no way contributed to the victim's death. From the lividity of the body, he had been dead for some period of time before Marcia Kelsey's body dropped on top of him.

Unlike Chambers, Marcia Kelsey had evidently died instantly, falling where she was shot. Hers was not a self-inflicted wound, although someone had gone to a good deal of trouble to make us think so.

The lack of powder particles ruled out suicide once and for all.

Baker's preliminary tests showed no sign of drugs or alcohol in either victim, but a final determination on that score would have to wait on the toxicology reports. Those take time.

"It says here Chambers was shot somewhere else and then dragged into the closet."

Kramer nodded. "That's right. That shows up in the crime lab report. The crime-scene team found trace evidence of blood in one of the floor seams in the entryway, near where his table and chair were set up. Liz, from the crime lab, told me they were really lucky to find it, because whoever did it stuck around long enough to do a pretty good job of cleaning up."

"So we're dealing with a real cool customer."

"And somebody who's compulsively neat," Kramer put in with a malicious smile. I knew he was thinking about Pete Kelsey's pristine garage. So was I.

"Did you get to the part where it says no semen?" Kramer added.

I scanned the page to where Doc Baker had detailed his sexual findings. Just as Kramer had said, there was no sign of sexual intercourse. No semen in the vagina or elsewhere.

"What about it?"

Kramer shrugged. "It's too bad, that's all. To get killed for nothing. I mean, if you knew you were gonna die, wouldn't you want to go out with a bang?"

"You're an incurable romantic, Kramer, with a real way with words," I said sarcastically. He grinned. I think he thought it was a compliment.

It occurred to me then that Detective Kramer, who was driving the car rather than studying his own copy of the reports, had a nearly total recall of everything written there. "What did you do, memorize the reports on the way down here this morning?"

"Not this morning. I changed my mind and picked 'em up on my way home last night after all, just in case there was something that needed our attention right away."

I had no delusions that if something had needed "our" attention, I wouldn't have heard word one about it until after the fact. Kramer would have handled it on his own. His silence about the logbooks was anything but the innocent oversight he claimed it to be. It's hard to like working with somebody like that, someone you can't afford to turn your back on. The book says you're supposed to be able to trust your partner. With your life. Fat chance.

Letting it go, I returned to the issue of two guns. That didn't make sense. "I still don't understand why we have two separate weapons."

"Who knows? Maybe the killer thought that if one gun was good, two were better."

Convinced there was nothing more to be gained right then by rereading either one of the two official reports, I turned to the third batch of papers. These turned out to be surprisingly good copies of the Seattle Security logbook pages for December thirtieth and thirty-first and January first.

I glanced down at the second page, the one for the first of January. It had been a holiday after all, and there were only two entries on the entire page: Marcia Kelsey had checked in at eight P.M. There was no check-out time following her name. Andrea Stovall had signed in at eleven and out again at eleven-fifteen.

That certainly answered one question. No wonder we were on our way to see Andrea Stovall. The presence of her name in the register on the same day at around the time of the killings made her a person of interest, someone we needed to interview.

Without further comment, I gathered the pieces of paper together and shoved them back in the envelope. We rode in silence for several blocks, with Kramer driving and me steaming. The pattern behind his behavior was beginning to emerge. He had known about the logbook sheets being ready when he called me the night before. He had known the autopsy reports were ready as well and had lied to me about them on the phone. He had picked them up on the way home and must have spent much of the night studying them. Fortunately for me and unfortunately for him, the vital information he'd been searching for, details that would have given him a crack at being a Lone Ranger hero, hadn't been there.

I was learning the nature of the beast. Look to thy butt, Beaumont, I warned myself firmly. This guy's a weasel who'll kick ass and take names later if you give him half a chance. I didn't like the idea of being pitted against both a murderous crook and an untrustworthy partner at the same time. That didn't make for very good odds. The only way to win in a situation like that is to be smarter than everybody else, cagier, so I bit back any number of caustic comments and got back to the job at hand.

"So tell me. Who's this Andrea Stovall?"

A self-satisfied smirk lit up Kramer's face before he answered, and I wanted to backhand him. "The head of the SFTA," he answered.

"What's that?"

"The Seattle Federated Teachers' Association."

"The union? She's head of the teachers' union."

Kramer smiled. "I thought you'd like that touch."

"So why are we meeting her at the school district office?" In fact, we were just then pulling into the parking lot on Lower Queen Anne.

Detective Kramer glanced at his watch. "You're right. Her office is up in Greenwood, but her secretary told me she has a meeting here at nine-thirty. We're supposed to see her before that."

As we got out of the car, I could see I was dealing with another instance of Detective Kramer's behind-the-scenes machinations. The district office was probably a whole lot more convenient meeting place for all concerned, but it had taken a hell of a lot of arranging. I said, "You must have been one busy little beaver this morning."

Everywhere I turned, I could see Kramer was deliberately holding out on me, keeping me in the dark, but if I complained about it to Sergeant Watkins or Captain Powell, they would laugh themselves silly. How could I complain about a partner so willing to work, so eager to take on extra jobs and lessen my burden, right? Right. I didn't give Kramer the satisfaction of saying a word about it. Instead, I went along with the program and acted as though everything was on the up and up.

"Were they here together? And if so, why would the head of the teachers' union be cozying up to the district's head of labor relations in a secret midnight meeting?"

"Why don't we ask her?" Kramer responded.

Jennifer Lafflyn—Ms. Lafflyn, if you will—the previous day's miniskirted number, was seated demurely at the large reception desk in the school district office. A thick cloud of flowery perfume tainted the atmosphere ten feet in any direction from her desk. She seemed totally recovered from the previous day's emotional roller coaster.

"Good morning, Ms. Lafflyn," Kramer said with oily deference when she looked up from her switchboard and saw us standing there. "We're here to see Mrs. Stovall. Her secretary said that you'd know where to find her."

I don't know if Kramer actually remembered Jennifer Lafflyn's name and preferred salutation or if he had taken his cue from the nameplate on her desk, but his underscored use of the word "Ms." earned him a warm smile from the lady in question. The guy walking three feet behind him, me, that is, was totally invisible.

Jennifer rose quickly to her feet. "Of course," she said. "One moment. Please wait right here."

She turned and disappeared down a long hallway. Her slight but well-built figure was poured into a tightly belted, short black sheath over black panty hose. She may have thought of her basic black getup as appropriate mourning attire, but it was short, exceedingly short.

Kramer leered after her, watching her every move. "Maybe when we're done here, I'll offer to give her a lift downtown so we can get those fingerprints we need. And I'll throw in an early lunch."

He wasn't just talking about lunch, either. "You'd better watch that stuff, Kramer," I warned him. "She looks like she could blow all your fuses and never turn a hair."

Ms. Lafflyn came tripping back down the hallway right then. "They'll be meeting in the conference room. Mrs. Stovall's in the room next door, fourth door on your left."

I've always had this image of union presidents as tough-talking, cigar-chewing guys in baggy pants and rolled-up shirtsleeves who negotiate heavy-duty secret deals in smoke-filled rooms. With my introduction to Andrea Stovall, that particular stereotype was about to be pleasantly shattered.

The woman sitting in the small office was a tiny, immaculately dressed blonde with her hair cut in the short, free-falling style preferred by figure skaters. She had pixielike features combined with the solid handshake of a born politician. She would have been pretty had it not been for the deep shadows under her eyes, ravages of sleeplessness that even the most deftly applied makeup couldn't entirely obliterate.

"Sorry we're so late," Kramer said as she motioned us into chairs. "We had trouble getting transportation."

She shrugged. "That's all right, but we'd better get started right away. What can I do for you?"

"This won't take long," Kramer assured her. "It's about Sunday night. We noticed that you were signed in and out on the logbook."

Andrea Stovall nodded. "That's correct. You said as much on the telephone. What about it?"

"The only other person we have any record of working that night, other than the security guard, the only other person who signed in, was Marcia Louise Kelsey, a woman who died under mysterious circumstances that same night."

"I know all about that," Andrea said wearily. Her whole body sagged and the smooth veneer of her face contorted with grief. "Marcia Kelsey and I were friends. I can't get over what happened. It's such a terrible tragedy."

"Actually, Mrs. Stovall," Kramer said, "that friendship is one of the things we wanted to ask you about, as well as what you were doing at the district office the night before last. Isn't it odd for the head of the union and the head of labor relations to be buddies, as it were?"

"We started out teaching together years ago, and we became friends then. Through the years our jobs grew in different directions, but the friendship stayed."

"What about Sunday night?" I asked.

"I came down to check on her."

"You knew she was going to be working that night?"

"Not really, but . . ."

"But what?"

"I just thought she might be, that's all." Andrea Stovall dropped her eyes and wiped imaginary dust off the desktop in front of her. Even though we were treating her with kid gloves, this line of questioning was making Andrea Stovall very nervous. I wondered why and decided to get a little tougher.

"Look, Mrs. Stovall," I said gruffly. "It was the middle of the night on one of the worst nights we've had in years. The streets were a mess, yet you expect us to believe that you came all the way down here on the off chance that Marcia Kelsey might be here as well? That doesn't make sense."

"It doesn't matter if it makes sense or not. That's what happened. I was worried about her and came to check on her. She wasn't here, nobody was. I thought . . ." She paused.

"You thought what?"

"Since her car was still in the lot, I thought maybe Pete had come by and given her a ride home."

"Was the guard on duty?" I asked.

"Probably, but I didn't see him or anyone else, not a soul."

"What time was that?" Kramer asked.

"I don't remember exactly. Around eleven. I wrote it down in the logbook, both the time in and the time out. If you don't believe me, you can ask Rex."

She broke off and bit her lower lip while an embarrassed flush crept up her neck and across her cheeks. Clearly she had blurted out something she hadn't intended to.

"Who's Rex?" I asked.

"Rex Pierson, the manager of my building."

"What building is that?"

"I live at the Queen Anne. It's just up the hill from here."

The Queen Anne wasn't a building I recognized by name. Next to me, Detective Kramer shifted uncomfortably in his chair. There was a good deal the two of us didn't agree on, but he was getting the same reading from Andrea Stovall that I was.

"How exactly did you get into the building, Mrs. Stovall?" I asked. "You said you couldn't find anyone, not even the security guard. Weren't the doors locked?"

Andrea Stovall clasped her hands and placed them on the desk in front of her, but not before I noticed a sudden, uncontrolled trembling.

"Are you cold, Mrs. Stovall?" I asked, feigning sympathy. "Your hands are shaking."

"No," she said quickly, "I'm fine." But under her makeup, the color of her skin had paled.

"You still haven't told us how you got into the building," I prodded.

She swallowed. "I have a key," she said in almost a whisper. "I used that to let myself in."

Detective Kramer's jaw dropped, and so did mine. Giving the head of the teachers' union a key to the district offices sounded downright crazy, like giving the Big Bad Wolf his own private key to the henhouse.

"You mean the head of the teachers' union has a key to the building?" Kramer demanded.

"I probably shouldn't have," Andrea Stovall conceded, "but I do. I've had one for years. I still sign in and out, the way I'm supposed to. Remember, that's how you found me, from the sign-in sheet. Besides, I was sure Marcia was still here, because her car was parked in the lot outside, but when I couldn't raise the guard with the bell, I let myself in."

"There's a bell?" Kramer asked.

"A night bell, so that if the guard is in some other part of the building, he can still hear that someone's at the door."

"Tell us about the car," I said, switching gears. "You said it was still parked in the lot?"

"She drove a Volvo, a green Volvo station wagon," Andrea Stovall answered gratefully, relieved to move away from any more questions about her unauthorized possession of a building key. "It was right there in the lot when we drove up."

"We? You mean you and this Rex person?" Kramer asked.

She swallowed. "That's right."

"And he's your apartment manager, right? How did he get dragged into this?"

"He offered me a ride, and I accepted."

"In the middle of a snowy night? To come check on someone you didn't know for sure would be here?"

Andrea nodded.

"Why?"

Suddenly Andrea Stovall dissolved into tears. "Because I was worried about her. Because I was afraid."

"Afraid of what?"

"That something might happen to her. And I was right, goddamn it! I was right to be afraid."

Some women cry daintily and prettily. Andrea Stovall wasn't one of them. Her nose and eyes turned red while her face puffed up instantly.

There was a gentle knock on the door just then, and Doris Walker poked her head into the room, looking questioningly from one face to another. "Sorry to interrupt," she said apologetically, "but

Dr. Savage and the others are waiting. Would it be possible for you to finish this later?"

Without waiting for us to answer, Andrea Stovall reached down and scooped up both a purse and a briefcase that had been sitting on the floor beside her. "Tell them I'll be there in a minute. I've got to fix my face."

With that, she bolted from the room and Doris closed the door behind her, leaving Kramer and me alone. I'm sure we could have stopped her, told Doris Walker that Andrea Stovall was unavoidably detained and kept the interview going, but the interview had raised some interesting questions, disturbing questions.

What exactly was the relationship between Marcia Louise Kelsey and Andrea Stovall? More than Andrea had let on, of that I was sure. She had said she was "afraid" for Marcia. Why? It hadn't been just a general fear of someone working late and alone in an otherwise deserted office building. The fear had been more specific than that, and strong enough to make Andrea enlist her apartment manager's help when she went to check.

We'd be talking to Andrea Stovall again, but before we did, we'd need to do some checking on our own. When homicide detectives ask questions, it's always a good idea to have some idea in advance what the real answers ought to be. It keeps you from being suckered quite so badly.

"What's with her?" Kramer asked, still staring at the closed door.

"She's hiding something," I said. "Something that happened the night of the murders, and she's scared to death we're going to find out what it is, which we'd by God better do before we talk to her again."

Kramer nodded and we both rose to go. At least we had found one point we could agree on, and in this case, that counted for progress.

CHAPTER 12

ON THE WAY BACK DOWN THE HALL, I STOPPED OFF LONG enough to use the rest room. I had thought Kramer was joking about taking Jennifer Lafflyn back downtown with us. By the time I reached the receptionist's desk, she was wearing her coat, and a substitute receptionist had been pressed into service.

"Wait a minute," I said. "As long as we're here, shouldn't we talk to Kendra Meadows?"

"Suit yourself," Kramer replied. "Now's when Ms. Lafflyn can go, and I offered to take her."

Which gave me a clear choice of taking it or leaving it. "See you later," I said. I turned to the substitute receptionist. "Is Kendra Meadows in?"

"One moment. I'll check. What did you say your name was?"

Unlike Jennifer Lafflyn, the formidable lady who appeared at the top of the stairs a few moments later was dressed for a very respectable funeral. Kendra Meadows was a middle-aged black lady whose thick, wavy hair was turning gunmetal gray. She was large, in every sense of the word, what the purveyors of women's clothing call "queen-size." Almost as tall as I was and thickly built, she was attractively dressed in a generously cut wool suit, the skirt of which covered her legs halfway down her calves.

Moving with ponderous grace, she came down the stairs while her undergarments whispered in that peculiarly feminine rustle of nylon on nylon.

"Detective Beaumont, is it?"

Kendra Meadows' welcoming smile revealed a wide gap between her two front teeth. No doubt the school district's dental insurance would have covered a set of braces for the middle-aged lady had Kendra Meadows ever stopped to consider such vain nonsense desirable.

She held out her hand. When I gripped it, her handshake was firm enough to make me wince.

"Sorry about that," she apologized, catching what must have been a pained expression on my face.

"It's nothing," I told her quickly. "I hurt my fingers a few months back. They still give me problems every once in a while."

"Too bad," she said with a sympathetic click of her tongue. "Well then, come along. I was just going back to my office." I followed her back up the stairs and down a long, narrow corridor into a large but nonetheless crowded and messy office. Like Marcia Kelsey, Kendra Meadows seemed to thrive in an environment with the appearance of total chaos. Not only the desk but the credenza, chairs, and several extra tables were piled high with stacks of file folders and loose pieces of paper. She cleaned off one of the chairs and motioned me into it.

Once Kendra Meadows had seated herself at the desk, she extricated a stack of papers from the general clutter and sat holding it, regarding me with yet another warm smile. Kendra Meadows' natural charm, so obvious in person, hadn't been at all apparent in her abrupt telephone manner.

"I took the liberty of making a preliminary list for you, Detective Beaumont," she explained, reaching across the desk and handing me several 8½-by-11-inch pieces of paper with neat handwritten lists of names, telephone numbers, and addresses on them.

"The first list is of the people who were here at the office on the morning in question, after the bodies were found. You'll find Mr. Jacobs there, but it would probably be better if you didn't try to contact Martin until I get a clear go-ahead from his doctor. You'll notice Jennifer Lafflyn is on that list as well. She's usually on the desk downstairs in the mornings, but she wasn't there just now."

"Right," I said. Under Jennifer Lafflyn's name were five more names I didn't recognize. "Who are the others?"

"The next few are on our substitute teacher scheduling crew. They come in every morning at five. Even though we already knew school was going to be canceled on Monday, those five you see there are the ones who still managed to make it in. They were here to help handle the extra volume of calls from anxious parents. I thought you'd be interested in talking to them. After all, one of them might have seen something without realizing it."

Kendra Meadows should have been a cop. She

paused and waited while I ran my finger down the list of names and telephone numbers.

"Is this the kind of thing you had in mind?" she asked.

"Absolutely, Mrs. Meadows. This is great."

"Kendra," she said. "Call me Kendra. Now, where was I? Oh, yes. The next list includes the names of most of the people here in the building who worked closely with Marcia Kelsey. Her secretary and the staff members who reported directly to her. That list also contains the names of those she reported to."

"Good," I said. "Having them broken down into groups like this will be a big help when we start the interviewing process. What's the next page?"

"That's a list of district employees from outside the building who probably worked with Marcia on a regular basis. Some are certified employees, some are noncertified. As director of Labor Relations, she wasn't just responsible for our dealings with the teachers' union. There are several other unionized entities as well. I've put the names of the unions as well as their addresses and phone numbers right there at the bottom of the page."

Halfway down this list I discovered the name, address, and telephone number of Andrea Stovall. I'm not sure how Kendra Meadows did it, but it struck me that her sources of information were very thorough. In all my years of doing homicide investigations, I had never before started a case with that kind of comprehensive background material on a victim.

I turned to the last page. On that one there was only one entry. Seattle Security. Poor dead Alvin

Chambers. His death kept being shortchanged at every corner of the investigation.

"This is all you had on the security guard?" I asked.

"Since he worked for a subcontractor, we don't have any specific information on him. I'm sure you can get that from Seattle Security."

Once more I paged through the extensive list. On further examination it proved to be even more impressive than I had at first thought.

"How did you manage to get all this pulled together in such a short time?"

Kendra Meadows laughed. "Of course, I had some help from the computer," she said, "but there are some things people do best, wouldn't you say?"

"I certainly would," I told her. "I can see it was a good deal of work. Thank you."

"You're welcome, Detective Beaumont." Kendra Meadows' dark eyes were suddenly serious. The good humor disappeared from her face and the laughter from her voice.

"You're right. It was work, hard work. I was here half the night, pulling it all together, but I'm glad to be of use. You see, I knew Marcia Kelsey. We weren't close, but I've known her for years. Something terrible must have gone wrong in her life. I can't imagine what it would have been. Do you know?"

I shook my head. "We're working on it, Mrs. Meadows. That's all I can say for right now."

"You must find out what happened, and quickly too, so we can all put it behind us and go on with the real job of educating children. It's impossible for children to learn to live nonviolent lives when they see well-respected adults behaving this way."

"That's true, Mrs. Meadows," I said, rising to go. "I couldn't agree with you more."

At the door to her office, I turned back. "One other thing. Do you happen to have a key to this building?"

She frowned. "Yes. Of course. Why?"

"Do many other people?"

"A few. Not many. It's bad for security."

"Did Marcia Kelsey have a key?"

"Probably. I could check the list. It won't take a moment."

Kendra Meadows heaved herself out of the chair, hurried over to a file cabinet in the far corner of the room, and extracted a file folder. She moved her finger down a piece of paper inside.

"That's right. Marcia had a key. It says so right here. And the locks were changed as of the first of October."

"Are all the people with keys on that list?"

"As far as I know."

"May I see it?"

She passed it to me without a murmur and I scanned down it to the S's. Andrea Stovall may have had a key, but her name did not appear on the master list.

"Thanks," I said. "That tells me exactly what I need to know. May I have a copy of this?"

Kendra Meadows smiled her gap-toothed smile and shrugged her broad shoulders. "Certainly. I don't see why not."

I left Kendra Meadows' office with wonderfully comprehensive lists of people to interview and with one real additional bonus—the sure knowledge that, for whatever reason, Andrea Stovall was a liar.

It was a lead. Maybe only a small one, but in this business, a small lead is a hell of a lot better than no lead at all.

I wanted to make a series of phone calls, fairly private calls, so instead of returning to the reception area, I went to the superintendent's suite of offices and threw myself on Doris Walker's mercy. She politely showed me into a small private office and then left me to use the phone, discreetly closing the door behind her. In view of what happened next, I was tremendously grateful for that closed door.

I called down to the department to check in and got hold of Margie. She sounded relieved to hear from me.

"It's a good thing you called in," she said quietly. "Watty's on the warpath. He's looking for you. And where's Detective Kramer? The prosecutor needs him in court this afternoon."

"Kramer's on his way downtown; in fact, he should be there by now. What's Watty pissed about?"

"How should I know? I'll connect you and let him tell you himself."

Sergeant Watkins came on the phone a moment later. "Where the hell are you, Beau?"

"At the school district office. I just finished interviewing Kendra Meadows, the lady in charge of Personnel. We also talked to the president of the teachers' organization." I was still operating under the faint hope that this could end up as a friendly conversation.

"Well, I'm glad to hear that you're finally working."

The word "finally," said with that peculiar emphasis, gave me the first hint that I was in deep trouble.

"Did you say 'finally'? What's that supposed to mean?"

"It means get cracking, Beau. It means stop playing around at this and get to work. I saw the reports. Paul Kramer wrote every damn one of them. You stuck him doing the reports; I know that for a fact. You also left him here working long after you went home. Where the hell do you get off treating him like some junior errand boy, sending him around picking up lab reports and autopsies? You think you're too good to do some of the grunt work, Beaumont? Detective Kramer's supposed to be your partner, a full-fledged goddamned investigator, not your personal gofer."

"Wait just a goddamned minute here, Watty. Did he tell you . . ."

"No, you wait a minute, Detective Beaumont, and don't interrupt. Just because Kramer's a dedicated cop, and just because he's low man on the totem pole here in Homicide, doesn't mean you old-timers get to take advantage of him and stick him with all the shit work. Do I make myself clear?"

"Perfectly," I responded bleakly.

From Watty's tone of voice, I could tell it was useless to object or offer any excuses or to suggest that things Kramer had done were things he had appointed himself to do without any kind of request or consultation from me.

"I want to see results, Beau," Watty continued. "I want to see reports on my desk with your signature on them. I want to know who you've interviewed and what was said. I want to know what kind of contribution you're making, because this is now, and always has been, a *team* effort, Detective, and don't you forget it."

With that, Watty hung up. It was a good thing Kramer was long gone, because if he hadn't been, I probably would have wrapped the phone cord right around his damn ass-kissing neck. I felt like one of those poor schmucks in the comics who suddenly has a lightbulb click on over his head.

So *that* was how Kramer was playing the game, and I'd walked right into the trap like a lamb to the slaughter.

For several minutes, I stood there seething, my hands shaking with rage, while the blood pounded in my ears. Eventually I got a grip on both myself and my anger. If Watty wanted interviews, then by God, I'd give him interviews, and after a moment's thought, I knew exactly where I'd start.

My mother was always one to do the worst things first and get them over with. Talking to Maxwell Cole was very low on my list of wonderful things to do. Unfortunately, other than talking to Charlotte Chambers, Maxwell Cole seemed like the next logical interview step.

But Charlotte Chambers didn't live on Queen Anne Hill, and Maxwell Cole did.

I knew Max lived only a few blocks away from the school district office. If he happened to be home, it would take only a few minutes to trudge on up there to see him. If not, if he was already at work, then the *Post-Intelligencer* office was located at the very bottom of Queen Anne, and I could maybe catch him there on my way back downtown.

I tried calling his office first. No luck. I was told he was ill, out for the day. I looked in the book, but as a public personage, Max naturally has an unlisted phone number. Since I'm hardly on a best-buddy basis with him, I'm not privy to his number any more than he is to mine. That left me only one viable alternative—to show up unannounced.

In the long run, it was probably just as well that I didn't call in advance. If I had warned him I was coming, chances are Maxwell Cole wouldn't have answered the door.

On my way past her desk, Doris Walker flagged me down, signaling for me to wait until she finished a phone call. "Dr. Savage wanted to know how to get in touch with you, in case anything comes up that he needs to talk with you about."

"Didn't I leave a card?" I asked.

"Not that I know of."

It was an oversight. As a penance, I scrawled both my home and cellular number on it in addition to the office one. After all, if the superintendent of schools couldn't be trusted with an unlisted phone number, who could?

CHAPTER 13

MAX COLE LIVES ON BIGELOW AVENUE NORTH, A GRA-
cious, gently winding, tree-lined street that curves
around the base of what's known as Upper Queen
Anne Hill. I used several sets of steep stairway side-
walks to make my way up to Bigelow from the school
district office on the lower part of the hill. The cold
but invigorating climb left me feeling a little winded
but quite virtuous by the time I topped the last set of
stairs and came out on the snow-covered street.

Max's house, which I learned had once belonged
to his parents, was a stately old Victorian set back
behind a pair of towering, winter-bare chestnut trees.
I walked up onto the covered porch and rang the
bell. A miserable-looking Maxwell Cole, wearing a
flannel robe and carrying a huge red hanky, answered
the door. His unwaxed handlebar mustache drooped
feebly, his eyes were red and runny. Obviously he
had caught himself a dandy of a cold.

"Hi, Max," I said cheerfully. "I just happened to

be in the neighborhood. How're the sick, the lame, and the lazy?"

He wasn't exactly overjoyed to see me. "What are you doing here, J.P.? Can't you see I'm sick?"

Actually, I could. There was only a frail hint of the old mutual antagonism in his voice. Feverish and haggard, he was too sick to carry off his customary obnoxiousness with any kind of believability.

"Just doing my job, Max, that's all. I'd like to talk to you about Marcia and Pete Kelsey, if you have a minute. May I come in?"

"Suit yourself," he said gruffly, pulling open the door with one hand while he used the other to stifle a sudden fit of sneezing. As I walked past him, the thought passed briefly through my mind that he was probably contagious as hell right then and I'd most likely end up with a case of pneumonia for my trouble. I accepted his reluctant invitation in the manner in which it was given and went on inside.

Max led the way into a spacious but overly furnished living room. The place was full of things that looked to me like genuine antiques, quality antiques. The only problem was there were far too many of them. And the room was boiling hot. Max had the thermostat set so high that it was sweltering in there.

He took a seat in an easy chair in front of a huge empty fireplace. Dropping my coat and gloves at one end of a chintz couch, I put as much distance between us as I reasonably could, settling at the far end of it and facing him across the wide expanse of an ornate, marble-topped coffee table.

"Wanted to have a fire in the fireplace this morning," he grumbled, "but wouldn't you know burning restrictions are in effect today? This is the kind of weather when you *want* to have a fire in the fireplace."

That was true. I didn't mention to him that this was exactly the kind of weather when *everyone* wanted a fire in his respective fireplace and that was precisely why it was a problem. Besides, had the room been any warmer, I would have died of heat prostration. I said a silent prayer of thanks for all those busy little environmentalists who had made burning restrictions possible.

"I'm sorry to disturb you when you're sick, Max," I began, "but I really do need to get some background information from you regarding this case. You're pretty much the only one I can turn to so far. I understand you've known Pete and Marcia Kelsey for some time."

Much to my surprise, Maxwell Cole slapped the sodden hanky over his face and burst into great lurching, choking sobs. It was several long, noisy minutes before he was able to speak.

"It finally hit home this morning that she's really gone," he mumbled miserably at last. "Yesterday, I was like in a dream, a fog. It wasn't real somehow, but today . . ."

The day before when I had encountered him in front of the Kelseys' house, I had very much doubted the veracity of his claim of family friendship, but there in that suffocatingly hot living room, with unchecked tears rolling down his pudgy cheeks and dripping from the ends of his sagging mustache, the depth of Maxwell Cole's grief was undeniable. As Max's story spilled out, I found myself missing the old familiar antagonism. His friend's death had taken all the fight out of him, and in spite of myself, I felt a certain grudging sympathy toward the man.

"From fifth grade," he added brokenly. "That's how long we were friends. Her family came to Seattle from southern Utah, someplace around St. George, I believe. They moved to the Hill the summer Marcia and I were between fourth and fifth grades. She liked to read and so did I. We met at the library branch up on Garfield Street. We both had permission to check books out of the adult section. All summer long we passed books back and forth. Marcia always turned down the corners of the sexy parts. She was a lot better at finding them than I was."

He smiled sadly, tugging with both hands on the wispy ends of his drooping mustache as though hoping to massage them into some kind of order. It didn't work.

"We were like that," he went on. Max crossed two fingers and held them out in front of him for a moment to show me what he meant before letting them fall limply back into his lap.

"I never had a sister," he said, "and Marcia never had a brother. We were both only children. She was like a sister to me."

"You stayed friends from then on?" I asked.

"More or less. You know how kids are. We had a big fight during eighth grade. I can't even remember now what it was about, but we didn't speak for most of that year. We patched things up once we got to high school, though. We were in journalism together, and our senior year we were coeditors of the *KUAY.*"

"The what?"

"The _KUAY_," he repeated. "Queen Anne High's weekly newspaper. That's where I first got interested in journalism. Chris was there too. He did sports."

"Chris?" I asked. "Who's he?"

"Chris McLaughlin. Her first husband. You didn't know about him?"

"No."

"Well," Max said firmly. "Christopher McLaughlin was a creep, the absolute scum of the earth as far as I'm concerned. I never could see what she saw in him other than sex maybe. He seduced her early on, the night of the junior/senior prom, as a matter of fact. She told me about it at the time, we were that close, and I worried that maybe she'd get knocked up. Of course, that was long before anyone knew she was a Downwinder."

"A what?"

"A Downwinder. Haven't you ever heard of them?"

I shook my head. "They're the people who lived downwind from the Nevada Test Site during the late fifties, when they were still doing aboveground nuclear testing," he said.

"What does that have to do with anything?"

"Marcia was staying out on her grandparents' ranch when they set off a particularly dirty test. Unexpected winds blew the radioactive crap right across her grandparents' land. Both grandparents eventually died of cancer. The doctors later attributed Marcia's sterility as well as her female difficulties to that, although nobody's ever proven it in court. You know how that goes."

Max paused for a moment, then hurried on.

"Anyway, that's why it was so wonderful when Pete showed up with a ready-made family."

"You said Chris McLaughlin was her first husband. What ever happened to him?"

Maxwell Cole snorted derisively. "Who knows? Who cares? Marcia left him in Canada and came back home. Good riddance, as far as I'm concerned. Her folks were absolutely delighted to think she had finally come to her senses and left the creep. They helped her get an annulment—that cost them a pretty penny—and they also helped Marcia get back into school at the university. They weren't wild about Pete to begin with, but they got along fine with him eventually. If it hadn't been for him, they probably would have missed being grandparents altogether."

While Max was speaking, I began putting together a rough chronology. Max and I were almost the same age. That meant Marcia Kelsey and Chris McLaughlin were too. Back then there had been only one reason why someone of my generation would disappear into the wilds of Canada and stay there— the Vietnam War.

"So Chris McLaughlin was a conscientious objector?" I asked.

Max nodded. "So he claimed. How'd you guess?"

"It figures," I said.

"Chris was one of the very early models," Max continued. "He took off for Canada in 1967 and dragged Marcia along up there with him. He married her on the way, just to put a good face on it, I guess, but her folks were heartbroken.

"I still don't know everything that went on while they were up there. Marcia and I were always close, very close. We told each other secrets that we wouldn't share with another living human being, but she never talked to me about those years in Canada, not the details anyway. It must have been pretty bad. She hinted around about drugs and some kind of commune living arrangement. I'll say this much for him. When it came to scuzzy low-life stuff, Chris McLaughlin was always ahead of his time."

"So how did she meet up with Pete Kelsey?"

Max shrugged. "Kismet. Fate. Whatever you want to call it. I hadn't seen her for almost three years when she just happened to drop by the house to say hello and to tell me that her annulment had been granted. She came by to say she was a 'free woman.' Pete Kelsey was there that afternoon, giving my mother an estimate for a remodeling job she wanted done. As soon as they laid eyes on one another, Pete and Marcia hit it off. I've never seen anything like it, and Marcia was wild about Erin. You've heard of whirlwind courtships? Theirs took the cake. They got married three weeks to the day from the time they met. A justice of the peace married them right in this very room, here in front of the fireplace. I was the best man, and my mother was the matron of honor. We took care of Erin while they were off on their honeymoon."

"It sounds almost too good to be true."

"I think that's what the Riggs thought at first, that Marcia had screwed up again."

"Who are the Riggs?"

"Marcia's folks. LaDonna and George Riggs. He's retired now. They spend their winters in Arizona and their summers in Gig Harbor. Like I said, to begin with, they weren't wild about the idea. For one thing, Pete wasn't Mormon, and Marcia was, in name at least. She was always way too wild for her own good. She's what they call a Jack Mormon. Much to her folks' surprise, though, after the wedding, Pete didn't raise the least objection to George and LaDonna taking Erin along to church with them. They ended up with a good Mormon grandchild after all. Erin is quite devout. She takes it all very seriously. She's all set to go on a mission next year after she finishes her degree."

"What can you tell me about their marriage?"

Max eyed me speculatively. "What did Pete tell you?"

"That it wasn't all a bed of roses."

"No, I suppose not," Max agreed. "They've had their troubles just like everybody else, but what can you expect? They come from such different backgrounds."

"What exactly is Pete's background?"

"His folks divorced when he was very young. He was on his own by the time he was sixteen, so you can see how he and Marcia would be coming from opposite ends of the spectrum, with her family solid and stable, and his anything but. Anyway, they were both a little on the wild side when they got married, and I think maybe they both fooled around some on the side—Marcia more than Pete, perhaps—but that was always just surface stuff. Those were meaningless relationships. There was never anything that came close to breaking them up. Those two shared something very special between them, a real bond. I always envied them that."

This was a somewhat different marital report card than the one we'd gotten from Pete Kelsey himself.

"So you knew about their so-called open marriage?"

Max looked startled. "Pete called it that?"

I nodded and Max drew a long breath. "I knew about it, as much as an outsider ever knows about those kinds of things, but like I said, those occasional dalliances didn't mean that much to either one of them. They both cared about staying together, not only for each other but for Erin as well."

"What if one of them did?" I suggested, letting a hint of Paul Kramer's pet theory loose in the room for the first time. "What if one of those dalliances turned serious? Would Pete Kelsey have become violent about it?"

"You're implying . . . No. No way. Not on your life."

I heard what Max said, but declarations of that sort from good friends are to be taken with a grain of salt.

"Did you and Marcia stay close through the years?"

"Not so much lately," Max admitted ruefully. "Pete and I have become good friends over the years, and we keep in touch. I try to go down to the Trolleyman every once in a while when I know he's there. I tip back a pint of bitters, and Pete and I have a chance to shoot the breeze."

"How long has he worked for the Trolleyman?"

"Off and on for as long as they've been open. He likes it, he's good with the customers, and he's dependable. They flex with him when he has a remodeling job."

"What's his background, do you know?"

"Not really. He came from Ottawa originally, I

believe. When he did that work for my mother, he was just starting out and struggling. All he had then was his green card and a whole lot of talent. After he and Marcia married, of course, he became a naturalized citizen."

"Where'd he go to school?"

"To college, you mean?"

I nodded and Max shook his head. "I know he went somewhere, but I'm not sure where. Started out as a history major and decided he didn't like it. I don't think he ever graduated. And for the kind of thing he does, he certainly doesn't need a degree. His work speaks for itself. Believe me, he makes a very good living doing remodels when he feels like it. He can pick and choose his jobs, too. He's a craftsman, you see, someone who understands wood. That's rare these days."

"What about Erin?"

Max's face clouded over. "Erin's one sweet kid, and she couldn't have loved Marcia more if she'd been her real mother."

"You'd say Marcia was a good mother then?"

"The best. Not according to her mother, maybe. Not in the old-fashioned motherhood-and-apple-pie sense. LaDonna Riggs still believes a woman's place is in the home. I don't think she ever approved of the fact that Pete did most of the cooking and cleaning. Marcia may have been sloppy as hell, but she was an interested mother, a concerned mother, and a smart one.

"She exposed Erin to the arts, to the kinds of plays and books and performances that most kids never have a chance of seeing. Marcia recognized Erin's intelligence early on and encouraged her every step of the way. Erin finished up her undergraduate degree at the U-Dub here in Seattle in three years flat, and now she's down in Eugene working on her masters in English lit."

Max paused. "She's my godchild, you know. Did anyone tell you that? She was almost two when I first met her, but Pete said she didn't have a godfather because he'd never thought of it. I was deeply honored. It's probably the closest thing I'll ever get to being a parent, I suppose," he added somewhat wistfully.

"Are you in touch with Erin?" I asked.

He nodded. "She writes to me at least once or twice a month. In fact, Pete asked me if I could go down and pick her up from the airport this morning and I hated to turn him down, but with this cold, I told him I'd better not. I wouldn't want her to catch it."

"Have you ever heard of someone named Andrea Stovall?"

Max frowned. "Andrea Stovall," he repeated. "It sounds familiar. I'm sure I've heard the name, but I can't place it."

"The Seattle Federated Teachers' Association," I said. "Now does it ring a bell?"

He nodded. "That's right. She's the president, isn't she?"

"Yes. Did Marcia ever say anything to you about her?"

Max paused to consider. "Wait a minute. Now that you mention it, I think I may have met her once

at a Christmas party at Pete and Marcia's. As I recall, I didn't like her much. Dykish females tend to
rub me the wrong way."

"Dykish? She didn't strike me that way, and I
thought she was married."

"Divorced," Max answered. "A lot of times they
get married, but it's just for show and it doesn't last.
Don't look so surprised, J.P. It's not like they have to
go around wearing a sign or something."

An errant thought crossed my mind. "What about
Marcia Kelsey?" I asked.

Now it was Max's turn to be surprised. "Marcia?
A les? No way. She was a fun-loving girl, all right, but
strictly heterosexual. If that's what you're thinking,
you're barking up the wrong tree."

This time it was my pager that went off and interrupted the process. Max directed me to the kitchen
phone, which was far enough away to be out of earshot
When I called in, I was given Ron Peters' number.

"There you are," he said when he heard my voice.
"Amy gave me strict orders to get in touch with you
early today, but I've been stuck in a meeting all morning long. We just got out."

"What do you need?"

"We wanted you to come to dinner tonight. Amy's
doing a pot roast. It should be good."

A pot roast? Real home cooking? It was too good
to resist. "What time?" I asked.

"What time can you make it?"

My after-work AA meeting would last from five-
thirty to six-thirty in the basement of a downtown
church across from Denny Park.

"Is seven too late?"

"No. That'll be fine. See you then."

Ron started to hang up, but I stopped him. "Wait a minute, Ron. There's something I need some help with."

"What's that?"

"Do you remember hearing anything about a series of bomb threats at the school district office last fall?"

"Bomb threats? I don't remember anything about it."

"Me either," I told him, "but they happened, and they didn't get reported. What I want to know is who buried those reports and how they did it."

"Sounds like something that's right up my alley," Ron said. I could hear a smile lighting up his face, an echo of the old enthusiasm leaking into his voice.

"That's what I thought. By the way, don't try checking directly with the Firearms and Explosives guys," I warned. "We don't want to get Sparky's tail caught in a wringer on this one."

"Don't worry," Ron Peters responded with a laugh. "I have my own sources, and I'll be the soul of discretion. See you at seven."

I left the phone and went back into Maxwell Cole's living room. He was leaning back with his eyes closed. For a moment I thought he had fallen asleep, but he sat up as soon as he heard me pause in the doorway.

"Did Pete tell you about the harassing phone calls?" Max asked.

"Yes."

"And he told you that Erin had been getting them too?"

"Yes."

"Is it possible the phone calls and the murders are related?"

As a loyal friend of Pete Kelsey's, Max was gently trying to lead me away from pointing an accusing finger in Pete's direction. Under the circumstances, I probably would have done the same thing. He was also fishing for information.

"I wouldn't know about that," I replied evenly, trying not to let any information slip into my words or intonation. "It's much too early to speculate."

"Well, I think they are," Max declared forcefully, maybe trying to convince himself as much as he wanted to convince me. "When you find the person making those phone calls, you'll find the killer. You mark my words."

It always sounds so easy when somebody else says it. So easy and so simple. Saying it and doing it, however, are two entirely different things.

"Right, Max," I said, picking up my coat and showing myself to the door. "We'll have to see about that."

We'll just have to wait and see.

CHAPTER 14

WHEN I STEPPED OUT ONTO THE COVERED PORCH OF Maxwell Cole's Victorian home, it was such a relief to be out of the hot house that I thought at first it was much warmer. It wasn't. I was just overheated from the inside out.

My growling stomach said it was lunchtime, and I listened. Rather than go back down the way I'd come, I decided to trek on across the summit of Queen Anne Hill to the upscale little business district at the top of the Counterbalance, the steepest part of the hill, where heavy weights had once been used to aid trolleys going up and down Queen Anne Avenue.

By eleven-thirty I found a comfortable chair in a trendy café called Après Vous and was stuffing myself with a mouthwatering Tower Burger, named after the cluster of radio towers, including one still covered with Christmas lights, that had sprouted like three gangly weeds across the crest of the hill behind the restaurant.

I chewed my food and mulled over my conversation

with Maxwell Cole. I couldn't get beyond the uneasy sense that something was strangely out of kilter in what I was learning about Pete and Marcia Kelsey. There was no one thing I could point to, no one blatantly obvious discrepancy, just an overall sense that what I had discovered about them so far was somehow dim and slightly out of focus. I couldn't get a clear picture of either one of them.

According to Pete, the marriage had been wrong, at least as far as he was concerned, for a considerable period of time. Yet he hadn't left. And if, as Max had told me, Marcia had flitted from one meaningless relationship to another, then it hadn't been right for her, either. Yet something had compelled them to stay together. What was it? And did this elusive "something" have anything to do with the murders at hand? The only way to find out was to gather more information.

While downing my second and third cups of coffee, I wrote up a detailed report on everything I had learned from Kendra Meadows and an equally detailed version of Max's interview. If Watty wanted reports, I'd plant my butt on a chair somewhere and give him reports until the damn cows came home.

Over dessert I studied my lists of things to do and people to see, both the ones I had made and the ones given me earlier that morning by Kendra Meadows. I tried to prioritize those things that needed to be handled first.

Speculating about Pete and Marcia Kelsey's kinky marriage was intriguing as hell, but I didn't want to be as guilty of neglecting Alvin Chambers as everybody else was. He was inarguably part of the puzzle.

He was also equally dead, and Charlotte Chambers' next-of-kin interview was still missing.

That at least was something I could fix, another little trophy I could lay on Sergeant Watkins' desk to say what a good boy am I. And in keeping with my good-boy persona, I made one pro forma call to the department to check on whether Detective Kramer had turned up for his court appearance or if he would be joining me for the afternoon's labors. Luckily for him, the son of a bitch was stuck in court for the remainder of the day and possibly for much of the rest of the week. I was free to work on my own for the afternoon with a totally clear conscience.

I walked out of the restaurant fully prepared to head back down to the department and check out a car to take to the North End. Instead, providence stepped into the picture in the guise of a battered Farwest cab.

The ancient green hulk of a taxi was stopped directly in front of me as I stepped out onto the sidewalk. It was disgorging an improbable number of laughing, baby-gift-carrying women on their way to a noontime shower. Without a moment's hesitation, I climbed into the newly unoccupied taxi and directed the driver to take me north to Charlotte Chambers' Forest Grove apartment complex.

The heavily traveled streets weren't nearly as bad as they had been earlier. Sand, slightly warmer temperatures, and friction from passing vehicles had combined to turn most of the roadways to lumpy slush, although driving conditions would probably still change for the worse once the sun went down for the evening.

When we reached the Forest Grove Apartments, I could see that someone had made a halfhearted attempt at scraping clean the driveway down into the complex. Nonetheless, I had the cabbie drop me on the street and I walked the rest of the way.

The rickety stairway and handrail leading up to the Chambers' apartment had also been scraped clear of snow, but the layer of ice that remained on the slick wooden steps was far more treacherous than the snow would have been.

From inside, I could hear the noise of an industrial-strength vacuum cleaner. No one answered my first knock, or the second. I waited until the vacuum went off before I tried again. This time the door opened immediately, and a wizened man stood before me.

"Yes?" he asked.

I handed him my card. "I'm looking for Mrs. Chambers," I said.

He glanced uneasily over his shoulder. "Charlotte isn't here just now," he said. "She's expecting some family members to arrive from out of town, and the wife and I are waiting here in case they come before she gets back."

"I see. Can you tell me where she is or when you expect her?"

The man looked back into the room. "I can't say for sure," he replied. A woman wearing an apron and carrying two bulging garbage bags appeared over his shoulder.

"Who is it, Floyd?" she asked.

"A policeman," Floyd replied uncertainly. "He

wants to know where Charlotte is and when she'll be back."

"Well," the woman said impatiently. "Let him in. Don't just stand there with the door open. It's cold outside. And go ahead and tell him where she is. If Charlotte Chambers isn't ashamed of herself, she certainly ought to be."

Floyd stepped back from the door and motioned me inside. Gravely he held out his hand. "The name's Patterson. Floyd Patterson, and this is my wife, Alva."

"How do you do, Mr. Patterson," I said, glancing over his shoulder into the room behind him. The curtains were open, and an almost miraculous transformation had taken place in the dingy little apartment. It was clean, almost spotlessly so. The dirty dishes were gone, as were the collection of boxes and the wads of clothes. The unmistakable back-and-forth tracks of a vacuum cleaner marched virtuously across the orange and green shag carpeting.

"Well?" Alva Patterson said expectantly to her husband. "Are you going to tell him or am I?"

"The movies," he murmured.

"Pardon me?" I asked, not understanding.

"Charlotte's at the movies."

"Right down here at the Oak Tree," Alva Patterson sniffed. "The so-called bargain matinee. She took the bus. If it weren't for Richard, we wouldn't be here at all, but I can't imagine him coming home and finding this place the way it was this morning, and with his mother not here besides."

She shook her head disdainfully and clicked her tongue in matronly disapproval. "Those two men deserved so much better," she added with a sniff. "Both Richard and his father."

"So there's a son?" I asked. "I wasn't aware they had any children. Mrs. Chambers didn't mention it yesterday when we talked to her."

Floyd Patterson nodded. "They have a son, all right. Richard's in the Navy. Stationed in Norfolk, but he's been on a cruise in the Mediterranean. He's getting hardship leave and should be arriving home sometime today. Maybe not until this evening, with the way the weather's been, but I told him we'd stay around here and come pick him up once he gets in. Charlotte doesn't drive, you see, and it's way too expensive for him to take a cab all the way here from Sea-Tac."

"Driving's not all that woman doesn't do," Alva Patterson remarked pointedly, and flounced off toward the kitchen with a stack of overflowing garbage bags still in hand.

Patterson motioned me toward the couch. "Won't you have a seat, Detective Beaumont?"

I moved toward the sagging couch. It too had been thoroughly vacuumed. The stray popcorn leavings from the day before had disappeared completely. No dust rose from the cushions as I lowered myself onto them.

"I take it you and your wife are friends of the family, Mr. Patterson?"

Floyd hung his head. "Of Alvin more than Charlotte, I'm afraid. Charlotte's, well . . . she's always been difficult."

"You can say that again," Alva offered tartly from the kitchen, where she was furiously scrubbing the counter. The odor of undiluted bleach wafted into the living room. "You should have seen the parsonage after they moved out. I tell you it was criminal."

"Now, Alva," Floyd cautioned mildly. "Remember, judge not . . ."

"That's easy for you to say, Floyd," Alva snapped, cutting him off in midsentence. "You menfolks didn't have to clean those filthy bathrooms. The women did. And the kitchen! We found roaches in some of the kitchen cupboards, can you imagine? And don't you think for one minute that I'm here working today because of Charlotte Chambers. Absolutely not. I'm doing this for Richard so that when his friends stop by to visit, he won't have to be embarrassed."

"So you're members of the church where Alvin Chambers used to be the minister?" I asked, directing my question to Floyd.

He nodded. "That's right. The Freewill Baptist down in Algona. I've been deacon there for fifteen years. I was on the committee that hired Pastor Al when he first came to us ten years ago. I hated to see him go when he left, especially for a job like that. It's such a terrible waste, but then . . ." Floyd left off and shrugged. "It was just one of those things, I guess."

"Why did he leave?" I asked.

"Because of the remodeling," Patterson answered without hesitation. "It was all because of that."

The fall from grace of numerous televangelists as well as that of a few of the less reputable local clergy had prepared me for the worst. I wouldn't have been the least bit surprised by the recounting of any number of peccadillos, but the word "remodeling" definitely wasn't on the list of what I expected to hear.

"Did you say remodeling?" I asked.

Patterson nodded sadly. "It was all so silly. We . . ." He paused. "The church had finished paying off the mortgage. In fact, we celebrated with a mortgage-burning at the annual dinner. I remember Pastor Al telling me how much he was hoping we'd be able to spend some of that extra money on a new outreach program that he had in mind. Mission work we could do in our own backyard, right there in Algona. But at the very next board of directors meeting, someone came up with the idea of remodeling the sanctuary, and that's what the board voted to do. Remodel. I think it broke Pastor Al's heart."

Alva Patterson appeared in the kitchen doorway, drying her hands on the front of her apron.

"It wasn't just that, Floyd, and don't you sit there and say it was."

"Now, Alva," Floyd cautioned, holding up his hand.

"Don't you 'Now, Alva' me," his wife returned. "You know as well as I do that the remodeling was just the straw that broke the camel's back. The real problem was Charlotte. She was the problem then, and she's the problem now."

Without warning, Alva Patterson pulled the skirt of the apron up to her wrinkled face and sobbed into it. "That poor man. Whatever did he do to deserve the likes of her for a wife! It's not fair. He should have had better!"

At that precise moment, my pager went off. Floyd Patterson directed me to the kitchen telephone, where I dialed Margie's number.

"Beaumont here," I said.

"I'm glad you called right back," Margie said. "Detective Kramer telephoned before court went into session and wanted me to get in touch with you. He said to tell you 'Bingo.'"

"Bingo? What the hell does that mean?"

"Beats me. That's all he said."

I wondered, had he learned something important during the course of his lunch with Jennifer Lafflyn or had the fingerprints from Pete Kelsey's spoon shown up somewhere on the AFIS system? It was just like my friend Kramer to play games and not tell me exactly what was happening.

"Where's Kramer now?" I asked.

"In district court. Court was just then being called to order. He said he'll probably be there all afternoon. Do you want me to try to get word to him?"

"No. Don't bother," I said. "I'll handle it myself."

Damn! Charlotte Chambers' next-of-kin interview was going to have to wait a little longer. I flung the phone back on the hook and turned back toward the living room, where a still-sobbing Alva Patterson stood leaning heavily against her husband's comforting shoulder.

"What is it?" Floyd Patterson asked.

"Something's come up," I told him. "I've got to go back to the department. Do you know where the phone book is?" I asked. "I need to call a cab."

"Don't bother with that," Floyd said. "I'll be glad to give you a lift. Alva can stay here to handle the phone calls if Richard's plane should come in before I get back."

It was a generous offer, and I was happy to take him

up on it because time was of the essence. I rode back downtown in an aging Mazda.

"Alva's right about Charlotte," Floyd told me, once we were alone in the car. "She's a sick woman, and I'm sure Pastor Al was burdened by it, but where could he go? We always expect our ministers to help us when we have problems, but who helps them when they get into trouble?"

He shook his head sadly and lapsed into silence. I was relatively certain Floyd Patterson himself hadn't pulled the trigger, but he was nonetheless carrying a heavy burden of guilt over what had happened to Alvin Chambers.

"You knew him well?" I asked.

"As well as anyone, I suppose," Patterson replied. "We had the whole family over to our house for dinner several times in the early years. And our two sons ran around with Richard some, but after Charlotte got so bad, it was hard to invite them over together."

"What happened to her?"

Patterson shook his head. "I don't know exactly. It was sort of gradual. She stopped going out much, except to movies, and she started putting on so much weight. Pastor Al told me once that he had tried to get her into counseling for depression, but she refused to go."

"So you and he remained friends in spite of it?"

"Yes."

"What can you tell me about him?"

"He was a kind man, a good man," Patterson declared firmly. "And it's terrible for him to have been gunned down that way. Where will all this godlessness end?"

"This isn't easy to ask, Mr. Patterson, but to your knowledge, did he ever fool around?"

"Fool around? You mean with other women? Absolutely not! I'm telling you, Pastor Al was a God-fearing man, in the strictest sense of the word. He believed adultery was a sin, plain and simple. Just because he left our church didn't mean he left his calling."

I might have pointed out that being a man of the cloth hadn't prevented any number of other ministers from doing things they shouldn't have, but Floyd Patterson was clearly affronted by my question and he was, after all, going miles out of his way to give me a ride.

"I'm glad to hear it," I said placatingly. "In the course of an investigation like this, it's important for us to have some idea of what kind of man he was."

"I already told you," Floyd replied. "Pastor Al Chambers was a good man, a good man through and through."

Floyd Patterson dropped me off in front of the Public Safety Building. Inside the lobby, waiting for the slow-moving elevator, I wondered if Detective Kramer had actually picked up an AFIS report or if he had just called in to check on it. Instead of going directly back to my cubicle on the fifth floor, I stopped off on four.

Tomi Nakamoto, one of the clerks who works in the AFIS section, used to work in Homicide. We're still buddies.

I stopped at the counter and waited until she looked up. When I waved, she smiled broadly. "How's it going, Beau? Long time no see."

"Fine. Did Detective Kramer pick up that report on our crook, Pete Kelsey?"

Tomi got up and walked to another desk, where she riffled through a stack of papers in a wire basket. She shook one out of the pile.

"Nope," she said, walking toward the counter. "Here it is. He said he'd be in for it later, but you can go ahead and take it now, if you like."

"Thanks," I told her. "Kramer's busy in court. I want to get cracking on this right away. You do good work."

"I know." Tomi beamed, her dark eyes flashing humorously behind wire-framed glasses. "You dicks couldn't get along without us."

I waited until I was back out in the elevator lobby before glancing down at the piece of paper in my hand. When I did, my first reaction was that Tomi must have made a mistake and given me the wrong report. Pete Kelsey's name wasn't on it. I studied the paper for several long moments before the truth of the situation slowly began to dawn.

Pete Kelsey wasn't Pete Kelsey at all. His real name was Madsen, John David Madsen, from Marvin, South Dakota. He was, in fact, PFC John David Madsen, who had gone AWOL from his unit in Southeast Asia on the fifteenth of March, 1969, and who had subsequently been declared a deserter on April fifteenth of that same year.

Holding the report in my hand, I almost laughed aloud, not because Pete Kelsey wasn't who he said he was and not because he was a wanted fugitive. That was clearly no laughing matter. What was funny was that we now knew Pete Kelsey was a wanted man, but thanks to Detective Paul Kramer, we couldn't do a damn thing about it.

Because Kramer had picked up that spoon and the damning fingerprints in the course of an illegal search.

The joke was on Kramer, and it served him right.

CHAPTER 15

I HURRIED UP TO THE FIFTH FLOOR AND SAT AT MY DESK poring over the AFIS report as if reading the same black-and-white words over and over again would somehow unlock the secrets hidden behind them, because the words gave the bare-bones skeleton of a hell of a story.

John David Madsen, alias Pete Kelsey, had been on deserter status from the United States Army for more than twenty years. Why?

Picking up the phone, I dialed South Dakota information. As I waited for the operator to answer, I thought about how a son's or brother's or husband's sudden reappearance after so many years of unexplained absence might affect the family he had presumably left behind. But the information operator came up empty.

If John David Madsen had any surviving relatives, they were no longer living in the vicinity of Marvin, South Dakota, wherever the hell that was.

Then, since I had come up empty-handed on the

first try, I made another wild stab at it. This time I dialed Ottawa information, asking for either a Madsen or a Kelsey. Again, no Madsens, but three Kelseys were listed, one of which was a Peter. It sounded to me like one of the oldest phony ID tricks in the book—assuming the identity of a long-deceased child.

I jotted down the telephone number, but it took several minutes to work up nerve enough to dial it. The woman who answered sounded elderly and frail, and I berated myself for being an uncaring bastard even as I laid the groundwork for asking the painful questions.

"Is this Mrs. Peter Kelsey?" I asked.

"You'll have to speak up a bit. I can't quite hear you."

I upped the volume. "Is this Mrs. Peter Kelsey?"

"Yes it is. Who's calling, please?"

"My name is Beaumont, Detective J. P. Beaumont, with the Seattle Police Department."

Had I been on the other end of the line, I probably would have demanded that my caller offer some further form of identification or verification. Mrs. Peter Kelsey did not.

"What can I do for you, Detective Beaumont?" she asked.

"This may be difficult for you, Mrs. Kelsey," I said gently, "but I'm working on a case where someone has been living under an alias for many years. It's entirely possible that this person has taken the name and assumed the identity of someone in your family."

"Yes," she said. "I see. Go on."

"What I'm calling for, Mrs. Kelsey, is to see whether or not there was a child in your family named Peter Kelsey, a child who died at a very early age."

The sharp intake of breath answered my question in the affirmative long before she spoke, her voice quavering tremulously. "Yes. He was my youngest," she said, almost in a whisper. "My baby. He died of whooping cough when he was only three months old. I sat up with him all night in the hospital, but there was nothing anybody could do. Nothing at all. He died at five past seven in the morning."

I was struck by the fact that even after all those years, the exact time of her child's death was still engraved in her heart and brain. Mothers are like that, I guess.

She paused, waiting for me to say something. While I was still fumbling ineptly for an appropriate comment, she continued. "You say someone is living with my little Peter's name? Someone there in Seattle?"

I didn't want to drag this particular Mrs. Peter Kelsey, an innocent bystander, any further into the ugly morass. By just making the phone call, I had already inflicted far too much damage.

"It's a police matter now, Mrs. Kelsey," I said. "Knowing what you've told me, I'm sure we'll be able to straighten things out in no time."

"But this person," she insisted stubbornly. "Has he done anything wrong, I mean anything that would reflect badly on my Peter?"

Aside from being the scum of the earth—a deserter and a suspected killer—how much more wrong can you get?

I said, "It's nothing serious, Mrs. Kelsey. Don't worry. Everything will be fine."

With that, I rang off. I had said the soothing words, but I didn't believe them, not for a moment. I put down the receiver, but before I had begun to think about what to do with this new information, the phone rang again.

"Beaumont here."

"Detective Beaumont?" It was a man's voice, tight and tentative and uncertain.

"Yes." I tried to keep the impatience out of my voice.

"My name is George, George Riggs. You don't know me but . . ."

I recalled the name from Max's story. "You're Marcia Kelsey's father."

"Why, yes. That's right." I could tell he was enormously relieved at not having to complete his awkward introduction.

"What can I do for you, Mr. Riggs?"

"I'm calling because my wife, Belle, I mean, La-Donna, asked me to. We're here at Pete and Marcia's house with Erin, our granddaughter. Pete had told us about you, I mean, he had told Erin at least, and he showed her your card. So when we found it, LaDonna said we should call you right away. That's why I'm calling. To see if you can come over. If you would, I mean. We need to talk to you."

I suspected George Riggs was a shy man, a person of few words, who didn't much like using the phone to talk with complete strangers. His nervousness broadcast itself through the telephone receiver with such force that what he said was almost unintelligible. The desperation was not.

"Of course, Mr. Riggs. I'll be right over."

"You know where the house is? The address?"

"Yes, I do. Is this an emergency, Mr. Riggs?"

"Oh no, nothing like that, but if you could come as soon as possible . . ."

"It may take half an hour or so," I reassured him, "but I'll be there just as soon as I can."

"Thank you so much. I'll tell Belle that you're on your way."

The garage gods were with me. I checked out a car in record time and was parked on the snow-covered street below the Kelseys' house in something less than twenty minutes.

Sidewalk, stairs, and porch had all been carefully shoveled clean of snow and ice. The red-bowed holiday wreath had disappeared from the front door, which was flung open wide by a ravishing young nymph with a wild mop of uncontrolled red hair, vivid green eyes, and milk white skin. Something about the cheekbones and the set of her eyes seemed vaguely familiar to me, but that was only a passing thought, which disappeared as soon as she spoke.

"I'm Erin," she announced. "Are you Detective Beaumont?" I nodded. "Thank you for hurrying," she added. "Gran is worried sick." She turned away from me and called back over her shoulder, "He's here."

An older woman appeared in the doorway to the dining room. She was angular and spare, with her arms clasped nervously around a narrow waist. She moved swiftly across the room, reaching out a hand in greeting.

"Thank you for coming so quickly," she said. "I'm LaDonna Riggs, but everyone calls me Belle. As soon as I found it, I told George to call you. I wanted that thing out of the house immediately."

I looked from the older woman to the younger one. "What 'thing' are we talking about?" I asked.

"Why, the gun, of course. Didn't George tell you about it on the phone?"

Now an older man wearing jeans and cowboy boots stepped into the dining room doorway. Sidled more than stepped. He stood there, leaning against the jamb with his hands shoved deep in his pockets.

LaDonna Riggs turned to face him. "Why didn't you tell him about the gun, George? I told you to tell him."

George Riggs shrugged his shoulders. "I must've forgot, sweetheart. I can't always remember everything, you know."

"What's all this about a gun?" I asked.

"Daddy and I came over to get Marcia's things to take down to the mortuary," Belle Riggs explained. "She wasn't married in the temple, you see, so she doesn't have any temple clothes, but we found her a nice white dress to be buried in all the same. And I wanted to find her some nice white underwear, too. New underwear. Marcia was always particular about her undies, and I knew she'd have some nice things put back. She was a saver, you know. That was one thing she was good at. She'd buy bras and panties on sale . . ."

"Gran," Erin interrupted impatiently. "Just tell him about the gun."

"Well, I'm trying to. Anyway, I checked her bottom drawer, thinking that's where she'd keep any new things she hadn't worn yet, and that's where I found the gun. It was there under a stack of panties that were still in their plastic containers."

"Maybe you'd better show me," I said.

Erin led the way up a carpeted stairway and into a cheerful master bedroom. The bed was made, the pillows plumped under a Wedgewood blue spread. I wondered if Pete Kelsey had made the bed—I still couldn't adjust to thinking about him in terms of John David Madsen—or if that was something Belle Riggs had handled before she went searching for her dead daughter's underwear.

The bottom drawer of a sleek teak dresser still stood open. I walked over to it and peered inside. The rough checkered handle of a .25 Auto Browning was partially hidden under a stack of shrink-wrapped panties. The barrel was completely visible. It was an old-fashioned gun, well made—almost quaint—the kind of weapon an eccentric Auntie Mame type might have packed in a dainty purse. Old-fashioned and quaint maybe, but at point-blank range, very, very lethal. I recalled from my cursory reading of Doc Baker's autopsy that the misshapen slug that had severed Alvin Chambers' spinal cord before tearing through his internal organs had been from a .25-caliber something.

"It's not Marcia's," Belle Riggs was declaring firmly to the room in general. "It certainly isn't Marcia's. She wouldn't have allowed a thing like that in her home, to say nothing of in her underwear drawer."

I took a deep breath and turned to Erin. "Where's your dad?" I asked.

"Mrs. Damon, one of the ladies he did some remodeling for a few months ago, called early this afternoon. One of her pipes had burst and she wanted to know who to call. She didn't want to bother Dad, and she didn't want him to go over, but he did anyway. He should be home any time now."

"Did anyone here touch this?" I asked.

"No way!" Mrs. Riggs responded at once. "I wouldn't let anyone near it. You'll take it with you, won't you?"

Of the three people in the room, Erin, young as she was, seemed most in possession of her faculties. "Can you find me a shoe box?" I asked her.

"A shoe box?" she repeated with a puzzled frown.

"Yes. A shoe box and some string."

Erin nodded and hurried away.

"What do you need that for?" Belle Riggs asked indignantly. "A shoe box, of all things."

"I can't tell whether or not this weapon is loaded. I'll have to secure it in the box in order to take it down to the crime lab."

Erin returned at once with the shoe box. "The string is down in the garage. I'll be right back."

Carefully I picked up the Browning, holding the grip gingerly between my thumb and forefinger as I placed it in the box. Television detectives to the contrary, lifting guns with pencils to preserve fingerprints is not only dangerous—you never know whether or not it's loaded—it ignores the reality that the rough surfaces on most pistol grips are totally unsuitable for fingerprinting techniques.

"The crime lab?" Belle Riggs asked suddenly as though the words had finally penetrated her consciousness. "You don't think this is connected to what happened. That's impossible. It couldn't be. I just wanted the thing out of the house."

"It's possible," I said grimly.

Much as it pained me to admit it, mounting circumstantial evidence made it look more and more as though Detective Kramer was right, and Pete Kelsey was our man. As the saying goes, I may be dumb, but I'm not stupid, and I wasn't about to ignore facts that jumped up and hit me in the face.

Erin returned, carrying a ball of string and a pair of scissors. I punched holes in the bottom of the box and immobilized the gun, tying it off with a piece of string. At my request, Erin once more disappeared, returning this time with a Magic Marker. Across the top of the box I scrawled the words, "Possibly Loaded," in huge red letters.

A dismayed Belle Riggs had retreated to the bed. She sat on the edge of it, rocking back and forth in a dazed sort of way. George came on into the room and sat on the bed beside her, consolingly patting her hand.

"Now, Mama," he said. "Don't you worry. It's going to be all right."

"But, George, how can they possibly think that Pete . . ."

Erin had been out of the room during the first exchange, but now she was back. Squatting on the floor in front of me, she looked at me across the gun-laden shoe box, her green eyes flashing fire.

"My father didn't do this," she said in a calm, measured voice that belied the smoldering anger in her eyes. "I know my father. He couldn't."

There was a whole lot about her father that I knew that Erin Kelsey didn't. Somebody was going to have to tell her, and I didn't want that person to be me.

"Who else besides your father has access to this room?"

"No one, except me, I guess," she answered.

"What was your mother's maiden name?" I asked.

"Riggs," Erin Kelsey replied firmly. "What kind of question is that?"

"Your real mother," I said. "What was her name?"

For the first time, Erin Kelsey's lower lip trembled as she answered. "Marcia Riggs Kelsey *was* my real mother, Detective Beaumont. She was the only mother I ever knew. She changed my diapers and bandaged my knees and taught me how to drive. My birth mother's name was Carol Ann Gentry Kelsey."

"Where was she from?"

"Ottawa, like my dad."

"Have you ever met any of your Canadian relatives?"

Erin shook her head. "No. None of them. My dad was sort of an orphan and there was some kind of trouble with my mother's parents when my parents got married. I think my birth mother was disowned. That's why we ended up living in Mexico, and that's where we were when the car wreck killed my mother. But what does any of this have to do with this gun? I don't understand."

"I'm just trying to put together some background information."

"What kind of background information?" Pete Kelsey asked suddenly from the bedroom doorway, startling us all. "What's going on here?"

I hadn't heard or seen him arrive, and I have no idea how long he'd been standing there in the doorway. He was still wearing heavy work boots and his sheepskin-lined denim jacket. His eyes took in the entire room in one long, sweeping glance.

Mrs. Riggs leaped off the bed and rushed to the door. "Oh, Peter, I'm so glad to see you," she gushed breathlessly. "We found a gun in Marcia's bottom drawer. I don't have any idea where it came from, but I wanted it out of the house right away, so I . . . we asked Detective Beaumont here to come pick it up. So he was . . ."

"A gun?" Pete Kelsey's question interrupted his mother-in-law's harangue. "In Marcia's drawer?"

Erin and I both stood up, leaving the shoe box sitting forgotten on the floor between us.

"Good afternoon, Mr. Kelsey," I said calmly. "I'll need to ask you a few questions about this." I made no move to draw my weapon. In that crowded bedroom, that could have been deadly for any one of us.

"Daddy," Erin began, cutting me off in midsentence and taking a halting step toward the doorway. Her action, inadvertent or not, effectively blocked my path to the door.

With a stricken look on his face, Pete Kelsey paused, but only for a fraction of an instant, then he turned and bolted back down the stairway. George and Belle Riggs, Erin, and I all leaped for the door like panicked patrons in a crowded theater responding to a shout of fire. We all jammed into the narrow doorway at once, and I heard the front door slam behind Pete Kelsey long before I ever managed to untangle myself from the others.

Breaking free at last, I pounded down the stairway behind him, but to no avail. By the time I reached the front porch, he was gone. I had no way of knowing if he had escaped on foot or if he was driving his Eagle. I turned to go back into the house to call for assistance, but a determined Erin Kelsey barred my way.

"No," she said firmly, standing before me with her arms folded across her chest and her chin raised in fiery defiance.

"What do you mean, no?"

"You're not coming back inside this house without a search warrant."

"But I need to know if your father's in his car or on foot."

"That's your problem."

I backed off because I could see she meant it. "What about the gun?" I asked.

"It'll still be right there where you left it when you come back with a warrant," she said. "Nobody here is going to touch it, but if that's what you think, if you believe my father's a coldblooded killer, I'm not going to lift a finger to help you. My grandparents won't either."

I couldn't blame her for putting up a fight, and there wasn't time to explain that asking someone questions wasn't necessarily the same as accusing him of murder, but standing there on the porch arguing about it was splitting hairs and wasting precious time. I hurried back down to my car and radioed for help, feeling foolish that I didn't know if our quarry was on foot or traveling by car.

Several uniformed patrol officers responded, arriving within minutes. One street at a time, we combed the immediate area at the far north end of Capitol Hill, but it was useless.

By then Pete Kelsey had disappeared completely into cold, thin air.

CHAPTER 16

In the wintertime it's dark in Seattle by four-thirty in the afternoon. By then it was clear to all concerned, including the chase-crazed members of the news media, that Pete Kelsey had successfully eluded our efforts to find him.

At that point, despite the fact that he had fled the house on Crockett rather than answer any questions, and despite our learning that he had lived his entire life in Seattle under an assumed identity, we still only wanted him for questioning. The presence of the gun in his bedroom was certainly a strong link, but it would take a laboratory analysis to tell us whether or not that gun was the missing .25 from the murder scene. If the weapons proved to be one and the same, the web of evidence against Pete Kelsey would become a whole lot stronger.

I left the physical search for Pete Kelsey in the hands of a squad of patrol officers as well as a K-9 unit. They were all much younger than I, and they were all, including the dog, a whole lot better-dressed for the still icy weather.

Returning to the Public Safety Building, I set the necessary wheels in motion to obtain a search warrant for Pete Kelsey's house on Crockett. Since the warrant wasn't immediately forthcoming and since there wasn't a damn thing I could do to speed up the process, I headed back to my cubicle to finish documenting exactly what had happened during the course of that day, and in what order, while it was all still relatively fresh in my mind.

I had completed the first page of the final installment and was almost finished with the second when an irate Detective Kramer materialized in my doorway. He was outraged. It's a good thing I'd had time enough to cool down.

"What the hell do you think you're doing, grabbing" that AFIS report from Tomi?" he demanded.

"My job, Kramer," I responded. "I was just doing my job. I got word from Watty that you were being overworked, and I thought I'd help out by picking it up for you."

But Kramer thundered on as though I hadn't even opened my mouth. My wonderfully effective use of irony fell on totally deaf ears.

"I go by the fourth floor to pick it up on my way back from court," Kramer continued, "and Tomi tells me you got it from her hours ago. You've been sitting on it all this time!"

I kept trying to stay cool and rational, to not get suckered into a confrontational mode, but Kramer was sorely tempting me.

"I haven't exactly been sitting around on my duff,"

I pointed out reasonably. "As a matter of fact, I've been dragging my freezing ass all over Capitol Hill looking for your friend and mine, Pete Kelsey."

"Give me the damn report, Beau. I want to see it."

"Wait a minute, aren't you the very same guy who somehow neglected to tell me about the logbook sheets when you talked to me on the phone last night?"

"That was an oversight," Kramer snapped.

"What the hell do you think this is? I've been busier than a one-legged man at an ass-kicking contest, Kramer. I barely got up here with that damned AFIS report of yours when George Riggs calls to ask me to come pick up the gun. What would you have done, ignore him? If you're pissed that I didn't take the time to ship you your mail before I went high-tailing it out of here, that's too damn bad, and as far as I'm concerned, you can stay pissed all day."

Belligerently, Kramer held out his hand. "I don't know anything about a gun. I want that report, Beaumont."

"I haven't had a chance to copy it yet," I responded heatedly, because by then, my hackles were up too. "When I get around to it, believe me, you'll be the first to know."

Just then Sergeant Watkins appeared, drawn as inevitably to the sound of raised voices as iron filings to a powerful magnet. He paused in the doorway and peered at us both from over Detective Kramer's burly shoulder. "What's going on here, guys?" he asked.

"You could call it a slight procedural difference of opinion, Sergeant Watkins," I replied. "It's no biggie."

I modified my tone slightly, answering the question as evenly as possible. Detective Kramer, still seething, said nothing.

"Anything I can do to help?" Watty asked, looking back and forth between us.

"Sure thing," I told him. "We need all the help we can get."

I shuffled through the impressive stack of papers that had collected throughout the day in the much-folded manila envelope Kramer had given me early that morning. The pile now contained not only the autopsy results, but also the duplicated logbook pages, the school district lists from Kendra Meadows, as well as the AFIS report. I separated out the last two sets of papers and handed them past Kramer, placing them directly in Watty's hands.

"Give these to Margie to copy before she leaves, if you could. Detective Kramer here will need his copies, of course, but I'd like to have the originals back. Now, if you two will excuse me, I've got to finish up this report and head out of here. I've got a meeting at five-thirty."

"Sounds reasonable to me," Watty said. He dropped copies of my two earlier reports onto my desk. I'd left them on his as I came past. "Much better, by the way," he said. He glanced down at what I was doing.

"Is that about the thing on Crockett?" I nodded. "Too bad Kelsey got away," Watty continued, "but you handled it as well as anyone could under the circumstances. You can't use deadly force in a room full of people."

With that, Watty took the copying for Margie and

left. As far as he was concerned, all was forgiven, at least for the moment, at least until the next time Kramer was able to sucker me. And if I was more careful, maybe that wouldn't happen.

"I won't forget that," Kramer snarled. "Now, what the hell's all this about Kelsey, and what went on up on Crockett?"

"I didn't think you were interested, but we found a .25 Auto Browning in Marcia Kelsey's underwear drawer."

"You did what?"

"I tried to tell you earlier, but you weren't listening. Pete Kelsey's mother-in-law found it in her daughter's dresser drawer along with a whole bunch of Marcia Kelsey's brand-new bras and panties."

I had finally succeeded in getting Kramer's undivided attention. "No shit?" he asked.

I nodded.

"Well, where is it?"

"Still back at Kelsey's house, secured in the bottom of a shoe box, and sitting on the floor in Pete Kelsey's bedroom."

"Is it the same gun that killed Alvin Chambers?"

"It could be, but I don't know yet, not for sure, because it still hasn't come down here to the crime lab. My guess is that it's the murder weapon, all right, at least one of them."

"So you found the gun, then what happened?"

"While we were looking for a way to secure it, Kelsey himself showed up. As soon as he saw the gun, he took off like a shot."

"And you let him get away?"

"You have a wonderful way with words, Kramer. Kelsey got away, but you heard Watty. I didn't *let* him. You wouldn't have had any better chance of catching him than I did."

I shoved the first part of my report in his direction. "Since you haven't gotten a look at your copy of the AFIS report yet, maybe you should start by reading this, and for your information, Pete Kelsey's real name isn't Pete Kelsey."

"It's not? Who is he then?"

"Shut up and read."

While Kramer dropped heavily into a chair and started reading, I returned to working on the rest of the report. Before he had completed the first page of the one report, Margie came into the cubicle, bringing the others. Kramer read those as well with such absorbed concentration that I had completed the second and final page of my report, cleared the top of my desk, and was standing behind the desk with my coat on before he glanced up.

A deep frown scarred his broad forehead, but for the moment, his quarrel with me was entirely forgotten. I had to give the devil his due. Detective Kramer focused on the case almost to the exclusion of everything else, including his petty feud with me. That meant I had to shape up, too.

"What's this character hiding?" Kramer asked musingly while rubbing the stiff bristles of his five-o'clock shadow. "It must be something serious for him to have been hiding out for more than twenty years. That's a long time. A capital crime, maybe? The statute of limitations would have run out by now on something less than that."

I nodded. It was a good point, and one I hadn't thought of in precisely the same way.

Kramer referred once more to the first page of my report. "It says here you couldn't find any of John David Madsen's South Dakota relatives when you called looking for them."

"Not through information. And not by that name. That's not to say they don't exist, however. There may be others, but it'll take someone on the spot to track them down."

"And as soon as Kelsey saw you were there with the gun, he took off?"

"That's right."

"He probably figured we were getting too close to the truth. Now that I think about it, what if Marcia knew about whatever it was and was threatening to expose him? Maybe that's why he knocked her off."

I could see where his line of reasoning was going, and reluctantly, I had to agree it made sense. "Whatever it is, it could also explain why he stuck it out in an otherwise unsatisfactory marriage, but why two guns?" I asked. "And why leave one at the scene and leave the other one hidden in a place where, once found, it would inevitably point suspicion in his direction?"

"That's pretty damn stupid," Kramer agreed. "Think about it. If we hadn't already stumbled on this AFIS report, we certainly would have once the gun was found, and if he's hidden out under cover for this long, you'd think he'd be smarter than that."

It was interesting to realize that for the first time during the investigation, Detective Kramer and I seemed to be operating on similar wavelengths. As he was inching away from his conviction that Kelsey *had* to be the killer, I was moving toward it. With any kind of luck, we'd meet somewhere in the middle.

"So what's going to happen?" Kramer asked. "Do you think he'll try to go back to the house?"

"I doubt it. I've made arrangements for a twenty-four-hour surveillance team, though. As near as I can tell, there are only two ways into the house—the passage up from the garage that leads into the pantry and the front door, both of which are visible from Crockett."

"It sounds like that daughter of his wouldn't be above helping him out if she got a chance. Aren't you worried that she'll try to deep-six the gun or mess with it in some way?"

"I can't say for sure," I told him, "but my guess is no. She gave me her word, and I think she'll honor it and let us take the gun when we show up with the warrant. Actually, she's doing us a favor. That way there can be no question later about whether or not that gun was illegally removed from the premises."

"When is the warrant supposed to be ready?"

"Later this evening, maybe. Otherwise, not until tomorrow morning. Do you have to be in court again tomorrow?"

"Yes. From ten o'clock on."

"Maybe, before you go there, we could pick up the search warrant and go collect the gun. Then, while you're in court, I'll see about tracking down some of the loose ends. I'll go to work on the Kendra Meadows information and take another crack at seeing Charlotte Chambers."

I looked up at the clock on the far wall. Five-eighteen. "I'm late for that meeting," I added. "I've got to get out of here right now."

I didn't tell Kramer exactly what meeting I was late for, and I knew I was laying myself open for more criticism about not keeping up my end of the investigation, but at fifty-one AA meetings in as many days and counting, I didn't want to have to start over on my ninety meetings in ninety days. Especially not when the only thing holding me back was sitting around chewing the fat with Detective Paul Kramer.

He nodded absently. "Sure," he said. "That's fine. Go ahead." He seemed lost in thought, and I don't think he even noticed when I stepped past him and left the room.

Watty and I ended up in the stairwell together. When he noticed me glancing at my watch, he asked if I needed a lift.

Because I live downtown, most of the people at the department who know me realize I usually don't drive my car to work. Some of them, like Watty, routinely offer me rides. If the weather's good, I say thanks but no thanks. This time the weather was rotten, and I grabbed it.

"You late for something?" Watty asked.

"A meeting," I said. That's all I said, but it was enough. Watty nodded knowingly.

"Good," he said. "Glad to hear you're still working on the problem. Now, if you and Kramer can just get this case wrapped up, I'll get the two of you off each other's backs."

He dropped me at Seventh and Denny and headed

for the freeway. I trekked through a snowy and deserted Denny Park, slipping into the meeting a full ten minutes late. It was overly warm in the church hall basement, and it was almost impossible to concentrate on what was being said, because by then all I could hear in my head was the siren call of Amy Fitzgerald-Peters' legendary pot roast.

When the meeting was over, I hurried home, showered, and dressed to go downstairs. I paused in front of the mirror, debating whether or not to leave my pager at home. Eventually, though, I decided to take it along. If somebody came up with Pete Kelsey during the course of the evening, I didn't want to miss out on the action.

Dinner at Ron Peters' downstairs apartment was every bit as wonderful as I'd anticipated. It was delightful to sit in the warm glow of happiness in that newly blended little family. I chowed down on the home-cooked grub and listened to the girls' endless prattle about whether or not there'd be school the next day. They were finally getting sick of their much-extended Christmas vacation.

When the meal was over, Amy directed Heather and Tracie at clearing the table and then took them off to get ready for bed, leaving Peters and me alone to talk.

"I don't like being stonewalled," Ron said quietly as soon as the girls disappeared down the hallway. "I don't like it at all."

For a moment I thought that maybe he and Amy were having some kind of difficulty. "Who's stonewalling you?" I asked.

"I'm talking about the bomb threats," he said. "I

don't know who it is exactly, not yet, but I can tell you this. They're real, and they have pull with a capital P."

"What do you mean?"

"I made a few inquiries today, and that's all it took. Before the afternoon was over, Captain Harden called me into his office and let me know in no uncertain terms that members of the media relations team have absolutely no business helping someone from the homicide squad with one of his investigations."

"If Harden told you to back off, you must have stepped on some toes."

Ron Peters smiled thinly. "Presumably so. In fact, now that you mention it, it's the first chance I've had to step on someone's toes since they stuck me in this chair. It felt damn good. What's the next move?"

Peters had caught the scent and was raring to go. "Whoa down a minute. If you're already in hot water with Hardass Harden, there's not going to be any next move for you, buddy-boy. Just forget I ever mentioned it. Forget the whole thing."

Peters' smile disappeared. "Drop it? Are you kidding? Like hell I will! Tracking that bomb threat information was more fun than I've had in a long, long time. It felt like I was back in the real world again, back making a meaningful contribution for a change instead of writing one of the chief's prepared statements. It was fun, dammit, and I liked doing it."

Tracie and Heather reappeared at his side, clad in matching long flannel pj's. Their teeth were freshly brushed and their damp hair still smelled of shampoo and conditioner. After collecting ritual hugs and kisses from their dad, they made an obligatory pass by me on their way back to the bedroom. Peters watched wistfully after them as they walked away.

"I want my life back, Beau," he said quietly. "My whole life."

I knew what he meant, and I couldn't blame him. I worried that he might lapse back into one of the black moods that had plagued him in the early months right after his injury and before Amy Fitzgerald had appeared on the scene. The only weapons I had at hand were the kind of meaningless platitudes that come so easily to people who aren't in chairs.

"You're not doing so badly," I pointed out. "You've got Amy and the girls. What more do you want?"

The look he turned on me was one of barely suppressed fury. "I'll tell you what I want. I want my old desk back, the real one, on the fifth floor. I know everybody at the department thought they were doing me one hell of a favor by finding me a slot in Media Relations, but it's just not good enough. I want to go play with the grown-ups, Beau. I want to be a detective again."

The idea of Peters getting back on the homicide squad wasn't even a remote possibility to begin with. Going against a direct order from his immediate supervisor would make the possibility that much more remote.

"So drop the damn bomb threats business then," I told him. "That's an order, and not from me either, from Harden. If you want to be a detective again, pissing off Old Hardass isn't the way to go about it."

"In other words, you want me to forget all about it? Pretend it never happened, just like that?"

"You bet."

Amy returned to the dining room just then. Seeing her, Peters bit back another angry retort. Amy paused uncertainly in the doorway, sensing the tension in the room and looking questioningly from one of us to the other.

"You two talking shop?" she asked.

"Were," I said uncomfortably, standing up and pushing back my chair, "but we're finished now, and I've got to get home. Thanks for dinner. It was delicious."

"So early?" Amy protested. "You've made yourself a stranger around here."

"I know, but I still have a few calls to make before I turn in. You tell that husband of yours to keep his nose to the grindstone and not go getting involved where he shouldn't."

She paused by Peters' chair and stood there, affectionately resting her hands on her husband's broad shoulders and gently kneading the back of his neck.

"I can't," she replied with a smile.

"Why not?"

"Ron and I made a prenuptial agreement."

"A prenuptial agreement? What does that have to do with the price of peanuts?"

She smiled again. "He doesn't tell me how to be a physical therapist, and I don't tell him how to be a cop. That's fair enough, isn't it?"

She said it softly enough, and the smile on her full lips didn't change, but I knew she'd landed a blow.

Hospitality or not, pot roast or not, Amy Fitzgerald-Peters had put me in my place.

Maybe deservedly so. Probably deservedly so. After all, I was the one who had started it.

CHAPTER 17

EARLY WEDNESDAY MORNING, A STEEP HILL COMBINED with a patch of black ice, a lightly loaded Metro bus, and a fully loaded bread truck all conspired together to help us to locate Marcia Louise Kelsey's missing Volvo.

The bus, turning off Denny Way onto Broadway, was shoved sideways by the out-of-control truck. The bus skidded backwards, taking out three parked cars as it slid back down the hill and inflicting a good deal of damage along the way. Fortunately, nobody was hurt.

The investigating officer on the scene realized almost immediately that the middle squashed car belonged to Marcia Kelsey. Due to the murder investigation and Pete Kelsey's subsequent disappearance, that missing Turbo Volvo was right at the top of the Patrol Division's high-priority list.

Nobody lost any time. As soon as the patrol officer radioed in with the information, Dispatch called me. It was only six-fifteen, and the phone call woke me out of a sound sleep.

"Detective Beaumont?"

The voice wasn't one of my usual early morning callers. "Yeah," I mumbled. "Who is this?"

"Lieutenant Congdon with Dispatch. One of our patrol officers found that Volvo you were looking for, if you still want it, that is."

That got my juices flowing. "You'd better believe I still want it. Where is it?"

"Just west of Broadway, up on Capitol Hill. The tow truck driver's on the horn right now. He's been in touch with the owner, and they want it towed to a repair shop up in the University District, but I told him I thought the vehicle was involved in a homicide investigation and that I'd have to check with you first."

Patrol doesn't get nearly the credit it deserves. The detective divisions would be lost without them. Routine traffic stops pick up more crooks by accident than detectives do on purpose, but those guys, the ordinary foot soldiers in the war on crime, don't show up in the press unless they screw up and shoot somebody they shouldn't have. Or unless somebody shoots them. The only time patrol officers get to be heroes is when they're dead.

"Good work, Lieutenant. You're absolutely right. Thanks for checking. Tell the officer on the scene to impound that vehicle and have it taken into the garage to be searched. Nobody's to touch it until after the crime lab team goes over it, you got that?"

"Got it," Congdon replied.

"And thanks," I told him.

"Sure thing," the lieutenant replied. "Always glad to help out."

"How long do you think it'll take to bring it in?"

"About half an hour or so. Not too long."

"Good," I told him, glancing at my watch. "I'll be there by then, too."

I hurried in and out of the shower and was one leg into the process of putting on my pants when the phone rang again. This time it was Ron Peters.

"Your calling me early in the morning like this seems just like old times," I said, holding the phone pressed to my ear with one shoulder while I used both hands to zip up my pants and fasten my belt. "What's happening?"

"Tell me everything you know about the bomb threats," he said quietly.

I didn't like the dangerously calm way he spoke, and it wasn't a request so much as it was a direct challenge.

"Look, I thought we went over all that last night. Captain Harden told you to back off. That strikes me like very good advice."

"I'm not interested in well-meaning advice, Beau, not from Harden and not from you. And I'm not backing off, either. I'm a cop, Beau, a cop who's sworn to uphold the law. Bomb threats to public property aren't something that ought to be swept under the rug, but in this case, not only are we not supposed to investigate it, the public isn't supposed to know about it either. I won't work that way."

"But . . ."

"No buts, Beau. With just the few phone calls I made yesterday before Harden chewed my ass, I found out that somebody across the street is behind this thing, someone very close to the top in city government. I want to find out who that person is and what they're up to. If somebody in this department's in on it, if they're dirty, too, then I want to know about that as well. I don't like crooked cops, and I particularly don't like crooked cops who work for crooked politicians."

"What about Harden?"

"You mean about him ordering me to lay off? I won't do anything about the bomb threats during my shift, but nobody tells me what I can and can't do during my off hours. So tell me what you know, or I'll have to track it down myself. That might create some real waves."

And so I told him, because, God help me, I felt exactly the same way he did. During the next ten minutes, I recapped for Peters everything I had learned from Dr. Kenneth Savage and from Doris Walker as well, including all the details I could recall from Sparky Cummings' off-limits file.

"Do you still think this has something to do with your two homicides?" Peters asked when I finished.

"I can't say. Maybe the only real connection is that the security guard who was killed wouldn't have been at the school district office if it hadn't been for the bomb threats back in September. Whether or not the bomb threats have anything directly to do with his death still remains to be seen."

"But you don't have any specific evidence that links the two?"

I laughed. "The only thing linking them so far is pure old J. P. Beaumont cussedness."

"That's good enough for me," Peters replied with a chuckle of his own. "I'd better get going."

"Don't stick your neck out too far, Ron," I cautioned. "You've already had it broken once."

"I noticed. Believe me, I'll be careful."

By the time I got off the phone with Peters, my half hour of travel time was almost gone. I was still too damn stubborn to want to bring my shiny 928 out of hiding to take its chances of being smashed to pieces on icy streets. Instead, I ran a full block and a half and crossed against a *DON'T WALK* light to catch up with a bus. Phone call and bus notwithstanding, I still beat the tow truck to the garage by several minutes.

I tagged along after the driver while he unhitched the crunched remains of the Volvo, dogging at his heels and asking questions.

"Was it locked?" I asked.

"What, this Volvo? Hell no, it wasn't locked. Somebody from an apartment building around there said it had been parked there ever since the storm came through on Sunday night. Funny, ain't it," he added with a bucktoothed grin. "Just goes to show some people don't even think these here hummers are good enough to steal. I don't like 'em much myself."

Peering in through the windows after he left, I caught sight of a piece of yellow paper protruding from under the plastic seat belt clip on the driver's side. It looked like another one of those Post-it telephone messages. I was eager to read it. Whatever was written there might very well contain information that would point us in the right direction.

But I had to wait, because nobody, including me, was allowed to touch the vehicle until after the crime-scene technicians did. Eventually the techs showed up, and I paced the floor impatiently while they methodically went through their interminable preliminary procedures. Forty-five long minutes later, they finally let me have a look—look but don't touch—at the piece of wrinkled yellow paper.

Whoever had driven the car last had sat on the note, probably without even being aware it was there. The paper was crushed and wrinkled, the pencil marks smudged. The message on it hadn't been written so much as scrawled in obvious haste.

"Mar," it said. "Somebody's been talking to Pete. I don't know who. Be careful. A."

I knew who Mar was. That had to be Marcia Louise Kelsey. And I knew who Pete was too. So who was A? Alvin Chambers? But then I realized there was one other possibility as well, one other A name in the equation—Andrea Stovall, the lady from the teachers' union with an unauthorized set of keys to the school district office.

A flurry of questions eddied through my mind. I remembered Andrea Stovall's obvious discomfort when we asked her about her unsuccessful attempt to see Marcia Kelsey the night of the murder. And I remembered the way she had bolted from the room, using her meeting as an excuse when, as a friend of the victim, she would logically have wanted to help us.

I stood there in the garage for some time, thinking about the message itself and what it meant. According to Pete, Marcia's romantic escapades were a known quantity to him and had been for years, so what was it that someone had told Pete Kelsey in only the past few days that he hadn't known before? What was it that had been damaging enough to set him off? And who was doing the talking?

I remembered Andrea Stovall telling us that the reason she went to the school district office was that she was afraid, afraid for Marcia Kelsey's safety and well-being. Since she hadn't found Marcia in the building, she could have placed the note on the windshield, but that meant whoever had driven the car away from the office, presumably the killer, had also seen the note. If it was Pete, why hadn't he gotten rid of such a potentially damaging item?

My instinct about the importance of the paper in the car had been right, but now the problem was finding out who had authored it. Alvin Chambers was dead, so getting a sample of his handwriting wouldn't be too difficult. If, however, Andrea Stovall had written the note, I would have to be somewhat less direct.

I was already fully convinced Andrea Stovall was concealing something important about that night, something she hadn't wanted to tell us. It was high time we asked her about that, and this time no urgent summons to some lightweight meeting was going to keep her from answering my questions.

Leaving the crime lab folks to continue their painstaking search of the vehicle, I dashed up to my cubicle, intent on obtaining those two separate but equally critical samples.

My first call went to the Seattle Federated Teachers' Association office in Greenwood. The secretary there told me that Mrs. Stovall had called in sick and probably wouldn't be in for the remainder of the week. My second call, to Andrea's home phone number, went unanswered. She may have been home sick, but she wasn't taking calls, not even after fifteen rings.

I put down the phone and thumbed through my notebook until I came to the name of Andrea Stovall's apartment manager, Rex Pierson, the man who had so kindly consented to give her a ride down to the school office the night of the murder. It was possible that this Pierson guy might have a sample of her handwriting on a note or lease agreement in his office.

Andrea hadn't given me a phone number, but telephone books work far more often than they don't. I flipped through the pages—Q, R, P, Pe . . . I turned to the next page, the Pi's, and glanced at the bold-faced heading at the top of the page to make sure I had the right one.

And that's when I saw it. The name was printed in heavy capital letters across the top of the column indicating the beginning and ending words on the page: *Piedmont—Pioneer*. And just below the column heading was the first name: Piedmont, Jonas A., 8445 Dayton Avenue North.

I felt like someone had splashed a bucket of icy water down my entire body.

The phone book was eight months old, and the bold-faced name had been lying in wait for me all that time like a coiled but invisible snake waiting to strike. In all those months, I had never before had occasion to use that particular page, had never stumbled over that unwanted and unlooked-for piece of my personal history. Seeing my grandfather's name there in black and white hit me with the same power as a fist plowing into my gut.

Against my will, I sat there staring at the line while the name, address, and phone number seared themselves indelibly into my brain.

"What's the matter, Beau?"

Guiltily I looked up first and then back down, like someone caught doing something he shouldn't. I had been so stunned by seeing my grandfather's name that I hadn't heard Ron Peters' wheelchair whisper up to the doorway of the cubicle.

I closed the phone book with a decided snap—I didn't want Peters to see which page it was open to—and tried to brush off the incident with a casual laugh. "I think I just saw a ghost," I told him.

"Really? How's that?"

"My grandfather. I just stumbled across his name here in the phone book when I was looking for something else. I didn't even know he was still alive."

Peters seemed surprised. "I didn't realize you had any relatives still living here in the city."

"Me neither," I told him.

"Well, that's great. You two should get together. I'll bet you'd have a great time."

"Sure," I said, but I didn't mean it. "What brings you here?" I asked, changing the subject.

"I figured I'd better bring you the paper," Peters said. "I know good and well you won't buy one yourself."

He handed me a neatly folded copy of the local section of the *Post-Intelligencer*. "Take a look at this."

"Husband Sought in Double Homicide," the banner headline read.

"Wait a minute," I objected. "We just want him for questioning at this point. There's some circumstantial evidence, but the way this lead is written, it makes it sound like we know for sure Pete Kelsey did it."

"That's not all, either," Ron Peters answered grimly. "I think maybe you'd better read the whole article."

And so I did:

"Late last night city and state authorities continued to search for a Puget Sound area man who disappeared in the aftermath of a double homicide that took the life of his forty-four-year-old wife and that of a fifty-year-old school district security guard. The brutal murders have left Seattle's educational community stunned and grieving.

"Peter Kelsey, forty-four, a freelance contractor and sometime bartender, is being sought in connection with the slayings of his wife, Marcia Louise Kelsey, head of Seattle Public School District's Labor Relations department, and of Alvin Chambers, a night watchman employed by Seattle Security. The killings occurred in the district's Lower Queen Anne area office building late Sunday night.

"Unconfirmed reports from unnamed sources both inside and outside the school district have indicated that Mr. Kelsey became irrational upon hearing rumors that his wife was conducting an illicit relationship with another female member of the school district staff."

That one stopped me cold. "A female? As in AC/DC?" I remembered Pete Kelsey's startling reaction when Kramer had told him about Alvin Chambers. He had said Marcia was always full of surprises, and she continued to be so. Maybe he was surprised to hear that his wife had been with a man rather than another woman.

"Read on," Peters said.

"'I know all about those godless women,' Mrs. Charlotte Chambers, widow of the slain security guard, stated in an airport interview late last night, where she had gone to meet her son, who is on emergency leave from the U.S. Navy. The younger Chambers flew home to attend his father's funeral.

"'Alvin told me all about them. He was a man of God, you see, even if he left the ministry. He was burdened seeing the way those two women carried on. It's a sin and goes against all the teachings of the Bible. It troubled him—he wanted to bring them God's love and forgiveness, but they weren't interested. I tried to get him to report them, but he wouldn't. Alvin was a great one for judging not, you see. So he just prayed about it, is all, and now he's dead and so is she.'

"Alvin Chambers spent fifteen years as pastor of the Algona Freewill Baptist Church before leaving the ministry to accept a position with Seattle Security.

"Mrs. Kelsey, a longtime employee of the Seattle Public School district . . ." The article continued with a rehash of the murders themselves as well as capsule biographies of both Marcia Kelsey and Alvin Chambers.

"Do you think it's true?" Peters asked when I finished reading and looked up. "About the other woman,

I mean. That's going to be pretty rough on the family, especially if they didn't know about it before."

"I think they knew," I said quietly. "At least one of them did."

I remembered the stark warning scrawled on the Post-it found in Marcia Kelsey's Volvo. I handed the folded newspaper back to Ron Peters. "I think somebody spilled the beans, just before the murders. I don't think he approved."

I went on to tell Peters about the warning message on the note found in Marcia Kelsey's smashed car. I had just finished when Margie poked her head around the doorway and peeked into my cubicle. "There you are, Beau. Good to see you, Ron. How's it going?"

She rushed on without waiting for Peters to give a real answer to her pro forma question.

"Detective Kramer was looking for you a little while ago, Beau. He picked up the search warrant early and said to tell you that he was going on up to the Kelseys' house, that you could meet him there if you want to. He said he had to hurry because he's due back in court at ten again."

"Fine," I said.

Margie frowned. "Are you going to meet him there or not?"

"I've got my own stuff to handle. Tell him he's a big boy and he can take care of the search warrant all by himself."

"Where will you be?"

Margie's sometimes as bad as a dormitory housemother.

"I'll be dropping by Seattle Security and going up to Queen Anne Hill to see a lady named Andrea Stovall."

Margie started away, then stopped. "She called, by the way. Did Detective Kramer tell you?"

"Andrea Stovall called here?"

"Neither you nor Kramer were in yet. I had nearly finished taking her message when Detective Kramer came in, and I turned her over to him. He probably rushed out and forgot to give it to you."

Right, I thought. Sure he did. I smiled engagingly at Margie. "You wouldn't happen to remember any of that message, would you?"

"Let me go get my book."

Margie writes her messages in a book that makes a carbon copy of each one. She returned carrying the spiral-bound notebook. "Erin called to tell me about her dad, to warn me. I've decided to leave town for a few days, just as a precaution, but . . ."

"But . . . ? That's it? She didn't say where she was going or how we could get in touch with her?"

"I told you. Detective Kramer came in just then, and I gave the phone to him. I'm sure he has the rest of it." The phone on Margie's desk began to ring, and she hurried to answer it.

"What are you going to do?" Peters asked after Margie left.

"First off, I'm going to try to get those two handwriting samples. I'm sure I can get a sample of Chambers' writing from Seattle Security, and I've got the name and address of Stovall's apartment manager at a place called the Queen Anne. When I finish with those, I may track down that worthless Kramer down in District Court and clean his clock."

With an acknowledging nod, Peters deftly maneuvered his chair back out through the doorway. "You do your thing, and I'll do mine," he said. "I have to read the chief's prepared affirmative-action statement to the press at ten A.M. It's going to be boring as hell, but it's a job, and it beats doing nothing."

He wheeled his way on up the corridor, with me trailing behind. "That's where she lives, the Queen Anne? It seems like a pretty nice place."

"You know where it is?" I asked.

"Sure. Amy and I thought about getting an apartment there until you talked us into staying awhile longer in Belltown Terrace. It's really convenient, right across the street from the girls' school."

I still couldn't place the building in my head. "I've got the address," I told him. "I'm sure I'll be able to find it."

At that, Ron Peters laughed aloud. "Your memory must be failing, Beau. It's not that difficult. It's old Queen Anne High School. Somebody redid the whole thing and turned it into apartments."

As soon as he said it, I did remember. In fact, I had picked up Tracie and Heather from John Hay Elementary on numerous occasions, but the name of the apartment building directly across the street had somehow slipped my mind. Probably deliberately slipped my mind. As far as I was concerned, Queen Anne High School was forever that, imprinted in my memory as a teeming, cheering gym—the site of my single high school basketball triumph, a last-second dumb-luck basket that won the final regular season game the year I was a senior.

The *UP* elevator appeared right then, and Peters wheeled himself into it.

"Thanks for jogging my memory, Ron," I called

as he disappeared into the elevator. "Where would I be without you?"

I headed back toward my office, happy in the knowledge that with Ron's help, there was no need to look up Rex Pierson's number. I knew where I was going and would simply show up on his doorstep at the Queen Anne unannounced.

I was relieved that for now the *PI* page of the phone book would continue to be off limits, because I wasn't tough enough to look at it yet, and I didn't know if I ever would be.

CHAPTER 18

I DIDN'T HEAD OUT OF THE BUILDING AS SOON AS I IN-
tended. Instead, I got stuck making phone calls,
spending time talking with various law-enforcement
authorities in Grant County, South Dakota. We
needed to know something more than just a name
about John David Madsen, aka Pete Kelsey.

After my request for information had been passed
around the sheriff's office there for some time while
I cooled my heels on hold, I finally ended up talking
to Undersheriff Hank Bjorensen, a man who had
actually attended high school with John David Madsen, although Bjorensen had been two years younger.

What he told me was every bit as baffling as all
the other puzzle pieces involved in what the media
was now calling the school district murders.

According to Bjorensen, John David was the only
child of a local and once well-to-do farming couple
from the nearby town of Marvin, a couple named Si
and Gusty Madsen. John David had graduated from
Milbank High School as valedictorian of his class

and had gone on to an appointment to West Point. Shipped to Vietnam as a second lieutenant immediately after graduation, he had mysteriously disappeared during an R and R period in Saigon. The Army listed him first as AWOL and later as a deserter.

"That whole episode almost drove the old man crazy," Bjprensen said. "Si Madsen was one of those old-time God-and-country men. He set out to prove the Army was wrong, insisting that his son should have been listed as an MIA, not as a deserter, but you know how that goes. The bureaucracy wears you down, grinds you down. They have all the time in the world; Si didn't.

"It was like an obsession with him, took over his whole life until he hardly knew which end was up. To the Army he probably wasn't much more than some pesky gnat. Mrs. Madsen died about five years ago. Old Si kept right on after it for a while, writing letters to his congressmen, writing letters to the editor, but when Gusty died, that took most of the spunk out of him. I think he just lost heart, finally, and gave up. After he died, the farm went to a niece and nephew on his wife's side."

"Are there any other living relatives?" I asked.

"Not as far as I know, other than the Lunds, the cousins I told you about, the ones living on the farm. But like I said, the Lunds are on his mother's side. On his father's, John David was the only child of an only child, so he was the last of the line as far as the Madsens are concerned. Do you want me to call Ruth Lund and see if she knows of anyone?"

"No, I don't think that will be necessary," I replied.

"So tell me. Why's a big-city cop from Seattle interested in all this ancient history?"

Waffling, I said, "I'm working a case that might be connected."

I didn't want to admit straight out that I knew for sure John David Madsen was alive and well and living as a fugitive somewhere far away from Marvin and Milbank, South Dakota. Making an informal inquiry was fine, but at that point I could see no need of officially involving another jurisdiction. After successfully eluding his past for over twenty years, I was relatively certain that South Dakota was the very last place where a missing Pete Kelsey/John David Madsen would show up.

When I hung up a few moments later, I sat there in my office cubicle staring at the phone as if the answers to my questions were somehow encoded into the touch-tone numbers if only I had the ability to divine them.

What would have driven a gung ho, patriotic West Point graduate to disappear off the face of the earth as far as both his family and country were concerned? A My Lai incident or some other wartime atrocity? That might have been enough to send him AWOL, but what had driven him underground and kept him there for so many years after the war was over, while in the meantime, back home, his parents died with no word or clue about what had happened to him? What had made someone with a good family leave them all behind without a backward glance? And why would someone with a fine mind, perhaps even a brilliant one, hide out in a lifetime's worth of low-status, craftsman-type jobs that required some skill, certainly, but didn't begin to tap his intellect?

No matter how long I stared, the impassive face of the telephone gave me no answers to these troubling questions.

In the course of homicide investigations, I often encounter unexpected pieces of people's past lives. Sometimes those secrets come from the victim's side of the aisle, sometimes from the perpetrator's. Often these pieces of history have little or nothing to do with the case at hand. But in this instance, and for no logical reason I could pinpoint, I had the uncanny sense that Pete Kelsey's hidden past had everything to do with my unsolved double homicide.

I called down to Seattle Security and was told that Fred Petrie, the owner, was in a meeting and would be out in about half an hour. I figured there was just time enough to pick up a fresh turkey sandwich from Bakeman's, see Fred Petrie on the way, and make it to a noontime browh-bag AA meeting in one of the missions in Pioneer Square.

Carrying a paper sack containing my made-to-order sandwich—turkey on whole wheat bread with sprouts, cranberry sauce, and mustard—I headed on down Cherry and First, briskly threading my way through a chilly Pioneer Square until I came to Seattle Security's office in a decrepit building just east of the Kingdome.

Seattle Security was still in the exact same location it had occupied years earlier when I had sometimes moonlighted as a security guard to supplement my meager Seattle P.D. salary.

Within minutes of giving my name to the receptionist, I was shown into the private office of Fred Petrie. Instead of the familiar, portly-bodied and bald-headed countenance of Fred Senior, I encountered Fred Junior, the new owner and much younger son of the original.

I remembered Freddie Petrie from those earlier days as a whiny, miserable adolescent, a loudmouthed and none-too-talented Little League player who dreamed of one day making it in the Majors. He hadn't made it. From the looks of things, he was having a difficult enough time just trying to fill Fred Senior's unambitious shoes.

As I listened to him rail on, I was struck by how little he had changed. He was still the very same spoiled and obnoxious shit he had been as a child. Longhaired and clad in a ragged shirt and scruffy tennis shoes, he looked as though he should still be knocking around on some high school campus carrying a civics textbook instead of hanging out in an office with his name on the door and a brass plaque on the desk that labeled him president and CEO.

When I gave him my card, he didn't remember me from Adam, but then, why should he? After all, security guards are a dime a dozen. Just ask Alvin Chambers.

But I will say this much for Freddie Petrie. He, at least, was prepared to talk about Alvin Chambers.

"I know why you're here, Detective Beaumont," he said with a doleful shake of his head. "It's a terrible thing. In fact, I still can't believe it happened. We've been in business in this same location for nearly forty-five years, and this is the first time we've ever had an on-the-job fatality."

"I'm aware of that," I said. "I worked for your dad years ago when I was first on the force."

Petrie looked up at me. "Oh, did you?" he asked vaguely and without much interest.

"How is your father, by the way?"

"You know him?" he asked.

It was a dumb question, and I couldn't quite believe he had asked it. Back in those days everybody at Seattle Security knew everybody else. It had been a typical mom-and-pop operation, with Fred Senior handling the hiring and scheduling, and his wife, Mazie, doing the books and payroll.

"I knew them both," I said.

"The folks are off enjoying themselves, cruising the Bahamas," he said resentfully. "I wish I were too. Seems like I'm always scrambling for money these days. I'm buying out their interest, at least I'm trying to. Having somebody die on the job like this is going to send our insurance costs out of sight."

I knew for a fact that Fred Senior would have been far more worried about Alvin Chambers' family than he would have been about his company's insurance premiums. Fred Senior was a likable guy, a people person. With the changing of the name on the office door, Seattle Security's bottom line had changed as well. It made me feel old and more than a little sad.

"What can you tell me about Alvin Chambers?" I asked.

It's always best to start interviews with nonthreatening, mundane questions and gradually ease into more substantial inquiries. I figured it would be best to ask for the handwriting sample only after Fred Junior had gotten used to giving me what I wanted. It's the old door-to-door salesman's technique of getting the customer accustomed to saying yes.

Petrie shrugged. "Not much. Been with us about six months or so. Hold on while I go get his records."

Freddie was away from his desk for only a few moments. He returned carrying a file folder, thumbing impatiently through its loose paper contents as he sat back down.

"Like I said, he was only with us for six months. Bounced around from location to location in the beginning until we put him on the school district job about two and a half months ago. He really settled into that one. Seemed to like it a lot."

Fred Junior smiled at me indulgently as though I might need some further clarification. "These older dudes generally prefer that, you know. They like going to the same place day in and day out. They like doing the same thing over and over. It's like they want the continuity. The younger ones like moving from place to place, doing the rock concerts, the more far-out stuff."

Freddie's smiling condescension said far more than he realized about where he lumped me. I was right in there with all those unfortunate "older dudes." That kind of categorizing didn't endear him to me, and it probably didn't endear him to his father, either.

"Where did he come from?" I asked.

Petrie consulted the file. "Algona Freewill Baptist Church. He came to us after fifteen years in the ministry."

"Why?" I asked.

"Why'd he leave the ministry?" Petrie inquired. I nodded and Fred Petrie shrugged. "Says here he left for personal reasons, but it doesn't go into exactly what."

"Did you do any kind of background check?" I asked.

"We called his references, I'm sure," Petrie answered. "We always do that. If anything negative turns up, we don't hire 'em. Since we did, he must have checked out. We hire lots of people around here, Detective Beaumont, and when we do, we don't go digging into their reasons for leaving a previous job. People come here asking for work, and we're glad to have 'em. We're always looking for people, especially these older ones. They're usually more dependable."

"You still pay minimum wage?" I asked.

"To start out. Al Chambers was doing some better than that, of course, because he'd been with us awhile."

"Doesn't it strike you as curious that a man with his background would leave the ministry and come to work for minimum wage?"

"He must have had his reasons, but like I said, that was Chambers' business, not ours. We've always got more jobs than we can fill. Supply and demand."

"Could you tell me how it happened that Mr. Chambers ended up with the school district job?" I asked. "Did he ask for that one in particular?"

"Just rotated into it, as far as I know," Petrie answered. "One guy quit suddenly, and we needed somebody to take his place that very night. It was Al's regular night off from another job site over in

Bellevue, but he jumped on the chance to take an extra shift. Once he had been there, at the school district, I mean, he liked it, especially since there was usually some overtime available with that job. He kept it from then on. I got the impression that he needed the extra money from those overtime shifts."

"Speaking of money, will there be any insurance?"

"Some, but not much. We only carry a small death benefit. Ten thousand, including double indemnity."

"Did you ever hear any rumors about Chambers becoming involved with someone from the school district?"

"Involved? As in romantically?" Freddie stifled a snort of incredulous laughter.

"Yes. Did any of the other guards he worked with mention anything to you about it?"

Petrie shook his head. "Nope. I never heard anything like that at all, but it doesn't really sound right to me either. Preach to her maybe, but Al Chambers didn't strike me as the type to mess around with another woman, although I don't suppose you can always tell that just by looking, can you?"

The wolfish grin and conspiratorial wink that accompanied that last statement made me think that Fred Petrie Junior wasn't entirely blameless on that score himself.

"So you've got someone else scheduled into the school district office for tonight?" I asked.

"We sure do. We covered it last night, as a matter of fact," he said. "We're having to pass it around again some. It'll take time for us to find someone to take that shift on a permanent basis again. The overtime doesn't seem to have much appeal at the moment."

"I can't imagine why, but tell me, how does that coverage break down?"

"You mean in hours?"

I nodded.

"During the week, one guy comes on at four and another at midnight until eight in the morning."

"And on weekends?"

"If the guys working it don't mind, we break it into two twelve-hour shifts. That's what Al liked. I mentioned that before. It gave him a crack at overtime every week. He always took it, too."

"So Saturday and Sunday, he would have worked eight to eight?"

"Right."

"And who was his opposite number?"

"That I'll have to check on the time cards."

Again Petrie left the room. When he came back he said, "There were two guys. Sam Burke on Saturday, and Owen Randall on Sunday. Here are their names and phone numbers in case you want to talk to either one of them."

I shoved the proffered piece of paper into my notebook. "Would it be possible to have a copy of that application?" I asked.

"You mean Chambers' job application?"

I nodded. "It would be a big help."

"I never had a request like that before," Petrie said dubiously. "I mean, if the guy's alive, then his application is confidential, right? But after he's dead, what does it matter?"

I kept quiet and gave him a chance to make up his

own mind. "I don't see that it would hurt anything," he said finally. "Wait here. I'll go make a copy."

Petrie left the office briefly for the third time, taking the application with him. Actually, there probably could have been confidentiality problems, if someone had found out about it and had wanted to make trouble, but I wasn't going to mention it, and I doubted Petrie would either. He came back in and handed me a barely legible copy.

"The copier's a little low on toner right now," he said. "That's the best I can do."

"It'll be fine," I told him. I glanced down at the precise printing on the application. I'm not a handwriting expert, but even to my unpracticed eye, it didn't seem likely that Alvin Chambers' neat hand was the same one that had written that hastily scrawled message.

Folding the copy and putting it into my jacket pocket, I rose to go.

"Wait a minute," Petrie said. "Aren't we going to talk about the gun?"

"Which gun?"

"The one Chambers was wearing. It belongs to us, I mean. To Seattle Security. We own it, and we issued it to him. Will we be able to get it back? Guns aren't exactly cheap, you know."

Fred Petrie Junior was back worrying the bottom line. That .38 may have been Seattle Security's rightful property, but as far as I was concerned, it was first and foremost a murder weapon, and murder weapons are sacred.

"I wouldn't hold my breath if I were you," I said. "It could be some time before you see it again, if ever."

"Damn," Petrie muttered. "If it's not one thing, it's three others."

I went back out on the street and walked up to the mission. Another day another meeting, although going didn't make me feel particularly virtuous. Once again, there was talk about families and the kind of pain people deliver to one another in the name of love.

And as I listened, it crossed my mind that Pete Kelsey and I both had something in common. For whatever reason, we had both turned our backs on our blood relatives. Lars Jenssen's son, Danny, had been dead for years before Lars finally came to his senses. The same was true for the Madsens. Now that their long-lost son had resurfaced, Si and Gusty Madsen had gone to their rewards.

But Jonas Piedmont, my crusty old son of a bitch of a grandfather, wasn't dead, at least not yet. And what, if anything, was I going to do about it?

CHAPTER 19

AS SOON AS THE MEETING WAS OVER, I WENT BACK TO the department long enough to grab a car and set out for Andrea Stovall's place on Queen Anne Hill. As I drove up to the apartments, I noticed that somebody had spent a lot of time and effort in scrubbing the grime off the face of the old high school building. Its gray facade looked almost tawny in the hazy winter's light.

I parked on Galer and went up to what had once been the main entrance, only to find that use of that particular door was limited to residents only. All others were directed to use the courtyard entrance.

As I started around the building, walking on a cleanly shoveled sidewalk, a school bell rang across the street, and John Hay Elementary's children, bundled from head to toe, came racing outside for a chilly recess. I didn't wait to see if I could catch sight of Tracie and Heather. It was too damn cold.

The Queen Anne had been done up in spades, complete with a *porte cochère*, which, I believe, is French for a covered driveway designed to keep passengers out of the rain. Set smack in the middle of the circle was a solidly frozen fountain of sculpted lions with fangs of icicles dripping from their fierce muzzles. If the rehab folks had been paying attention, they would have used Queen Anne High's grizzly mascot instead of lions to create their driveway fountain, but then again, rehab developers as a species have never been known for their sentimentality.

I was headed for the main doorway when I encountered a man in coveralls who was standing on a tall ladder under the portico. He was busily taking down a long plastic garland that had been draped over the doorway.

"I'm looking for Rex Pierson," I said.

"That's me," the man replied, looking down at me a little curiously but making no move to climb back down the ladder. "Are you the fella who called about the vacancy?"

"No. I'm not."

He went back to working on the garland. "What can I do for you?"

"I'm a police officer," I said. "Detective Beaumont, with Homicide."

In many situations the word "homicide" causes an immediate reaction. This was one of those times. "Be right down," Rex Pierson said, bringing the garland with him.

While he was still on the ladder, it had been impossible to tell how big he was, but once he was on the ground, I realized that Rex Pierson was a giant of a man—six seven at least—with forearms like small tree trunks and hands the size of serving platters.

He carried the tangle of garland as far as the glass doors of the building, punched a code into the security phone, and led me inside, where he dropped the garland in a large heap along with several others on the carpeted entryway floor.

"What's this all about?" he asked me, wiping his chilly hand on the leg of his coveralls before extending it to me.

"I'd like to talk to you about Sunday night," I said. "About your giving Andrea Stovall a lift down to the school district office."

"Well, of course I gave her a ride," he said. "I mean I couldn't very well let her go down there all by herself, not after what happened." He squatted down and began straightening the garlands.

"What exactly did happen?" I asked.

"Well, after that crazy bastard came bustin' in here and practically knocked her door down, I wasn't about to leave her alone."

"What crazy bastard?"

"Why, you know, the guy you cops are lookin' for, the one whose wife got iced just down the hill here. In fact, I started to call you about it, but my boss said to let it be. Said it would be bad if prospective tenants heard about it, so I kept my mouth shut, but I've been thinkin' to myself that maybe he did her first, his wife I mean, and then came lookin' for Mrs. Stovall. Or maybe it was the other way around. At any rate, by the time we got down there, it was already too late."

"Too late for what?"

"To warn her, his wife, that her husband was on a tear and looking for her."

"Maybe you'd better tell me exactly what happened. From the beginning."

"The alarm in the building went off, right around eleven I think it was. Since I'm a resident manager, the alarm sounds in my unit, so I went looking to see what was going on. We've had a break-in or two, but nothin' very serious. Somebody had come in through the front door, pried it open and come in, but there wasn't any sign of them on this floor, so I go up in the elevator, stopping on each floor and listening.

"Up on five I hear this crazy guy pounding on the door and squalling for somebody to open up. So I go up to him and ask him what seems to be the matter. He's raving away that his wife's in there, in that apartment, and that if they don't open up, he's going to break the mother down.

"So I call through the door to Mrs. Stovall—it was her apartment, you see—and ask her if she's okay, and she says she is but that there's nobody in there but her, that she's all alone. Then this guy starts yelling again, saying that she's lying, so I ask Mrs. Stovall real nice and quiet-like if she'd mind opening the door so he could see for himself that his wife wasn't there, and she did. She opened it right away, and this guy goes barging in like he owned the place.

"I wasn't worried about that, although I think Mrs. Stovall was. You see, I can handle guys like him. They're no problem. Anyway, he went stormin' through the apartment, lookin' in closets and bathrooms and out on the balcony and even under the bed, but just like Mrs. Stovall said, there wasn't anybody there. She was all alone.

"After he finishes lookin', I tell this guy that maybe he made a mistake and that he should get the hell out. He starts out the door and then he turns and looks back and tells Mrs. Stovall that if she ever breathes a word of it, he'll take care of her."

"He threatened her? Those were his exact words?"

"Near as I can remember. Anyway, he left then, without any more hassle. I wanted to call the cops, but Mrs. Stovall was all shook up, cryin' and shakin' and she says that she has to go down to her office and warn her friend—Marcia was her name. That's what she said, gotta go warn Marcia."

"And you offered to take her?"

"Wouldn't you?" he returned.

"I suppose I would," I replied. "So what happened then?"

"I take her down to the office, you know, the school district office, just down the hill here. She points out this Marcia's car in the parking lot and says she must still be there. She jumped out of the car before I even had it stopped good, and she went inside."

"How?"

"What do you mean, how? The way most people do, through a door. She let herself in with a key, but she came back out a couple minutes later and said she couldn't find anybody there, but she brought a note out with her and put it on the driver's seat in the other lady's car."

So consulting a handwriting expert wasn't going to be necessary in order to learn who had written the warning note. "A" was indeed Andrea Stovall. What I wanted to know now was exactly what Pete Kelsey had just found out and didn't want Andrea Stovall to tell.

Pierson had finished straightening the tangle of garlands and was now busily wrapping them around a huge wooden spool. It was one of those spools the phone company uses for storing and transporting cables. Most people couldn't have hefted it by themselves, but Rex, muscles bulging, lifted it as though it were a child's plaything.

I stood there for a moment watching him. "No one reported the disturbance to the police, did they?"

Rex shook his head. "Mrs. Stovall said not to. He settled right down as soon as I got there. Most people do." He smiled, and I saw what he meant. On my best days, I wouldn't have been a physical match for Rex Pierson, and neither would Pete Kelsey.

"By the way, is she here?" I asked.

"Who? Mrs. Stovall. Could be. I haven't seen her today. She's usually at work by now, but then, I've been busy taking down the decorations. You can try giving her a ring on the security phone if you like. She might be there."

I tried the phone, but if Andrea Stovall was inside her apartment, she still wasn't answering. I was sure, her sickness-excuse to the contrary, that she had indeed gone out of town and was lying low someplace. I could only hope that Kramer knew where.

Hanging up the phone, I turned to Rex. "Do you mind taking me up to her apartment?"

Rex Pierson stopped what he was doing and looked me straight in the eye. "That's not legal."

"But what if something's happened to her?"

His eyes bulged. "You don't really think something's happened to her here, do you?"

"We should check."

He nodded wordlessly and led the way to the elevator. Wide school hallways had been broken up by strategically placed walls. Polished floors had been covered over with carpet. Only an occasional bulletin board or trophy case and the broad, glassed-in stairways gave any hint that the place had once been a school.

An unopened newspaper lay on the floor in front of the door to Andrea Stovall's unit. A clutch of worry gripped my stomach. Supposing Pete Kelsey had made good his threat against Andrea.

I glanced at Rex Pierson. Obviously concerned about the same thing, he was already reaching for the key ring at his belt. "I can't let you in there," he cautioned, "not without an official warrant or something, but I can go in myself and check if you want."

He went in and came out a few moments later. "Nothin's wrong that I can see," he said.

For the moment, there wasn't anything more to be done. We went back down to the entry, where I handed Pierson one of my cards. "If you see her, give her my card and ask her to call me, would you?"

"Sure thing," he said.

I started to leave, and then thought of one more question. "Did you ever see Marcia Kelsey around here?"

With studied concentration Rex Pierson carefully fastened the last piece of garland with a five-inch tie-wrap. None of that garland was going to unravel from the spool until Rex Pierson was ready for it to unravel. Eventually he looked up at me and answered the question.

"I don't want to say nothin' against somebody," he said, "I mean nothin' that would get anyone in trouble."

"I'll try to keep whatever you tell me in strictest confidence," I said.

He nodded. "Well, sir, you see, I haven't been here in the building all that long. When it comes to a job like this, it takes time to connect people and faces and names. Know what I mean?"

I nodded.

"Well, for a couple of months, I thought she was one of the residents."

"Marcia Kelsey? You mean she was here that much?"

He nodded. "I recognized her from the picture in last night's paper. And if she was married all that time, I can kinda see how her husband might be just a little bent out of shape, know what I mean?"

Indeed I did, but even so, murder is never the answer.

Thanking Pierson for his help, I left. On the way back to the department, I stopped off at the Doghouse for a quiet cup of coffee. It was after the lunch hour proper and the place wasn't very crowded. Glad to be away from the hubbub of the fifth floor, I used the privacy of a dimly lit booth to write another report for Sergeant Watkins. This one detailed my interviews both with Freddie Petrie at Seattle Security and with Rex Pierson.

The good thing about writing reports is that it forces you to gather your thoughts, forces you to sift through what you think you know and helps clarify what you don't.

It was time to draw the logical conclusion that Andrea Stovall and Marcia Kelsey had been lovers, with or without Pete Kelsey's knowledge. That was an understandable triangle, an age-old pattern for trouble, but a triangle did nothing to clear up the problem of Alvin Chambers. Where did he fit in?

I was sorry I had returned Ron's copy of the *P.-I.* I did my best to recall exactly what Charlotte Chambers had said in the article about those "godless" women. Those were Charlotte's words, not Alvin's, but clearly Alvin had known what was going on between Andrea and Marcia. He had known and didn't approve. From the sound of it, he would have been reluctant to be associated with those kinds of people, so once more I came back to the same old question: What the hell was Alvin Chambers doing in that damn closet?

I thought about everything Rex Pierson had told me. His comments put a far different light on Pete Kelsey's claim that he and Marcia had shared an "open marriage." Evidently there were some things they hadn't been so open about, some things Pete Kelsey wasn't prepared to ignore or forgive. But if Marcia had been that unhappy with the marriage, and if Pete had been that miserable as well, what the hell had kept them together? Why hadn't they called the whole thing off and split? Their marriage had evolved beyond the tie-that-binds stage into something more like a noose—and every bit as deadly.

The beep of my pager startled me out of this reverie. The call-back number was Peters'. He's probably busy tracking the bomb threats on his lunch hour, I thought with annoyance, but I went to the noisy phone booth by the cash register and called him back.

"What's up?" I asked.

"Beau, where are you?" Ron Peters sounded anxious.

"At the Doghouse, having coffee. Why do you want to know?"

"Hold on a minute. Let me check something out."

He put me on hold while I entertained myself watching the Wednesday afternoon crush of lucky lottery players line up for their individual cracks at winning four million bucks, that week's Lotto prize.

Eventually Peters came back on the line. "Okay," he said. "I got hold of him and he's on his way to see you. Wait right there."

"Who's on his way?"

"Maxwell Cole. He came up to me this morning right after the press briefing and asked if I knew where to find you. I told him I didn't have a clue and that he should check with Margie, but he was adamant that he didn't want to be seen on the fifth floor. He said it was important. He insisted that he talk to you privately. Nobody else would do. I told him I'd try to locate you, but this is the first I've had a spare minute."

"He's coming here?" I asked.

"That's right. He said he'd be there in ten minutes or so."

"Okay," I said. "I'll wait here."

I went back to the booth, and Wanda brought me another cup of coffee. I had barely taken off the top layer when Maxwell Cole came steaming in the door, huffing and puffing and out of breath. Hurriedly he looked around the room. Relief showed on his face when he finally caught sight of me.

He rushed over to me, hand outstretched in greeting. "Thank God you're still here, J.P.," he said, easing his heavy bulk into the booth across from me. "I didn't know if you'd wait or not."

Wanda approached the table to offer coffee, which Max accepted with a grateful nod. He still looked sick enough that he probably shouldn't have been out of bed. His nose was bright red, and his eyes were watery.

"What's the matter, Max? Is something wrong?"

Nervously chewing on one end of his drooping mustache, Max glanced anxiously around the room as if checking to see if anyone was listening. When he spoke, it was in a confidential whisper. "I need your help, J.P."

"With what?"

He swallowed hard before he answered. "With Pete."

"With Pete Kelsey? Do you know where he is?"

Max nodded. "I do. When he saw the paper this morning, I thought he'd tear the place apart. I've never seen him like that."

"Reading the paper set him off?"

"Of course it did. I mean, the things that woman said!" Max answered indignantly. "I can't understand how they could print such terrible things about Marcia. They're not true. They couldn't be. If they were true, don't you think I'd know it? I can't imagine what those damn editors were thinking of!"

He shook his head miserably and sneezed into a wrinkled, much-used handkerchief. It was almost comic to think of Max being so offended by something printed in his own newspaper. No doubt it was the first time someone he truly cared about had been on the receiving end of hatchet-job reporting. Dishing it out is always a whole lot easier than taking it, but this was no time to revel in the irony of it all. Maxwell Cole knew where Pete Kelsey was, and I wanted him to tell me.

"Where is he?" I asked. "At your house?"

"He's willing to turn himself in," Max said. "But there's a condition."

"Suspects don't get to name conditions, Max. You know I can't make any deals."

"But he doesn't want much," Max pleaded. "Marcia's funeral is tomorrow. All he wants is your guarantee that he'll be able to go to that."

"Come on, Max. We're talking homicide here."

"Please, J.P. I swear to you, no matter what you think, Pete didn't kill Marcia. He couldn't have." Max's voice broke as he finished, and he buried his face in his hands.

Maxwell Cole looked so troubled, so miserable, that I couldn't help feeling sorry for him. Pete and Marcia were no doubt his best friends in the world, and what had happened to them was tearing him apart. I gave him a moment or two to pull himself back together.

"How well do you know Pete Kelsey?" I asked finally when Max looked once more as though he were capable of speech.

"Jesus Christ, J.P.!" Max exploded. "We already went over that! I know him like my own brother."

"Did you ever hear of anyone named John David Madsen?"

"No. Who's that?" Max asked with a frown.

"If you don't know John David Madsen, Max, then you don't know Pete Kelsey, either. Where is he?"

"At my house. He came there yesterday afternoon. I swear to God, I didn't know you were looking for him until the paper came this morning."

"Is he armed?" I asked.

"Of course he's not armed. What kind of a fool do you think I am?" Max demanded.

"Are there any weapons in the house?"

Maxwell Cole thought for a moment and then said, "Well . . ."

His hesitation told me what I needed to know. I stood up, dropping a fistful of change onto the table. "Where are you going?" Max asked.

"To call for a backup. Kelsey got away from me yesterday. That's not going to happen twice."

"No deal then?"

"No deal."

Maybe Pete Kelsey wasn't asking for much, but it was far more than he was going to get.

CHAPTER 20

IT WAS DONE WITHOUT SIRENS OR FANFARE. AND without any reporters, either.

Two cars, one marked and one not, accompanied Maxwell Cole and me back up Queen Anne Hill to Max's house. I had told him that under no circumstances would he be allowed to approach the house, but while I was busy strategically placing my six backup officers, Max slipped away from me and made a beeline for the front porch. He was opening the door before I realized what he was up to, and by then it was too late to stop him.

Leave it to Maxwell Cole to blow my cover. One way or another, Kelsey/Madsen now knew we were there. We had lost whatever small advantage might have been gained by the element of surprise. If he chose to make a stand, to force us to come in after him, Max's huge old house stood there like an impenetrable fortress. And then there was always the possibility that Kelsey would take Max hostage and attempt to use him as a bargaining chip.

While I was still assessing the situation and trying to determine whether or not to summon the Emergency Response Team, the door opened and both Max and Kelsey stepped outside onto the wide front porch. Kelsey walked with both hands held high over his head.

Quickly I moved to intercept them, my whole body tense and alert for any sign of trouble. In one hand I gripped my new Beretta and fervently wished it was my trusty old Smith & Wesson.

"Step aside, Max," I ordered, motioning him away with a sideways jerk of my head. He complied, but not without argument.

"Put the gun away, J.P. I told you there wouldn't be any trouble. I told you Pete was ready to turn himself in."

Kelsey/Madsen was looking me straight in the eye. "Will I be able to go to Marcia's funeral?" he asked.

"I already told Max that we don't make deals, Madsen. Now, up against the wall, feet apart and hands over your head. You're under arrest."

For a long moment Pete Kelsey didn't move. He leveled his ice blue eyes at me in a steady, unblinking stare, but the working muscles across his jawline told me that my use of his real name had hit home. At last, when he dropped his eyes, his whole body seemed to sag. He started to lower his hands.

"Hands up, Madsen!" I barked again, putting real menace in it this time. "I said move it!"

He did move then, but slowly, as though he were in some kind of uncomprehending trance. As soon as he turned his back to me, I stepped behind him and propelled him toward the house with a swift shove to his shoulder. He had gotten away from me once, and I wasn't going to allow him the slightest opportunity to do it again.

"I didn't do it," he said quietly, almost under his breath. Standing behind him, I was the only one who heard him speak. "No matter what you think, Detective Beaumont, I didn't kill my wife."

As soon as Max and Kelsey had appeared on the porch, my backup officers had abandoned their positions, and converged behind me. Now two of them, their weapons drawn, sprinted up onto the porch, shoving Max aside as they did so. While one of them kept Kelsey covered, another did a quick pat-down search, finishing by cuffing Kelsey's arms tightly behind him.

"He's unarmed," the pat-down officer reported.

Relieved, I nodded. "Good."

"I told you," Max said indignantly.

Holding Kelsey by the arm, one of the officers spun him around so the two of us stood facing each other. It's a moment I've lived through a thousand times when hunter and hunted, captor and captive, come face-to-face. Maybe it's due to the adrenaline pumping through my system at those times, but years later, although the names have long since disappeared, I can still recall those moments and those faces with absolute clarity.

Some murderers, especially repeat offenders, swagger when they're caught, their faces haughty with contempt because they know there's no such thing as life in prison and no such thing as the death penalty either, no matter what the lawbooks say. They know there are plenty of ways to slip through plea-bargaining cracks and plenty of attorneys who will help them do it. They're sure they'll walk away without doing any time at all, and usually they're right.

The inadvertent ones, drivers in vehicular manslaughter cases, drunks who kill without meaning to in the course of a barroom brawl, don't swagger and are usually scared shitless when we pick them up. The domestic violence types—people who kill their husbands and wives and kids—are often still angry when they're arrested: angry at the victims for causing their own deaths and angry at the cops for catching them doing it.

A very few killers are grateful to have their crimes finally out in the open—a few but not most. Unlike the others, they make no protestations of their innocence because they want the nightmare to be over.

Despite his claim of innocence, what I saw on Kelsey/Madsen's face was just that kind of relief. No fear, no bitterness, no animosity—just a profound resignation. I wondered if, after so many years of living a lie, he wasn't grateful that the other shoe had finally dropped.

We stared at each other for some time. I was the one who spoke first, and then not to him but to the other officers.

"Read him his rights," I said, "then take him downtown to the fifth floor so we can take his statement. Have someone call the Criminal Investigations Division down at Fort Lewis to find out what they want us to do with him. His ID will give his name as Kelsey, but his real name is Madsen, John David Madsen. For the moment the only charge against him is desertion."

Maxwell Cole's mouth dropped open a foot. I think he had missed it the first time I called Pete Kelsey by his real name.

"What's this?" he demanded. "What's going on?"

"This man is a deserter," I said, "from the United States Army. We're holding him for them."

"Wait just a minute," Max objected. "Pete's never even been in the Army in his life. This is crazy."

"Let it go, Max," Kelsey said tersely, his voice almost a low growl. "Stay out of this."

"But . . ."

"I *said* let it go," Kelsey repeated.

Rebuffed and hurt, Maxwell Cole ducked back as though he'd been slapped. Meanwhile, Kelsey/Madsen turned to me. "How'd you find out, Detective Beaumont? Fingerprints?"

"Does it matter?"

He gave a short, harsh snort and shook his head. "No, I don't suppose it matters at all."

He looked back at Max, who stood to one side wringing his hands helplessly. "There is something you can do for me, Max. Go tell Erin, so she doesn't find out about this from somebody else. Tell her I love her no matter what and not to worry."

"Is that all you want me to do? Jesus Christ, man! Don't you want me to get you a lawyer or something?"

"I don't need a lawyer, Max. I don't *want* a lawyer. Just go talk to Erin. Do that for me, please."

By then the other officers were ready to lead him away, and Madsen went without protest. Max stood on the porch watching them go, shaking his head in stunned silence. He didn't speak until the last of the three cars had disappeared around the curve in the street.

"How come you called Pete by another name?" he asked at last.

Considering the situation, I figured I owed Max at least a partial explanation.

"Because John David Madsen is his real name, Max. Pete Kelsey is a fraud, a phony. He's lived under an assumed name for as long as you've known him."

"No," Max said, and then, a little later, "Why would he do a thing like that?"

"Who knows?"

"But he's my best friend," Max objected, as though he hadn't heard me. "Why would he pretend to be someone he wasn't?"

"I intend to find that out, Max, and when I do, I'll be sure to let you know."

"I guess I'd better do like he said and go tell Erin."

"First I'm going to need a statement from you."

"About what?"

"About last night. About what happened when he came here."

Max nodded. "All right then, but let's go inside before I catch pneumonia."

We went into the house and he led the way into the furniture-crowded living room where we had sat the day before. I took out my notebook.

"What time did he get here?"

"I don't know. Seven-thirty, eight. I don't know for sure. I was reading and not paying any attention."

"And how did he get here?"

Max shrugged his shoulders. "I thought he came

by car, but I didn't see it outside on the street any-place this morning, and it's not there now. All I can tell you is that it was dark when he turned up on the doorstep, and I let him in."

"What did he say?"

"He asked if he could stay over. He said Erin was staying with her grandparents, but that the phone calls and the reporters were driving him crazy. He had to get away."

"What did you do?"

"Got drunk. Sat around and talked and got drunk. Not roaring, just enough to dull the pain a little."

Some pains take more dulling than others. I know that myself from firsthand experience.

"What did you talk about?" I asked.

"Mostly Marcia," Max answered. "Marcia and Erin. That's all he wanted to talk about, his family, espe-cially the old days when they first got married and they were so happy together. Pete talked. All I did was listen."

"What did he say?"

"Nothing really. Nothing and everything. I didn't know until last night, though, that they must have been having lots worse troubles than either one of them let on. He said that before she died, he knew he was losing her. He had worried about what kind of effect a breakup would have had on Erin—he's always been more concerned about Erin than himself."

"Even though the parents were having their diffi-culties, you'd say he still had a good relationship with his daughter?"

Max nodded. "He's always treated Erin like she was made of spun glass. Nothing's too good for his

Erin. That's the way it's always been. You'd think being raised like that, with two adoring parents, that Erin would be spoiled rotten, but she isn't.

"Anyway, to go back to him and Marcia, he said that he wouldn't have *liked* losing her, but that he could have accepted it eventually. He said he wished to God she were still alive." Max broke off, sniffling into a fresh wad of Kleenex he pulled from a box on a nearby table.

"It's this damn cold," he mumbled. "My nose just keeps running."

I knew it wasn't only his cold that was making Max's nose run and eyes water. The Kelseys were Maxwell Cole's good friends, his best friends, and slowly but surely they were being wrested from him. Max was just about at the end of his rope, but I had to press on anyway. Besides, I suspected that keeping him talking was actually doing him a favor. Answering my questions was the only thing preventing him from falling apart completely.

"So he said he knew he was losing his wife. Did he say how exactly?"

Max shook his head. "No, and I didn't push him, and you wouldn't have either. He was grieving, J.P. He was in pain, actual physical pain, I think. I listened to what he had to say, but I didn't pry, although after what I read in the paper this morning, maybe . . ." Max's voice drifted into a troubled silence without finishing the sentence.

"You said you didn't know we were looking for him until this morning?"

"That's right. As soon as he got here last night, he asked me to turn off the radio and leave it off. He also asked me not to answer the phone. He said he was afraid people might track him down here, and he didn't want to talk to anyone else."

"Tell me what happened when he saw the paper this morning."

"Now, *that* was scary," Max declared. "In all the years I've known him, I've never heard Pete Kelsey say a cross word, never heard him raise his voice in anger, but when he read that article, the libelous things that security guard's wife said, I thought he was going to lose it completely. He picked up that brass poker over there by the fireplace. I was afraid he was going to rip the place apart."

"What stopped him?" I asked.

Maxwell Cole, flabby and perpetually out of shape, would have been no match for the work-hardened muscles of Pete Kelsey.

"I talked him out of it," Max said gravely. "I told him to think about Erin instead of himself. And that's when he agreed to turn himself in. Just like that. He put down the poker and sat down and told me to go find you. He was very specific about that. He said he'd talk to you and nobody else."

"Why? There are two detectives on the case. Why not Detective Kramer?"

"Pete didn't say. Maybe he liked you better, thought he could trust you or something. There's no accounting for taste, you know." Max gave me a feeble grin.

"While you were talking, did he mention anything about going to the school district office Sunday night looking for Marcia?"

"No."

"Or looking for her anywhere else?"

"No."

"Did he say anything at all about that night?"

"No. Nothing."

"Did he ever mention Vietnam to you?"

"No. Why should he? He was a Canadian citizen. My mother sponsored him when he applied to become a citizen. Why would he have had anything to do with Vietnam?"

"What was his first wife's name?"

"His first wife? Why do you want to know that?"

"It might be helpful."

"I don't remember," Max said. "That's a long time ago, you know. I'm not sure I ever knew her name. I don't think he ever told me. It was such a tragedy that he didn't talk about it. I think it hurt him too much to think about it."

"Or else it never happened," I suggested grimly.

"You mean you think that was a lie as well?"

Gradually the full extent of Pete Kelsey's betrayal was beginning to sink into Maxwell Cole's consciousness. A friendship of twenty years' standing was tumbling down around his ears like a house of cards.

"Why not?" I returned. "Since everything else was, why not that, too?"

"I can't take it all in," Max said. "I can't understand it. I don't want to understand it." Abruptly Max stood up. "I hope that's all the questions for now, because I need to hurry over to see Erin." He started out of the room and then paused and looked at me. "Do you suppose she's still at the Riggs' place? That's right here on Queen Anne."

"You can check," I said. "My guess is that no matter what Kelsey said, Erin stayed where she was last night. At home. And the grandparents probably stayed with her."

With a sigh and a shake of his head, Max continued on into the kitchen to use the phone. I followed behind. Without having to look it up in the book, he punched in the Riggs' phone number. He let it ring and ring, but there was no answer. He dialed another number, again from memory.

"Hello, George," he said at once. Suspicions confirmed. The grandparents were indeed still at the house on Crockett. "Is Erin there?" Max asked, and after George responded, Max added quickly, "No, no. Don't get her. This is Max. Maxwell Cole. I'm coming over to see her. Tell her to wait for me." He paused and then added fiercely, "Don't let her listen to the radio or watch television while she's waiting."

There was another pause while George Riggs asked a question. "Yes, there's something wrong," Max acknowledged reluctantly, "but I don't want to talk about it over the phone. Just have Erin wait there. It's very important."

I followed Max out the door and down the walk to his waiting Volvo. He moved with a wooden, stiff-legged gait, like an aging, overweight toy soldier. I didn't envy him his errand. He was going to have to deliver the news that the last bastion of Erin Kelsey's world was collapsing.

Not only was her mother dead and her father in jail, her father wasn't who he had always claimed to be. That meant Erin wasn't who she thought she was, either.

Both Max and Erin had been betrayed by Pete

Kelsey's web of lies and deceit. Both would be wounded by it.

Watching Maxwell Cole drive dejectedly away through the gray and suddenly overcast day, I wouldn't have bet money either way about which one was going to be more hurt.

It was a moment after Max had driven out of sight before I realized I was standing there aching for him, and even while it was happening, I couldn't quite believe it.

If, two days earlier, any one of a dozen people had tried to tell me that before the week was out, I'd be standing on Maxwell Cole's doorstep feeling sorry for that poor, miserable bastard, I would have laughed in their faces and called them outright liars. Or crazy.

But they weren't, because I was.

CHAPTER 21

IT WAS WELL AFTER FIVE BY THE TIME I GOT BACK TO THE department. To get to my cubicle, I had to walk directly past Captain Powell's fishbowl. Normally his glass-enclosed office would have been deserted at that hour, but on this particular afternoon it was standing room only. Captain Powell himself was there, along with Margie and Sergeant Watkins. Detective Kramer had assumed center stage and was busy playing uproar.

"So I get outta court," Kramer was noisily complaining. His voice rumbled through the open door and down the hallway as I came toward them. "I get outta court, and what do I find? Without saying a word to me, Beaumont has arrested this suspect, this Pete Kelsey character, and locked him up on some ancient charge of desertion. The booking paper doesn't say word one about what's going on with our case."

"And where's Beaumont in all this? Nowhere to be found, that's where. Can't raise him on the radio.

Can't get him to respond to his pager. The guys who brought Kelsey in tell me they left Detective Beaumont up on Queen Anne talking to some lousy reporter. His own partner can't find out a damn thing, but he's got time to give some cretin reporter a goddamned blow-by-blow interview."

No one seemed aware of my stopping in the doorway, except for Captain Powell, who looked at me with one eyebrow raised quizzically. The half smile on his face made me think he was glad to see me. He nodded and gave a brief, welcoming wave, but when he didn't speak, I did.

"I take it somebody here's looking for me?"

Kramer swung around, his face simmering with suppressed anger. "You're damn right I am! Where the hell have you been? Why didn't you answer your pager?"

"I've been working, Kramer. How about you?"

Casually I reached across him and passed Margie the two reports I had completed in the Doghouse earlier that afternoon. "Make two copies of those when you have time, would you please, Margie. Give one to Sergeant Watkins and the other to Detective Kramer here. He'll want to read them too."

"Was your pager off, Detective Beaumont?" Captain Powell asked mildly. The captain isn't the flappable type. If he had been, I would have been bounced out of Homicide long ago.

I took the pager out of my pocket and checked it. Sure enough, the switch had been turned to off. I turned it back on.

"Sorry about that, Captain," I said. "I don't have

any idea when that happened. I must have accidentally switched it off the last time I used it."

Captain Powell smiled. "No problem."

"But it is a problem," Watty objected. "The point is, you were totally incommunicado for well over an hour while people were looking for you, Detective Beaumont. Your *partner* was looking for you. This squad isn't set up to consist of several dozen lone wolves. Teamwork, remember?"

Here I was, back in the wrong with Watty one more time.

I tried to explain my actions. "Look, Watty, I was talking to Max—Maxwell Cole—trying to find out as much about Kelsey as I could before I came back down here to interview him. That's standard procedure. The more you know *before* you question a suspect, the better your chances are of uncovering something important."

Sergeant Watkins stood up with an impatient shake of his head and moved past me into the hallway, where he stopped to deliver his parting remark. "That's all very well, Beau, and I'm sure we'll see whatever you learned detailed in your reports, but in the meantime I want you to remember that you owe it to this department and to your fellow officers to stay in contact at all times. That's why the city invested all that money in electronic pagers. Leave the son of a bitch on! Do we understand one another?"

"Yes."

Watty nodded curtly to Captain Powell and the others, then he disappeared down the hallway, with Margie trailing fast on his heels. I could feel my ears glowing hot and red in the bright fluorescent lighting. Tongue-lashings should never be a spectator sport, and Detective Kramer was enjoying my discomfort.

Captain Powell, too, must have noticed the smug look on Kramer's face. "That'll be enough of that, Detective Kramer. Sit down, both of you, and let me know a little of what's been going on today. I don't want to have to wait for written reports."

So I told them briefly what I'd learned from Freddie Petrie and Rex Pierson. When I started telling them about my Doghouse meeting with Maxwell Cole, Kramer began squirming impatiently in his chair. He was still operating under the illusion that Max and I were long-term best pals, but the captain knew better than almost anyone in the department that the connection between me and Maxwell Cole was anything but cordial.

"We knew, going in, that Max has been friends with Pete Kelsey for twenty years, and with Marcia Kelsey for a lot longer than that," I explained. "Last night, after Kelsey ditched us at the house on Capitol Hill, Kelsey went to Max's house and asked to spend the night."

"So your friend Cole was harboring a criminal," Kramer said.

"He's not my friend," I objected, "and he was doing no such thing. Cole didn't know what had happened over on Crockett, because Pete Kelsey didn't tell him. Cole knew nothing about our finding the gun, and he had no idea Kelsey was a fugitive."

"And I suppose next you're going to tell us that Max had no idea about Kelsey's deserter status."

"Actually, that's true," I said agreeably. "He knew Kelsey, not Madsen, and Kelsey was a Canadian. Why should he think the guy's a deserter? The first Max knew about any of this was this afternoon."

"Sounds to me like you blabbed everything you know. The entire city will be dissecting our case over breakfast and the morning *P.-I.* tomorrow. Terrific!"

Detective Kramer could piss me off in less time than anyone I know. My ears were no longer glowing, but I had an idea my blood pressure was sneaking up.

"Look, Kramer," I snapped back at him. "It wasn't that kind of interview. You already know that Maxwell Cole is intimately involved with this case, that he's the one who introduced Pete and Marcia years ago. He's not going to be writing a story about this. His involvement here is strictly personal, not professional. I wanted some insight into their relationship, and Max gave it to me."

When I realized I was defending Maxwell Cole in public, no one could have been more surprised than I was, including Captain Powell.

"Some relationship!" Kramer snorted. "That broad was screwing everything in pants and some that weren't. What he writes about that isn't going to help our case either. People will read about it and think her husband's a hero, that we ought to give him a medal."

Captain Powell was losing patience. "You *do* have a point, Detective Kramer," he said placatingly. "But from what you're telling us about the friendship between Cole and the Kelseys, it seems highly unlikely that Mr. Cole will put anything in his column that would in any way jeopardize the investigation. So are you two going to interview Kelsey now?"

"That was my plan," I replied. "I don't know about Detective Kramer. You'll have to ask him."

"I'm in," Kramer said.

Powell turned to Kramer. "Oh, by the way, did you ever have a chance to tell Detective Beaumont about what the search warrant turned up this morning?"

With that one quiet question, Powell changed the entire tenor in the room, took me off the hot seat and put Detective Kramer there in my place. He was already squirming as he stammered his answer. "I tried, but like I said, I couldn't raise him on the pager."

"What?" I demanded, enjoying the idea that Powell's knife could cut both ways. We'd been so busy discussing what I hadn't told Kramer that no one had mentioned what he might not have told me.

"A casing," Kramer replied sullenly. "A .25 CCI-Blazer casing in the same underwear drawer where they found the gun."

"That's not all," Captain Powell prompted. "Tell him the rest."

"And a pair of trousers, blue with light blue piping."

"Chambers' uniform?"

Kramer nodded. "We're pretty sure. Charlotte Chambers' son is going to bring her down here this evening to see whether or not she can identify them."

"Where were they?"

"Out in Mr. Clean's garage. The trousers had been

freshly laundered, and the shoes had been cleaned and polished. The lab's checking the shoes especially for blood."

"And then I have some additional news for both of you," Powell put in. "The answer to the question of why there were two guns used instead of only one. The Browning jammed on that hollow-point ammo with only one shell expended, so the killer had to find himself another weapon. Chambers' .38 was the only one available."

Powell finished and was quiet while I assimilated what we'd learned. "It sounds like a pretty tight case," I said at last.

"Tight!" Kramer yelped. "It's not just tight, it's foolproof, open and shut. Kelsey had motive and opportunity both, we found the murder weapon and some of the victim's clothing in the man's house, so will you tell me why the hell desertion is the only damn thing on his booking sheet?"

"Because that's all we know for sure so far. How about if we go talk to the man and see if we can find out anything else."

"Good idea," Captain Powell said.

They brought Pete Kelsey/John David Madsen to one of the windowed interview rooms on the fifth floor. He was wearing jail-issue orange coveralls, matching slippers, and an air of stubborn determination.

"Good evening, Mr. Madsen," I said cordially as he took a seat at the bare wooden table. "Is your attorney meeting you here?"

"I don't have an attorney," he answered, "and my name is Pete Kelsey. That's what I want to be called."

"But you have been read your rights, haven't you, Mr. Madsen?" I continued, pointedly disregarding his wishes. I wanted to put the man on notice that this wasn't a walk in the park and it was high time he paid attention.

"You know you have the right to counsel and if you can't afford one, an attorney will be appointed for you?"

"I already know all that. Just tell me what you want to know."

"How long have you known your wife was having an affair with Andrea Stovall?" I asked bluntly.

"It's always been there, in the background. The security guard was a surprise, but I've known about Andrea from the beginning."

"What changed?"

Kelsey/Madsen stared at me blankly. "What do you mean, what changed?"

"Just exactly that. Andrea tried to warn your wife that you were on a rampage because of something you'd been told. What did you know then, the night of the murder, that you didn't know before?"

Kelsey hunched his shoulders. "I didn't want all this to come out, to become so much public gossip."

"What did you find out that night?" I insisted.

"That she was leaving me. After all these years, she had decided to go live with Andrea as soon as school got out."

"How did you find that out?"

Suddenly a dam broke somewhere inside the man's previously unflappable calm. He buried his face in his hands. "Oh God, I didn't want any of this to come out. Why are you insisting on bringing it out? I knew it would hurt George and Belle and Erin if they ever found out the truth, and as long as Marcia kept her part of the bargain, it didn't matter that much to me."

"You still haven't answered the question," I insisted.

"A phone call," he said.

"A phone call? You told us about some threatening calls, harassing calls."

Kelsey shook his head. "I didn't tell you about this one, because I hoped you'd never find out about it. The call came on Sunday night, quite a while after Marcia left."

"Who was it?"

"A woman, I didn't recognize the voice, laughing hysterically. She told me Marcia was going to run away with Andrea, but all the while she kept laughing and laughing, like it was the funniest thing she had ever heard."

"You're sure you didn't recognize the voice?"

"No. At first I thought it was Erin. I was afraid she was having car trouble and was calling for help, but it turned out not to be her at all."

"So who was it?"

"I don't know. She didn't say. Wouldn't say, but what was scary was how much she knew, or seemed to know. She said Marcia wasn't working at all, that she was at Andrea's. She even told me where Andrea lived. In all the years, I've never known that, never wanted to. That's not all, either. She said that Marcia was going to break her word to me, her promise, and go live with Andrea."

Pete had said the words in a rush, and now he was silent.

"Did she tell you anything else?"

"No. She couldn't."

"Couldn't? Why not?"

"Because she was laughing, Detective Beaumont, laughing hysterically! I've never heard anything like it."

"What did you do after the phone call?"

"What do you think? I went to find them."

"Why?"

"To try to get her to change her mind, but she wasn't there. I tried the office first, then Andrea's apartment, and later I tried the school district office again. So then I went by the school district. Nobody answered my ring the first time, and when I went back the second time, her car was gone. Actually, it's probably a good thing I didn't find her."

"Why?"

"Because I didn't trust myself, Detective Beaumont. Because I might have killed her. I was right at the end of my rope. Later on, after I cooled off, I got to thinking that if the person who called was wrong about them being together at the apartment, maybe she was wrong about the rest of it too. Maybe Marcia wasn't going to leave me after all."

Kramer was shaking his head in obvious disgust, but I didn't give him a chance to say anything.

"Why didn't you tell us any of this before?"

"I was hoping no one would find out, that what went on between Marcia and Andrea Stovall would be a secret that Marcia would take to her grave so no one else would have to be hurt by it. But that didn't work either. It was all over the paper this morning. I couldn't believe it when I saw it."

"So how did the murder weapon get in your bedroom, Mr. Madsen?" Detective Kramer asked.

"I don't know," Pete replied.

"And what about Alvin Chambers' trousers and his shoes?"

"What about them?"

"We found those in your house as well, out in your garage."

"I don't know," Pete began. "I can't imagine, unless somebody's trying to frame me."

"Who would do that? Who would be interested in framing you for the murder of your own wife?"

"I told you, I don't know. It's a nightmare."

"Tell me why you stuck it out with your wife for so long, Mr. Madsen or Kelsey or whatever you call yourself," Kramer continued. "I sure as hell wouldn't, not under those circumstances."

Pete Kelsey's eyes hardened. "We made a bargain, Detective Kramer," he said. "I'm a man who keeps bargains."

"Sounds like a hell of a bargain to me," Kramer returned derisively. "What did you get out of it?"

Had I been Pete Kelsey, I think I would have tried to belt that smart-mouthed son of a bitch. Either that or I would have clammed up. Pete Kelsey did neither.

"It was good enough for me," he answered softly. "I got what I wanted."

"And what was that?"

Pete Kelsey held Kramer's eyes when he answered. "I got a family," he said. "A family and a country."

"Wait a minute. We already know you're John David Madsen, you already had both a family and a country, so cut the bullshit."

"That's not true," Pete replied. "When I met Marcia Riggs, I was a man without a country, a man who had cut all ties with the past and with my family. Marrying Marcia gave me both. I owed her for that, no matter what. It's a debt I can never repay."

"You paid, all right, bud," Kramer said under his breath. "You paid through the nose, and when you got tired of paying, you got rid of her."

"I didn't," Kelsey said, half rising in his chair. "I did not!"

Suddenly there was an urgent pounding on the door to the interview room. Kramer turned and opened it. Uncertain of his welcome, the evening desk sergeant stood warily outside the door. "Excuse me, Detective Kramer, but . . ."

"I demand to see my client," said a confidently assertive voice. With that, Caleb Winthrop Drachman the Third stepped past the desk sergeant and Kramer and marched into the interrogation room as if he owned the place.

Cal Drachman, with his polka-dot bow-tied image is a young (thirty-five-year-old) rising star in Seattle's criminal defense circles. At least among those defendants who for some reason or other don't qualify for a public defender. Cal Drachman III is far too busy with his burgeoning practice and making a name for himself to ever consider working for free. You could rest assured that if Cal Drachman appeared in a case, someone was footing a considerable bill.

Cal stopped in front of Pete Kelsey and smiled down at him, holding out his hand.

"Cal's the name," he said pleasantly. His offhand demeanor made it seem as though interrogation-room introductions are entirely ordinary. In his kind of work, maybe they are.

"One of my partners is an old friend of your father-in-law's. He and Belle wanted me to come see how you're doing."

"Fine," Pete said, "but . . ."

"Are they treating you all right?"

"Yes, but . . ."

"Good. Glad to hear it. Glad to hear it."

While he had been speaking to Pete Kelsey, he had been smiling warmly, but now, as Drachman turned back to us, the smile disappeared.

"I've only just now been called in on this case. Naturally, there'll be no more questions until I've been allowed to consult with my client. What are the charges?"

Drachman knew as well as we did what the charges were, but he wanted to hear it from our own lips. He wasn't going to stand for our skipping any of the required steps or empty gestures.

"Desertion from the United States Army," I said.

"And when did this alleged desertion take place?"

"March of 1969."

"My goodness, that's some time ago," Drachman said, shaking his head. "Over twenty years. Surely the Army isn't still interested in pursuing this after all these years."

"We've alerted the CID down at Fort Lewis," I told him. "Someone from there will be in touch to let us know what to do next."

Caleb Drachman smiled. "So that's all then? I mean those are the only charges against my client at the moment?"

"So far."

"Very good. What's your name?" Drachman asked, looking at me through stylishly thin-framed horn-rimmed glasses.

"Beaumont," I responded. "Detective J. P. Beaumont."

"Very well, Detective Beaumont." He frowned and scratched his head. "You're in Homicide, aren't you?"

"Yes."

"But my client isn't charged with any homicide, isn't that also correct?"

"Yes."

"Good. Bearing that in mind, I'm sure you'll agree with me that since there's nothing more serious against my client than this twenty-year-old desertion beef with the Army, then it's perfectly feasible for Mr. Kelsey here to attend his wife's funeral tomorrow afternoon. I've been given to understand that those are his wishes."

"I don't agree with anything of the kind," I began, but Cal Drachman cut me off before I could go any further.

"Excuse me, Detective Beaumont. He has not been charged with anything more serious than this. It's water under the bridge. I believe there's a good chance that the Army will decide to drop the charges altogether. If that happens, it wouldn't look very good if you had decided to keep him from attending his own wife's funeral, now would it? Now, I think that would seem downright criminal."

Cal Drachman shook his head sadly and waved me aside. "You go on, now. I want to consult with my client. I'll let you know when he's ready to talk to you again. He won't be meeting with you without me, is that understood?"

In the old days, when I was a kid and played cops and robbers with the kids on my block, there weren't any lawyers in the game. Nobody would have stood still for being a lawyer; you were either a good guy or a bad guy. Some days the good guys won and some days the bad guys did.

I wonder if things are different now, if nowadays when kids play that game, there aren't some who actually want to be lawyers. If not, they're missing a good bet, because these days, it's the lawyers who call all the shots.

WE HAD SENT PETE KELSEY BACK TO THE JAIL AND WERE almost ready to go home when Richard Chambers and his mother showed up around seven. Richard was a lean, handsome kid with a short, military-style haircut and ramrod-straight posture. When we had last seen Charlotte Chambers, she had been weeping uncontrollably in the reception area of the medical examiner's office. If I expected a next-of-kin interview with a still-weeping widow, however, I was in for a big surprise. Charlotte Chambers wasn't crying anymore. She was mad as hell.

"It's all those women's fault," she raged. "I know it is. It's their wickedness that caused Alvin's death. He should have done something to stop them. When he didn't, God punished him, plain and simple."

"Now, Mother," Richard crooned, patting her shoulder soothingly and trying to steer her away from the subject, but Charlotte Chambers wasn't about to be placated or diverted.

"You know it's true. If you ignore evil, it sneaks

into you and starts eating at your own soul. That's what it does, you see. Alvin was infected by the evil around him, by the godlessness around him. That's why he's dead."

"When did he tell you about this?" I asked, trying to move away from her aimless tirades and extract some useful information. "About the two women, I mean."

"I don't know exactly. How would I remember a thing like that? I didn't write it on the calendar. He probably knew about it long before he mentioned it to me. He wouldn't have done that if I hadn't heard him praying about it. Alvin always prayed aloud, you see. It's a habit he sort of got into being a pastor and all, and I sort of got in the habit of listening. Me and God. Whenever Alvin set about praying, me and God were always both listening away, Him up there and me in the other room."

"Did he tell you how he found out about them?" Kramer asked.

Charlotte shook her head. "Nope. He never did."

I considered this whole line of questions and answers distasteful. I didn't like delving into someone's private prayer life, asking questions of a third party over what Alvin Chambers had wrongly believed was a confidential conversation between him and his God.

It soon became apparent that no matter what questions we asked, Charlotte, like cagey politicians being interviewed on talk shows, always came back to the answers she wanted to give, to her private agenda. No doubt she had handled the newspaper reporters the same way, but they somehow hadn't connected with the idea that Charlotte was several tacos short of a combination plate. They had reported her every word in grim detail. As a result, Erin Kelsey and her grandparents were reaping the whirlwind of Marcia's indiscretions.

Given a choice, I much prefer interviewing killers to interviewing bigots, and I soon found myself agreeing with Alva Patterson's noncomplimentary opinion regarding her former pastor's widow—no matter what sins poor Alvin Chambers might have committed during his lifetime, he had deserved better than Charlotte.

Finally, giving the interview up as a lost cause, we escorted Charlotte and Richard Chambers downstairs to the crime lab, where we asked them to examine the shoes and trousers that had been removed from Pete Kelsey's garage early that morning.

Richard declined and hung back, but Charlotte knew just what to look for. She reached into the front pockets of the trousers and pulled them inside out.

"It's Alvin's," she announced confidently and at once.

"How do you know?" I asked, and she showed me the pockets. The seams at the bottom of both pockets had come undone, and both had been mended— with a series of staples stuck through the cloth.

"Alvin always fixed his pants himself," Charlotte told us. "And he always did it this way. I don't sew, you see. My mother never taught me."

Apparently Alvin's mother never taught him either, but he had figured out a way to get the job done.

The shoes were tougher. Charlotte studied them for some time without being able to make a decision.

They were the right size, but other than that, there were no identifying marks on which to form an opinion. I told her that was all right. Besides, I had every confidence the crime lab would be able to figure it out from trace evidence without the need of a separate identification from a family member.

I turned to Kramer. "Any more questions?" He shook his head. "Why don't you take your mother home then, Richard," I suggested. "She probably needs the rest."

The truth of the matter is, we were the ones who needed a rest. Richard Chambers probably could have used a break as well, but Charlotte was his mother, and he was stuck with her.

I dragged myself home on a bus. The weather was definitely warming, but I was too tired to pay much attention. I let myself into my apartment thinking I'd have a long, quiet evening all to myself, but that wasn't to be.

The blinking red light on my answering machine tells me how many messages are waiting. This time it wasn't too bad—there was only one light flashing when I finally arrived home around eight o'clock that night. As I played the tape back, the voice I heard belonged to Ron Peters.

"Call as soon as you get home," he said. "I'll come right up."

Noting a certain urgency in the tersely worded message, I called back right away. Ron Peters, without either Amy or the girls in tow, showed up at my door a scant three minutes later. I peered up the hallway toward the elevator lobby to see if anyone else was coming with him, but he was definitely alone.

"This isn't a social call?" I asked.

"Hardly."

Peters wheeled himself over the threshold into the apartment. I had been in the kitchen pouring myself a seltzer. I offered one to Ron, but he shook his head and led the way into the living room, where he parked his chair next to the window seat. That particular spot offers a panoramic view of Puget Sound, which, even at night, teems with lighted ferries, tugboats, and other shipping traffic.

I reached to turn on a light, but Peters stopped me. "Leave it off," he said. "We can see outside better this way."

The light stayed off. I settled comfortably into my old leather recliner, which creaked under my weight. "So what's up, Ron?"

"You want the good news or the bad news?" he asked.

"Good," I said. "If I have a choice, I always want the good news first."

"I've located the kid behind the bomb threats."

That grabbed my attention. My second wind blew in full force. "Hot damn, Ron! That's not good news, that's great news. Who is it?"

"That's the bad news," Peters returned grimly. "His name's Todd Farraday."

The name was indeed bad news, bad enough to take my breath away. There may have been lots of other Farradays living in the Puget Sound area, but I knew of only one for sure, a lady named Natalie Farraday, who happened to be Seattle's newly elected mayor.

"He can't be any relation to . . ." I began, but Peters cut me off.

"He is," Ron said. "He's fifteen years old and Her Honor's only son."

I whistled under my breath. "No wonder the case was under wraps. Let me guess. He was doing the threats. When mama-san figured it out, everybody down the line got their marching orders to keep it quiet, and everybody played ball, right?"

Peters nodded. "That's right, everybody, up to and including the media. But then, Natalie Farraday's been a media darling since she first ran for city council. If this had been her opponent's kid, you can bet it would have been a different story.

"The way I heard it was that once Her Honor found out what he was up to, she was so pissed that she's kept him under virtual house arrest ever since."

"How did you find all this out?"

"I've told you over and over, Beau, it doesn't hurt to become friends with a reporter every once in a while. There are times when they really can help."

"Why did he make the threats, and how?"

"How is the easy part," Peters replied. "They live up on Kinnear, just a few blocks west of Queen Anne Avenue. So it was no trouble at all to scoot down to the school district office, do the dirty deed, and then make tracks for home again. As to why, I wouldn't even hazard a guess."

"What you're saying is that this was done just for the hell of it by some stupid punk who can't even spell?"

"Actually, that's the funny part. According to what I can find out, Todd Farraday is now and always has been an honors student. That's one of the reasons his mother was able to convince everybody that, except for the glass breakage, it was nothing more than an innocent prank. She's already paid for the broken windows, by the way."

"False reporting of crimes is a crime, not a prank," I said.

"Unless your mama's the mayor," Peters returned.

We sat there silently for several moments, watching two slow-moving ferries lumber past each other as they approached the Coleman dock.

"Chances are he has nothing whatever to do with my homicides, then."

The idea that the bomb threats and the murders were somehow connected had always been a long shot, but it had been *my* long shot and it hurt to have to give it up.

"Probably not," Peters agreed.

Again we were silent for a time. "But wouldn't you like to tweak him a little?" I asked. "Just for the hell of it?"

In the gloom of the darkened room, I saw Peters' ghostly face turn in my direction. "What do you mean tweak?"

"Actually, I mean scare the living shit right out of him, make him think we've connected him to something that his mother won't be able to hush up or fix. Having a homicide detective turn up on his doorstep might light a fire under that little jerk's privileged ass."

"Now, Beau," Peters cautioned. "Let me remind

you, his mother *is* the mayor, duly elected by the people of this city."

I grinned back at him through the darkness. "That in itself will make the look on his face worth the price of admission."

"It could also get you fired."

"That's all right. Think about it. There's a certain justice here, Ron. You know as well as I do that some of the guys go down to the Central District and bust kids for a hell of a lot less than false reporting. The way I see it, if I scare the shit out of this spoiled creepy kid over something he *didn't* do, it'll even the score a little. What do you think?"

"Is my answer on or off the record?" Peters asked.

"Jeez, they've already taught you the finer points of PR double-speak, haven't they? It's off the record, Ron; now, tell me."

"I think it's a hell of a fine idea. I only wish I could be there to see it."

"Want to ride along? Maybe I'll go right now. You said he lives just up the hill." I started to get up and then stopped. "Wait a minute. I can't do that, not without having his actual address."

"I just happen to have it right here," said Ron Peters with a grin. "What are we waiting for?"

Down in the garage, Peters heaved himself into the rider's side of the low-slung 928. Once he was inside, I loaded his chair into the hatch. It stuck out some, but I fastened it in with a collection of bungee cords. With the hatch open, however, it was going to be a mighty cool ride.

The engine roared to life as soon as I turned the key in the ignition. It was none the worse for all its storm-enforced rest. By now the streets were pretty much clear. We drove up Queen Anne to Kinnear with no difficulty.

Had the Farradays' house been on the north side of Kinnear, it would have been impossible for Peters to be in on the interview, because all of those houses seemed to have a minimum of fifteen to twenty steps leading up to their front doors. The Farraday house, however, was on the downhill side of the street.

It was a huge, old-fashioned brick place with four white columns lining the front porch. With the exception of a single step leading up onto the porch, it was a straight shot from the street into the house.

I brought the chair around from the back and helped Peters back into it. Once settled, he looked at the house appraisingly. "I don't think Natalie Farraday ran for office because she needed a job," he said. "Now tell me this. What do we do if the mayor happens to be at home?"

"Punt," I declared with a grin. "Punt and run like hell. Every man for himself."

CHAPTER 23

As it turned out, the mayor wasn't home after all. Todd Farraday himself—a bespectacled, pimply-faced, sallow-skinned, long-legged kid—answered the door. He opened it only a cautious crack and peered outside.

"Who are you?" he asked.

One look at this nerdy wimp, standing there in his ratty T-shirt and jeans and his equally ratty and untied high-tops, told me that he wasn't exactly what his mother had in mind when she brought her supposed bundle of joy home from the hospital fifteen years earlier.

"We're police officers. Are you Todd Farraday?" I asked, holding out my card.

"Yeah. Whaddya want?"

"I'm with Homicide, Todd. I'd like to talk to you for a few minutes."

"Homicide. What do you want to talk to me about?"

"A case I'm working on."

He backed away from the door, and a breeze pushed it open in front of us. "Wait a minute, I don't know anything at all about that."

My statement had been innocuously general, but his immediate denial was damagingly specific. I was instantly on the alert. "You don't know anything about what?" I demanded.

Realizing too late that he had inadvertently let something slip and trying to hedge his bets, Todd Farraday shrugged his shoulders. "I don't know," he said miserably in an unconvincing whimper. "I mean, I wasn't even there."

"You weren't where?"

"At the school district; that's what you're talking about, isn't it? You think I'm connected to those school district murders because of what happened last fall, but I'm not. I swear to God. My mother doesn't let me out of the house at night now, and I don't sneak out anymore, either."

"Is your mother home?" I asked.

Todd Farraday shook his head. "No. She's at a meeting down in Olympia. She won't be home until tomorrow afternoon. But don't talk to her about this, please. She'll kill me. She really will. She said that if I got into any more trouble of any kind, she'd send me to a military school in New Mexico. In Roswell. I was in New Mexico once," he added mournfully. "I hated it."

We were still standing on the porch. Todd had backed away from us across the polished hardwood floor of the vestibule.

"I think we need to talk about this," Ron Peters asserted quietly. "Can we come in?"

Todd looked at Ron Peters, and his eyes narrowed. "Wait a minute, haven't I seen you on TV?"

Peters nodded. "Probably. I work in Media Relations."

"You're not going to put this in the paper or on the news or something, are you? My mom would die, she'd just die, and so would I!"

"Todd, we just want to get to the bottom of this," Peters said reassuringly. "Could we come in please? It's cold out here, and we're letting all the warm air outside."

"I guess," Todd answered warily. "Come on in."

He stood there watching as we made our way inside and closed the door behind us. I looked at him hard. "I didn't tell you what case we were working on, Todd, but you guessed which one right away without having to be told. How come?"

He shrugged his shoulders again and turned sullen. "I dunno."

"You do know," I insisted, "and you're going to tell us."

"Wait a minute. You can't make me tell you anything. I know my rights."

I turned to Peters. "I guess we could just as well go then. We'll come back later on after his mother has time to make arrangements for an attorney to be present."

Todd Farraday's stricken face paled visibly. "Aw shit! Don't do that, please. I already told you. I didn't *do* anything. I wasn't even out of the house that night, and the guy who was . . ."

"What guy?"

"Just a guy, that's all. A friend of mine. He's the

one who told me about it, after it came out in the papers. He wanted to know what he should do. I mean, like he thought I had some kind of experience, you know?"

"What did he tell you, Todd?"

"He was skiing, late at night, and he wasn't supposed to. Jason got these new skis for Christmas, see, and he wanted to try them out. But his mother said later. They're going up to Whistler sometime this month, but the snow was here that night, and Jason didn't think it would hurt anything."

I remembered then, the ski trails imprinted in the snow in front of the school district's office the morning after the murders. Criminals working under the cover of night sometimes make the mistake of assuming it's still the old days, when kids used to go to bed and stay there once their parents turned out the lights and locked the doors. Nowadays, the lights go out—and so do the kids, without their parents' knowledge or consent.

More often than not, the kids themselves are up to no good, but having extra eyes on the nighttime streets when they aren't expected has worked in my favor on more than one occasion. A surge of excitement went through my body when I realized this was going to be another.

"Your friend Jason saw something?" Peters prodded gently.

Todd Farraday nodded. "And he asked me what to do about it, but he got in trouble the same time I did for sneaking out, and I told him to forget it."

"Did he tell you what he saw?"

Todd shook his head. "I wouldn't let him. I didn't want to know."

"What's Jason's last name?" I asked.

"Don't you understand? If I tell you, he's going to get in trouble again too. His mother probably won't even take him to Whistler. She'll end up telling mine, and I'll be in trouble anyway."

"Where does he live?" Ron Peters asked. "Around here someplace?"

Todd nodded. "A few blocks away. It's not far."

"Supposing you call him and tell him we're here. Tell him we want to talk to him. We need his help, but we don't want to get him in any more hot water. Tell him we'll do our best to keep it a secret from his mother. You two can make up a story that you need to get an assignment from him or something, can't you?"

Todd looked back and forth between us indecisively. "Prob'ly," he said. "At least I could try. Wanna come on into the living room and sit down?"

Obligingly, Ron Peters wheeled himself toward the arched entrance to the living room. The unthinking words were barely out of Todd's mouth when he realized what he'd said. Todd Farraday may have been a spoiled young punk, but he still had some vestiges of good manners left. His face flushed beet red.

"Sorry," he said, hurrying out of the room. "I'll go call Jason."

A full-length oil portrait of Natalie Farraday hung over the marble-manteled fireplace. She was a handsome woman, rather than a beautiful one, posing against a tree trunk. I was standing there admiring the painting when Todd came into the room and stopped beside me.

"Jason'll be here in a few minutes. He told his mom he has to return my Axis and Allies game."

"This is your mother?" I asked, knowing the answer but asking anyway.

Todd Farraday nodded.

"Did you want to hurt her? Is that why you did it?"

"I already *told* you, I had nothing to do with . . ."

"I'm not talking about the murders, Todd, I'm asking about the bomb threats. Why'd you make those calls? Why'd you throw those rocks through the windows?"

"But aren't I supposed to have my attorney . . ."

I turned on him savagely. "Don't give me that shit. You already know you've beaten the system. You know good and well I won't be able to touch you for that, but I deserve an answer, and, by God, I'm going to get it."

Suddenly Todd Farraday's eyes filled with tears. He sidled away from me and sank down sobbing on a nearby ottoman. "You don't know what it's like having a mother like my mom, a mother who always wants you to be perfect, who always says you have to set an example. The other kids, except for Jason, were all the time making fun of me. I just wanted to be one of the guys, you know what I mean? I just wanted to be treated like everybody else."

"But you *weren't* treated like everybody else," I countered roughly, wanting to rub his nose in it. "Your mother got you off!"

"I know," Todd Farraday responded bleakly, star-

ing down at his empty hands. "And that wasn't
fair, either. I wanted to be treated like any other
kid, but she said I'd better keep my mouth shut because having that on my record would wreck my
life."

Todd paused and looked up at me for the first time
since he'd dropped onto the ottoman. "It all back-
fired," he added, "and the other kids still make fun
of me."

The doorbell rang, and Todd got up to answer it,
walking with his shoulders slouched. God help me, I
couldn't help feeling sorry for him, too. Maybe quit-
ting drinking was turning me into some kind of
sentimental slob.

Jason Ragsdale was another scrawny kid, an over-
grown pup whose body had yet to grow into his feet.
He too was wearing the same teenage uniform of
ragged clothes and untied, ratty high-tops. These
kids didn't live on the pricey side of Queen Anne because they were poor, but you sure couldn't tell that
by looking.

"This is them," Todd said unenthusiastically. "I
told 'em you'd tell them what you saw."

Jason Ragsdale shuffled uncomfortably from foot
to foot. "I didn't see all that much, really. I mean,
I could have been mistaken."

"What did you see, Jason?" I asked, handing him
my card. "This could be very important."

He nodded and bit his lower lip. "If I hadn't almost
run into her, I wouldn't have seen it. That's why my
mother said no skiing in the city. She was afraid
I'd hit somebody, and I almost did. It scared me to
death."

"Tell us exactly what you saw," Peters urged. "Try not to leave anything out."

Jason shrugged and shook his shoulder-length locks. "I had been going up and down Fourth because there wasn't much traffic there, and I almost ran into her. She came out of the parking lot and was walking up the hill. I didn't know anyone was there. I flew past when she was right by the school district office, and I think, no, I'm sure, she had a gun in her hand."

"A woman?" I asked.

"No. Not a woman really. She wasn't very old, I mean not much older than me. She was wearing one of those knit caps, so I couldn't see her hair, but she was young, I know that much. I saw the gun, just in a flash, you know, as I went by. I told myself I was mistaken, but then, a few minutes later . . ."

He stopped dead in the middle of his story, swallowing hard, unable to continue.

"A few minutes later what?"

"I heard it go off, the gun, I mean. I pretended at first that it was just a backfire and that it didn't mean anything, but I was scared and I went right back home. Then in the morning, when I saw all the cop cars . . ."

"Why didn't you come forward before this?" I asked.

"Dunno. I was scared, I guess. More of my mother than anything else."

"Would you be able to recognize her if you saw her again?" Ron Peters asked.

Jason Ragsdale ducked his head and drew a line across the rug with the toe of his leather high-tops. "That's just it," he whispered. "I think I have."

"What do you mean?"

He reached into his hip pocket and pulled out a wadded piece of newspaper, which he straightened across the knee of his jeans before he handed it to me. "This was in the paper today," he said, pointing. "That's her. At least I think it is."

I looked down at the clipping from the *P.-I.* Staring back at me was a poor reproduction of Erin Kelsey's senior high school picture.

"You're going to have to tell your parents, Jason," I said at once. "If it turns out that you're an actual eyewitness, there'll be depositions to take, court appearances. Your parents will have to know."

He nodded. "It's all right," he said gruffly, his changing voice cracking under the strain. "I mean, I get mad at my parents all the time too, but I could never shoot 'em."

"Fortunately for society, most people can't," I said. "Most people come up with other, more civilized, ways of dealing with their problems."

For the next half hour, I went over in detail everything Jason Ragsdale could remember about the night of the murders. He was good on everything but the times, because he wasn't sure what time he had left the house. It was close to eleven by the time I finished the interview and he headed for the door.

"I'd better get going," he said. "I got school tomorrow."

"Will you tell your parents?" I asked. "It would probably be better if they heard it from you first."

He nodded. "I will."

"As soon as you do, I'll want to talk to them as well."

"How come? They didn't see anything."

"No, but you did, and the woman you saw may come back to this neighborhood looking for you. After all, you can link her to the scene of the crime at the time the murders took place. Your parents may want to take some precautions for your own protection."

"You mean she might come back looking for me?" Jason's eyes grew wide.

"That's right."

"Shit, man. I never thought of that. I'll tell 'em. First thing in the morning."

Jason Ragsdale got up and started toward the door but stood there before it indecisively for a moment, shifting back and forth. He seemed suddenly very young and unsure of himself, a kid thrust out into a world where bogeymen, or women, as the case may be, were free to roam the earth.

"Would you like a ride home?" I offered.

He was too damn macho to admit to wanting a ride. "No. I'll be all right." With that, Jason Ragsdale hustled out into the night, pausing long enough to peer around cautiously before stepping off the porch.

As I watched him go, I was grateful that, for this one time at least, Jason Ragsdale had been where he wasn't supposed to be when he wasn't supposed to be there. And I was also thankful that despite all that, and even despite the bomb threats, Jason and Todd probably weren't such bad kids after all. Maybe in the long run there was some cause for hope.

And then I remembered Erin Kelsey, and I wasn't so sure.

"Are you psychic, or just plain lucky, or what?" Peters asked with a dubious shake of his head when he was once more seated in the 928 and I had finished loading his chair into the back. "I don't understand how you did that."

"How I did what?"

"Managed to figure out there was a connection between the bomb threats and the murders when no reasonable connection existed. How did you tie them together?"

"Pure dumb luck," I laughed, "because it wasn't exactly scientific, and it certainly wasn't the kind of connection I expected. Just you wait. In a couple of years, Tracie and Heather will be sneaking out in the middle of the night too."

"Like hell they will," Peters muttered determinedly. "Not my kids."

"I believe those come under the heading of famous last words," I told him. I'm equally sure those weren't words he wanted to hear.

A thoughtful silence followed. "You never suspected the daughter, did you?" Peters commented finally.

It was true. The idea that Erin Kelsey might be our killer still rocked me.

"No," I replied. "Never. That one came as a bolt out of the blue, although . . ." Suddenly a portion of Andrea Stovall's message came back to me.

"Although what?" Peters asked impatiently. "Don't leave me hanging in midsentence like that."

"Andrea Stovall. When she called down this morning and talked to Kramer to tell him she was leaving town."

"What about it?"

"She told him Erin Kelsey had called to warn her that her father was on the loose and might come looking for her."

"Nice kid," Peters said. "Sounds like she's trying to pin the rap on her daddy and buy him a one-way ticket to Walla Walla."

"That's the thing. She sure doesn't look the part."

"Looks can be deceiving, Beau. Where was she late Sunday night?"

"According to what her father told us, Erin had left for school in Eugene much earlier in the day. Sometime during the early afternoon, I think."

"That may be what she *told* him," Peters reasoned, "but since we have an eyewitness who puts her at the scene of the crime much later in the evening, she must have lied to her dear old dad. It's that simple. Did anyone say whether or not she and her mother quarreled while she was home for vacation?"

"Not that I know of."

"Have you gotten any other readings that things weren't okay between mother and child?"

"Not a glimmer," I answered. "Not from Pete Kelsey, Maxwell Cole, or the grandparents, either. The only thing I can figure is that Erin somehow must have learned the truth about what was going on between her parents and decided to get involved."

"And what exactly *is* the truth about her parents?" Peters asked. "Try to look at it through her eyes. First she finds out that for years her sainted mother has been messing around with other women on the side. Next she learns that her father isn't who or what he always said he was. I mean to tell you, this kid's world is flying into a million pieces, and where the hell does that leave her? Think about it."

"Up shit creek?" I suggested. "Lost? Angry?"

"All of the above," Peters responded. "Every damn one of them."

By now we were back in the parking garage at Belltown Terrace. I followed Peters as he deftly maneuvered his chair into the small confines of the P-3 elevator lobby and pushed the *UP* button.

"You want to stop by the apartment for a few minutes? Amy says there's just enough leftover New Year's eggnog to divide three ways. I'm talking straight eggnog here," Peters added with a smile.

I shook my head. "Thanks but no thanks. I think I'll pass. It's been a helluva long day."

Peters got off on seventeen, and I rode on up to the penthouse thinking that at last I would be able to crawl into bed and get a good night's sleep. That was not to be.

When you're up to your eyeballs in a case, it hardly ever is.

CHAPTER 24

IN THE APARTMENT, MY ALL-TOO-DUTIFUL MESSAGE-counting light was blinking furiously—six in all. A full deck. I was tempted to ignore the machine and go straight off to bed, pretending I'd never seen it, but I'm a detective, and I was working a case. In the end, I caved in and listened.

As soon as I began playing back the messages, I was glad I did. They were from two very different people, neither one of whom I would have expected to call me voluntarily—Andrea Stovall and Erin Kelsey.

The first was from Andrea Stovall. It gave her name and number, and that was all. I put the message playback on pause and returned Andrea's call before listening to any of the other messages. I tried dialing the number, only to be told that I had to dial a "one" first. That time the phone rang and was answered immediately.

"Semi-ah-moo," a cheery voice answered. "May I help you?"

"I'm calling for Andrea Stovall," I said.

"One moment please."

The phone rang and was answered on the second ring. "Hello?" Andrea Stovall said uncertainly.

"Detective Beaumont, Mrs. Stovall," I said. "You left word for me to call."

"I hope you don't mind me calling you at home. Doris—Doris Walker—gave me your card after the meeting. It was nice of you to leave one for me, considering the way I acted, but I was scared to death. My first thought was to run away. But now that Pete's in jail, I've been trying to figure out what to do. When I made up my mind to talk to someone from the police, I called Doris at home and she gave me your number."

"It's fine for you to call me at home, Mrs. Stovall, and don't worry about how you got the number," I said, short-circuiting an explanation that threatened to go on forever. "What can I do for you?"

She took a deep breath. "First, tell me the truth. He is in custody, isn't he? They couldn't report it on television if it weren't true, could they?"

"Is who in custody?" I asked, playing dumb. I knew good and well who she meant.

"Pete Kelsey. It said on the five-o'clock news that he had been picked up for questioning early in the afternoon."

"That's true, Mrs. Stovall. He is in custody. For the time being."

"What does that mean—for the time being? He's a killer, isn't he? You're not going to let him out again, are you?"

"Mrs. Stovall," I said patiently. "We're in the process of gathering information. It's important that we be able to speak to witnesses, and when they disappear on us . . ."

"I didn't mean to," she said hastily. "Disappear, I mean. Really I didn't. We're having the conference here later this week, and I thought it might be wise to come up early . . ."

"Mrs. Stovall, let's not pussyfoot around. You left word with Detective Kramer this morning that you were going out of town because you feared for your life, that Erin Kelsey had called you and warned you that her father was gunning for you."

"That's absolutely correct," Andrea Stovall returned. "She called early this morning."

"How early?"

"Five-thirty. Five thirty-five, actually. I looked at the clock when the phone woke me up."

"What did she say?"

"She was terribly upset, sobbing into the phone. I wanted so badly to go over to the house and take her in my arms, but I couldn't. I just couldn't."

I should imagine not, I thought. I said, "Tell me what she said."

"That there were terrible things in the paper this morning, things about her mother and me, and that Pete was coming after me."

"And you believed it was true?"

"Absolutely. After the other night, wouldn't you? As soon as I got off the phone, I packed a bag and came up here. I'm not the kind of person who takes chances."

"Aren't you?" I said.

There was a distinct pause and a distancing in her voice. "What does that mean?"

"Evidently things had gone along smoothly for years with whatever private arrangement the three of you had made. Who made the decision to change them all of a sudden?"

"Nobody."

"Nobody?"

"That's what I said. Nobody. Nothing was changing. Pete didn't care what Marcia and I did as long as nothing jeopardized the appearance of their marriage. He didn't want anything to upset Erin or Marcia's parents. And neither did Marcia."

"But I thought . . ."

"You thought what? That Marcia was going to come out of the closet and the two of us live together openly? She made a bargain with Pete Kelsey years ago. She never would have broken her word, and I wouldn't have asked her to."

"But somebody wanted him to think she would."

"What do you mean?"

"Somebody called him on the phone that night and told him she was leaving him."

"For me?" Andrea asked. "They lied." She added firmly.

"Were Alvin and Marcia friends?"

"No."

"Lovers then?"

"You haven't been paying attention."

"Did you and Marcia have a 'usual place'?"

I heard Andrea Stovall's sharp intake of breath. "How did you know about that?"

"Did you?" I insisted.

"Yes. We'd meet for lunch. In the Center House or by the International Fountain."

"Did you ever meet there on weekends?"

"No," she said. "We never did."

That meant that there was a chance that the note we'd found under Alvin Chambers' shoe was a plant, a note from another time that had been placed there to make the scene appear even more incriminating.

"This must be a nightmare for the family," Andrea Stovall said, "for George and Belle and especially Erin, and yet she was thoughtful enough to call."

"You're sure it was her?"

"Of course I'm sure."

"Did she say it? This is Erin?"

"She didn't have to. I know her voice, even when she's crying, and besides . . ."

"Besides what?"

"She called me Auntie Andy. Erin's the only one in the whole world who calls me that. The only one."

"Did you tell her where you were going?"

"No."

"Did she ask?"

"No. Why?"

I was thinking about the crumpled likeness of Erin Kelsey in Jason Ragsdale's sweaty paw. "Don't," I cautioned. "Don't tell anyone at all where you are, is that clear?"

"You think I'm still in danger, even though Pete's locked up?"

"You could be, Mrs. Stovall. I don't want to take any chances."

"Right," she breathed. "I understand. I'll be very careful."

"Is that all?" By now I had had to reset the *PAUSE* button a half dozen times in order to prevent my machine from continuing to play the messages.

"There is one more thing," she answered uneasily.

"What?"

"What happens if Pete Kelsey's crazy?"

"That's something a court of law would have to decide. Why, do you think he is?"

"Maybe."

"Why?"

"Because when I went looking for Marcia Sunday night, when I went into her office, he'd taken all her stuff."

"Stuff?"

"Her pictures. Pictures of Erin when she was little. Their wedding picture. There must have been half a dozen or so. They've been in every office Marcia's ever used at Seattle Public Schools. That's the first thing I noticed that night when I went looking for her. It was almost as though someone had removed everything that had made the office hers alone. If that's not crazy, I don't know what is."

"I don't know either, Mrs. Stovall, but let me sleep on it, and I'll be back in touch with you tomorrow. Will you be coming down for the funeral?"

"Should I?"

"No," I said. "I can't order you to stay away, but I think it could be dangerous for you if you showed up."

"That's what I thought too," Andrea Stovall conceded. "At the time of the funeral tomorrow, I think

I'll just go out on the beach here and say good-bye privately. That would probably be better for all concerned, don't you think?"

"By all means."

The next time the *PAUSE* button clicked, I let the much-interrupted messages continue playing. The next five were all from Erin Kelsey.

They started calmly enough with a very businesslike: "This is Erin Kelsey. Uncle Max just left. Please give us a call as soon as you can. We'd all like to talk to you about it."

The second message sounded a little more urgent, more uptight: "Erin again. Grandma and Grandpa had to leave. They wanted me to come home with them and spend the night, but I told them I wanted to wait here for your call."

By the third message, she was in tears, mumbling, difficult to understand. "Detective Beaumont, please call me back no matter how late you get in. I've got to talk to you right away."

In the fourth, her voice was empty and hollow, "Me again," and the fifth a desperate plea. "Please call me back. Please!"

When I dialed the number, she answered before the end of the first ring. "Detective Beaumont?" She sounded frantic.

"Yes, Erin, it's me. What's wrong?"

"I've got to talk to you. Right now. Tonight. Where can I meet you?"

"Erin, tell me what's wrong."

It was hard to connect that young, wretchedly distraught voice with the personality of a killer, but I couldn't afford to ignore Jason Ragsdale's eyewitness warning. In my own best interests—and in hers as well—I had to assume that Erin Kelsey was both dangerous and unpredictable.

She paused, drawing a ragged breath. "Everything's wrong, Detective Beaumont. My life is wrong. My mother is dead, my father is in jail for killing her. I don't understand it. I want somebody to explain it to me. I want somebody to tell me what's going on. Maybe I'm going crazy. Is that possible?" She ended the series of questions with an uncontrollable sob.

Unfortunately, if what Jason Ragsdale had told me was the truth, insanity was one of the few ideas that made absolute sense. While Erin continued to weep into the phone, I tried to strategize.

I've learned a few hard lessons over the years. One of the toughest is that, for me personally, a damsel in distress usually proves to be a one-way ticket to disaster. This time, for a change, I paid attention and refused to blunder in where angels fear to tread.

"Erin," I asked. "Do you have a car there at your house?"

"A what?" she asked, sniffling.

"A car. Transportation. Can you drive somewhere and meet me?"

"No. My car's still in Eugene. The police towed Mom's Volvo away, and I haven't seen Daddy's Eagle anywhere. Can't you come here?"

"No," I told her firmly, "I can't," although "won't" was a whole lot closer to the truth.

"Call a cab then," I continued. "Do you know the Doghouse Restaurant at Seventh and Bell?"

"I think I can find it. I've been there before a couple of times, after football games."

"The cabbie will know where it is even if you don't. Meet me there in fifteen minutes."

"What if I can't get a taxi that fast?"

"Get there as soon as you can. I'll wait."

For the second time that evening, I headed out into the night.

CHAPTER 25

I WAS SEATED HALFWAY DOWN THE WALL WHEN ERIN Kelsey rushed headlong into the restaurant. Once inside, she paused uncertainly and glanced around the room before catching sight of me and hurrying toward my booth.

If anything, she looked far worse than she had sounded on the phone. Her hair was pulled back into a ragged, disheveled braid of some kind. The yellowish light in the restaurant is never flattering to anybody, but her face, contorted by emotion, looked downright ravaged.

I made a quick strategic evaluation as she came closer. She was wearing jeans and a bulky, sheepskin-lined jacket, which she made no move to take off. Over her shoulder dangled a good-sized purse. Both of those factors meant that concealed weapons were a definite possibility. I kept my guard up.

"Can I get you something?" I asked as she slid into the booth opposite me. "Coffee, tea—a drink?"

She shook her head. "No. Just water."

I kicked myself then, remembering Max's description of Erin as a devout Mormon. But even at the time, the irony of the thought struck me. Devout? If Erin followed the rules about what she could and couldn't drink, wouldn't she also follow some of the others as well, some of the more important ones like "Thou shalt not kill," and "Honor thy father and mother"? Maybe Erin Kelsey was one of those people who scrupulously obeys all the little rules and ignores the big ones.

Unfortunately, I couldn't tell which she was, and both our lives hung in the balance of my making the right choice. I needed information.

"What's the matter, Erin?" I asked, trying to sound calm and reassuring, trying to win her confidence.

She shuddered and made a supreme effort to pull herself together.

"Who am I, Detective Beaumont?"

"What do you mean who are you?"

"You know what I mean, and don't pretend you don't. Uncle Max told us tonight that you're the one who found out Kelsey isn't my father's real name. So if his name isn't real, that means mine isn't either."

"Erin, what Max told you is true. Your father had evidently lived under an assumed name the whole time you've been growing up, but . . ."

"And why do other people know so much more about me than I do myself?" she interrupted.

Without warning, she opened her purse and reached inside. I readied my body to repel an attack, but instead of a weapon, she withdrew a long, narrow envelope and sent it spinning across the table toward me. I managed to grasp it in midair like some errant Frisbee before it could sail all the way to the floor.

"What's this?"

"Look at it," she ordered.

I did. It was a birth certificate. Erin Kelsey's birth certificate, saying she'd been born in St. Michael's Hospital in Toronto, Canada, to a couple named Peter B. and Carol Ann Kelsey.

"What about it?"

A flood of tears overflowed the long lashes and coursed down her cheeks. "It's a fake," she mumbled almost incoherently. "It's nothing but a fake."

"A fake? How can that be?"

"I don't know how. All I know is that it is."

"And how did you find that out?"

"Mr. Drachman. He told me earlier tonight that if he could do anything at all to help, I shouldn't hesitate to call, so I did. He said he had a friend or two in Toronto, and maybe they could do something even though it wasn't regular office hours."

"And he did?"

Erin nodded. "According to the records in Toronto, no Erin Kelsey was born in St. Michael's Hospital. I don't even exist. Maybe I'm a figment of my imagination." She giggled, almost hysterically. "I must have made myself up."

I studied Erin warily. She was treading dangerously close to the edge, her story sketchy and difficult to follow.

"You're satisfied that this is a fictitious birth certificate?"

She nodded. I had heard through the grapevine that

Caleb Winthrop Drachman, much like Ralph Ames, was no slouch when it came to getting things done regardless of regular office hours or bureaucratic red tape. And again like Ralph, international boundaries were not necessarily a problem. I had no doubt that his verification or lack of it was accurate.

"But what made you think to have someone check, Erin? Most people take their birth certificate's word for it. You didn't come up with that idea all on your own. Did Max tell you to do it?"

"No. The phone call."

"What phone call?"

"At first I thought it was the regular kind of call we've been getting, people calling to tell us how sorry they are, that kind of thing. This woman asked for me by name, so I thought it was someone who knew us, probably some friend of my mother's from work. Except it wasn't."

"Who was it?" I asked.

Erin paused and took a deep breath. "I don't know. As soon as she knew it was me on the phone, she said that she knew who I really was and then she started laughing, and she wouldn't stop."

"She laughed?"

"You should have heard her. But between times, she would say things. Like she said that if I was smart, I'd check out my birth certificate. I asked her what was wrong with it, and she said that was for her to know and for me to find out, and then she laughed some more."

Pete Kelsey had mentioned something about a laughing telephone caller, too. As I recalled, the person who had given him the wonderful news about his wife and Andrea Stovall had laughed like hell the whole time she was lowering the boom. What was going on?

"Was that all?"

"No. Not exactly." Erin paused, her eyes meeting mine, and a new urgency came into her voice, "She said that she had a message for Pete Kelsey. For me to tell him that he hadn't lost everything, not yet, but that he would and that when he did, it would be . . ."

"Would be what?"

"I'm trying to remember her exact words. "Payment in kind. That's it."

"What's that supposed to mean?"

"I don't know, Detective Beaumont," Erin said. "Do you?"

I shook my head.

Erin shivered again, holding her arms close to her body. "If you could have heard the way she said it . . . It was like listening to an icicle. Or a knife. She wasn't laughing anymore, not then. It was a threat, and it scared me to death. I mean, my father may have done something wrong, but I'm afraid for him. I'm really afraid. He's all I have left."

For the first time in the whole process, I was afraid, too.

"Did you recognize the voice?"

"No."

"So what did you do then, after you got off the phone?"

"What would you do? After what Max had just finished telling Grandma and Grandpa and me? I wanted to know for sure, to find out for myself, so I got out the birth certificate. Dad always keeps his important papers in the rolltop desk in his study. It looked all right to me, but I decided to call the hospital and check. They wouldn't tell me anything, so then I called Mr. Drachman. I already told you what he found out."

"Does he know you're talking to me?"

Erin shook her head. "No. In fact, he told me not to, said that whoever it was couldn't hurt my dad as long as he was in custody, but Mr. Drachman didn't hear her," Erin said. "He didn't hear the way she sounded."

By then, Erin's teeth had begun chattering so badly she could hardly talk.

"How about a glass of warm milk?" I suggested. "Maybe that would help."

Tears came to her eyes. "That's what my mother used to give me, but yes, I'd like that."

When the waitress brought the steaming cup, Erin held the thick white mug between her hands as if hoping to leach some of the heat out of it.

"Tell me about my father," she said.

"I will, but first, let me ask you this. What time did you leave for Eugene on Sunday?"

"Right after lunch. Around one or one-thirty. Why?"

"Did you go straight there?"

"We stopped once for a break in Woodland, at the Oak Tree. That's about halfway."

"Did you say 'we'?" I asked, sitting up and taking notice. It hadn't occurred to me before that Erin might have an alibi.

"Yes. My roommate was with me. Her name's JoAnne McGuire. Why?"

"Your father didn't mention you had a rider."

"He probably forgot JoAnne was riding along. Her parents live in Tacoma, so I picked her up on the way down I-5. Dad never even saw her."

"What time did you get into Eugene?"

"Almost nine. There was a big eight-car pileup on the freeway in Portland, and that held us up for quite a while. By the time we made it back to our apartment, they said on the radio that it was snowing hard in Portland, so we were just barely ahead of the worst of the storm."

If that was the case, it would have been impossible for Erin to reappear in Seattle two or three hours later. It didn't make sense.

"How can I get in touch with this roommate of yours?"

Erin jotted a number on a piece of paper from her purse and shoved it across the table toward me. "I'm sure she'll be at the funeral tomorrow if you want . . ."

Suddenly the anguished look returned to Erin's face. "Wait. Will my father be there too, Detective Beaumont? At the funeral? Mr. Drachman said he might be."

"He might," I agreed, "but I can't tell for sure yet. Why?"

"I know Grandma and Grandpa want him there desperately, but I don't. I don't ever want to see him again. What would I say? How could I face him? If he lied to me about who he is, he must have lied to my mother as well. And why should this woman on the phone know more about me than I know myself?"

"Does your father have any enemies?"

"No," she answered quickly, but then her eyes

misted over again. "But then, what do I know about it? Nothing, nothing at all."

She set the cup down and leaned back into the bench. I knew she was exhausted, and my heart went out to her. Possible killer or not, right then Erin Kelsey was far too worn out to be a danger to me or to anyone else.

"Come on," I said. "I'll take you home."

But she shook her head stubbornly, defiantly, as though the milk had somehow revived her and given back some of her spunk. "Oh no, you don't. You said you'd tell me about my father."

"I thought Maxwell Cole already told you."

"Uncle Max is a friend. He didn't want to tell us any more than he absolutely had to. You're not a friend, Detective Beaumont. You're a cop, and I want to know the truth. What did my father do? It must have been something terrible, something awful, for him to hide out all these years. Tell me. I've got a right to know."

"I can't tell you any more than Max did," I told her.

"Why not?"

"Because I haven't been able to find out anything else. According to what we've been able to piece together so far, your father was a smart kid who went off first to West Point and then to Vietnam. At some point in time, something snapped and he made up his mind to never go home again. His own parents died in South Dakota years later without ever knowing for sure whether their son was dead or alive."

"So he lied to them too?"

I nodded, and that was all Erin was willing to

hear. She stood up abruptly. "Did you say you'd give me a ride?"

"Yes."

"Take me home then, Detective Beaumont. I can't listen anymore."

I stopped briefly at the cashier's desk before following Erin outside, where I found her waiting for me on the sidewalk. She seemed to be listening to the muted city noises around her. Just then, far away from us, the chill night air was split by the haunting wail of a distant siren.

"My car's right over here," I said.

I led her around the mounds of ice and snow that still littered the parking lot. Once on the street, I headed the 928 for Denny Way and Capitol Hill. Erin was silent now, huddled miserably against the door. I knew that no matter how much it hurt, I had to ask her one more question.

"Did you talk to your Auntie Andy today?" I asked.

"Don't call her that!" Erin hissed. "She's not my aunt. I thought she and my mother were friends. And no, I didn't call her. I'll never speak to her again."

Once more, Erin Kelsey began to cry, weeping silently, her face covered with her hands. "I feel like such a fool," she mumbled through her tears. "Such a stupid, stupid fool!"

We drove on in silence. If Erin hadn't called Andrea Stovall, who had?

As we made our way down Broadway, I had to pull over to the side to wait for a blaring fire engine to rush past. Several blocks away from Boston, we began to encounter a whole phalanx of emergency vehicles—aid cars and fire trucks as well as police patrol cars.

By then, looking up the side of the hill, we could see the eerily leaping flames of a house fire surging into the air. Although the flickering glow was visible, the house itself was still hidden from view.

"It's my house, isn't it?" Erin Kelsey breathed with despairing certainty.

"No," I said. "Don't be silly."

When we reached the intersection of Tenth and Boston, a uniformed officer was diverting traffic away from the area. I stopped and hopped out of the car. I flashed my badge in his face and asked him if he knew the address of the burning house.

"Thirteen fifty-two East Crockett, I believe that's the address," he said.

Shock must have registered on my face.

"You know the house?" he asked.

I nodded.

"There's not much more I can tell you," the patrolman said sympathetically. "One of the guys from the fire department came by a few minutes ago and told me it's a total loss. No victims so far, but they're still looking."

"Arson?" I asked.

"Probably, but that's not official yet."

"I know."

I turned away from him and went back to the car to give Erin Kelsey the rest of the bad news. At least she hadn't been there when the fire started, although I felt sure that whoever did it had meant her to be.

Realizing that gave me pause. If Erin hadn't been meeting with me at the Doghouse when the fire broke out, she too could be dead, joining her mother as a youthful statistic in the realm of violent crime.

Suddenly I knew, knew in my gut, that whoever had called Pete Kelsey with the lie about Marcia and Andrea moving in together, whoever had called Erin and told her about the phony birth certificate, and whoever had called Andrea to say Pete Kelsey was gunning for her—those three separate, sadistic phone callers were all one and the same person.

Whoever it was, this laughing Cassandra had predicted that Pete Kelsey would lose everything, that it would be payment in kind for something, some crime he had committed in the past.

So far, Pete Kelsey hadn't lost everything. Not yet. Not quite, but he had come close—very, very close—and at this rate, he still might.

CHAPTER 26

AT ONE O'CLOCK THURSDAY MORNING, I DELIVERED A stunned and ashen version of Erin Kelsey to her grandparents' condo on Queen Anne Hill. The mounting losses left Erin numb, speechless, and beyond tears. She fell into LaDonna Riggs' comforting arms, but her grandmother's murmurs of sympathy and outrage fell on seemingly deaf ears.

Belle Riggs led Erin back into the apartment while George, hands stuffed deep in his pockets, walked me back to my car. He seemed to want to say something, and I stood with the door open waiting for him to get around to it.

"Marcia wasn't perfect," he said at last, clearing his throat. "I mean, the things they said about her in the paper . . ." He paused awkwardly, and shook his head.

"Well, we didn't know for sure, although I guess I always suspected. Maybe Belle didn't—she's always been naive about those kinds of things—but I did."

He sighed, and walked away a foot or two, looking

off over the side of the hill at a lighted grain ship being loaded at the terminal below us. The night was still, and the noisy clatter from the grain elevator conveyor belts filtered up the hill to where we stood. The air was noticeably warmer now compared to the arctic deep freeze we'd been locked into for the better part of the week, but it was still chilly to be outside dressed in nothing but shirtsleeves, as George was. The old man, however, seemed totally oblivious to the weather.

"But Pete now," he said thoughtfully, "Pete's all wool and a yard wide. I couldn't have asked for a better son-in-law. He's always been real steady—a good provider, a good worker, an old-fashioned family man—things that my daughter didn't necessarily appreciate. Don't get me wrong. I'm not saying he's perfect, and I didn't approve of him working in that bar off and on the way he did, but Pete's not Mormon, and I made it a point to stay out of his business. That's probably one reason why we always got along."

George Riggs' voice cracked with emotion, and he aimed a swift kick at a chunk of hardened snow and ice that had been pushed to the edge of the driveway.

"What are you telling me, Mr. Riggs?" I asked.

"I don't care what his real name is, Detective Beaumont. No matter who he is really or what he may have done in the past, no matter how it looks, I *know* Pete Kelsey never killed my daughter. He may have been provoked, but he didn't *do* it. He wouldn't. Do you understand?"

"Mr. Riggs . . ." I began, but he ignored me.

"What about the fire?"

"What about it?"

"You haven't said, but it wasn't an accident, now was it? It had to be deliberate. Pete replaced every inch of wiring in that house and brought it up to code. It was all old knob-and-tube stuff, and fixing it was one heck of a job. So now he's lost his wife and he's lost his house. What's next, and who's doing this? Who's got it in for Pete Kelsey?"

"I don't know."

"But it does look like somebody's out to get him?"

"Yes, Mr. Riggs, it is beginning to look that way, and I'm on my way down to the jail to find out what I can from Pete Kelsey himself. In the meantime, how about if I get the Patrol Division to send a unit up here, just to keep an eye on things."

"You mean a police guard?"

"Listen, Mr. Riggs, I don't want to alarm you unnecessarily, but there's already been one attempt on Erin's life tonight, and there could as easily as not be another."

"No," George said, shaking his head stubbornly. "No way. I believe I can handle it myself. The women are already upset enough as it is. Having police guarding the house would upset them that much more."

I left him then, but on my way down to the King County Jail, I called the Patrol Division anyway. Just to be on the safe side. They told me they'd handle it and be discreet.

In the jail, Pete Kelsey/John David Madsen was being held in Ten South, a cellblock reserved for suspects arrested in connection with serious crimes.

I waited in the small, pie-shaped cinder-block interview room while one of the night guards brought the prisoner from his cell. He arrived wearing his orange jumpsuit jail uniform and looking as though he'd been rudely awakened from a sound sleep.

"Detective Beaumont, what are you doing here?"

"I came to talk to you, Pete. I've got some bad news."

He blanched. "What is it? Has something happened to Erin?"

"No," I said. "Erin's safe for the moment, but your house isn't. It burned to the ground earlier tonight. I'm here to ask you the same question your father-in-law put to me a few minutes ago. Who's got it in for you?"

Kelsey dropped onto the only remaining plastic chair. "The house is gone?"

"Yes, completely, but Erin's all right. I took her to her grandparents' house. Fortunately, she wasn't home when the fire started. If she had been . . ."

"She'd be dead," Kelsey finished.

I nodded.

"Was it arson?" he asked.

"Probably, although right now it's officially known as a fire of suspicious origin. Once the arson investigators get inside, I'm sure they'll find all the telltale signs. So tell me, Pete, who did it?"

"I don't know. I can't imagine."

"Maybe this will throw some light on it. Erin had a call an hour or two before it happened, a threatening call from a woman who laughed all the while she was telling your daughter that you hadn't lost everything yet, but that you would. Does that sound familiar?"

He looked at me, his electric blue eyes searching mine. "Laughing?" he asked.

I nodded. "Laughing and saying that what's happening is payment in kind for something you did to her. So who is it, Pete? Tell me."

"It must be the same woman then, but I've no idea . . ."

I was losing patience. "Look, let's not play games. Someone's out to get you, any way they can. So far your wife is dead and your home has been destroyed. If somebody's decided to beat you out of everything, the way I figure it, there's only one thing left for them to take away."

I saw the stricken expression on his face and knew I'd landed a telling blow. "Erin?" he whispered.

"That's right. Erin," I said. "So are you going to help me or not?"

"I'll try, but what can I do?"

"Think, man. Who's got it in for you?"

"I don't know. I swear to God, I don't know."

"You must. This is somebody with a major grudge. Maybe you're not proud of it, maybe it's something you never wanted to see the light of day, but it's not something you would have forgotten."

"Detective Beaumont, I don't have any idea . . ."

"Is it something you're afraid would be self-incriminating and could be used against you in a court of law? Would it help if I called Cal Drachman down here?"

"No, don't do that."

"Talk to me then. It's someone from years ago, someone who knew all about Erin's birth certificate."

Pete Kelsey's head snapped erect. "What about her birth certificate?"

"That it's a fake, just like your name."

"But how could someone know about that? Erin didn't even know."

"She does now. Tell me, Pete, what are you hiding? I've got to know. Erin's life is at stake. Unless I know the whole story, I can't help."

He stared at me, his Adam's apple bobbing up and down in his throat. I kept quiet, knowing he was verging on spilling whatever it was.

"She's not mine," he said at last.

"Who's not yours?"

"Erin. I stole her, or rather we both did. Marcia and I."

It took a moment for that to soak in. "You stole her? You mean as in kidnapping?"

"Not exactly. It seemed like the right thing to do at the time." He gave me an odd look, as though it was some kind of joke, but I wasn't smiling. "If you'd only seen what was happening . . ."

"You'd better tell me about it, Pete. From the beginning."

"Did you ever play much poker?" he asked.

"Not me. People tell me I've got an honest face."

Pete Kelsey smiled hollowly. "Not me. I've always been a good bluffer, too good, in fact. I bluffed my way into and through West Point. My father was only second-generation American, and he wanted me to go all the way to the top. He wanted me to be a general or head of the Joint Chiefs of Staff. That was his idea of the great American Dream, that a farm kid from Marvin, South Dakota, could rise to the top.

"I was good at target practice, and I was good at tests—academic, personality profile, you name a test and I could pass it with flying colors. But I didn't find out about killing until after it was too late. Oh, I could talk a good game, but I couldn't kill worth a damn. Once I was in Nam, I froze up. I couldn't pull the trigger, not even to kill someone who was out to kill me. And our guys were counting on me, leaning on a bent reed, so I managed to steer clear of actual combat and took off the first time I got a chance."

"Where did you go?"

He shrugged. "All over. I knew I could never go home. My father couldn't have stomached having a coward for a son. It was better that I simply disappear. That way he never knew."

Pete Kelsey stopped in the middle of his story and looked at me questioningly. "How is my father, Detective Beaumont? You must have talked to him by now."

"Your father's dead, Pete. Both your parents are. Years ago."

He swallowed hard and nodded. "Thank God. At least I won't have to face them." For a moment he buried his face in his hands. When he looked up, he seemed dazed. "Where was I?"

"You were telling about what you did after you left Vietnam."

He nodded. "I bummed around for a while, first in Asia and then later in South America. I wanted to come home, to the States, I mean, but I didn't dare. The closest I came was Mexico. I ended up tending bar in a little place in Baja called Puerto Peñasco."

"Where?" I asked.

"Gringos call it Rocky Point. It's sort of a poor man's Acapulco. Anyway, I was bartending in a little beachfront bar there. The guy who owned it thought having a gringo tend bar would pull in the money. That's where I met Chris McLaughlin."

"Marcia's first husband?"

Kelsey nodded grimly. "That worthless bastard."

"I thought they were in Canada. Is that where you met Marcia?"

"No, Marcia wasn't there. By then she was already back home with her parents. Chris was the only one I met, although that wasn't the name he was using at the time. I didn't find out his real name until much later."

"What was he doing there?"

"Buying drugs," Pete Kelsey answered. "Buying drugs, drinking too much, letting himself run off at the mouth. One day when he was half-drunk I heard him telling somebody that having the baby along made his work a piece of cake. He called her his little mule. He said he could put whatever he wanted in with that baby and carry it back and forth across the border with no difficulty because the *Federales* never searched her."

"His own baby?"

"That's right," Kelsey answered bitterly. "Chris McLaughlin was a nice guy. A helluva nice guy."

"So whose baby is Erin really if she wasn't Marcia's?"

"Chris McLaughlin and another woman's, Sonja, I think her name was. They all went to Canada together, but Marcia didn't know that Chris and Sonja were already married. The way I heard it, he had this fantasy about starting his own patriarchy—you know, the old one-man-many-wives routine? Except it didn't work out quite the way he planned. I think Marcia liked Sonja more than she did Chris, and I think she would have stayed if it hadn't been for the drugs."

"Both Chris and Sonja were into the drug scene?"

Pete nodded. "That's why Marcia came back home to Seattle."

"But you still haven't explained how you ended up with Erin."

"I knew from what I overheard in the bar that McLaughlin was there to pick up a load and take it back. He was only supposed to be there for a week or so. To make it look like an ordinary vacation, he hired himself a Mexican lady to take care of the baby and then he settled down to having a hell of a good time. He found plenty fun, all right, in all the wrong places. He disappeared and turned up three days later down on the beach with a knife stuck between his ribs.

"In the meantime, the baby-sitter, a cousin of the guy who owned the bar, came looking for him too. She was afraid what would happen to her if the cops found her with an Anglo baby with no father anywhere around. I think she was worried about kidnapping. She brought the baby and all her stuff to the bar, and while I was looking through the bags, in among the false bottoms, I found a stash of phoney IDs."

"Including one for Pete Kelsey?" I asked.

Pete nodded. "Pete and Erin Kelsey and my deceased wife. I also found a half-written letter to Marcia in an address book. From the sound of it, he had planned to assume Pete Kelsey's ID and disappear, from his drug connections and from Sonja as well."

"So you took the baby and the ID and came to the States masquerading as a Canadian citizen?"

"That's right. It was a ticket home and I used it. I thought, from the letter, that Erin was actually Marcia's baby, but I found out differently. She was as outraged as I was by Chris and Sonja using the baby to smuggle drugs, and between us we came up with the idea of getting married and keeping Erin ourselves. Marcia was the one who thought of letting Maxwell Cole believe he was introducing us and playing cupid. She worked behind the scenes and engineered my getting the remodeling job at Max's mother's house. He always took full credit for our getting together."

"And it made things seem like they were all on the up-and-up," I added.

"That's right," Pete said.

My heart went out to poor duped Maxwell Cole. He had spent twenty years taking credit for bringing Pete and Marcia Kelsey together without ever knowing how completely they'd played him for a fool. It made Erin's calling him "Uncle Max" seem pitiable rather than laughable.

"So you two set out to raise Erin as your own?"

He nodded. "Marcia and I made an agreement that we would stick together for Erin's sake, no matter what. It was like an old-fashioned arranged marriage, I suppose. We were both happy enough at first, but keeping that bargain got harder as the years went on, especially after Marcia met Andrea. It never occurred to me that Marcia would really run off with her."

"Maybe she wouldn't have," I suggested.

Pete Kelsey frowned. "What do you mean?"

"According to Andrea Stovall, the woman on the phone told you a lie. She said Marcia had no intention of breaking her word to you."

Pete Kelsey's hard jawline went slack. "You mean she told me that just to make trouble?"

"And it worked, too, didn't it?" I returned.

He thought about it a moment before nodding his head. "Yes," he answered bleakly. "I guess it did."

I took a second to try to organize my thoughts. "You're sure Chris McLaughlin died in Mexico?"

"Yes, I saw him. I didn't stay around afterward, though. I took Erin and headed for the border."

"What happened to Sonja?"

"I don't know. We never made any inquiries for fear of drawing attention to ourselves. Marcia went ahead and let her parents get the annulment, even though she already knew Chris was dead. The rest you know."

"Where did they live in Canada?"

"In a commune-type arrangement someplace up near Nanaimo on Vancouver Island in British Columbia."

"You're sure this Sonja was Erin's real mother?"

"As far as I know."

"What was her last name?"

"McLaughlin too. He was a bigamist. That's how come Belle and George were able to get an annulment without any problem. Actually, they probably didn't even need to, but they wanted to wipe the slate clean."

"And Marcia couldn't have shown up with an annulment, a clean slate, and a baby."

"By then Marcia had already had a hysterectomy. Erin was our only chance at having a child of our own." Pete paused for a moment and seemed to mull an idea.

"Are you thinking that maybe after all these years, Sonja has come after us and she's behind all this?"

"It's possible."

"Would she hurt her own daughter?"

"I don't know."

"Can you stop her? I don't care what happens to me as long as you keep her from hurting Erin."

"We'll try," I said.

Pete Kelsey reached across the table and grasped my hand, squashing it in a powerful grip.

"Do more than try, Detective Beaumont," he pleaded. "Once Erin finds out about all this, she may never want to see me again, but I can't stand for her to be hurt anymore. Maybe she isn't my real daughter, but she's the only daughter I've ever had."

Extricating my hand, I went to the door and signaled the guard that I was ready to leave. I was about to walk out when I remembered about the fruits of Detective Kramer's search warrant and something else Andrea Stovall had mentioned.

"Who else besides you and Erin had keys to your house?"

It was a closing-the-barn-door question in view of the fact that the house had burned to its foundations, and if there hadn't been so much other pain winging around the room, it might have been a painful one, but I asked it anyway, and Pete answered without hesitation. "We're the only ones, other than Marcia."

"Were Marcia's keys in the envelope of personal effects from Doc Baker's office?"

Pete Kelsey frowned. "No, I'm sure they weren't."

"And the garage door opener?"

"No. That wasn't there either. Isn't it still in the car?"

"I don't know. I'll have to check. One last thing, Pete." Calling him John David Madsen right then would have amounted to kicking him while he was down.

"What's that?"

"Did you happen to take the pictures of you and Erin that were hanging in Marcia's office?"

"Why, no. Aren't they still there?"

"No. I'm sorry to say they're not."

That was the final straw. "I was hoping we still had those," Pete Kelsey croaked. "I was hoping there was something left, but it's gone, isn't it? It's all gone."

And he buried his face in his arms.

I left then, quickly, feeling my own eyes fill with tears.

I was still sniffling when I reached the front desk. "I must have caught a cold somewhere," I said to the guard, who eyed me quizzically as I stopped long enough to sign out.

Maxwell Cole's goddamned cold, but of course, it wasn't a cold at all.

CHAPTER 27

BY THREE O'CLOCK IN THE MORNING, I WAS BACK AT MY desk with an armload of work to do and with no intention or need of going to sleep. I called Paul Kramer, and got him out of bed. He squawked at first, but he listened intently to what I had to say. By the time I finished briefing him, he was up and moving and ready to go looking for Sonja McLaughlin, wherever she might be, because Sonja McLaughlin sounded like someone with a lifetime's worth of axe to grind. And that was just the kind of person we were looking for.

I certainly don't like receiving middle-of-the-night calls, and I don't like making them either, but I made some that morning. I rustled up the crime lab folks who had inventoried Marcia Kelsey's car. Sure enough, no keys and no garage door opener had been found in the vehicle.

It took some fast talking to get past JoAnne McGuire's mother in Tacoma, but finally Erin's roommate came on the phone. In a voice still thick with sleep, she corroborated Erin's story of their drive to Eugene the previous Sunday—complete with departure time, the stop in Woodland, the wreck in Portland, and the snowstorm by the time they finally reached Eugene.

That meant Jason Ragsdale was mistaken when he said he had seen Erin Kelsey at the school district office sometime Sunday night, but I was convinced Jason, the unauthorized midnight skier, had seen someone, someone who looked like Erin Kelsey and carried a gun. If she wasn't Erin, who was she?

I hit the wall about five-thirty and went home for a shower and a nap. By ten that same morning I was back in the office and in as good a shape as could be expected for someone running on three hours of sleep, five cups of coffee, and one hot shower. Coming into my cubicle, I was delighted to find a fully recovered Big Al Lindstrom sitting there big as life with his huge feet propped on his desk, munching complacently on an apple.

"Welcome back. Are you ever a sight for sore eyes," I told him.

"You mean you missed me?"

"Are you kidding? I've been stuck working with Paul Kramer the whole time you've been gone."

Big Al grinned. "You think you've had it bad. With Molly sick, I had to do all the cooking. I musta lost ten pounds. By the way, there's a message there for you. Came in about five minutes ago."

The message, written in Big Al's barely decipherable scrawl, directed me to call Caleb Drachman's office—at once.

"Good morning, Detective Beaumont," Drachman

said cordially, once I had him on the line. "I've got a court order for you. I'm sending a copy over by messenger service to make sure you have it. Since the funeral starts at two, I wanted you to have plenty of time to make arrangements."

"What arrangements?"

"They're all listed in the court order."

"Look, Mr. Drachman, how about saving us both some time and telling me what it says?"

"Certainly. I've talked to the criminal investigations folks down at Fort Lewis. They say the only charge pending against my client is one of simple desertion. They're running an all-volunteer Army these days, and they don't want any bad PR. In addition, I've talked to Mr. Kelsey several times this morning. From what he's told me about what happened last night, I would assume the chances of your charging him in connection with his wife's murder are somewhat less today than they were yesterday."

"Forget the buildup, just tell me what I need to know," I put in impatiently.

At once Caleb Drachman switched gears. "My client's wife's funeral is today. He is to be released long enough to attend the services, and it is to be done as unobtrusively as possible. Do I make myself clear?"

"Completely," I replied.

"Good. There are to be no restraints and no obvious police presence. The judge ordered one guard. I suggested someone from the jail, but for some reason, Mr. Kelsey would like you to be there. I personally am strongly opposed to that idea, but I have agreed to abide by my client's wishes, if it's all right with you, of course," he added.

If I'd had any lingering doubts about the kind of legal-beagle, Open-Sesame power Caleb Winthrop Drachman could wield, they were totally removed. On those occasions when prisoners are allowed to attend funerals, they usually do it under the aegis of a conspicuous police guard, and they do it wearing restraints—if not leg shackles, then at least handcuffs concealed under a raincoat.

"Well?" Drachman prompted.

"Well what?"

"Will you do it or not?"

"I'll do it," I said.

"Good. I'll call down to the jail and tell them to have him ready by eleven. The visitation starts at noon. I'm sure he'd like to be there for that as well."

"Do what?" Paul Kramer asked, walking into the cubicle and picking up part of what was being said. He asked his question while Drachman was still speaking.

I hung up the phone. "Take Pete Kelsey to his wife's funeral," I said. "Drachman got a court order."

"It figures," Kramer said. "Better you than me, though. I hate funerals. By the way, I've got some bad news for you."

"What's that?"

"We're barking up the wrong tree. Sonja McLaughlin didn't do it."

"How do you know that?"

"She's dead. I've been in touch with the authorities in B.C. Sonja McLaughlin died about two years ago in an insane asylum in Vancouver."

"She went crazy?"

"Evidently. I've got the Royal Canadian Mounted Police looking for next-of-kin who might be able to tell us more. They say there's a daughter but that she's dropped out of sight."

"Her daughter's been out of sight for twenty years," I put in dryly, but Kramer shook his head.

"No, there's another one, two years younger than Erin. That's the one they're looking for."

"And maybe we should be too," I said, feeling that sudden surge of excitement that says you're finally on the right track.

Kramer didn't pick up on it immediately. "What do you mean?"

"Remember? The Ragsdale kid identified Erin Kelsey as being on Queen Anne Hill even though we have a witness that puts her in Eugene at the very same time. And Andrea Stovall thought it was Erin on the phone, calling to tell her that Pete was on the warpath. After all, if the two girls have the same mother and father, maybe they look alike and sound alike as well."

Kramer considered that for a moment and then nodded slowly. "You could be right. I'll keep after it."

Kramer left, and Big Al rolled his eyes in my direction. "What did you do to Kramer? He's almost civilized."

"For the moment," I said, gathering up to leave. "But it's probably not permanent."

"Where are you off to?"

"Back home to get my car and then to the jail to pick up our prisoner."

"And take him to a funeral? Have fun, but it doesn't

sound like a picnic to me," Big Al said, settling comfortably back in his chair. "It's the kind of duty I'm happy to miss."

I picked up the 928 at Belltown Terrace then drove back down to the jail. I waited in the lobby while a guard brought Pete to the sign-out desk. He arrived there looking somber and subdued. Someone, probably George Riggs, had seen to it that despite the fire, Pete Kelsey had a set of suitable clothing to wear to Marcia's funeral.

"Where to?" I asked.

"Magnolia. The church is on McGraw. Do you know where it is?"

I nodded.

We went out to the car without saying anything more until we were well under way. "Tell me about Sonja McLaughlin's other daughter," I said.

Pete seemed surprised. "Daughter? What other daughter?"

"One who must be two years or so younger than Erin."

Pete Kelsey shook his head. "I never knew about another daughter. She must have been born after Marcia left Canada and came back to Seattle. What about Sonja? Where's she?"

"Dead," I told him. "She died about two years ago."

"So it's not her then," he said forlornly. "We're still not getting anyplace."

"What about the daughter? Could she be behind all this?"

"What would Sonja's daughter have against me or Erin, either one? How would she even know we exist?"

"Beats me," I said, and Pete Kelsey lapsed into silence. "By the way," I added, "before we get there, I want to establish some ground rules. You don't go anywhere without me and vice versa. Understand?"

"Yes," Pete replied. "I understand."

Overnight Lars Jenssen's promised blanket of warm, moist air had moved in from the ocean, breaking the cold snap's icy grip. Now, as we stopped in front of the church, heavy rain began to pelt the ground around us, visibly melting the snow as it did so.

I had never attended a Mormon funeral before, and I didn't know quite what to expect. Clearly it was going to be very well attended. Although we got there a good two hours before the funeral was scheduled to start, the church's parking lot was already full of cars, with the overflow spilling up and down both McGraw and Condon.

I was searching in vain for a parking place when Erin Kelsey came dashing out from under the protection of the entryway and motioned for me to pull up directly behind the hearse.

As soon as the car stopped, she wrenched open the passenger-side door and pulled Pete Kelsey out. Once he was upright, she fell crying into his arms. "Daddy, Daddy, Daddy," she whimpered. "The house is gone. Completely gone. I've been so scared. I've missed you."

So much for her not ever wanting to see him again.

Over the back of Erin's head, I saw tears of gratitude well up in Pete Kelsey's eyes. This wasn't the time for him to tell Erin that the man whose real name she didn't know wasn't her father either. That would have to come later, much later, and I hoped to God I wouldn't have to be around to see it.

"Come on," Erin said suddenly, pulling away from Pete's embrace and leading us determinedly toward the church. "We're in the Relief Society room. Grandma and Grandpa are already there. So's the Bishop."

Belle Riggs came to the door to greet us. Like Erin, Belle drew Pete Kelsey to her and held him close. There were tears in her eyes as well, but a brave smile warmed her lips.

"Remember," she said to Pete. "She's just gone on ahead. We'll all meet again. Come on." She took Pete by the hand and led him into the room. "Let me introduce you to the Bishop."

That left me little choice but to follow along behind. The visitation and funeral that followed were unlike any I'd ever attended before. The music was stirring, uplifting, and the eulogy made it sound as though Marcia Kelsey was waiting on the other side of a door somewhere, marking time and waiting for everyone else to show up.

Maxwell Cole, serving as one of the pallbearers, listened to that, shook his head, and sniffled noisily. I don't think the idea of meeting Marcia Kelsey somewhere in the Great Beyond offered him much consolation.

When the graveside portion of the service was over, everyone returned to the church, where a women's group called the Relief Society served lunch. Standing with the family throughout the afternoon, I was introduced to everyone. I met JoAnne McGuire, Erin's roommate from Tacoma, and saw most of the school district people I'd met during the course of the investigation.

By four, it was beginning to get dark and things were winding down. It was almost time to take Pete Kelsey back to the King County Jail. I looked around the room for Erin, intending to tell her good-bye, but I didn't see her.

"Where's Erin?" I asked Pete.

He too glanced around the gradually emptying room. "I don't know. She was here a little while ago."

JoAnne McGuire overheard our exchange. "She's in the rest room, with her cousin," Erin's roommate told us lightly.

Pete's eyes met mine. "Erin doesn't have a cousin," he said warily.

JoAnne looked startled. "Why, of course she does. I left them there together just a minute or two ago."

"Where?" I demanded.

"Look," JoAnne said, pointing. "There they are now, just going out the door."

Sure enough, I turned just in time to see two women, arms linked together, slip out the front door.

"Erin, come back," Pete called, panic edging into his voice. If they heard him, they didn't stop.

I headed after them, racing for the door at a dead run. I didn't have to look back over my shoulder to know that Pete Kelsey was right on my heels.

CHAPTER 28

WE REACHED THE OUTSIDE ENTRYWAY JUST IN TIME TO see the taillights of a small, foreign-made car speed away from the curb half a block away. Rubber tires squealed on the rain-slicked street. It was them, had to be.

Without a word, I dashed for the 928, with Pete pounding behind me.

There are only two ways off Magnolia Bluff—one to the north, near Ballard, and one to the south, heading back toward downtown Seattle. The Magnolia Bridge soars high above Piers 90 and 91, stocked with multicolored ranks of newly imported Japanese cars.

Our quarry was headed south. I told Pete how to call for help on my cellular phone while I drove like hell.

I careened up Condon, hoping I could manage to hit Garfield before they did. Wonder of wonders, it worked! We were already stopped at the corner of Thorndyke and Galer when a yellow Datsun B-210 came skidding around the curve on Galer. I was pretty sure it was the right car, but I didn't dare ram them for fear it wasn't. Instead, I waited at the intersection until they went past.

Their faces were caught in the light from a street lamp, and I could see it was them. Erin was driving, with someone else leaning close beside her, watching for pursuers in the rearview mirror. Only after they flew past did I realize who the other person was, Jennifer Lafflyn, Ms. Jennifer Lafflyn, the antagonistic school district receptionist.

"I'll be damned," I muttered, swinging into the lane behind them, nearly forcing an oncoming driver off the road. "So that's who it is!" The other driver leaned on his horn.

"That's somebody you know?" Pete Kelsey demanded.

I was too busy driving to answer, afraid that if they once crossed the bridge, they'd lose us in the snarl of rush-hour traffic. I thought they'd hit the bridge and floorboard the gas pedal. Instead, just as they gained the entrance to the bridge, the brake lights came on, and the car skidded to a stop.

I was right behind them. It took every bit of skill I could muster to keep from rear-ending them. I did, but the guy behind, an old man in a Buick Regal, wasn't so lucky. He crashed into the back of my poor little Porsche. Metal crumpled and glass shattered. We were shoved in a smoking heap against the concrete rail of the bridge. Fortunately the rail held.

A quick glance in Pete Kelsey's direction told me we were both all right—stunned maybe, but not broken. The bent doors wouldn't open, but one of the windows had shattered and disappeared. We wiggled out through the empty opening.

I expected them to be long gone. Instead, the Datsun was still there, parked haphazardly on the shoulder of the bridge, lights still on and doors flung wide open. In the glare of the headlights, we could see two figures making for midspan of the bridge, lumbering awkwardly along together like Siamese twins joined at the shoulder.

"Stop!" I shouted after them, but they didn't pause, didn't even slow down.

Pete Kelsey tried his luck. "Erin!"

One of the runners seemed to stumble and stopped, pulling herself free.

"Daddy!" Erin screamed back. "Help me. Please. She's got a knife."

But just then Jennifer grabbed Erin from behind and spun her around. For a moment they struggled together, then Erin was once more being yanked forward, and once more we gave chase.

In midspan, the girls stopped again and swung around to face us. Jennifer was holding Erin with one arm across her neck while the other held a knife near her throat. Orange light from the sodium vapor lamps glinted off the blade.

"Don't come any closer," Jennifer warned, her voice tight and shrill.

An alert driver, coming from downtown, had seen the trouble and had stopped his car on an angle, effectively blocking both lanes. Behind him and behind us on the Magnolia side, honking horns blared from the building tie-up. A traffic helicopter circled far overhead. But the middle of the bridge was a rain-drenched, eerily lit no-man's-land with four people locked in a life-and-death struggle.

For several long seconds no one moved.

"Let her go," Pete Kelsey said softly but firmly. "Let Erin go."

"No. I won't," Jennifer answered stubbornly, stepping backward and dragging Erin along with her. "She's coming with me."

"Let her go!" Kelsey repeated.

Despite Jennifer's warning, Pete and I both took a cautious step forward. We were only ten yards or so away now, close enough to see the wild desperation on Jennifer's face and the abject terror on Erin's.

"Stay back!" Jennifer ordered.

Pete stepped forward again as though he hadn't heard her. "Why?" he asked. "Why are you doing this?"

Jennifer stared hard at him, her eyes focused on him alone. "To get even."

"For what? What did Erin ever do to you?"

Taking advantage of the byplay between them, I edged away from Pete's side so Jennifer wouldn't be able to see us both at the same time.

"Not her," Jennifer spat back at him. "You! You took everything we had. You left my mother pregnant with no husband, no job, no nothing."

"How could I?" Pete objected. "I never knew your mother. I didn't take anything."

We both inched forward again, closing the distance between us and the girls.

"You did," Jennifer insisted. "You killed my father, stole my sister, and destroyed my mother. She never got over it. Never! Not until the day she died. I was there, but it was always the other one she wanted. This one. The one she lost."

Jennifer tightened her grip on Erin's shoulder and shook her for emphasis while her eyes remained fixed squarely on Pete Kelsey's face.

"I didn't kill your father, Jennifer," he said gently, soothingly. "He died in a knife fight in Mexico with some of his drug-dealing friends. And Marcia and I kept Erin because we didn't want her raised by the kind of person your mother had become."

"Liar! They weren't like that, you know they weren't, and my father wasn't a drug-runner, either! He was a kind, wonderful, loving man. Mother said so. He would have given me anything I wanted if you hadn't murdered him. I saw the police report, I know what it said, but you're the one who did it, and that's the truth."

By now there was a distance of only five or six feet between us and the girls.

"What other fairy tales did your mother tell you?" Pete asked softly.

The question threw Jennifer Lafflyn over the edge.

"It wasn't a fairy tale!" she exploded. "It was the truth. You stole my future from me and gave it to your precious Erin. You gave her everything and left me with nothing. Now you're going to pay. Do you hear me? You're going to pay the same way I paid."

Pete Kelsey never lost his cool, never raised his voice. "How did you pay, Jennifer?"

"That's not my real name, but real names don't matter, do they?"

"How did you pay?" he repeated.

"I lost everything, and you will too. If you just

would have come into the office that night, the way I planned, it would have been all over, and it would have been just you and Marcia. You could have saved your precious Erin and your house, too. At least she would have had a place to stay, which is more than you left me, but now it's too late."

She started to laugh then, the same maniacal laughter both Pete and Erin must have heard before. It was chilling. Terrifying.

Suddenly she jerked Erin to one side and headed for the guardrail. I knew if she once reached it, we'd lose them both, that they'd fall to their deaths among the hundreds of parked import cars on Pier 91 far below us.

I leaped in from the side and grabbed for Erin's arm. As soon as my hand closed around her wrist, I dragged both of them back toward the centerline. For a long moment we hung there, caught in a desperate tug-of-war. I heard the sickening pop of joint and tendon and knew we'd dislocated Erin's shoulder. She yelped with pain, but even as she did, we tumbled back into the center of the roadway. I had managed to pry Erin loose from Jennifer's deathlike grip.

"Put down the knife, Jennifer," Pete Kelsey ordered quietly, calmly. "You need help. We'll get it for you."

"No," she said. "I won't."

Warily Jennifer backed away from him, swaying back and forth like some cornered wild animal, her eyes locked on him and him alone. One hand still held the menacing knife while the other lovingly caressed the guardrail.

"Daddy, be careful," Erin sobbed. "She's crazy. She'll kill you. She said she would."

Just then, Jennifer Lafflyn sprang forward, holding the deadly knife in front of her. Pete Kelsey jumped back and dodged to one side, but not quite fast enough or far enough. The knife plunged into his side and he crumpled to the ground.

Shoving Erin away, I went to help, but before I could reach them, Jennifer Lafflyn vaulted over the guardrail.

Her terrible scream keened up to us from the enveloping darkness. It was a long, long fall, and the piercing cry seemed to go on forever, ending with the sickening crunch of metal and explosion of glass as she crashed into the roof of one of the Nissans parked far below.

Jennifer Lafflyn died instantly, taking an unsuspecting thirty-five-thousand-dollar sports car with her, but for long moments afterward, echoes of her piercing scream reverberated off the walls of the bluffs around us. The gruesome sound of her going seemed to linger forever.

In my worst nightmares, I hear it still.

I'm sure I always will.

CHAPTER 29

THE DOCTORS AT HARBORVIEW HOSPITAL REMOVED Pete Kelsey's damaged spleen, and by nine o'clock that night we knew he was out of danger. George and Belle Riggs took Erin Kelsey, her shoulder bandaged and her arm in a sling, home with them. Nobody said much about Jennifer Lafflyn.

While I was at the hospital, Kramer had gotten a search warrant and gone through Jennifer's apartment. I wanted to wait up and see what he found, but I was too damn tired. I dragged the beat-up old body home and put it to bed.

The next morning, when I climbed out of bed, I ended up hopping on one foot. During the melee on the bridge, I had reactivated my bone-spur. It's hell getting old.

I was slogging my way through reports when Detective Kramer showed up. "Want to take a trip down to the evidence room and see the jackpot?" he asked.

"Good stuff?" I asked.

"Good enough," he returned. "Her real name is Julie McLaughlin, by the way. The Royal Canadian Mounted Police up in Vancouver came up with that late last night after you went home."

We went down to the crime lab, with Kramer dashing off ahead and me limping along behind. At Kramer's request, the evidence clerk brought out a stack of several boxes. The first contained half a dozen framed pictures—the missing ones from Marcia's office. On each, the glass had been hammered to pieces, and all faces in the pictures themselves had been totally obliterated by smears of red ink.

When we took the top off the next one, it contained nothing but wastepaper. "You brought the trash along?" I asked. "Isn't that being a little compulsive?"

"Some trash," Kramer said. "It's all Marcia Kelsey's. Notes, correspondence, grocery lists—things she tossed in her office trash can without thinking about them and which were rescued and studied by Julie McLaughlin as she was making her plans."

"So this wasn't something she dreamed up overnight."

"Hardly. She's been working on it for a long, long time with single-minded determination, probably since her mother died. Maybe since before her mother died. Look at this."

He held up a page from a phone book. It was old— yellowed and crumbling. It must have been at least ten years old. The name that was circled in heavy black ink was that of George F. Riggs, listed along with a Queen Anne address and phone number, not of the Riggs' new condo, but of their old address, the place where Marcia had lived as a child.

"This is how she tracked them down?"

"Evidently."

"I can see that it wasn't that hard to find them, since she had the name and address of Marcia's folks, but how did she end up working for the school district?"

Kramer smiled. "That's easy," he said. "Blackmail. She showed up at Marcia's office, threatened her with exposure, and told her she needed a job. I already checked that out with Kendra Meadows in Personnel. Marcia Kelsey was listed as a reference on Jennifer Lafflyn's job application. The other two names and addresses don't exist at all as far as I can tell."

Detective Kramer may be a pain in the ass at times, but in this case, he had done some astute thinking. I could finally see how it all came together.

"So she settled down to work for the district, and spent all her spare time spying on Marcia Kelsey and gathering information."

"And garbage," Kramer added. "There's a lot of damning stuff dropped into garbage cans these days. Here's something else."

He handed me a small, invitation-sized envelope. Inside was a thank-you card with a handwritten note that said:

Dear Alvin,

I can't thank you enough for all the help and advice you've given me about "the problem." You're right.

> *What they do isn't any of my business. That's be-*
> *tween them and God. He'll have to punish them*
> *for it.*
>
> *Jennifer*

The last almost made me laugh. "And in case God
forgot, she was fully prepared to take up the slack,
but from the sound of this, it seems like she and
Alvin Chambers were pals. Do you think she meant
to kill him?"

Kramer shook his head. "We'll never know for sure.
I think Marcia and Pete Kelsey were the real targets.
Chances are Chambers walked in on her when he
shouldn't have and she decided to incorporate him
into the program."

That made sense. It was one more piece in a foolproof recipe for posthumous character assassination.

There was a separate box filled with nothing but
clothing, and a final container with two items, a garage door opener and a set of keys.

"Marcia's?" I asked.

"According to the monogram on the key chain.
Too bad we're not taking this one to trial. You hardly
ever get a case with this much damning evidence. It
would be open and shut."

I disagreed with Kramer there. Wholeheartedly.
No matter what the evidence, murder trials are never
open and shut, and they always add immeasurably
to the pain of the people left alive. Pete and Erin
Kelsey, Belle and George Riggs, and Andrea Stovall
didn't need their names and lives dragged through any
more mud. They had already been through enough.

Back upstairs in my office, I filled out enough reports to choke even Sergeant Watkins. Kramer was going around the floor, thumping his chest and telling anybody who would listen what a great job we'd done. I didn't think we were all that slick. After all, Pete Kelsey was in the hospital with a knife wound, Erin's shoulder was dislocated, and my foot hurt like hell.

Around noon the insurance adjuster turned up to give me the verdict on the Porsche. She recommended that it be totaled, but I'm a sentimental slob and wanted a second opinion. Eventually she gave me a check and let me have the wreck towed to Ernie Rogers' garage on Orcas Island on the condition that if the rebuild job came to more than the check, the difference was coming out of my pocket. Fair enough. We'll have to see what happens.

About five that afternoon, just as I was getting ready to leave the office, I had a call from Maxwell Cole inviting me to meet him for tapas at a place called Café Felipe near Pioneer Square. Max sounded real low, and I figured he could use a little cheering up. Besides, I was in the mood for Mexican food, so I agreed to meet him.

It turns out, however, that tapas are Spanish, not Mexican. They could just as well have been Greek, for all I knew. There wasn't any of it that I recognized, but it was all delicious. In my frame of mind, liberal doses of garlic on everything were just what the doctor ordered.

I may have been wrong thinking Café Felipe served Mexican food, but I was right about Max. He was lower than a snake's vest pocket. Brooding over

everything he had learned about Pete and Marcia
Kelsey in the last few days, Maxwell Cole was still in
a world of hurt.

"How come Marcia never let on?" he asked plain-
tively. "How come she and Pete let me spend all these
years thinking I was the one who introduced them?"

"They needed you to help create their fictional
life," I told him. "And for twenty years, it worked.
Have you seen Erin?"

He nodded.

"How's she taking it?"

"All right, I guess. After all, Pete's the only father
she's ever known, and he almost got himself killed
trying to save her."

"Look, Max," I said, "you and Erin both have every
right to feel betrayed, but Pete Kelsey's always been
your friend, the same way he's always been Erin's
father. Right now he needs both of you in his corner.
Don't let what happened in the past rob you of the
present."

Max thought about it for a while, then nodded.
"You're right," he said.

Brightening a little, he added, "By the way, Caleb
Drachman called today and said he's arranging for
Pete to get a general discharge. At first the Army
said he'd have to come to California to be processed,
but considering the circumstances, they're sending
the processing to him here. By the time he gets out
of Harborview, he'll also be out of the Army."

"Good," I said, and meant it.

Having given Max a rousing little pep talk and
after loading up on garlic, I went off to an AA
meeting. While there, I started thinking about how

easy it is to hand out advice and how hard it is to take it.

A month later, at the end of my ninety meetings in ninety days, I left the Sunday morning breakfast group that meets up near Northgate. Driving my insurance-company loaner, I inexplicably found myself in the 8400 block of Dayton Avenue North.

It was one of those balmy January days, the kind that trick trees into blossoming and sucker crocuses into popping up out of the ground. During the intervening weeks since I had inadvertently stumbled on the name and address in the phone book, I had driven past the place several times, always thinking about Pete Kelsey and the family he had abandoned in South Dakota.

For a time I stood on the sidewalk examining the place. It was hardly more than a clapboard cottage, with shaded front windows and a roughed-in wheelchair ramp going up the two shallow steps onto the front porch.

I had driven past on numerous occasions, but this was the first time I had stopped. There was an old white dog lying on the front porch. She thumped her tail once or twice, but she didn't get up until I rang the bell, then she got up and limped over to the door. I guess she figured if I got in, she would too.

After I rang the bell, I stood there on the porch with my heart thumping wildly in my chest. I don't know what I expected. It was several moments before I heard anyone moving inside the house. At last the knob turned and the door opened.

I stood looking down at a bent-over little old lady. Over a cotton housedress, she wore a full-length apron, made from the same pattern my mother had always used.

"Yes?" she said, peering up at me through thick glasses.

I swallowed hard, unable to say anything. Then she stepped closer to me and studied my face.

"Why, Jonas!" she said.

I thought for a moment that she was calling to her husband, my grandfather, but then she reached up and grasped the lapels of my jacket.

"Jonas? Is it you?"

For a moment, my knees wobbled under me. No one had called me Jonas in the twenty years since my mother died. With a clawlike grip on my wrist, the old woman dragged me into the house. The dog shuffled inside as well.

In the doorway of the tiny living room sat a man in a wheelchair. One side of his face was frozen into a permanent grimace, but the resemblance between us was uncanny. I was, as they say, the spitting image.

The dog went over to the man and eased her head up under a useless, stroke-bound hand. The woman led me forward. My legs seemed made of wood.

"Jonas, look who's here. Can you imagine after all these years?"

My tongue was welded to the roof of my mouth, but the old woman was used to doing all the talking in the household. I don't think she even noticed.

"Your grandfather had a stroke two years ago," my grandmother was explaining unnecessarily, "so he doesn't talk much. I always told him you'd come someday, didn't I, Jonas? I told him I wouldn't go against his wishes and go looking for you, but that if you ever came here . . ."

She reached up with the hem of her apron, and wiped her eyes. It's hard to think of a wrinkled old lady in terms of radiant, but her transparent skin fairly glowed. In her aged features I caught echoes of my mother's much younger and almost forgotten face.

Laboriously the old man lifted one hand and began making mysterious motions with it. He seemed to be drawing a square in the air.

"Oh," my grandmother said. "You want me to get the box?"

There was an almost imperceptible nod from the man in the chair. The old lady bustled out of the room, leaving the two of us to examine each other in thick silence.

When she came back, she was carrying a box, an old-fashioned hatbox. It was so full that the cover wouldn't quite shut. The corners were held together with tape so old that it had turned brown and brittle.

She put the box on the dining room table and then came back and pushed the old man's wheelchair over to the table.

"Well," she said to me. "Are you coming or not?"

Obediently I followed them to the table and sat on the chair she indicated, watching with fascinated attention as she removed the cover from the box. It was full to the brim of newspaper clippings. The last, only three days old, was a *P.-I.* article discussing my court appearance as the investigating officer in a drive-by shooting.

For the next several hours we went through layer

after layer of yellowing, crumbling paper. It was like an archaeological dig through my life. My grandmother hadn't discriminated. It was all there, good and bad, honor roll listings the few times I made it as well as some of the occasional snide remarks from Maxwell Cole's column. It included a picture, yellowed and poorly printed, of my winning basketball shot in the Queen Anne High School gym years before. At the very bottom of the stack was an even-longer-ago shot of me and two other dazzled cub scouts shaking hands with Smokey the Bear.

Looking through that box of clippings was a peculiar and humbling experience. All those years when I was feeling sorry for myself because I was so alone, because I didn't have a family like other kids did, somewhere in Seattle a little old lady was hunched under a lamp, clipping newspapers and carefully hoarding whatever tidbits she managed to glean there.

Just thinking about it made a huge lump grow in my throat.

My grandmother fixed lunch for all of us. Patiently she fed thick, hearty soup to the old man before she ate her own. I stayed until three o'clock in the afternoon.

When it was time to go, my grandmother walked me out onto the porch. She stopped on the top step, and seemed to be searching for words. For a woman who had talked nonstop all day, I was surprised when she grew strangely quiet.

"Your grandfather and I grew up in a different world," she said finally. "Your mother was headstrong, willful. He wanted the best for her, wanted her to live by his rules. She wouldn't. She defied him, and he never forgave her for that. There was a terrible quarrel. He vowed to never let her set foot in this house again, and she didn't. You see, your mother was every bit as stubborn as he was."

She paused for a moment and wiped at her eyes with a corner of her apron. I recognized the gesture as another echo from the past. My mother used to do the same thing.

"I never went against your grandfather's wishes. That wasn't my place, so I never saw your mother again, either, but I did start keeping my box. My treasure chest, I call it. Two years ago, right after his stroke, a nurse pulled it out from under the bed and asked him what it was. I was afraid he'd make me get rid of it, but instead, he wanted me to read the stories to him, show him the pictures. Since then, he's wanted to look at it almost every week. Thank you for coming today, Jonas. It's an answer to my prayers."

With tears in my own eyes, I hugged her, held her close, then left her standing there on the porch. As I drove away, what had happened long ago between my mother and my grandfather no longer seemed important. A heavy but invisible burden had finally been lifted off my shoulders.

Lars Jenssen is right. Forgiveness *is* a two-way street. And it's good for you besides.

Don't miss a single one of *New York Times* bestselling author J. A. Jance's novels featuring Seattle private investigator J. P. Beaumont, whom *Booklist* calls "a star attraction."

UNTIL PROVEN GUILTY

"J. A. Jance is among the best—if not the best!"
Chattanooga Times

The little girl was a treasure who should have been cherished, not murdered. She was only five—too young to die—and Homicide Detective J. P. Beaumont of the Seattle Police Department isn't going to rest until her killer pays dearly. But Beaumont's own obsessions and demons could prove dangerous companions in a murky world of blind faith and religious fanaticism. And he is about to find out that he himself is the target of a twisted passion . . . and a love that can kill.

INJUSTICE FOR ALL

"J. A. Jance does not disappoint her fans."
Washington Times

It was a scene right out of a Hollywood "slasher" movie—a beautiful woman's terrified screams piercing the air, a dead body sprawled at her feet, blood staining the pristine sands of a Washington beach. But the blood is real, and the victim won't be rising when a director yells, "Cut!" In one horrific instant, a homicide detective's well-earned holiday has become a waking nightmare. Suddenly, a lethal brew of passion, madness, and politics threatens to do more than poison J. P. Beaumont's sleep—it's dragging the dedicated Seattle cop into the path of a killer whose dark hunger is rapidly becoming an obsession.

TRIAL BY FURY

"Jance delivers a devilish page-turner."
People

The dead body discovered in a Seattle Dumpster
was shocking enough—but equally disturbing was
the manner of death. The victim, a high-school
coach, had been lynched, leaving behind a very
pregnant wife to grieve over his passing, and to
wonder what dark secrets he took to his grave. A
Homicide detective with twenty years on the job,
J. P. Beaumont knows this case is a powder keg and
he fears where this investigation will lead him. Because the answers lie on the extreme lethal edge of
passion and hate, where the wrong kind of love can
breed the most terrible brand of justice.

TAKING THE FIFTH

"Jance's [novels] show up on bestseller lists. . . .
one can see why."
Milwaukee Journal-Sentinel

There are many bizarre and terrible ways to die.
Seattle Homicide Detective J.P. Beaumont thought
he had seen them all—until he saw this body, its
wounds, and the murder weapon: an elegant woman's
shoe, its stiletto heel gruesomely caked with blood.
The evidence is shocking and unsettling, even for
a man who prowls the shadows for a living, for it
suggests that savagery is not the exclusive domain of
the predatory male. And the scent of a stylish killer is
pulling Beaumont into a world of drugs, corruption,
and murder to view close-up a cinematic dream at
its most nightmarish . . . and lethal.

IMPROBABLE CAUSE

"Jance brings the reader along with suspense,
wit, surprise, and intense feeling."
Huntsville Times

Perhaps it was fitting justice: a dentist who enjoyed
inflicting pain was murdered in his own chair. The
question is not who wanted Dr. Frederick Nielsen
dead, but rather who of the many finally reached
the breaking point. The sordid details of this case,
with its shocking revelations of violence, cruelty,
and horrific sexual abuse, would be tough for any
investigator to stomach. But for Seattle Homicide
Detective J. P. Beaumont, the most damning piece
of the murderous puzzle will shake him to his very
core—because what will be revealed to him is nothing less than the true meaning of unrepentant evil.

A MORE PERFECT UNION

"In the elite company of
Sue Grafton and Patricia Cornwell."
Flint Journal

A shocking photo screamed from the front pages
of the tabloids—the last moments of a life captured
for all the world to see. The look of sheer terror
eternally frozen on the face of the doomed woman
indicated that her fatal fall from an upper story of
an unfinished Seattle skyscraper was no desperate
suicide—and that look will forever haunt Homicide
Detective J. P. Beaumont. But his hunt for answers
and justice is leading to more death, and to dark
and terrible secrets scrupulously guarded by men of
steel behind the locked doors of a powerful union
that extracts its dues payments in blood.

DISMISSED WITH PREJUDICE

"She can move from an exciting,
dangerous scene on one page
to a sensitive, personal,
touching moment on the next."
Chicago Tribune

The blood at the scene belies any suggestion of an "honorable death." Yet, to the eyes of the Seattle police, a successful Japanese software magnate died exactly as he wished—and by his own hand, according to the ancient rite of *seppuku*. Homicide Detective J. P. Beaumont can't dismiss what he sees as an elaborate suicide, however, not when something about it makes his flesh crawl. Because small errors in the ritual suggest something darker: a killer who will go to extraordinary lengths to escape detection—a fiend with a less traditional passion . . . for cold-blooded murder.

MINOR IN POSSESSION

"One of the country's
most popular mystery writers."
Portland Oregonian

All manner of sinners and sufferers come to the rehab ranch in Arizona when they hit rock bottom.
For Seattle Detective J. P. Beaumont, there is a
deeper level of Hell here: being forced to room with
teenage drug dealer Joey Rothman. An all-around
punk, Joey deserves neither pity nor tears—until he
is murdered by a bullet fired from Beaumont's gun.
Someone has set Beau up brilliantly for a long and
terrifying fall, dragging the alcoholic ex-cop into a
conspiracy of blood and lies that could cost him his
freedom . . . and his life.

PAYMENT IN KIND

"Any story by Jance is a joy."
Chattanooga Times

It looks like a classic crime of passion to Detective J. P. Beaumont: two corpses found lovingly entwined in a broom closet of the Seattle School District building. The prime suspect, Pete Kelsey, admits his slain spouse was no novice at adultery, yet he swears he had nothing to do with the brutal deaths of the errant school official and her clergyman-turned-security guard companion. Beau believes him, but there's something the much sinned-upon widower's not telling—and that spells serious trouble still to come. Because the secret that Pete's protecting is even hotter than extramarital sex . . . and it could prove more lethal than murder.

WITHOUT DUE PROCESS

"Jance paints a vibrant picture,
creating characters so real you want to
reach out and hug—or strangle—them.
Her dialogue always rings true, and the cases
unravel in an interesting, yet never contrived way."
Cleveland Plain Dealer

What kind of monster would break into a man's
home at night, then slaughter him and his family?
The fact that the dead man was a model cop who
was loved and respected by all only intensifies the
horror. But the killer missed someone: a five-year-
old boy who was hiding in the closet. Now word is
being leaked out that the victim was "dirty." But
Seattle P. D. Homicide Detective J. P. Beaumont isn't
about to let anyone drag a murdered friend's reputation through the muck. And he'll put his own life
on the firing line on the gang-ruled streets to save a
terrified child who knows too much to live.

FAILURE TO APPEAR

"Jance's artistry keeps the reader
guessing—and caring."
Publishers Weekly

A desperate father's search for his runaway daughter
has led him to the last place he ever expected to find
her: backstage at the Oregon Shakespeare Festival.
But the murders in this dazzling world of make-
believe are no longer mere stagecraft, and the blood
is all too real. The hunt for his child has plunged
former Seattle Homicide Detective J. P. Beaumont
into a bone-chilling drama of revenge, greed, and
butchery, where innocents are made to suffer in
perverse and terrible ways. And many more young
lives are at stake, unless he can uncover the villain
of the piece before the final, deadly curtain falls.

LYING IN WAIT

"[Jance] will keep the reader up nights."
Pittsburgh Post-Gazette

Else Didriksen is no longer the beautiful, troubled teenager who disappeared from Detective J. P. Beaumont's life thirty years earlier. Now she is a homicide victim's widow—frightened, desperate, and trapped in a web of murderous greed that reaches out from a time of unrelenting terror. And the dark, deadly secrets that hold Else prisoner threaten to ensnare Beau and new partner, Sue Danielson, as well—and to rock their world in ways they never dreamed possible.

NAME WITHHELD

"[Her work] can be compared to the work of
Tony Hillerman and Mary Higgins Clark.
J. A. Jance can stand tall
even in that fine company."
Washington Times

There are those who don't deserve to live—and the
corpse floating in Elliott Bay may have been one of
those people. Not surprisingly, many individuals—
too many, in fact—are eager to take responsibility
for the brutal slaying of the hated biotech execu-
tive whose alleged crimes ranged from the illegal
trading of industrial secrets to rape. For Seattle Detective J. P. Beaumont—who's drowning in his own
life-shattering problems—a case of seemingly jus-
tifiable homicide has sinister undertones, drawing
the haunted policeman into a corporate nightmare
of double deals, savage jealousies, and real blood
spilled far too easily, as it leads him closer to a killer
he's not sure he wants to find.

BREACH OF DUTY

"A thrill . . . One of Jance's best."
Milwaukee Journal-Sentinel

The Seattle that Beau knew as a young policeman is disappearing. The city is awash in the aromas emanating from a glut of coffee bars, the neighborhood outside his condo building has sprouted gallery upon gallery, and even his long cherished diner has evolved into a trendy eatery for local hipsters. But the glam is strictly surface, for the grit under the city's fingernails is caked with blood. Beau and his new partner, Sue Danielson, a struggling single parent, are assigned the murder of an elderly woman torched to death in her bed. As their investigation proceeds, Beau and Sue become embroiled in a perilous series of events that will leave them and their case shattered—and for Beau nothing will ever be the same again.

BIRDS OF PREY

"[A] fast-paced thriller . . . Vivid and well-drawn."
Tampa Tribune

The *Starfire Breeze* steams its way north toward the Gulf of Alaska, buffeted by crisp sea winds blowing down from the Arctic. Those on board are seeking peace, relaxation, adventure, escape. But there is no escape here in this place of unspoiled natural majesty. Because terror strolls the decks even in the brilliant light of day . . . and death is a conspicuous, unwelcome passenger. And a former Seattle policeman—a damaged Homicide detective who has come to heal from fresh, stinging wounds—will find that the grim ghosts pursuing him were not left behind . . . as a pleasure cruise gone horribly wrong carries him inexorably into lethal, ever-darkening waters.

PARTNER IN CRIME

"*Partner in Crime* will have fans of J. A. Jance
hopping in anticipation with just three little words:
Beau meets Brady."
Seattle Times

The dead woman on a cold slab in the Arizona
morgue was a talented artist recently arrived from
the West Coast. The Washington State Attorney
General's office thinks this investigation is too
big for a small-town *female* law officer to handle,
so they're sending Sheriff Joanna Brady some
unwanted help—a seasoned detective named
Beaumont. Sheriff Brady resents his intrusion, and
Bisbee, Arizona, with its ghosts and memories, is
the last place J. P. Beaumont wants to be. But the
twisting desert road they must reluctantly travel
together is leading them into a very deadly nest of
rattlers. And if they hope to survive, suddenly trust
is the only option they have left. . . .

LONG TIME GONE

"Brims with richly drawn characters,
atmospheric locales, and more twists and turns
than a bucket of snakes. . . . *Long Time Gone* is
crisply written and filled with suspense."
Tucson Citizen

A former Seattle policeman now working for the
Washington State Attorney's Special Homicide
Investigation Team, J. P. Beaumont has been handpicked to lead the investigation into a half-century-
old murder. An eyewitness to the crime, a middle-aged
nun, has now recalled grisly, forgotten details while
undergoing hypnotherapy. It's a case as cold as the
grave, and it's running headlong into another that's
tearing at Beau's heart: the vicious slaying of his
former partner's ex-wife. What's worse, his rapidly
unraveling friend is the prime suspect.

Caught in the middle of a lethal conspiracy that
spans two generations and a killing that hits too
close to home—targeted by a vengeful adversary
and tempted by a potential romance that threatens
to reawaken his personal demons—Beaumont may
suddenly have more on his plate than he can handle,
and far too much to survive.

FIRE AND ICE

"A gripping tale that's easily one of her best."
Publishers Weekly (✻ Starred Review ✻)

In Seattle, six women have died terrible deaths—wrapped in tarps, doused with gasoline, and set on fire—their charred remains unceremoniously scattered in various dump sites around the city. Investigator J. P. Beaumont is working overtime to unravel a killer's grisly pattern. In the Arizona desert, Sheriff Joanna Brady of Cochise County investigates the cold-blooded slaying of the elderly caretaker of an ATV park, heartlessly run over and left to die—the innocent victim in a brutal turf war . . . or possibly something far more sinister.

Two cases separated by thousands of miles are drawing closer together by the hour—and drawing Beau once more into Brady country. Sparks flew the last time they joined forces. This time, it'll be murder. . . .

JUSTICE DENIED

"Jance's success . . . lies in the strength of
her characters and the craftiness of her stories.
[*Justice Denied*] has plenty of twists and more than
enough hard-boiled banter to keep fans reading."

Booklist

The murder of an ex-drug dealer ex-con—gunned
down on his mother's doorstep—seems like just another turf war fatality. Why then has Seattle Homicide Investigator J. P. Beaumont been instructed to
keep this assignment hush-hush? Meanwhile, Beau's
lover and fellow cop, Mel Soames, is involved in
her own confidential investigation. Registered sex
offenders from all over Washington State are dying
at an alarming rate—and not all due to natural causes.

A metropolis the size of Seattle holds its fair share
of brutal crime, corruption, and dirty little secrets.
But when the separate trails they're following begin
to shockingly intertwine, Beau and Mel realize that
they have stumbled onto something bigger and
more frightening than they anticipated—a deadly
conspiracy that's leading them to lofty places they
should not enter . . . and may not be allowed to leave
alive.

BETRAYAL OF TRUST

"San Francisco has Dashiell Hammett,
Boston has Robert B. Parker,
Fort Lauderdale boasts John D. MacDonald . . .
Seattle has J. A. Jance!"
Seattle Times

When her teenage grandson is discovered with a snuff film on his phone, the governor of the state of Washington turns to an old friend, J. P. Beaumont, for help. The Seattle private investigator has witnessed many horrific acts over the years, but this one ranks near the top: a girl strangled to death while an unseen camera looks on. Even more shocking is that the crime's multiple perpetrators could all be minors.

Along with Mel Soames, his partner in life as well as on the job, Beaumont soon discovers that what initially appears to be a childish prank gone wrong has much deeper implications, reaching into the halls of state government itself. But Mel and Beau must follow this path of corruption to its very end, before more innocent young lives are lost.